Praise for A Blackened Mirror

Graham (*Black Ships*) recalls the legacy of Taylor Caldwell and Mary Renault in this smart series launch, humanizing history from the perspective of deeply imagined, unironically presented characters. //...this slow-building introduction to complex intrigue will please readers looking for vivid historical fare with just a touch of magic.

— *Publishers Weekly*

Ancient Greek and Roman rituals lie like a palimpsest beneath the streets of a Rome resplendent in full Catholic regalia in this tale of ambition, desire, intrigue and enchantment. La Bella Farnese is a compelling heroine, and author Jo Graham casts her Renaissance spell with a deft hand.

— Jacqueline Carey, award-winning author
of the *Kushiel Universe* series

An addictively rich, vivid and lushly written Renaissance fantasy // Jo Graham's writing style is beautiful, as always, and her storytelling is utterly compulsive from beginning to end.

— Stephanie Burgis, author of
Masks and Shadows and *Snowspelled*

Once again, Graham proves herself a master of historical fantasy—this time, the Italian Renaissance, portrayed in all its glorious complexity. Giulia Farnese is the ideal protagonist, ardent, ambitious, sharp of wit and tongue, willing to risk everything. I devoured the book, and cannot wait for the rest of the series

— Melissa Scott, legendary pioneering SFF author
and winner of multiple genre awards

Jo Graham returns to magical history with a fresh take on some of Rome's most notorious. Witty and loving, with sharp edges in all the right places.

— E.K. Johnston, #1 New York Times Bestselling Author

Jo Graham skillfully brings life in Renaissance Rome and Italy to life... // It is a highly enjoyable read, perfect for those who want to get to grips with the skullduggery of life in Renaissance Rome and the Curia.

— Dr. Katharine Fellows, Oxford University, author of "Diplomacy, Debauchery and Devils: the ecclesiastical career of Rodrigo Borgia"

Jo Graham's *A Blackened Mirror* showcases the breadth of her writing talents... // Graham gives us a fresh and underappreciated perspective on the life and times of late 15th century Rome, with a strong heroine, rich worldbuilding and language; clever, refined and immersibly readable.

— Paul Weimer, SFF book reviewer and Hugo finalist

Vivid characters, especially the charming and indomitable young Giulia Farnese herself, bring to life a story of conspiracy, intrigue, and Renaissance magic—Jo Graham's *A Blackened Mirror* is a wonderful adventure.

— K.V. Johansen, author of the *Gods of the Caravan Road* epic fantasy series

Also by Jo Graham (selected works):

Black Ships

Stealing Fire

The Order of the Air (series, Melissa Scott co-author)

The Calpurnian Wars:

Sounding Dark

Warlady

A BLACKENED MIRROR

Being the First Part of
the Memoirs of the Borgia Sibyl

Jo Graham

First edition published 2023

For information, address
Athena Andreadis
Candlemark & Gleam LLC,
38 Rice Street #2, Cambridge, MA 02140
eloi@candlemarkandgleam.com

Library of Congress Cataloguing-in-Publication Data
In Progress

ISBNs: 978-1-952456-14-5 (print), 978-1-952456-15-2 (digital)

Cover art by Alexandra Torres Ferrer

Editor: Athena Andreadis

www.candlemarkandgleam.com

For Janet Frederick Rhodes,
teacher, mentor and friend,
because this is the book she always wanted me to write.

Facilis descensus Averno;
noctes atque dies patet atri ianua Ditis;
sed revocare gradum superasque evadere ad auras,
hoc opus, hic labor est. — Virgil

The Borgia Family Tree in 1489

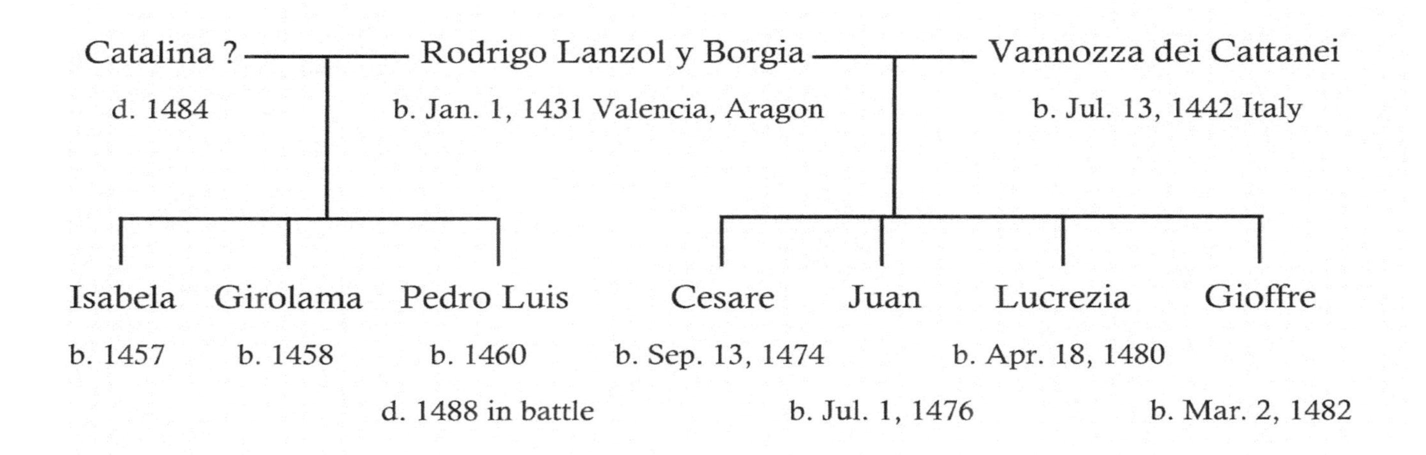

Some of the dates are unknown and a matter of conjecture

The Church Hours

As recognized in Rome in the 15th century

In the Renaissance, timekeeping for people in cities depended on church bells which were rung at specific hours of the day. A day began at sunset and went around until sunset the next day. Here are the hours as referenced in A Blackened Mirror.

Vespers: the Vespers bells rang at sunset, whatever time that was. In other words, what time Vespers is varied depending on the season. In Rome that's as early as 4:41 at midwinter. On June 22, the midsummer's eve of the last chapter of the book, sunset is not until 8:49 pm.

Compline: an hour after Vespers. Thus, "dinner after Compline" means anything from 6:00 to 10:00.

Vigil: two hours after midnight, so approximately 2:00 am.

Lauds: at dawn, which again means that it moves around. At midwinter, that's 7:02 am. At midsummer, it's 5:01 am. Thus, on June 22 if you come home at Vigil and are up for Lauds, you get three hours sleep!

Prime: an hour after dawn, generally the beginning of the working day.

Terce: the third hour, or two hours after Prime.

Sext: three hours later, so at midwinter it's about 1:00 pm and at midsummer at about 11:00 am, so noonish.

PEOPLE, PLACES AND THINGS

Ash Wednesday: the Catholic holy day marking the beginning of Lent forty days before Easter.

Barbaro, Ermolao: a leading Neoplatonist scholar and humanist, translator of many ancient Greek works into Latin. Rodrigo Borgia was one of his first patrons.

Borgia, Cesare: the oldest son of Rodrigo Borgia and Vannozza dei Cattanei. At the beginning of *A Blackened Mirror* he is fourteen years old and has just begun his studies at the University of Pisa.

Borgia, Gioffre: the youngest son of Rodrigo Borgia and Vannozza dei Cattanei. At the beginning of *A Blackened Mirror* he is seven years old and lives with his mother.

Borgia, Juan: the middle son of Rodrigo Borgia and Vannozza dei Cattanei. At the beginning of *A Blackened Mirror* he is twelve years old and lives with his mother.

Borgia, Lucrezia: the daughter of Rodrigo Borgia and Vannozza dei Cattanei. At the beginning of *A Blackened Mirror* she is nine years old and has just moved out of her mother's house to live with Adriana de Mila a few blocks from her father's house.

Borgia, Pedro Luis: Rodrigo Borgia's oldest son by a relationship before Vannozza, he was killed in service to the Spanish crown a year before *A Blackened Mirror*.

Borgia, Rodrigo: Cardinal, Vice-Chancellor, and Dean of the College of Cardinals, he is a power in the Vatican despite being

Spanish and a foreigner who is not connected to the ruling families of Rome. He is from Valencia, where he has amassed considerable estates and wealth. He is the patron of various Humanist and Neoplatonist writers, is a notable collector of ancient art, and is known for his lavish lifestyle. He is a member of the Humanist faction in the College.

Bracciano: a major fortress a day's ride from Rome held by the powerful Orsini family as the personal property of the head of the family, Virginio Orsini, known as Lord Bracciano.

Burchard, Johann: chronicler of the papal court.

Caetani, Giovanna: Now holding the castle of Montalto, she is the widow of Pier Luigi Farnese and the mother of Giulia and her brothers and sister.

Canale, Carlo: Vannozza dei Cattanei's husband.

Cardinal: the highest officials of the Catholic Church besides the pope, they are appointed for life to the College of Cardinals. It is their vote that elects one of their peers to be pope.

Carnival: the season from Epiphany on January 6 to the night before Ash Wednesday, in Rome a season of revelry and license before the seriousness of Lent.

Colonna: one of the great families of Rome.

Condottiero: a mercenary soldier of purportedly noble birth who sells his sword and supposed military acumen to the highest bidder.

Cybo, Franceschetto: a Roman nobleman, the illegitimate son of Pope Innocent VIII.

Dei Cattanei, Vannozza: once the foremost courtesan of Rome, she became the concubine of Rodrigo Borgia nearly twenty years ago. They had four children together before they parted. She is now happily married to Carlo Canale and has a considerable business as a real estate manager and owner of a working vineyard.

Della Rovere, Cardinal Giuliano: Papal Legate to France and one of the most powerful cardinals, he is considered a leading contender for the papacy when it next becomes vacant. He is a member of the Traditionalist faction but is considered by some members to be too much of an opportunist rather than a true believer.

De Mila, Adriana: Rodrigo Borgia's cousin, widow of Ludovico Orsini and stepmother to Orsino Orsini. She lives in Palazzo Orsini de Ponte, a fine house not far from the Vice-Chancellor's Palazzo.

Farnese, Alessandro: the oldest son of Pier Luigi Farnese and Giovanna Caetani; his parents managed to afford a good education for him at the University of Pisa so that he could have a career in the Church. At the beginning of *A Blackened Mirror* he is nineteen years old.

Farnese, Amadeo: the youngest son of Pier Luigi Farnese and Giovanna Caetani, he died in 1487 at the age of not quite two.

Farnese, Angelo: the third son of Pier Luigi Farnese and Giovanna Caetani, at the beginning of *A Blackened Mirror* he is eight years old.

Farnese, Bartolemeo: the second son of Pier Luigi Farnese and Giovanna Caetani, at the beginning of *A Blackened Mirror* he is thirteen years old.

Farnese, Girolama: the youngest daughter of Pier Luigi Farnese and Giovanna Caetani, at the beginning of *A Blackened Mirror* she is a year and a half old.

Farnese, Giulia: the oldest daughter of Pier Luigi Farnese and Giovanna Caetani, she is fifteen years old at the beginning of *A Blackened Mirror*.

Farnese, Pier Luigi: the former Lord of Montalto, father of Giulia and her brothers and sister. He had been a condottiero for many years before he inherited Montalto unexpectedly at the age of 39. He died of the summer sickness in 1487.

Ficino, Marsilio: a leading humanist writer, founder of the Neoplatonist movement. He was the tutor of Lorenzo de Medici and now leads an academy of young writers and artists in Florence. Among other things, he has translated and introduced the writings of Hermes Trismegistus, and as such is the father of Hermetic magic in the western magical tradition.

Gonfaloniere: the title of the general in charge of the Papal Armies.

Humanist faction: a faction in the College of Cardinals that favors the expansion of Renaissance thought, including the translation of ancient pagan writers like Plato and Pliny and their inclusion in the curriculum of the universities. The Humanists support the spread of printing and literacy.

Medici: the ruling family of Florence, merchant bankers and patrons of the arts.

Miglio (plural = miglia): a measure of distance, about a mile.

Montalto: a small fortress north of Rome along the ancient Via Aurelia near the seashore.

Orsini: one of the great families of Rome.

Orsini, Cardinal Giovanni: one of the leading members of the powerful Orsini family and a Cardinal of the Catholic Church.

Orsini, Orsino: a young man of the Orsini family, son of the late Ludovico Orsini and stepson of Adriana de Mila. At the beginning of *A Blackened Mirror* he is sixteen years old.

Orsini, Virginio (Lord Bracciano): head of the powerful Orsini family, he is the Lord of Bracciano, a substantial castle, and a wealthy landowner. He is also the Gonfaloniere of the Papal Armies, appointed by Pope Innocent as his military commander.

Osteria: a restaurant or tavern.

Pluto: the Roman god of the underworld, the equivalent of the Greek Hades. He is also called Father Dis.

Pope Innocent VIII: born Giovanni Cybo, he was elected pope five years before the events of *A Blackened Mirror* and has been in ill health for much of his reign. Part of the Traditionalist faction, he published the *Malleus Maleficarum*, which authorized the investigation and persecution of witchcraft, and encouraged the founding of the Spanish Inquisition.

Proserpina: the Roman goddess of the underworld, the equivalent of the Greek Persephone. She is the spring maiden who descends to the underworld and then returns over and over, thus creating the cycle of the seasons.

Savonarola, Friar: Florentine monk and preacher who is becoming a force in Florentine politics. He is extremely conservative and opposes the humanism of the Medici.

Sforza: one of the most powerful families of Italy.

Sforza, Cardinal Ascanio: a member of the College of Cardinals from the powerful Sforza family, he is the brother of both the Duke of Milan and the Queen of Naples.

Sorellina: little sister.

Summer sickness: an endemic and serious disease, probably malaria.

Tarocchi: a card game with four players that is the ancestor of bridge, but also the deck itself which is the precursor of the modern tarot deck.

Traditionalist faction: a faction in the College of Cardinals which seeks to limit the spread of non-Christian ideas, including ancient pagan books and art. They oppose the translation of ancient works and the expansion of printing and literacy.

Treschi, Dionisio: a Florentine scholar and would-be magician.

Via Aurelia: the ancient Roman road going northward from Rome passing through Montalto on the way to Pisa.

Chapter One

Montalto, Italy, 1489

So you will not believe me blameless in all that befell me, it began with something forbidden. My grandmother had told me where the old tombs were, across the little Fiora River that made its way to the sea less than two miglia away. The tombs, she said, were older than the Romans, remnants of the people who came before. They had been places of old pagan magic. They might even lead to the underworld itself. If a maiden dared to go into them and ask, she might see a vision of her future husband. Or she might never return.

I suspect, now, that these were the sort of cautionary tales that adults tell to daring young girls so that they will not climb around in crumbling ruins; but of course as a child I believed it and went nowhere near the place. If the summer sickness had not come, if my father had not died, if my grandmother had not died, if my baby brother not quite two years old had not died, perhaps I would have forgotten all about it until I was old enough to tell my own children to leave the ruins alone. But those things happened. The summer sickness came and tore us apart.

The marshes near the sea were known for pestilence. Perhaps that is why the Romans built an aqueduct that brought fresh water from inland to us, thinking the water here bad. Even so, from time to time the sickness came. I washed mountains of stained linens for my brothers, for I had it in the beginning and they later. I laid my youngest brother out for the grave myself, washing his little body and dressing him in a white gown. My mother was too feverish to get out of bed, and my tears fell on him as I fastened the cap over his curls and I prayed that I would not bury her and the child unborn, too. I saw our old steward to his grave. I saw the priest to his grave after. I tried not to think of my father's and my grandmother's bodies there in the dark. I say these things so you will know that the underworld held no terrors for me. I was well acquainted with death.

My mother lived, and so did I. My brothers Bartolomeo and Angelo lived. My oldest brother, Alessandro, was away at school and did not contract it. My mother's survival was a wonder, for she gave birth to my sister, Girolama, not seven weeks later. We were what was left. The town had been decimated, too, not just those who lived in the rather shabby and small keep in the center of town that passed for a castle.

And yet we went on. I fed Girolama on goat's milk because my mother had none. Alessandro came home from the university and took care of us all. He was meant to be a priest and Bartolomeo the heir, and he saw Bartolomeo confirmed in his rank as Lord of Montalto as soon as my little brother could walk enough to stand before people. Summer ended. Cooler weather came. The sickness had passed through like a flame, leaving scorched ground behind but burning on toward the horizon. We went on, and if our winter nights were full of tears, there was too much to do during the day to let them flow.

How should I do so many things with my own hands? Our name is an old one, but nothing to the great families. Once we were distinguished, but by the time I was born all our holdings had shrunk to the little castle at Montalto, two miglia from the sea on a hill above the river and the marshes, set amid farmland. My father had been a notable soldier in his youth, condottiero and master of men, but he stood not so far above that he did not see to the care of his own horses, to the state of his own olive groves, or to the health of our own cattle. We worked. When I sat by the fire and sewed at night, it was not fine embroidery but clothing for my brothers.

Alessandro and I leaned on one another, and somehow we managed. We were two of a kind, people said, alike as twins though he was the elder, tall and dark haired and clever and beautiful. He stayed a year, all his studies deferred, and I wondered if he would lose out on them entirely. But when the harvest came in the next year there was enough for him to go back to Pisa and finish school. I envied him. He set off north riding on the box of a merchant's wagon, his trunk in the bed behind him, and I wished I could go with him.

Of course not. For me it was another day. I would mend and direct the scullery maid and chase my brothers around and around and change Girolama's clouts and so on until I fell into bed after Compline to begin it all again at dawn. This would be my life unless I married a man with more money. It was, I thought, a doubtful proposition. My dowry was small. Now I had no father to arrange a good match, and Alessandro knew no one except university students and priests. My mother had no time or energy to see to it, and besides she needed me here with her. It might be that I would stay ten years or more, until Bartolomeo was grown and married, my youth fled, my maidenhood withered on the vine. I might stay a maiden aunt in his household, tending my nieces and nephews, changing their clouts and laying their bodies out for the funeral if they died, never seeing more than five miglia from home.

And yet the road that ran past our walls was the Via Aurelia. North, it went to the university at Pisa, but south it cut straight as the old Romans had built it, a little more than sixty miglia to the walls of Rome. There was the center of the world. There was the center of Christendom. There were palaces and princes and pope, all the wonders of the world. And here was I, sixty miglia away in what might as well be another country across the great seas. Each day we saw merchants and pilgrims, prelates and nobles, passing our doors. There was good money to be made in tavern keeping, for all must lodge and eat, and only the noblest could beg our hospitality in the castle. Which meant there were always more than we could afford, and while one might charge mendicant priests for lodging, one could not charge great nobles. One had to behave as though serving roast goose and fine wine was but a trifle.

By the time winter was waning, by the eve of Ash Wednesday, I was reckless with despair. That was why I tried the tombs.

I slipped out just after dinner carrying a basket with leftover bread and a pomegranate, from those left in the storage bins in the cellar. The night was fine and cool, the stars bright, a breeze bringing a hint of salt from the sea. I pulled my cloak over my hair and made my way rapidly through town, looking like someone in a hurry to get home. If anyone saw my face they would recognize me, of course, but hopefully no one would. The water whispered around the deep-sunk pillars of the bridge that carried the Via Aurelia over the river.

On the other side I turned off the road to the right, climbing up the little hills that overlooked the river. My father had always said it was an ideal place for a fortification. Perhaps that's what it had been long ago. Perhaps once that had been the old town and our Montalto the new town, but whatever conquerors or scourges had swept through in two thousand years, the old town was long deserted. Its houses were gone but its tombs cut deep into the hills.

The footing was treacherous. The sun was down now, only lingering twilight, and I made my way cautiously among the tumbled stones, careful of my lantern, the candlelight glowing through the pierced metal. There was the entrance, a dark hole a little more than my height, an open mouth that went into the hill.

I took a deep breath, pushing the hood of my cloak back. This was the moment of decision. Even small magics, like trying to see your future husband's face, were forbidden. I should have to confess it and do the penance, but that was less worrying than what might be inside. Was it truly the entrance to the underworld?

Aren't all tombs, I thought, as though something had whispered it behind me. *All graves are death's doorway*.

And so I plunged into the dark. My lamp made a little pool of light around me. It cannot have been far. The hill was not large, and yet it seemed to me that I walked a long time. There were pillars with flaking paint, carved figures limned in colors still bright, men with shields and swords battling lions. There were stone sarcophagi but any bodies which had lain in them were long gone. If this tomb had held treasure, it had been stolen long ago. The treasure which remained was on the walls.

Down, and down again. One gallery after another opened ahead, until I came to the heart of it and stopped in awe. Life-size, a couple stared back at me. They shared a couch, he leaning on one elbow, she sitting beside him facing forward with his arm around her. She wore a bridal garland on her head, a bunch of lilies in her hand, her saffron gown falling in graceful folds. Some water had gotten in, making a pool in front of them no deeper than my hand. The light reflected off its surface, as did they. In his hand he held a pomegranate.

I knew them. I knew the story. I had shared Alessandro's tutor until he went away to school, and of course he had the classics. "Proserpina," I said, "Queen of the Underworld, I am sorry to disturb your rest."

The echoes ran round galleries and columns. "…rest…rest… rest."

I laid the bread and the pomegranate carefully on the ground before them, against the wall where they would not be in the water. "My name is Giulia Farnese," I said. "I am a maiden of the town above. I have come to ask you to show me my husband. I need…"

I stopped, my voice breaking. "…I need a good husband if I am ever to leave here."

Her painted eyes watched me. He did not look at me. His eyes were only for her, forever admiring his bride. And yet it seemed that her eyes held compassion. It was a trick of the light, surely, the candle flame flickering through the piercings of the lamp. So many months, and no person to share it with since Alessandro left. I could not burden my mother further. She had so much to do and was sunk in grief, losing husband and mother-in-law and child at the same time. How could I ask her for anything?

"Proserpina, Persephone, Lady of the Dead," I said. "I need your help." I poured it out to her, every sorrow and pain that tore my heart, and then every hope and dream. A handsome husband who would take me to Rome or some other great city. Learning, art, beauty, pleasure, books and plays and a man who adored me. Beautiful children to grow up healthy and clever, clients and servants to depend on me as they had my father at Montalto, rulership and glamor and power and love. Most of all, love. I ached for love. I yearned for love like a young bird for the sky. Most of all I feared the cage, the cloister, the prison of remaining a maiden aunt. And I would die for love, to be wanted and precious, treasured and listened to, courted like a great lady and kissed like my lips held absolution.

At last I stopped. Tears were running down my face. "Please, Proserpina. Please show me my husband's face so that I can find him." I looked into the pool, or rather at the reflections on the surface of the water.

All I saw was the candlelight. I stared at it, willing it to change. It shifted, wavered. *Streaming torches, torches in the darkness. A procession through a great city. A swirl of scarlet, a bull lying bleeding on the pavement, a sword of fine Toledo steel. A garden in the sun, a fly crawling on the skin of a purpling fig….*

"No," I said. "My husband's face. The face of my husband

who will love me!" I bent my will to it. "Show me!"

A silver tissue mask in the shape of the moon, a cradle surmounted by white lace curtains, a fireplace and beaded slippers, gold and white....

"My husband's face!" Images swam, but there was no man's face. *A hand with a ring with a great ruby, a sword, a pack of playing cards dashed from a table....*

"Am I to have no husband then?" I demanded, my voice thick with tears. "Then grant me anything but the cloister! Anything!"

Go now. I heard it like a whisper. *Go now. Even now your time comes.*

I turned and ran from that place, half-blind with tears. The lantern shook, the light flashing over pillars and painted walls, until at last I emerged with the candle guttering onto the dark hillside. I stopped, breathing hard.

There were torches on the road. A great party of riders were approaching the bridge at a walk, outriders carrying torches before them. There must be twenty armed men with no wagons behind. The flickering light illuminated their colors, red and white.

I stood stunned for a moment. A great lord and his party. At this time of night they would surely stop in Montalto. We would need to give them hospitality. Mother would be looking for me, needing me to get rooms ready for the illustrious among them.

I blew out the candle and ran. I could not get to Montalto ahead of them, but I must not be too far behind. Mother would be frantic if I could not be found. Along the broken hillside and across the bridge I pelted. They were in the town ahead of me, but I caught up with them in the square before our gates, men and horses milling around while my mother made a speech of welcome from the steps, a yellow gown thrown on over her cotta and laced quickly in the front. I caught the end of it as I slipped up, trying to look as though I had just come outside as well. "...we bid you welcome to Montalto," she said. "My Lord, we will prepare a meal if you would enjoy it."

The leader was a big man on a white horse, with dark red velvet beneath his steel breastplate. "There's no need for such fuss, Madonna. A plain repast will do. We have been on the road all day and have far to go tomorrow. If we may eat and seek our beds, that is best for soldiers such as we."

"Of course," my mother said, trying not to sound relieved that a banquet would not be expected. Her eyes fell on me. "My daughter, Giulia, will show you to the best guest chamber so that you may refresh yourself. Pray, consider it our honor to welcome you as though this were your home."

That was laying it on rather thick, I thought. He must be someone extremely important. Red and white, the Orsini colors. He glanced at me, then gestured to his squire. "Take my things where the lady says. I will be up in a few minutes."

"This way," I said courteously, hoping that the maidservants had at least gone ahead to light a fire. The squire burdened himself with his lord's luggage, and I led him in and up by the broader stair. The castle had not been built all of a piece to a design, but had rather had bits put on over the years wherever it suited someone, and nothing made any architectural sense whatsoever. Finding two matching windows was a feat. We went around a corner and I opened the door. The room was chilly, but at least the fire had already been lit. "I hope this will suit your lord," I said.

"Very nicely," the squire said. He was younger than I, with a broad, homely face.

"I beg your pardon," I said, "But I arrived late outside. Who is your lord?"

He looked at me like I was inordinately stupid. "Virginio Orsini, Lord of Bracciano," he said. "Gonfaloniere of the Papal Armies."

"Yes. Of course." I felt myself blushing. The general in command of all the Pope's forces, a lord and great landowner, head of the powerful Orsini family—and I had asked who he was!

My next thought was to wonder if he had any sons. Of course he had sons. But certainly he would not consider me for any of them with so poor a dowry and no connections. Perhaps the squire was not promised? Surely the gonfaloniere's squire was well born. I favored the squire with what I hoped was a stunning smile. "If there is anything you need?"

"Not that I know of, thank you," he said. He did look gratifyingly stunned. "I'll go down and get the rest of My Lord's gear."

"Of course," I said, with what I hoped was a modest and curious glance. Or maybe I just looked nearsighted. I heard him clomping down the stair. I looked around the room to see what else was missing. The bed was made neatly. Was there water for washing in the pitcher? He would want to wash his face and hands after the road. I went over to the basin on its brass stand.

A mirror hung above it on the wall, a small one but nicely framed, so that one could see one's face while washing. There was no water in the pitcher. I would have to have it sent up warmed from the kitchen. I looked up. My reflection caught my eye. No, not my reflection. She looked back at me as she had on the wall, hair like ruddy gold and a saffron dress, but not painted and static. She smiled, holding out something in her hand.

"What is it?" I said. Was she trying to tell me that the opportunity I had wished for was here? The squire? One of the other men? Her smile broadened. She opened her hand. "I don't understand," I whispered.

"Don't understand what?" A rough hand closed on my shoulder.

I started, looking up into the face of Virginio Orsini, lord of Bracciano. "My Lord!" I managed.

His hand held me tight. "What were you doing?"

"Seeing if there was water in the pitcher, My Lord."

His eyes were piercing. "You were speaking to the mirror."

"You mistake me, My Lord," I said. His hand closed tighter. Surely he was bruising me. He had heard. I could not pretend. "I thought I saw something there," I said quietly.

His chin lifted. "You see things in mirrors."

"No. Yes," I stammered. "Sometimes. Nothing important."

"And what do you do to make this possible?" Bracciano demanded.

"Nothing," I said. "I do nothing, My Lord. Sometimes I see something of no importance. Just a glance. It is nothing."

"What did you see now?" He did not release me.

"A lady in yellow," I said. "That is all. She did not speak." He was beginning to frighten me. "Please, My Lord."

"A lady in yellow." His expression was appraising. "And what else do you see?"

I cast about for harmless things I had seen. "That my mother will call me just before she does. That we will have visitors and need fodder for their horses. Nothing grave or great, My Lord Bracciano."

"Nothing grave or great indeed," he said. He let go of my arm, smoothing my rumpled sleeve. "And you are the young lord's sister?"

"Giulia Farnese, My Lord," I said with a curtsy. "Bartolomeo is my brother." I took a step back. "Shall I send warm water up so you may refresh yourself?"

"Yes, thank you." He turned away, taking his gauntlets off and dismissing me as thoroughly as a servant. I backed out and closed the door, then took flight to the kitchen. There was something about him I did not like. I would send a maid up with the water and keep clear of him, easy enough in the bustle.

It proved to be simple indeed. Bracciano took his meal in the guest room and retired. He and his men rode shortly after dawn, south toward Rome. I did not speak to him and only saw him when he was mounted to leave. *Well enough*, I thought. Whatever opportunity the squire might have offered paled compared to the unpleasantness of the master. We were well rid of them. By the time the sun rose above the battlements, they were gone. I went on with my work and thought nothing more of it.

For three weeks. I had been chasing my brother Angelo out of the henhouse when a maid came running to tell me that my mother wanted me. Dusting my hands off on my apron, I went in to find her in the room she had shared with my father, their big, curtained bed taking up half the room, a table and chairs by the fire. The table was now covered in papers. She preferred to do the business of the family in here rather than in my father's study. Now she had a letter in hand and looked at me incredulously. "Giulia, what do you know of this?"

"Of what?" I asked.

"This," she said and held the letter out to me.

It took me three times through for it to register. "This is an offer of marriage," I said. "For me to marry a gentleman named Orsino Orsini, cousin of the gonfaloniere. It says that he is a year my senior, of the highest blood and impeccable character. An Orsini."

"Do you know this man? Was he here with Bracciano?" my mother demanded.

"Not that I know of?" I was utterly astonished. "I spoke only a few words with Bracciano, and none concerned marriage or this kinsman or anything!" I looked at the letter again. "Do they know the size of my dowry?"

"Certainly they must," my mother said. "It is no secret that we are not wealthy. Giulia, I hardly know what to say!"

"We must write to Alessandro and ask him to come," I said. "He will know what to do." And yet I thrilled at the thought. A great marriage, a great house, an unknown man who might have seen me and fallen in love though I was unwitting, or else I had impressed his kinsman so much that I seemed a match for this Orsino. My life was beginning.

Alessandro arrived a week later. He perused the letter at length, then sighed and looked at our mother. "It seems a legitimate offer," he said. "Properly written and sealed, signed in Bracciano's own hand."

"And the bridegroom?" I asked.

"He has no need to sign if the head of his family does it for him," Alessandro said. "Besides, he is only a year older than you, apparently." He leaned back in the chair which had been our father's. "I asked at the university when I got your letter. He hasn't been at school in Pisa, but I do have a friend from Rome who confirmed that he is a young man of the Orsini, though not of the main branch of the family. His family has a fine palazzo near the Vatican. His father died recently and Orsino is the heir."

"The heir?" Mother said disbelievingly. "The heir of what?"

"The palazzo, certainly." Alessandro shook his head. "Giulia, your beauty must have impressed Bracciano."

"Great lords do not marry their kinsmen to girls with no lands and little dowry because they are pretty," my mother said tartly. "There's something here."

"Montalto," I said.

"You are not the heir and you have three brothers ahead of you," Mother said.

"But he is the gonfaloniere," I said. "And Montalto overlooks the Via Aurelia and the northern trade route."

Alessandro nodded. "Useful. It's a strong point worth securing. Your marriage would tie us to the Orsini."

"Securing against whom?" I asked.

"The Colonna. Or maybe the Sforza." Alessandro frowned.

"The great families of Rome are always at war with one another. They war over lands and over the papacy itself. All of them have family members in the College of Cardinals, but the Orsini have the gonfaloniere as well, at least at the moment. Virginio Orsini holds his commission from the pope himself, but he serves at the pope's pleasure. Another pope might not keep him. And right now the Orsini have all but exiled the Colonna. Having a grip on the Via Aurelia could be useful to them, especially if they had to pressure the pope into keeping Bracciano on if he didn't want to."

I nodded slowly. "And Bartolomeo would never hold Montalto against my husband or his kin."

"That makes sense," my mother said. "Marry a young kinsman to you, and Bracciano has something he wants with no trouble."

"If that's the reason," I said, "then I think we should take this offer."

Mother looked at me like I was insane. "Of course we have to take it," she said. "Do you think we can go around rejecting the Orsini? But it is good to know why."

"Yes," I said. Being married for my brother's lands was not romantic, but perhaps my husband would be. He was young and rich. Surely this marriage was not of his choosing either. If I could win him over, be a good wife to him, we might have a very happy life. *Proserpina*, I thought, *I will thank you all my days*. And yet, remembering her smile, I was more uneasy than I might have been.

Chapter Two

Alessandro and I arrived in Rome on the twelfth day of May, 1489, to present ourselves for the signing of the marriage contract. I make no secret that I was awed by the beauty and size of the city. Alessandro attended the university in Pisa, so he considered himself a man of the world, and yet I could tell that he too was out of his element. In Montalto one saw the same faces every day. Here, one might go a lifetime without encountering the same person more than once, or so it seemed.

We passed directly in front of the Castel Sant'Angelo, the ancient fortress of the popes which had once been the mausoleum of the Roman emperor Hadrian, though it seemed somewhat in disrepair as it brooded above the Tiber. The bridge we crossed upon was as old as the one at Montalto, though much more crowded. It seemed that one had to practically push one's way across, though the crowd made way readily enough for a litter carrying an old man in long red robes. "A cardinal!" I said to Alessandro. "A real cardinal!" The old man looked neither left nor right, but simply looked straight ahead as his bearers pushed through the crowd, who seemed unimpressed.

"I expect it's a common sight in Rome," Alessandro said. He was trying to sound sophisticated, but he didn't fool me.

In his dark blue doublet, with a sword at his side, Alessandro looked quite splendid. The pale blue trimmings on his sleeves had not cost as much as they seemed, because the laces were made of the same cloth as my cotta, which I wore beneath a gown of same dark blue velvet as his doublet. I suspect, in retrospect, that we looked like twins in a play, each wearing part of each other's costume.

Palazzo Orsini de Ponte was a very fine building in golden stone, three stories high, with a roof of red tile. There were no first-floor windows on the street, though there were above, including a beautiful balcony around the side. There was a tall, arched entrance with heavy oak doors currently standing open to an elegant portico with a hanging lantern. Beyond, one could see the clipped bushes of a garden. "I am supposed to live here?" I whispered. It was not bigger than Montalto, but much grander and far better maintained.

"Courage, Little Bird," he said. I think he said it as much for himself as for me.

"Does that make you Great Bird?" I asked. "Avis minor and major?"

He smiled as I meant him to. "It means we're two of a kind," he said. I squeezed his hand.

We were admitted, an elderly and very dignified servant escorting us. To the right of the portico was the main stairway, broad and elegant. I lifted my skirts carefully so as not to slip on the marble stairs. In a moment I would meet my betrothed. I would learn what my life would be. In a moment I would transform. I would become a woman, not a child.

At the top of the first flight we turned right, following the servant. Alessandro put his arm beneath my elbow and I let my hand rest on his forearm as we entered a grand room with an elaborately coffered ceiling painted with fantastic flowers and animals. "Signore Alessandro and Donna Giulia Farnese," the old man announced.

There was a group of richly dressed people at the far end on the polished floor, a table set up with the contract upon it. I looked for the bridegroom. There was only one man it could be. He was tall—good—though he seemed to be stooping as if to make himself smaller. Only a year my senior, he was reedy, an impression that was not helped by red and white particolored hose and a red doublet with the sleeves slashed in white. He looked something like a harlequin puppet at a fair.

The woman next to him in a rich red gown looked as though she was keeping him from bolting. Well enough. That must be his mother, Donna Adriana de Mila. She was as dark as he was fair, quite beautiful and surely not yet forty. To her right was the one face I did recognize, and I dropped into a low curtsy. "My Lord Bracciano," I said. "I am honored."

Alessandro bowed deeply. "I am doubly honored, My Lord, that you receive us into your home and your family."

He laughed. "This is not my home." He spread his hands expansively. "This little palazzo was the home of my kinsman, the late Ludovico who died on Ash Wednesday. Now it is the home of his son, Orsino. Orsino, greet your bride."

The young man stepped forward slowly. He did in fact manage to look at me. "I give you greetings, Donna Giulia." He stared at my feet.

Perhaps he was just shy. If his heart was beating as fast as mine, how could he speak? I must set my husband-to-be at ease. After all, if he could barely look at me, how was this marriage to be consummated in a day and a half? I addressed him as warmly as possible. "Orsino, I am delighted to finally meet you," I said. "I am fortunate to have such a young and handsome husband, and I know that we will be very happy together."

"Um," Orsino said with a gulp. He turned, whacking me in the knees with his sheathed sword.

"I'm fine," I said quickly. "How funny!" I attempted a witty giggle. Alessandro's eyes widened. Too much. I was trying to be welcoming, not dizzy.

"Let's get on with the contract then," Bracciano said, gesturing to the elderly priest who unrolled the contract and laid it on the table. "If you would care to glance at it, Signore Farnese?"

"Of course," Alessandro said, and bent over it. Presumably it was just like the draft that had been sent to my mother.

I glanced around the room. It was large and elegant, but strangely devoid of furniture. Other than this table, there were six chairs arranged along the wall under the windows and a pair of wrought-iron floor candlestands. The only silver was a pair of candlesticks on a cabinet at the far end. The floor gleamed with polish but there was no rug. The coffered ceiling was painted but there were no curtains on the windows which stood open to catch the morning air.

My dowry of three thousand florins was due to Donna Adriana. The rest was entirely standard, yet Alessandro perused each word. I waited, attempting to make eye contact with my husband. He looked everywhere but at me.

His mother bent toward me. "You must excuse Orsino," she whispered. "It has not been long since his father's death."

Her husband's death. Indeed, this contract must have been rushed into the moment his father was in the grave. I wondered why. Yes, of course he would need an heir, but surely three months was hurrying? If I were some girl he had loved and waited for because his father disapproved, or because he could not marry until he inherited, it would all follow.

But he had never laid eyes on me before today, and he was young to marry himself. It seemed likelier that he should wait until he was well-established and then marry a girl more than a year younger than himself. Actually, not even a year. My birthday was only two months away. Still, what did I know of the way things were done in great families? The Orsini were the most powerful family in Rome, even if he was a lesser cousin of Bracciano, who was head of the family. They numbered not only the gonfaloniere among them, but also various lords and worthies, including a cardinal. Perhaps his fortune was so great that he must secure an heir as soon as possible? And yet for such a prince I would be no great prize. In fact I would be barely tolerable, a pretty face and an old name but no fortune or illustrious connections.

"Of course, Donna Adriana," I whispered back. "I am so glad to have your guidance, since I will be far from my own mother."

Her painted lips lengthened in a rueful smile. "You may not be glad of it when all is said and done."

"The contract seems to be in order," Alessandro said.

"You may sign then," Bracciano said, and Alessandro bent and signed the contract on my behalf.

And with that I was married. The vows tomorrow before a priest were a formality. This was supposed to be the moment when I changed. I looked at Orsino. "I am your wife," I said.

"Er," he said.

"Congratulations," Bracciano said heartily. He clapped Orsino on the shoulder. "I'll see you tomorrow. I've other business today. Remember what I told you?" He turned the clap into holding him by the shoulder, looking into his eyes as one would with a child one wished to remember instructions.

"Yes, My Lord," Orsino said.

"You're clear on that?"

"Absolutely," Orsino assured him. He looked down at his feet.

"Tomorrow then," Bracciano said, releasing him. He nodded to my brother. "My felicitations."

The priest began packing up his ink. "Well," Donna Adriana said with a forced smile. "Let me show you to your rooms. I hope you will stay tonight, Signore Farnese?"

"I would be delighted," Alessandro said with a little bow. There was a crease between his brows. "I hope to see Giulia settled." Orsino had left as soon as Bracciano did. There was no one in the room five minutes later except the priest, his mother and us. I took a deep breath. This wasn't the wedding. It was simply the contract. Surely tomorrow would be better.

My rooms were on the third floor, nearly above the room where the contract had been signed. As was appropriate to a wife, I had a sala of my own, which is to say a sitting room; and behind it, a more private camera for sleeping. However, the sala had nothing in it but two chairs and a small table. There was no carpet. There were no other pieces of furniture. Perhaps they had thought I would bring those things as dower goods? I felt myself flush with embarrassment. I had brought nothing but my clothes and some linens and a gold ring which had been my grandmother's.

The bedroom was small but lovely, and half-filled with a huge, curtained bed. The draperies were moss-green and gold, beautiful but not new, hanging from the ceiling rather than the bed itself as was the new fashion. Perhaps they had been the bridal fittings for Orsino's parents? The linen sheets were soft. The room was so small that it could only hold a clothes press and a basin on its stand. There was a fireplace, but no room for chairs before it. If one wanted to sit, one would have to sit on the bed.

The window looked on the inner courtyard, a perfect garden around a statue of a woman. A nymph, perhaps? I could not really tell anything about her from above, save that her feet were set among clipped rosemary bushes. There was a little paved area around her, a trio of chairs facing the grass. I could smell the rosemary from the window.

I took a deep breath. So this was my home. It did not feel like it. But then I would have to learn to love it. I tried to imagine myself and Orsino strolling in the garden in the evening, hand in hand, but somehow the picture would not come clear. A movement caught my eye and I turned.

Along the wall opposite the window was a bronze washbasin on an iron stand. Above it was a mirror. The garden was reflected in the mirror, paths and statue. A little dark-haired girl ran across the grass, her hair flying. She stopped, looking up at me, smiling.

I spun around, turning back to the window. The garden was empty. *Not again, not here*, I thought. *Not these glimpses, tantalizing and terrifying*. I was a woman grown, a bride, a wife. No more dreams of this. I willed myself to look at the empty garden. There was no child there.

And yet I heard a step behind me. The door squeaked on its hinges. There was the sound of quick young feet on the landing outside. I flung the door open in time to see a flash of coral skirts at the stair turn, a small slippered foot. "Wait!" I said, charging around the corner.

A little girl stood on the step, older than the one I had seen in the garden, eight or nine rather than three. She was the most beautiful child I had ever seen. Her hair was true gold, a river of perfect spun silk down her back, and her eyes were the lambent color of the sky. She was impossibly lovely, a flush on her cheeks that matched the coral color of her gown. Then she smiled. "I wanted to see the bride," she said. "But they said I was too young to come to the signing."

"I am the bride," I said. Perhaps she was my husband's sister? I had brothers aplenty, but my only sister was a toddler. "I'm Giulia. Who are you?"

"Lucrezia," she said. "I've only lived here for a few weeks, and it's very lonely. I hope we'll be friends."

"I hope so too," I said. Her candor was utterly charming. I could not help but respond in kind. "I am afraid I will be lonely too. Are you Orsino's sister?"

She laughed. "No, silly! He doesn't have any brothers or sisters. I'm Lucrezia. Donna Adriana is my father's cousin and I've come to live with her."

"So you're a poor relation?" I felt a sudden sympathy for her.

She sat down on the step. "No, I'm a rich relation." She held out a hand. "Come sit with me and tell me everything."

"I don't know what to tell you," I said.

"Where did you come from?"

"Montalto," I said. "It's a town north of here near the sea." A wave of homesickness washed over me. "I miss walking barefooted on the sand."

"I've never been to the sea," Lucrezia said, and so I told her about it. I spun Montalto out for her, every beauty I recalled, every stone and every ruin, every fishing boat pulled out on the beach, every breath of wind across the marshes where they rose to fields. My father had taught me to hunt with a bow in those marshes, shooting at waterfowl. I missed him still, for all he had been dead nearly two years. She listened, smiling at all the right parts.

At last I finished. "So that is who I am. I have come to marry Orsino."

"Do you love him?" she asked.

"I have only just met him," I temporized. "I am sure I will come to love him as we know one another."

"I wouldn't," she said, wrinkling her nose. "He's not very handsome and he's not very good at lessons. A man should be one or the other, don't you think? Either he should be handsome or clever. Both preferably. But one or the other is absolutely necessary."

I started laughing. "I feel very sorry for him now, with you to matchmake for him!"

"I didn't matchmake," she said seriously. "That was the gonfaloniere. He told Donna Adriana that Orsino was going to marry you and she asked my father and he said he saw no impediment to the match though he saw no good reason for it. And Donna Adriana said that My Lord Bracciano wanted it, and so it was."

"Ah," I said. I shifted on the step. "Who is your father?"

"Donna Adriana's cousin," she said. "Cardinal Borgia."

That explained something at least. "So you're the illegitimate daughter of a priest?"

"Of a cardinal," Lucrezia said proudly. "He's the vice-chancellor, which means he handles the Vatican's diplomatic relations. And of course I'm illegitimate. Priests can't marry."

"Yes, I know that," I said. "Everyone knows that."

"When Donna Adriana's husband died, she asked my father to help her because his relatives didn't want her to have anything, not even the house. They said it was all Orsino's and she should leave," Lucrezia said, dropping her voice.

"But she's Orsino's mother," I said.

Lucrezia shook her head. "She's his stepmother. His mother died when he was born and his father married her when Orsino was three. His family hated her." She made big, significant eyes at me.

"Why?" I asked cautiously.

"Because she's Spanish, like me," Lucrezia said. Her voice dropped to a whisper. "They say we're marrano."

"Ah," I said. That was a horrible slur, to call someone a Jew or a Moor. Yet this radiantly blond child certainly did not look like a Jew or a Moor, not that I had ever met one. How would one tell if such a thing were true or not? And would it matter?

"Anyway, they hated her but he married her anyway. Only they didn't have any children, so there's only Orsino. My father says that her husband was barely in the ground before his relatives started trying to throw her out of the house. So he helped and it all got straightened out and Orsino lives here with his stepmother and now his wife. And me," she finished. "So that I'll get polish."

"You seem very polished already," I said. Truly, she was more self-possessed than I, if quite a little gossip.

"Thank you," she said. She jumped to her feet. "Have you seen the house yet? I could show you everything."

"That would be lovely," I said, and got up feeling that at least I had one friend here.

The wedding the next day was sparsely attended, at least in comparison to what I had imagined. There was no procession, no white horse hired to carry the bride to her new home. There were only fifty guests and it took place in the saletta of the house, not in a church as I had expected. Alessandro escorted me. There was a nervous young priest to preside, though I noticed two red-robed cardinals among the guests, which perhaps accounted for his nervousness. However, he was nothing compared to Orsino, who seemed to have difficulty remembering his own name without prompting.

I, at least, managed my own name correctly, as well as his. The priest stepped on my foot. Orsino stared at the top of my head rather than into my eyes. His hand was clammy on mine. We did not touch at any other point.

Ten minutes, and it was done. We went into the sala for the wedding dinner. There were no musicians or entertainers of any kind. I had not expected a play, but surely one or two musicians were not out of the question! Even in Montalto there was dancing at a wedding. The tables were not dressed with flowers, the food itself being the only ornament. I sat between Orsino and his mother with little conversation from either. His mother kept jumping up to attend to one thing or another, and I gathered that most of the servants had been hired for the night and weren't used to the house. As the dinner ended, I looked for Lucrezia who had not dined but must surely be about. Of course she was. She was hanging on the arm of one of the men in red, his back to me. She saw me and waved, motioning to me. I began to thread my way through the people.

"Giulia Farnese." I looked up at an expanse of red and gold doublet into the face of Virginio Orsini, the Lord of Bracciano.

"My Lord," I said with a curtsy. "I have you to thank for my good fortune. I cannot express my gratitude."

"You are very fortunate," he said. His expression was inscrutable.

"I am sure that Orsino and I will be very happy together." It couldn't be a sin to say it as a fact when it was only a hope, could it?

He snorted, looking over my shoulder at Orsino across the room. "He's good for something."

"My Lord?"

Bracciano glanced down at me. "As are you. I'm sure you will be useful in the days to come."

"I am delighted to place myself at your disposal, My Lord," I said with another curtsy while my blood ran cold. What did he mean? I was quite certain in that moment that I did not want to be of use to him in any sense.

"I shall be out of the city for the summer. I'll see you in the autumn," he said.

"Of course, My Lord," I said, bobbing again. Was that ominous, or did I read too much into small talk about his plans?

There was a tug at my sleeve. "Giulia, I want you to meet my papa," Lucrezia said.

Bracciano turned, a suddenly affable smile upon his face. "Vice-Chancellor," he said. "I was surprised to see you here."

"Why should that be, My Lord? Surely I must make time to bless this union within our two families." The cardinal looked nothing like Lucrezia, except for something around the eyes. He was as dark haired as she was fair, black-eyed and with a shadow of evening beard, an ordinary looking middle-aged man splendid in scarlet robes. His tone was precisely as agreeable as Bracciano's.

"I am no kin to Donna Adriana de Mila," Bracciano said. "Save by a marriage now ended."

"Marriages are eternal," the cardinal said, putting his palms together. "Shall they not be reunited in Heaven? So therefore we are kin and good brothers together."

Bracciano flushed red. "I...."

"But I have not paid my respects to the bride," the cardinal said, turning to me despite Bracciano's choler as though he dismissed him. He bent over my hand politely, my fingers in his gloved ones. "Congratulations, Donna Giulia. I hope this day brings you great happiness."

He did not really see me. No one did. "I feel certain that it will," I said. My annoyance made me daring. "For what else might it do when I find myself in your august presence? Surely there will be no greater joy for me today except what the marriage bed brings."

He looked up then, his eyes meeting mine over my knuckles. Startled, yes, but laughing, as though a treat had suddenly appeared. "Then I wish you happiness in your marriage bed, dear lady. The rest of us will have to make do with your wit, a pleasant addition to the household."

"Do you find yourself here so often that it will impress you?" I asked.

"I am here quite often of late," he said, releasing my hand as Lucrezia pushed forward under his arm, her arm about his waist. "I see you at least twice a week, do I not, sweetheart?"

"Always," Lucrezia said. "My father always keeps his word. Except when he lies."

Bracciano snorted. He looked exceedingly put out. "Vice-Chancellor," he said with a sharp nod and disappeared into the crowd. I looked after him, thinking perhaps I should have handled all of this better.

"My apologies," the cardinal said quietly. "I should not have visited that unpleasantness upon your wedding."

"I gather you and My Lord Bracciano are well acquainted," I said.

"I am the vice-chancellor of the College of Cardinals," he said. "And he is the gonfaloniere, the general of the Papal Armies. We have been yoked together for many years. Soldiers always want money and rarely appreciate sound fiscal management." He shrugged ruefully. "But that is nothing to you." He looked at me keenly. "Do you know him well?"

"I met him once before yesterday," I said truthfully.

"Ah." He put his head to the side. "And yet he was quite determined you should marry his kinsman."

"It is a mystery to me as well, Your Eminence," I said. Did he wonder if I were Bracciano's mistress? Or whether Bracciano intended me to be? That was certainly not something I could ask a man of the cloth about.

"I told you she was very pretty," Lucrezia said, as though I were a pet she'd brought home.

"And you did not lie," he said, "but it is not tactful to say so to her face unless you intend to flatter."

Lucrezia looked indignant. "But you say it to women."

"That's different." He glanced sideways at me with a wink. "Let us leave aside Donna Giulia's beauty and ask her instead how she likes our Rome?"

"Very well, Your Eminence," I said, unaccountably flustered.

"I am glad," he said with another bow, seeing Alessandro making his way toward me. "Lucrezia, we must not monopolize the bride. Until another day, Donna Giulia."

"Of course," I said, and watched him lead his daughter away.

Alessandro came to my side. "Who was that?"

"Lucrezia, the little girl who lodges with Donna Adriana," I said. "And her father, Cardinal Borgia. She is quite precocious. I am sure she will remind me of home."

"I hope so," Alessandro said. He looked at me solemnly. "I hope you are happy."

And if I am not, I thought, *there is nothing you can do about it. You are nineteen and a university student, and Bracciano is the gonfaloniere. I must stand on my own in this.* "I am sure I will be," I said.

I had no friends or mother here, and it would hardly be appropriate for Alessandro to see me to bed, so I left the wedding dinner with no one but Maria, Donna Adriana's maid, to help me undress. Carefully, she laid away my best clothes and I changed my camisa for one I had not worn all day, a linen drawn so fine that it was almost transparent, yet gathered at sleeve and neck so that the volume of cloth concealed a little.

"You look lovely, my lady," Maria said. "Would you like me to brush your hair out?"

"Yes. Thank you." I was determined to acquit myself well. I sat down on the embroidered green coverlet and let her unpin my elaborate rolls, brushing my hair out until it fell smooth and soft to my waist. Would Orsino like it? I would find out soon.

As soon as the maid left, I followed my mother's very specific instructions. I chewed on three leaves of peppermint to make my mouth sweet, then spat them out in the toilet pot. I got out the little flask of good olive oil she had put among my things and lifted up my skirt, dabbing it carefully in the folds between my legs, with special attention paid to my passage. Mother had said it would make everything easier. Certainly the slipping sensation of putting it on was pleasant, or would have been if I hadn't been quite so nervous.

And how should I receive my husband? Should I climb under the covers and pretend to be sleeping? That seemed unappealing. Under the covers but sitting up, hands in my lap as though I awaited orders? Also unappealing. Lounging on the bed, one foot and leg daringly sticking out? Maybe? With the camisa tugged off one shoulder, ribbons undone? Too much. He would probably need more coaxing than that.

What if it didn't work? I sat up and considered the prospect. What if he didn't get hard? What if he was too shy to go through with it? Or couldn't get it in the right place? Normally one would expect a husband to have had a woman before, but Orsino couldn't be more than six months my senior, and if he'd had a woman before I'd eat my own camisa. One could help, couldn't one? Surely if I rubbed it or played with it, he'd be able to do the deed. Mother had intimated as much. Sometimes men needed help. Well, I decided, if Orsino needed help, I'd help. Surely we could figure it out together, as man and wife were supposed to do. After all, I was quite certain where everything of mine was, and if he was anything like my pack of brothers, he'd found his own already. The thing about having brothers was that one was clear on that.

I waited. And waited. Was he sick? Was he so nervous that he was drinking to get up his courage? That wouldn't help. Excessive drink robbed a man of his wits, my mother said, and of his ability to stand to stud. If he was drunk, I didn't know what I would do. I was considering possibilities when I heard a soft knock on the door. I flung myself into a provocative position. "Come in!" I trilled.

Donna Adriana opened the door. I sat up, pulling the coverlet up around me. She closed the door behind her, crossing the room and sitting down on the foot of the bed facing me. "Giulia," she said, "I thought you might be waiting, so I have come to talk with you."

"Of course, Donna Adriana," I said. "Where is my husband?"

"He will not be here tonight," she said firmly. "We have decided that you are both too young to consummate the marriage now."

"We?" My voice sounded both angry and incredulous. "You and Orsino?"

"Me and Orsino's relatives," she said. "Orsino has nothing to say about it. There is plenty of time in the future. For now, you will live together as brother and sister."

"I do not want a sham marriage," I said. "Donna Adriana, I

want my husband in my bed as is his right."

Her eyes roved over my face, and for the first time I thought I saw real sympathy in her dark eyes. "My dear, sometimes we women have no choices."

"You are his mother…" I began.

"I am his stepmother, and I am only a woman," she said. Adriana shook her head. "Giulia, you must know this was not my choice. But at least be glad that you will not have a terrible experience this night."

"What? Is your son an ogre then?" I demanded.

"He is young," she said.

"Then I can manage him," I said. "If he has never bedded a woman before, we will learn together." I felt tears coming to my eyes.

Adriana shook her head again. "I'm sorry, Giulia. For now you must remain a virgin. Surely it is not so terrible a fate." She smoothed the coverlet with one hand, a garnet and seed pearl ring upon it. "You have all your long life ahead of you. You can wait."

"It seems I have no choice," I said bitterly.

"No," she said. Her eyes were kind. "And that, perhaps, is the lesson about womanhood you will learn tonight. We are leaves in the stream, child. The current tosses us where it wills." She got to her feet. "Goodnight, Giulia. Try to rest."

She closed the door behind her and I flung myself among the fat pillows. I would have cried had I not been too angry for tears. What kind of husband lets his mother—his stepmother!—tell him not to bed his wife? A weak one.

I got up and paced over to the window, not opening it because of the spring chill, but looking out onto the garden. The last guests were leaving. The Lord of Bracciano was making his way through the garden, several men with him. Orsino's relatives. Bracciano. My eyes narrowed. I'd wager any money that Bracciano was the author of this prohibition. But why would he insist that Orsino marry me immediately and then leave me virgin?

I raised my head, looking out across the soft garden in the moonlight. "Mary, Queen of Heaven, help me," I whispered. Something was very, very wrong in the Palazzo Orsini de Ponte.

Chapter Three

Yet nothing terrible happened. Alessandro left the next day to return to Pisa, planning to stop at home along the way and tell Mother all the news. Of course that did not include the disaster of my wedding night. I could not bear to tell Alessandro. Either he would grab Orsino by the scruff of the neck and demand he get on with it, or burst out laughing. Neither was acceptable. So I said nothing, and he very rightly did not ask about the marriage bed.

The next few weeks settled into a state of tranquility so deep as to be dull. Each night the servants carried the table into the middle of the sala and the four of us sat down to dinner, Adriana and Orsino on the short sides and me and Lucrezia on the long sides. I tried to draw my husband out on his pursuits. Did he hunt? Not in the city, and he was rarely elsewhere. Did he boat? Not on the Tiber as it was pestilential. Did he fight? He was not destined to be a soldier. Did he like poetry or plays? Hardly, he was not destined to be a scholar. Short of asking if he liked wenching or brothels, I could think of nothing else. Orsino, it seemed, had no pursuits at all.

"Why do you not go to the university at Pisa?" I asked him one night. "You might find all manner of interests there."

Adriana looked at him across the table. "I do not think so, no," she said. Orsino did not look up from his plate.

"My brother goes to the university at Pisa," Lucrezia said brightly.

"Mine too!" I said. "Alessandro, whom you met when he was here for the wedding."

"Cesare just began," she said. "He means to take holy orders."

"So does Alessandro!" We monopolized the rest of dinner with a comparison of our brothers. Mine was several years older than hers, but this happy topic carried us along until we were leaving the sala together.

Lucrezia stopped me on the stairs. "You shouldn't suggest Orsino go to the university," she said quietly.

"Why not? He doesn't say much for himself, but he's hardly incapable of scholarship," I said.

"There isn't any money to send him," she said. "His father left almost nothing. It's not kind to suggest Donna Adriana send him when she can't."

"Oh." I felt my cheeks flame. I understood entirely what it was to be expected to afford things that one couldn't.

"Good night, Giulia," Lucrezia said, leaning down and kissing me. She hurried up, her little slippers quiet on the stone.

And there was another mystery, I thought. This lovely house, these beautiful things, and there was no money? Then who was paying for all this? Presumably Lucrezia's father paid for her fine clothes, but what about the rest? There was no man other than Cardinal Borgia who visited regularly or I might have suspected that Adriana had a protector, but if so it was surely not her cousin. Besides, when he visited he concerned himself entirely with Lucrezia, and his visits were in broad daylight in public rooms of the house.

What were we living on? My mother had impressed upon me the expense of nice things and how one might make do and still appear prosperous. We had fowl and fish, good wine and soft linens. I did not go to the markets or wash my camisas. There were maids to do that. Who paid them? Or more precisely, in what coin were they paid? I resolved to find out. I was certain that Orsino did not pay them.

After the feast of St. John the Baptist on June 24 it grew even quieter. Lucrezia was gone to visit her mother and go to the country with her until Assumption in August. Without her, the house was hot and silent. Cardinal Borgia came no more. Sometimes Adriana went out with some friend of hers, but she did not stay late. Orsino took to leaving early in the morning on business of his own, coming home in the heat of the afternoon. He avoided me on his returns.

Two weeks of this, and I went down into the kitchen when they were laundering. A maid was bringing down his shirts, and I stopped her, holding out a single silver soldo. I gestured to his shirt in her basket. "Drink or women?" I said.

She looked at me, looked at the shirt, then looked at the coin. "Women," she said.

I handed it to her. "Thank you," I said stiffly. So he would not bed me, but he would bed some trull? My head almost spun with rage. There was the bucket of warm, soapy water she intended to wash in. "May I have this?" I asked politely.

"Yes, my lady," she said. The other women had all stopped to watch as I picked the bucket up and carried it out. Orsino was practicing sword passes in the garden clad in shirt sleeves in the heavy heat of the day. He did not look around when I marched in.

"Husband!" I shouted. He turned around and I gave him the bucket of water full in the face. "Coward! Wastrel! Fornicator!" I yelled, "You think I'll let you get by with this? Do you? You make a fool of me and I will not have it."

"Giulia?" He stood there dripping.

"You will not bed your lawful wife but you go to brothels!" I threw the bucket at his head for good measure.

He fended it off with his forearm, ducking as it bounced overhead. "Only three times!" he said.

"Only three times! Only three!"

"I have needs," he said. I heard a titter. The maids had followed me upstairs and were now hiding behind their aprons pretending not to watch.

"I have needs too, you bastard!" I shouted. "It would serve you right if I went to a brothel myself!"

"You're my wife," he said. He was starting to look red in the face, angry in addition to ridiculous.

"I'll take a lover," I said. I heard my voice shake. "I'll stretch myself out for a lover, and you won't even know who he is."

Orsino went white. "You can't do that," he said quietly, pushing his wet hair back from his face.

"Watch me," I said.

"You'll destroy us both." He took a step toward me. He looked genuinely frightened. "Giulia, don't even joke about such a thing."

"I'm not joking," I said, but his fear did register on me.

"You can't do that," he said. "You have to stay a virgin or terrible things will happen."

"What kind of terrible things?" The most baroque imaginings flitted through my mind.

"My cousin..." he said. "I promised him."

"Bracciano? Why in the world does he care about my chastity?" I demanded. I had for a moment considered ancient curses and deadly monsters, and now it was simply that his kinsman would be angry.

Orsino looked miserable. "He does. And if I cross him, we'll lose everything. Giulia, I beg you. Don't do anything. We can't...." He broke off, looking behind me.

I turned around. Donna Adriana was approaching. "What is going on here?"

"Your son is an unfaithful, fornicating scum," I said. "And I am leaving him. I have had enough of this sham marriage and this ridiculous situation. I am going back to Montalto. My brother is coming from Pisa to get me." I hadn't actually written to Alessandro, but I would. I was shaking.

Her voice was calm, but her eyes were not. I would swear she too was frightened. However, when she spoke it was evenly, for my benefit and that of the gaping servants. "Giulia, come into my camera and we will discuss this privately. Orsino, put on dry clothes. You look ridiculous."

"Gladly," I said and followed her, my head held high. We went upstairs, through the sala and into her camera beyond. She closed the doors, then crossed the room to the broad balcony which opened from the opposite wall. I followed her, taking a deep breath.

It was a magnificent view. Rome baked in the heat, the tower of St. Peter's visible off to the left, while we looked down on the tile roofs of palazzos nearby. The entire city spread out before us, a haze of cooking smoke and heat rising from it, beautiful and close and real.

"You are an intelligent young woman," she said. "I see I have underestimated you." I remained silent. "When my husband died, his relatives claimed everything he had," she said. "By dint of my cousin's influence, I managed to retain this house but nothing else. I appealed to the head of the family, Virginio Orsini, Lord Bracciano, for help. He said the best thing would be for my son to make an advantageous marriage." Her hands were working together.

"I see that would be useful, Madonna," I said. "But I am not an advantageous marriage. My dowry was only three thousand ducats and I am heir to no lands."

She shook her head. "Bracciano said that he had found a good bride for Orsino. We were desperate. Do you understand? I had debts to pay, and my husband's incomes ended when he died. I agreed to the marriage."

"Not knowing it was so little money?" I asked.

"Not until the contract was on the table," she said. She gave a sigh that was almost a sob. "I thought he wanted Montalto."

I bent my head. "I have three living brothers," I said. "But my brother Bartolomeo is thirteen years old, and Montalto overlooks the Via Aurelia. It is true that he could never hold it against Bracciano or any other great lord. He would welcome him as a kinsman. And it is a strategic location."

"That is what I thought," Adriana said. "An alliance with my son as a pawn to give him access to a strong point. Well enough, except that the money was so little."

"What has this to do with chastity?" I asked.

She shook her head. "The day of the contract signing he took me aside very particularly and expressed his desire for you to remain a virgin. He went so far as to insist that if you did not, he would take this house regardless of my cousin. He would consider it an intolerable provocation if Orsino bedded you." She turned the ring around on her finger again, the only one I'd seen her wear, and it struck me it was garnets, not rubies. "You were still young enough that it was plausible that he felt you should wait."

"But most unlike him," I said dryly.

Adriana glanced at me sideways, for a moment her expression like the cardinal's. "Yes."

"You think he intends to make me his own mistress?" I asked. I was proud my voice was so level.

"I can think of no other explanation," she said. "Giulia, I am sorry."

I looked away. *You old bawd*, I thought. *You will be madam for me without a bit of regret. Or if you do regret, it is that it is the way of the world. It is what women are. We are leaves in the stream, and we go where we are bidden*. I could afford Bracciano's wrath no more than Adriana could.

I put my hands on the smooth stone of the balustrade. It was warm with sun, dreaming lazily in the noontide. *This is the moment*, I thought. *This is the moment I awaken, not in love but in pride.* Bracciano made my skin crawl, but if he wanted me, I would master him. I would learn what tricks there might be. I would enthrall him. If he sought my maidenhead, he would find that my blood bound him tighter than chains.

"Very well," I said to Adriana. "I will do this. You should have told me from the beginning so that I understood."

"I underestimated you," she said. "I will not again."

"Thank you, Donna Adriana," I said. "Now that we have this clear, I will seek my rooms." I wasn't certain how long my dignity could last.

"Of course." She inclined her head.

As I stepped from the sun-drenched balcony into the shadow, one thing still bothered me. Bracciano had never expressed the slightest interest in or appreciation for my person, not so much as Lucrezia's father had. If it was lust that motivated him, it was not lust for me. Which meant it must be something far darker.

And so the house returned again to dull tranquility. I understood now that Adriana had no parties because she could not afford them. There were no lavish dinners or entertainments of any kind, not unless it were absolutely socially necessary, which it presently was not. It was clear to me now that we were living on my dowry. What would happen when it ran out?

Adriana did grudgingly agree to pay for Orsino to train with a master at arms on the theory that Bracciano might reward him for his good service by finding a place for him in the Papal Armies. He had no qualifications or understanding necessary for any other kind of position that would make him useful to a patron. Perhaps training at arms would at least encourage the famed condottiero in the family to take him under his wing. Personally, I doubted it.

My birthday came and went without being marked except by a package from home. It contained a new camisa sewn by my mother and trimmed with ribbons, the kind of thing a young bride might wear for her husband. Thinking of the love and thought she had surely put into it, I felt a smoldering resentment that my husband would not even see it.

Orsino and I were barely speaking. Any hopes of a happy marriage seemed long in the past. Lucrezia remained with her mother longer than expected, and we ate as if it were Lent. I wondered how much of the cause was parsimony and how much was that the cardinal paid lavishly for Lucrezia's upkeep, enough to put dinner on the table for four people rather than one small girl. She would return two weeks after Assumption, when the summer heat began to wane and the grapes plumped on the vine. At home I would be looking forward to the harvest. At home I had work to do. Here I had none.

I haunted the house like a ghost. Indeed, in some fanciful moments, I wondered if future residents would see me here, wandering aimlessly from room to room, a young woman who had died of boredom. The house was a lopsided square with the garden in the center. The back wall wasn't ours; it belonged to the house behind on the opposite street, so we were really three sides of the square. The main stairs went up in the middle just beside the portico through all three stories, though there were servants' stairs at either end of the wings at the back. Right from the top of the stairs was Adriana's sala where we'd had the wedding, and through it her camera with the beautiful balcony. Next to it was the grand suite which had belonged to Adriana's late husband. It sat unused, sala and camera and study and dressing room.

My room was on the floor above hers, but on the third floor the hall had the exterior windows whereas the room windows looked onto the garden. Lucrezia's rooms were the mirror of mine on the other side of the stair. No one lived on the entire floor besides me and Lucrezia, something I found extremely strange. At Montalto I had shared a room with my grandmother until she died. After that

I had it to myself because I was the only girl except for the baby, who slept in my mother's room. My brothers were two to a room—Alessandro and Bartolomeo, Angelo and Amadeo. Poor people might sleep all in one room. You could see that we were wealthy since there were four bedrooms for a family of eight. This palazzo could have comfortably slept twenty, not counting servants' rooms.

On the ground floor there was the kitchen and laundry and pantries on one side and the saletta on the other, a little-used reception room where the candles were not even lit at night unless by Donna Adriana's order. There was also what must have been a porter's chamber or guardroom a few steps down just inside the front doors. However, there was no porter or guards at present, so it sat empty.

There was also a library presumably belonging to the late Ludovico, some twenty or so volumes. Gaps on the shelves showed where the most valuable books had been sold. What was left was not much. There was a single volume of Plutarch's *Lives of the Famous Greeks and Romans*, and I buried myself in it for the better part of a week, sighing over Alexander. Alexander was bold and gallant and clever, a lover of learning, a dangerous foe and a devoted ally. He was the model of all a man might be. I imagined him vividly, as though he were someone I remembered from early childhood. Was it possible, I wondered, to fall madly in love with a man dead nearly two thousand years? Or was that simply a mark of my frustration?

I was reading while walking downstairs. Because it was hot and I expected to see no one, I wore only my green cotta over my long camisa, my hair confined by a snood to keep it off my neck. I had gotten almost to the ground floor doors when they opened. Adriana was greeting someone with ceremony. Lucrezia was back and her father had brought her. Two manservants hurried in with her things, followed by the cardinal in a billow of scarlet and Lucrezia bouncing along talking at full volume.

I shrunk back, hopeful that they would simply pass without looking up the stairs and seeing me standing like a slattern. Unfortunately, Lucrezia had eagle eyes. "Giulia!" she shrieked, running to me and embracing me. "I missed you. I wished you could have been in the country with us. I told my mother all about you. I told my brother too. Not Cesare, he's still in Pisa. My other brother, Juan. And I told Carlo about you too. I told everybody you were my new friend."

Of course I could not simply disappear at that point. "I have missed you too, Lucrezia," I said, embracing her with Alexander in one hand. It was entirely true. I had wished she were back every day.

"My father came to get me," she said loudly. "And to tell Juan to behave. He was so rude to Carlo that now he's come to stay in the vice-chancellor's palazzo instead of with mother because she says she won't put up with it."

"Lucrezia, discretion," her father said quietly. He looked at me over her golden head, a conspiratorial glance. Her eyes were blue but his were a brown so dark they looked almost black. Perhaps her mother was fair? "Not every bit of personal business needs to be aired."

"I think your family's quarrels are private," I said, answering the cardinal with a smile.

"No, they're not. They were very loud!" Lucrezia said.

At that I laughed. "I am sure of that."

Her father inclined his head courteously. "And how is the bride? Happy in her marriage, I presume?"

My smile faded. "I am well, Your Eminence," I said stiffly.

"Forgive me," he said. "My question was inappropriate."

"Not at all, Your Eminence." What else could one say?

He glanced down at the book in my hand. "You have found an old friend?"

"A new one," I said, lifting it so he could see. "Plutarch's *Lives*. Unfortunately, there is only one volume."

"Which one?" he took the book from me, his fingers brushing against mine. "The last volume, Agesilaus, Pompey, Alexander, Caesar, Demosthenes, Cicero, Demetrius and Antony. The best one, perhaps." He looked up at me, as he stood two steps below on the stairs. "Who is your favorite?"

"I confess myself mad for Alexander," I said, with what I hoped was sophistication rather than blushing absorption in a dead man.

"My favorite as well," he said. "When I was your age there were no printed copies. I parsed out each phrase in the college in Valencia, a boy of twelve imagining each majestic scene."

"I am sixteen rather than twelve, Your Eminence," I said. And yet there was something charming about imagining him as a boy. Was he like Lucrezia, or more restrained and disciplined?

"Of course," he said, inclining his head. "And delightfully so."

Was this mere courtesy, or did he mean it? I felt myself blushing and not at a dead man. "Were you a serious and scholarly boy?" I asked.

"I believe I was directionless and pleasant, or so my uncle said," the cardinal replied. "Unlikely to make much of myself without greater application."

"And so that is what you say to my brothers," Lucrezia said.

"Young men require motivation," he said, with that conspiratorial glance again. "Unlike young ladies, who one must scamper to keep up with." He nodded to me politely. "Good day, Donna Giulia. I trust I will see you about."

"I hope so, Your Eminence," I said, and was surprised to find that I did.

Two days later a complete six-volume set of Plutarch was delivered for me. I gaped at it. I had never owned something so expensive in my life. The first page of the last volume was inscribed to me.

"For La Bella Farnese, with hopes that she will enjoy her studies, Rodrigo Borgia."

I held the book open, incredulous with pleasure, and nearly missed what Lucrezia was saying. "...I'm to have a tutor come four days a week. My father says if you'd like to help me with my lessons you could. I wish you would. Won't you, Giulia?"

"A tutor?" I felt that I had missed something. Five more volumes. And the note.

"I'm having a tutor come," Lucrezia said as though I were slow. "Do you want to help me with my lessons?"

"You mean join you with your tutor?" I had studied with Alessandro when we were small, but when he went away to university the tutor had been dismissed. Bartolomeo and Angelo were too young, and there was no sense in paying a tutor for just a girl.

"It would be more decent if there were a married woman with me even though he's a priest," Lucrezia said. "Like a chaperone. But you could learn everything I did. Or more, since you're older."

"Was this your idea or your father's?" I asked.

"His," Lucrezia said happily. "I terrify priests."

There was something that seemed strange, however. "Your own tutor? Just for you?"

Lucrezia nodded. "Just for me. My father says I need a serious tutor to teach me mathematics and Latin and things like that so I'll be ready to go to school soon. It's a convent school and he says it's the best one for young ladies in Rome but they're very demanding and they don't take girls who are ignorant. So I'm to have a tutor and work very hard. After all, I'm nine years old now."

I supposed it made sense for the daughter of a churchman to go to a convent, though it seemed to me that Lucrezia was ill-suited to a life of contemplation. "Are you to be a novice?"

She laughed, her face getting a little pink. "Don't be silly! It's just a few years. I'm to be a lady. My father says I may yet be a queen! Not that it's likely, but I will certainly be a great lady."

I must have looked skeptical because she went on. "My parents want me to marry well. I need polish, so I'm to live with Donna Adriana in a noble household and have tutors and go to school. Mother says a rich husband expects those things and I'm to have all the opportunities she didn't have. I mean, I learned how to write and I can't remember before I could read, but Mother can't teach me anymore. She can read and figure but she uses a letter-writer when she needs to send a letter."

Which seemed a great deal to me for a—what? I was unsure of the words that wouldn't cause offense. "Your mother doesn't want you to follow in her footsteps?" I asked cautiously.

Lucrezia sat down, drawing her knees up beneath bright blue silk skirts. "As a concubine? Or as the wife of a commoner? She's married to Carlo now. He's nice. Really quiet, not like Papa."

"I'm afraid I don't understand," I said.

"I suppose they don't have concubines in Montalto," Lucrezia said. She took on the air of a tutor explaining something to a backward child. "There are three kinds of whores—streetwalkers, courtesans and concubines. Streetwalkers just go with whoever for money. Most of them have other jobs too but pick up some on the side. Then there are the courtesans, meretrices from the Latin. They have their own rooms or houses and men come to them. Some of them are poor and some are really rich. My mother used to be a courtesan a long time ago. But then she met my papa and she made him court her. He had to work hard, he says. She says she knows her own worth. So he made her a fair offer and bought her house and she became a concubine." Lucrezia tossed her blond hair. "A concubine has one man who lives with her and who provides for her and her children and is responsible. Lots of churchmen have concubines since they can't ever marry anyone. Papa lived with us for years until they ended. I've got three brothers."

It was not at all the way it was done in Montalto. Even if poorer people didn't always get married with a contract and everything because they didn't have any property, everyone knew they were husband and wife.

Lucrezia was going on. "Cesare is for the Church and he's at the University in Pisa just like your brother. Juan is going to have a great military career. And I don't know what Gioffre will do because he's only seven."

The university wasn't cheap, as I well knew. Cardinal Borgia was spending a lot of money on his children. "And you have a dowry," I guessed.

"Sixty thousand ducats," she said cheerfully.

I could not have heard correctly. "Sixty thousand?" My dowry was three thousand. Sixty thousand would buy two properties like Montalto with everything in them.

Lucrezia nodded matter-of-factly. "Yes. But ten thousand came from my other brother's will. Pedro Luis was a lot older than me. He had a different mother. He was in the service of the Spanish crown and got killed last year in a battle." She dropped her voice like her father might somehow hear. "So don't say anything about him to Papa. He and Pedro Luis were close and he was distraught." She seemed proud of the word. I wondered if it was her mother's.

"You knew him?" A much older bastard son with a different mother?

"I met him when we were in Spain two years ago. Papa took me and Cesare and Juan with him to Valencia. I met Pedro Luis and my sisters. They're even older. Isabella has two sons who are almost my age! My sisters are married. I didn't ask them how much their dowries were because Papa didn't have as much money when they were girls so it would be tactless."

"Yes," I said. Lucrezia was dowered like a countess.

She looked at me keenly. "How much was your dowry?"

"Three thousand," I said, feeling my face heat.

She looked dismayed. "I'm so sorry!"

"Don't be," I said briskly. "My family may not be wealthy, but we love each other."

"And that's more important," Lucrezia said. "Having a big dowry is nice, but I hope Papa doesn't marry me to someone awful who just wants the money."

That was likely. But then a small dowry didn't seem to have gotten me a good husband. "None of us choose who we marry," I said, "so we just have to make the best of it."

"That's what Donna Adriana says. But my mother chose. She picked Papa and Carlo both. So maybe it's better to be a concubine than a wife."

"I am sure your papa will choose a good husband for you," I said. I expected at that price he'd have his choice of bidders, and given how indulged Lucrezia was, I had no doubt the cardinal would choose someone he thought good.

Chapter Four

Autumn came, the first cool day of rain. It had just begun to darken when Donna Adriana came to my room. There was a fire lit, the last of summer's greenery dry and burning brightly on the logs. Her face was pale beneath her high-pinned hair. "My Lord Bracciano has sent a message," she said.

I turned. I could see my reflection in the mirror behind her, wavering slightly from the burnished surface as though I were underwater. I had not expected this summons, not precisely tonight, though I had dreaded it since summer ended. "I see," I said. My voice was even.

"He requests your presence at a party at his palazzo tonight," she said.

"I see," I said again.

Adriana's hands twisted together. "You might...plead illness," she said. "Moon sickness."

"That will only postpone the inevitable." The woman in the mirror looked quite composed. "It is better to do it."

She nodded sharply. "Brave girl. Then..." She opened her hand. There were three peppermint leaves.

"Thank you," I said. I took them. I chewed them and spat them in the pot.

"Shall I help you dress?" she asked.

"That would be very kind," I said. For all that I was steeled for the blow, it was harder now that I faced it.

My best clothes, the fine camisa with the blue cotta and the dark blue gown that went over it, elaborate sleeves with light blue lacing. My wedding clothes. Donna Adriana helped me pin my hair as though she were my mother. She said nothing. I said nothing, only winced when she pulled a roll too tight.

"His man said he would send guards to escort you," she said.

"Of course," I murmured.

I had a cloak against the rain, protecting hair and dress, while three of Bracciano's men escorted me through the streets. I do not know if I was frightened. It seemed a dream of darkness and rain, the city quenched.

His palazzo was much grander than Donna Adriana's. He was the gonfaloniere and a great soldier. Candles and lamps blazed brightly. I was led in through the main doors and upstairs like an honored guest. The room was a sala on the second floor, but the furniture had all been pushed back to the walls, the carpets rolled up and laid aside. There was nothing but bare boards and a three-legged stool that might have been brought from the kitchen set in the center of the room.

My heart beat faster. And yet this was unfathomable. If the lord of Bracciano intended some debauchery, this was a very strange way to go about it. I turned, nearly colliding with him. "My Lord, I do not understand," I said breathlessly. Perhaps an appeal based on ignorance or innocence?

There were seven other gentlemen, two of whom seemed to be fiddling with a censer that would not have been out of place in St. Peter's. Bracciano looked around the room with approval. "It isn't necessary for you to understand. Gentlemen, this is Donna Giulia, my young cousin's wife whom he has generously loaned to us."

"Charmed," one said, bowing politely. The others simply looked at me and continued with what they were doing.

"Gentlemen," I said with my head high. Their looks were

not rapacious. Rather, they seemed hardly interested in me at all. Generously loaned indeed! As though Orsino had any say in the matter! Bracciano was in his fifties, a great lord and perhaps the most famous condottiero living, Gonfaloniere of the Papal Army. Surely he had better things to do than disgrace a young cousin's virgin wife. If he wanted women, he could have them by the dozen. This did not make sense. These men did not seem drunk or as though they sought entertainment with a woman.

I took a deep breath. Best to take the bull by the horns, as it were. "My Lord Bracciano," I said quietly, "I shall be better able to aid your purpose if I understand what it is. It is of course my honor and my pleasure to assist so distinguished a member of my new family. May I call you uncle? I feel already that you are." I looked up at him through my lashes.

He glanced down at me, his brows knitting as though he actually saw me for the first time. "You see things in mirrors. This is an operation which requires such."

Two of the men had chalk in hand and had begun to mark out a large square on the bare floor with the stool at the center of it. A chill ran down my back. "My Lord, is this witchcraft?"

Bracciano harumphed. "Witchcraft is folly entered into by old women. This is science. The celestial spheres in their movements hold secrets of what the future will hold. They show nexus points where one or another path may come to pass. The ancients knew this when they consulted Pythian Apollo and other shrines. Their lost knowledge is lost no longer. By means of certain principles, their knowledge may be applied."

"My Lord, I have little learning," I said carefully. "I do not see how I may aid you. I am a simple young woman and know nothing of science or the world."

"That is the essence of it," he said. He rubbed his chin with one hand, his eyes on the preparations rather than on me. "You are a vessel to be filled. You are a Dove. That which we contact can speak through you and relay their wisdom."

"My Lord, that frightens me," I said quickly.

"Full possession isn't necessary," he said. "The entity we summon will speak to you through the mirror and use it to show you the answers to the questions we pose. You will relay them to us."

My hands were shaking. I stilled them. There was little point in protest. He was hardly going to let me leave. "I understand, My Lord," I said.

"Good," he said brusquely. It would be easier if the Dove cooperated rather than resisted. He left me then, going to talk to one of the men who was chalking the square. I took a deep breath. Congress with demons was a mortal sin. If seeking a vision of my future husband was terrible, how much worse was this? And yet with no way back, there was only forward.

"Donna Giulia, if you will come sit on the stool now?" a younger man asked. I carefully lifted my skirts so they did not brush the chalked symbols as I stepped into the square. I sat on the stool, back straight. "Hold this, if you would," he asked, and put something into my hands.

It was a hand mirror, but not like any I had seen. It was all metal, bronze darkened by age, a smooth circle on a handle shaped like some kind of flower on a stem. It was old, as old as the tombs where I had sought Proserpina, cool and dark. It did not reflect my face or the room behind me. I held it in my lap, putting my feet up on the rung between legs of the stool like a child who helps in the kitchen. The stool was too tall for me. My sleeves were pale, shining dully in the candlelight. The mirror did not shine.

Now they were chalking symbols around the outside of the square. Greek letters? Probably, but I had no Greek. Alessandro had not begun when he had left for school and his tutor was no longer needed. I sat quietly. Now they were speaking in that tongue, now putting a circle around the square. There were more symbols, more addresses to the unseen. It was very cold. It should not be, not when I wore ordinary clothes for an autumn night, not in a room full of candles with nine people. I was shivering in the center of the square. The circle just touched the corners of the square. They all stood outside it, a young man kneeling to fill in the spaces between square and curve with more letters. His voice was monotonous. It made me sleepy for all that the cold pierced. My hands were cold on the mirror. I was freezing into ice.

Bracciano spoke aloud. "*Ecce*!" he said. "*Venite*!" *Behold! Come!* A long shiver ran though me, enough that I nearly fell off the stool. "Look into the mirror," he commanded. "Look."

I looked. It was not my reflection that looked back. It was a shape of mist that might have been a face. It had two eyes and a mouth, though the mouth flowed to the side as though it meant to grimace or smirk. It looked at me, and it was amused, like a cat with a mouse discovered in the middle of the kitchen floor, far from any hole.

"Asmodeus, you are bound to answer our questions," Bracciano said.

Its smirk grew. "I will answer," it said. It pleased it to do so. It relished the pain it could cause.

"What does it say, Donna Giulia?" he demanded.

"He will answer, My Lord," I said. To my surprise my voice was even.

"Consider well, My Lord," the young man said to Bracciano. "A spirit of this sort will exhaust the Dove."

Bracciano nodded. "How long shall Pope Innocent live?"

The thing in the mirror smiled. "Not three years," it said.

"Not three years," I said aloud.

Bracciano shrugged. "Can you be more specific? Show her."

The surface of the mirror wavered. An old man with a long beard lay in a bed, a cap pulled down around his ears. His breath was harsh. Figures like shadows moved around him. His hands were clasped on his breast, a rich coverlet pulled up beneath them. His chest barely moved.

"I see him on his deathbed," I said. And yet there was nothing to tell me when it might be. I simply watched him breathe.

"When?"

"I do not know, My Lord," I said. "There is nothing to tell me."

"Look, then!"

I looked. A red sleeve, as though a cardinal bent over him. A servant standing with a basin. "There is nothing that could not be on any day," I said.

"Yet within three years," one of the men said.

"Anyone could have told us that," another said.

Bracciano changed course. "Shall my cousin, Cardinal Orsini, put on the papal tiara?"

For a moment the mirror swam. I saw a group of cardinals disputing. They talked, their faces angry, their hands empty. "I do not see the tiara or your cousin," I said.

"Make it show you," Bracciano directed.

I saw slips of paper, black smoke rising. That was easy enough to interpret. "My Lord, I see only black smoke," I said. "I think it is not possible to answer whether your cousin shall be elevated or not."

"This is useless," one of the men said. "She makes up answers that are not answers."

Bracciano shook his head. "Whenever it happens, I will be ready. Asmodeus, will I have one hundred thousand florins to expand the Papal Army?"

The answer was clear enough. I saw an empty pay chest, Bracciano pacing furiously before a window. "No, My Lord." My arms were beginning to cramp. My voice shook. It was like having ice in my veins.

The young man saw. "Just one more, My Lord. We must close the circle before she faints."

Bracciano nodded shortly. "Who is the man who stands between me and the prize?"

The mirror swam again, a man's face appearing. Dark eyes looked up as though he could see me, not young but mobile and pleasant, deep graven lines and an expression that looked vaguely amused. A day's growth of beard on his chin was as much gray as dark. A red hat came down on his forehead.

"Who is it?" Bracciano demanded.

My arms shook. The man smiled. He half-turned, as though to some comment out of sight, then glanced back with a knowing look. "I do not know," I lied.

"What do you mean, you don't know?"

He lifted a hand, ruby ring flashing, and said something I could not hear. "I do not know, My Lord," I said. The demon laughed. "I do not know. I have never seen him before this moment." My hands shook. The mirror dropped from them, hitting the floor on the edge and landing face down.

"We must close the circle," the young man said urgently. "Before the Dove breaks it. We may repeat the operation at the next auspicious time."

Bracciano nodded sharply. "Do it."

I huddled on the stool, my arms crossed to hug myself, shivering, as they spoke many words and erased symbols. As soon as they had removed the circle that encased the square, the young man entered, raising me up and leading me out. His eyes were concerned. "Are you well?"

"Dr. Treschi, you are overconcerned with our Dove," Bracciano said.

"It is very difficult to find a good one," Treschi said. "One must take care."

"I am sorry, My Lord," I said to Bracciano. Truly, I felt my strength return, but there was little good in showing him that. If he thought me spent, all to the good.

"You cannot name the man?" Bracciano said.

"He wore a red hat," I said. "But I do not know him. My Lord, I am newly come to Rome. I do not know most of the cardinals by sight."

That seemed to satisfy him. "Take her home," he said to one of the men. "See she comes to no harm. Donna Giulia, you will speak of this to no one."

"Of course not, My Lord," I assured him, and because he frowned, I added, "If I did, who should believe it? I am a silly girl and you the gonfaloniere!"

"True." He nodded then. "Until another time."

He let his man lead me out, two guards falling in to escort us through the streets. It was late, and the streets of Rome were not safe. Cloaked, I walked among my escort. It was not so cold as I had thought. The feeling came back into my legs.

A Dove. An empty vessel. And yet I had not told him all, nor could he compel it. He did not realize what I had concealed. I knew the man on sight of course. He was Lucrezia's father, Cardinal Borgia.

When I got home there was a light still burning in Donna Adriana's sala. She heard my step and came out directly. "Giulia? Are you ill?" she asked.

"Only cold," I said. "And wet. The rain…"

She put her arm around my back and guided me up the stairs. "I will call for Maria. She will put you to bed. There is a fire already in your room."

I confess that I was touched. It had not happened as she had anticipated, nor as I had, but it all seemed too complex to explain. Besides, some part of me thought, Bracciano would rather have it thought he despoiled his cousin's virgin bride than that he practiced magic which was surely strongly prohibited. Even I, who did not follow Papal politics as closely as many in Rome, knew that not five years ago the pope had published the *Malleus Maleficarum*, saying that sorcerers should be executed. And yet I could not accuse him. What proof had I? His cousin was a cardinal and he himself commanded the pope's armies. I was no one at all. I had no more recourse than I would have if he had raped me.

Adriana saw me into my room. Maria, her maid, was waiting, the fire built up so that it was warm and light. "Goodnight, Giulia," she said.

"Goodnight, Donna Adriana," I said. "And thank you."

I slept ten hours. When I woke the storm had blown itself out and it was a beautiful autumn day, sun streaming through the window. My eyes still closed, I stretched my hand out against the soft sheets. In the garden, a child shouted excitedly. "Mama, come and see!"

I turned my head. The only child here was Lucrezia, and as far as I knew her mother had never been here. I went to the window, but there was no one in the garden. *Not again*, I thought. I leaned against the casement and considered my situation.

Now I understood completely. Yes, bringing Montalto under Bracciano's control was something, but it was not the sole reason for my marriage. Now I knew why Orsino had been forbidden to touch me, though we were certainly both of an age for the marriage to be consummated. A Dove must be virgin. If he had one, bound to his house by marriage and honor, he should never need to search for one again. And now he expected me to earn my supper. He was supporting the household. Every gown and sweet I had was his to give or withhold.

I had no illusions that Donna Adriana had any power to gainsay him. If I told her what had happened, what would she do? Absolutely nothing, I thought. If she had been willing to act as Bracciano's procurer, she would not cross Bracciano.

Who else could I tell? Our parish priest? If he believed me, what could he do? He was an elderly man. How would he cross the pope's hand-chosen general? And most likely he would not believe me. It seemed too fantastic. The pope's gonfaloniere has been conjuring demons? No, that was out. Telling Orsino was not even a possibility. Lucrezia was a child.

Her father? I considered Cardinal Borgia more carefully. It did touch upon him. And it was plain from the conversation at my wedding that he and Bracciano were not friends. However, as one of the men there had said, I had told them nothing that anyone could not have guessed. Pope Innocent was an old man in poor health, and anyone might guess that he did not have three years further appointed to him. That it was not possible to predict who would be chosen next. All Rome knew that. That the vice-chancellor would not give the gonfaloniere an absolutely absurd amount of money from the Vatican coffers? No one knew that better than the vice-chancellor.

If he believed me. And why should he? In the light of day it seemed ridiculous. His good opinion meant something to me. I did not want him to believe me mad.

No, I thought, looking out into the serene garden, I had taken no hurt from the episode. In truth, it had not frightened me as much as it probably should have. I should have been terrified witless. Instead, I had refused to say what both the demon and Bracciano wished me to and had not been harmed. I had indeed learned something. I had more control than they did. They could not compel me, save in the ways in the world that Bracciano could—wealth and position.

I took a deep breath of the fresh air, cleaned of smoke after the rain. A Dove is not an empty vessel with no will of her own. Perhaps I should learn what the limits of their control were, men and demon alike. To converse with demons was a grave sin. If I could not refuse Bracciano, perhaps I could at least blunt his purpose. If he learned nothing of use from this, he would give it up. It was a great deal to risk his immortal soul to find out things everyone in Rome could tell him! Yes, I thought, that was the best course. I would tell no one, and if he sent for me again, I would reveal nothing useful to him. If I were less use than week-old gossip, he would grow tired of it.

Adriana sent for me later that day. I went to her camera, which was much larger and nicer than mine, with room for a writing desk as well as her big bed, the doors to the beautiful balcony open to let in fresh air and golden autumn sunshine. She looked up from her account book as I entered.

"Good morning, Donna Adriana."

The lines of her face softened as though she liked what she saw. "Are you well, Giulia?"

"Yes, Donna Adriana." She thought that Bracciano had taken me, of course. Perhaps she thought I had found it a sore trial and approved my stoicism. I could hardly explain.

"Good." She paused as though waiting for some further description. I said nothing, only clasped my hands at my waist like a dutiful daughter. "Well then." Her voice was brisk. "Did My Lord Bracciano make you an offer?"

"I beg your pardon?" I wasn't entirely certain what she meant.

"Did he offer you financial support? Give you a present?"

I could certainly answer that truthfully. "No, Madonna."

"He said nothing about money or household expenses? An allowance?"

A flush rose in my face, but it was anger, not shame. She wanted to know if he had paid me like the whore she thought I was. "No,

Madonna." I kept my voice even. "All he said was that he would see me again soon."

Her mouth tightened. "I see."

"Perhaps he thought he had already done me great good by arranging my marriage to Orsino," I said, my eyes wide and disingenuous. Did she even feel any guilt about playing the madam for her daughter-in-law? She thought herself better than Lucrezia's mother, but Lucrezia's mother had made it clear she wouldn't sell her off like this. I had the power to make Adriana squirm a little bit. "After all, an eligible young man with the Orsini name is a better marriage than a girl like me could expect."

Adriana had the good grace to look away. "It is customary for a gentleman to make some offer of support," she said. "Or at least to show his appreciation with a present."

"You mean send me off with a purse? No, Donna Adriana. Perhaps he feels he's already paid for me."

"There is no need to be crude," Adrian snapped.

"I beg your pardon," I said sweetly. "I misunderstood."

"That will be all," she said, and bent her head over her accounts. No doubt she'd like to see a hefty contribution to the household expenses rather than having to contrive to feed and clothe me while I brought in nothing. Except my dowry, but by now I understood how little it was by Roman standards. Bracciano could well afford to contribute but I knew he wouldn't—and would not have even if Adriana's suppositions had been true. After all, as I'd said, one way or another he had already paid for me.

Whether my answers discouraged Bracciano from further conjurings, or whether he simply sought some other method, I did not know. Perhaps he was too busy. Whatever the reason, Advent and Christmas came and went without another summons. It was not as cheerless as I expected. My mother sent greetings, of course. Alessandro sent me a book from Pisa, the rather risqué verses of the poet Catullus, which made me wonder what he was studying. Or perhaps it was that he thought I might take instruction? Who knew, I thought fondly, what Alessandro thought? Of all my family he was the most like me in temper. If we could talk, I would love to hear of his adventures in Pisa. I would wager they were not as chaste as they should be for a man about to be bound to holy orders! A year ago I'd caught him in the barn at Montalto with a girl. I supposed if he was going to take a vow of chastity, he should make the time before count. Not that there seemed a great deal of chastity among the clergy of Rome.

Lucrezia was gone two days to her mother and two days to the vice-chancellor's palazzo, returning loaded with sweets which she shared generously. By Epiphany we had resumed our usual pursuits, including the visits of her tutor, and Rome seemed wrapped in eternal gray drizzle, not cold enough to snow. We did not go out. I read Plutarch twice and the Alexander section more than that. Indeed, sometimes I went to sleep reading and had sensual dreams of the conqueror in my bed. I did not confess them. Lusting after a man not my husband seemed silly when he was long dead! Perhaps I suffered from what my mother had called over-ripe virginity. And yet my husband would not touch me without Bracciano's permission. It was enough to make one grind one's teeth.

One cold and drizzly day I wandered into Lucrezia's room, wondering if she were as bored as I. "We could play cards," she said, bouncing up to get them. "I have a nice deck my brother sent me." She opened a wooden box to show a neatly printed deck, each picture hand-colored. "We could play Tarocchi. Well, except that it takes four people."

I looked at the printed cards a little enviously. “I don’t know how to play,” I said. “We had chess at home, but my parents didn’t play cards.”

“My mama taught me,” Lucrezia said, plopping down on the bed and shuffling the cards expertly. “She said we should know how to play without losing money. I used to beat Cesare all the time before he went away to school. That’s why he sent me the cards as a present. It was kind of a joke but not really.”

I could see that knowing how to play cards without losing money would be a useful skill for a courtesan’s daughter. Or perhaps in Rome everyone played for high stakes? “You could teach me,” I said.

“Not Tarocchi,” she said. “It takes four people. It’s two pairs of partners and you take tricks and there are the special cards and some suits are ascending and some are descending.” I must have looked blank. “Or we could play two-handed Patience, but that’s boring.”

“I don’t mind,” I said.

Her eyes lit. “Or we could tell fortunes! Mama has a friend who can tell fortunes with cards. Mama says it’s made-up but I don’t think so. She told a friend of my mother’s that her baby was going to be a boy before it was born!”

She had an even chance of being right, I thought. Still, it was a diversion. “All right,” I said. “What do we do?”

Lucrezia handed me the deck. “You shuffle. Just shuffle a bunch of times. And you think about me. That’s what Signora Corsi says she does. And I think about what I want to know.”

“What do you want to know?” I asked. The cards felt firm and warm in my hands, printed pictures flickering past, four suits and the trionfi, the trump cards.

Lucrezia gave a little waggle, like a thoughtful puppy. “Will I have a handsome husband? Oh wait, that’s a yes or no question. Who will be my husband?”

I shuffled again. "Who will be Lucrezia's husband?" The cards blurred into one another, bits of drawing flipping past, a goblet, a horse, swords interwoven like a lattice.

"Then you deal three cards face down," she instructed, patting the bed. "One, two, three. What will happen first, second, third."

"When I'm ready," I said. The cards weren't yet. Another shuffle. They were definitely warm. There was the same sense of something I felt in mirrors, but calmer. Easier. They were paper. They were under my control. I took a deep breath. Lucrezia's husband. "One." I laid one on the cloth beside her hand. "Two. Three."

"Now you turn the first one over," she instructed.

I did. A young man was mounted on a horse, his cap ornamented with a brooch, a fat purse at his belt and a rain of coins around him. "And there he is," I said. My vision narrowed. The picture was just a black engraving on paper, but clear.

"The Knight of Coins," Lucrezia said with satisfaction. "Tell me about him."

"I don't know how to do this," I said. If there were meanings her mother's friend used, I had not learned them.

"Oh, just make it up!" Lucrezia said. "Just tell a story."

Freed from having to know, it was easy. "A young man," I said. "Dark haired and stubborn. Look how closely he grips the reins! He's rich. Look at that purse. The lord of fine lands." His heels were tight to his horse's side and he did not smile. "He likes to control things. Responsible. A solid husband." I glanced up at her.

Lucrezia seemed unimpressed. "And then?"

I turned the second card. It was another man on horseback, a blond man with a tabard of cloth-of-gold, a golden goblet in his hands. He had a weak chin. "Another knight. This one has a cup instead of money. Gentler, kinder. Maybe a little indecisive." I flipped the third card. "And another knight." He was dark, wearing full armor, his horse in barding as well, a bared sword in his hand, though he wore a lady's token on his breast. "A soldier. A chivalrous knight. Leader of many men, a lord to be reckoned with."

"Three husbands?" Lucrezia said skeptically. "Really?"

I shrugged. "It's made up, as your mother says."

"And you just drew three knights in a row?" She frowned. "I should not like to be twice widowed. Or maybe they're lovers."

"They might be lovers," I allowed.

Lucrezia scooped up the cards, putting them back in the deck. "Now your turn. Will you have a handsome husband?"

"I think we know that I do not," I said, and we both burst out laughing. "There is little point in trying to see that." I shuffled the cards again. "Maybe just a more general what will happen." The cards drew me, pulling me into their pictures. Shuffling again. One. Two. Three.

I turned the first card. A woman rode in a chariot drawn by two winged horses. Her gloves were red and she held the orb of the world in her hands. She looked regal, serene, though the horses reared and stomped, her gown patterned with lilies. The horses carried her away, but she smiled. "I do not know this card," I said quietly.

"That's one of the trionfi," Lucrezia said. "The Chariot."

"A chariot to bear you away to the underworld," I said. She looked out of the card at me, a smile like Proserpina's on the wall of the tomb in Montalto. "Proserpina, the Queen of the Dead."

"She doesn't look dead to me," Lucrezia said.

"In the story," I said. "With Pluto. You haven't done Ovid yet, have you?" She shrugged. Perhaps abduction was considered too mature a topic for her. Or the Latin was too difficult. I took a deep breath and turned the next card.

"The Pope," Lucrezia said. "You're all trionfi, like I was all knights." It was certainly the pope, enthroned with the papal tiara upon his head, his hand upraised in blessing. "Well, he's right here in Rome. I suppose the pope could have something to do with it. I mean, he's old and sick and doesn't do much, but he might."

"Yes," I said. I could not tell her about Bracciano, about how he asked for news of the pope's health by black magic, how he schemed at who the pope's successor might be. I could imagine all too easily how the pope might have a hand in my future, by his life or his death. Did I want to see the third card at all?

Wondering would be worse than knowing. I turned it. Like the pope, a figure sat enthroned, but the face beneath the papal tiara was a woman's. She wore golden robes, a staff in one hand, her chair set between the pillars of a mighty cathedral. "A female pope?" I asked. There was no such thing.

Lucrezia shrugged. "It's the second of the trionfi, after the magus. La Papessa. I guess it's to have pairs. Sun and Moon. Emperor and Empress."

"Our faith allows for no such thing," I said. And yet her face drew me.

"Maybe you're going to get an annulment and go to a convent," Lucrezia said cheerily.

"I certainly hope not!" I exclaimed. "I cannot imagine anything I would like less."

"Well," she said, scooping up the cards. "Mama says it's all made up. Let's play Patience." And so we did, though a sense of unease remained with me.

Chapter Five

It was into this state that the invitation burst like a thunderclap. Donna Adriana received an invitation for herself, her son, and her daughter-in-law to attend a masked Carnival revelry to be held at the vice-chancellor's palazzo. She read the invitation out at dinner. "It is to be on a classical theme," she said with satisfaction.

"What does that mean?" I asked. There were no masked revelries in Montalto.

"It means we must each come as a figure from classical history or mythology." Adriana's eyes were bright. I realized how much she also must hate penury and isolation. When her husband was alive, no doubt she had a lively social life with people who now spurned her without his income. In addition to losing a husband who apparently loved her, she had also lost her position in society. It was kind of her cousin to issue the invitation.

"I want to be a lion," Lucrezia said cheerfully.

"You are not anything," replied Orsino. "The invitation does not include you."

"It is my papa's party!" she protested, hands on hips.

"You are too young for Carnival revelries," Adriana said. "As your papa well knows."

"That is not fair," Lucrezia said. "I'm nearly ten!"

"I'm sorry," I said, "but these parties are for grown-ups. Would you like to help me make my costume? I have no idea what I can wear. Perhaps there are some old clothes that could be made over?"

"I'm sure there are," Adriana added brightly. She actually looked happy for a change.

"You could be the lion," Lucrezia said to Orsino.

In the end, Orsino was Achilles. He was not enthusiastic, but Adriana had the costume made from bits of things of his father's, and while it seemed a little large, he did look quite nice. "Not at all Achilles hiding among the maidens," I said mischievously. He didn't get the joke.

It was only four blocks to the vice-chancellor's palazzo. We heard the party long before we arrived. Despite the chilly night, the streets were full of celebrants, some of them masked. "Surely all these people aren't going to the party?" I asked. One of the men dancing in a half-mask to the tune of a street musician appeared to be the burly shoemaker whose shop was at the bottom of our hill.

"That's stupid," Orsino said. "Of course they aren't. The party is just for the gentleborn."

"Cardinal Borgia always provides entertainments and refreshments outside his gates when he has a party," Adriana explained. "The entire quarter enjoys it. And it is Carnival."

We were pressed back against the wall of a nearby house to make way for a procession, a litter and four guardsmen. I caught a glimpse of the richly dressed man within, deep in conversation with a lady on the other side of him. "Cardinal Ascanio Sforza," Adriana said with satisfaction. "He has the Sforza attending."

"Is that good?" I asked. I knew that the Sforza were one of the great families who vied for control of Rome and the papacy, but I thought them opposed to the Orsini.

"Rodrigo steers a course between rivals," Adriana said quietly.

"It's good for him, at least. There will be a great deal of politics tonight, but you need not concern yourself with it too much."

I wondered if Bracciano would be present. Probably. Surely it would be conspicuous for the vice-chancellor to fail to invite the gonfaloniere?

The plaza outside his gates was packed. We threaded our way through the laughing and dancing people. There were musicians to one side of the gates playing loudly, though their strains were nearly drowned by the crowd. Three large wheels were arranged on a platform, a pair of guards keeping people away from them. A third man came with a taper and lit a fuse, stepping back. One of them sputtered, and then began spinning, fireworks in red and gold lighting successively, sending a few sparks into the cheering crowd. I applauded madly. I'd seen Catherine Wheels at a fair once, but these were even better.

At the gates an attendant spoke briefly with Adriana and we were waved through, shedding stoles and cloaks to a young maid in the vaulted vestibule. The loggia itself was supported by graceful columns, hanging lamps illuminating the doors leading into the saletta. To the right a set of marble stairs curved up the loggia above, the wrought iron railing elaborately decorated with gilded bulls. We were directed to the left, through broad doors into the saletta.

If I had thought Bracciano's palazzo was splendid, it was nothing on Cardinal Borgia's. It was built in the latest style, with marble floors in three colors of traventine marble tile, and the most beautiful paintings on every conceivable wall surface. Where there were not paintings there were lavish hangings, fantastic birds and beasts inhabiting enchanted gardens. Light streamed out. The tables in the saletta were covered in finely woven carpets and a selection of gold plate that boggled the mind. Enormous pots held palm trees taller than I was, their fronds bending down to add to the lush display.

The saletta was crowded with beautifully dressed people, all jostling as they passed through into the rooms beyond. "All the great families are here," Adriana said with satisfaction. She wore moss green, her over-dress trimmed in golden embroidery and her sleeves a darker green, the color of woods in summer. She carried a little gold mask trimmed with a few wisps of grain. "It has been so long!" Her eyes flew around the room, marking every person she saw.

"I am glad," I said. For a moment she looked like a lively young girl. Her marriage had been a love match. Fortunate woman.

"You should enjoy yourself," Adriana said to me quietly. "Dance. Have fun. Don't worry if you don't know people. You look beautiful."

"Thank you," I said. I wore extremely simple white linen, and while it was appropriate to my persona, it seemed like nothing compared to the gowns of the other women. Sumptuous velvets and ethereal silks seemed the rule. I had a little white mask, my hair braided at the sides and left loose down my back like a maiden. Unbound, it fell below my waist, dark with a slight wave to it.

"Do I have to dance?" Orsino asked.

I left Adriana to remonstrate with her son and wandered the perimeter of the dancing floor, watching to see what they did. I had learned with Alessandro, but it had been more than a year since I had danced, and I did not know the steps to the newest dances. I could follow along, I thought. The figured patterns were slow enough and built on familiar steps.

Indeed, it was only a few moments before I was asked to join the next set by a young man wearing an enormous floppy gray wig above his mask and what appeared to be a toga made out of a bedsheet. We were in the fourth turn, our fingers touching, before I recognized him. "Dr. Treschi?" I asked incredulously. He seemed to have been the magus in charge of Bracciano's summoning, though he was the only one who had shown any concern for me.

He blinked at me through the holes in the mask. "Donna Giulia? You look—different."

"I am wearing a costume," I said. We turned again, as he gracefully managed his toga and I the fruit dangling on ribbons from my wrist. "Who are you?"

"Erastothenes," he said. "He was...."

"I know who he was," I replied. We went round again, hands touching. "I have not met any other mathematicians here tonight. There seem to be many gods, however."

"Everyone wants to be a god," Dr. Treschi said. "To be a philosopher is superior."

"What can I say to that?" I said with a smile. We went around again. He was not much older than Alessandro. It came to me that if I wanted to know what Bracciano intended, perhaps the person to cultivate was Dr. Treschi.

"Donna Giulia, I want you to know...." The dance swept us apart, partnering me with a tall man in a bronze breastplate. I curtsied to him and he bowed to me.

"Ajax?" I asked.

"Achilles," he said. "What is your name? You are a vision and I have never seen you before. Are you one of the Colonna?"

"I am an Orsini by marriage," I said, feeling I ought to get it out there that I was married. "Giulia Farnese."

"You are the most beautiful woman here tonight," he said, turning so that we passed side by side. "My heart is at your feet."

"In half a dance?" I said. "Your heart is feeble." And yet it was fun to play this game.

"You must be Venus," he said.

"No, wrong guess." I thought I saw rams' horns on a man with his back to me near the first of the laden refreshment tables. He seemed to have a lovely red-haired woman hanging on his arm, her lavender complementing his purple. Might they be Alexander and Roxane?

We turned in the set again, the changing figures partnering me with a young man crowned in Dionysian vines. He said something to me that was lost in the movement.

The man across the room turned. Alexander, certainly. Cardinal Borgia was decidedly not wearing a bedsheet. He wore a long tunica bordered in purple and gold, a purple cloak flung over his left shoulder, a golden mask that covered only his eyes attached to a gilded helmet with ram's horns. The mask was somehow somber. His eyes met mine and for a moment I thought he didn't know me, so intent and admiring was his gaze. Like a cat suddenly seeing something pounceable, I thought. The dance turned me away, and when I could look back he was gone.

"Would you like to visit the refreshment table?" the Dionysus I was with asked me as the set ended. He offered me his arm to lead me into the next room.

"Yes, thank you," I said. As I might have expected, the table was laden with silver platters lavishly filled with every good thing, but I simply had a glass of wine. I was hot from dancing and it was nicely chilled in deep cellars, ruby-colored and sweet and not watered at all.

"It's odd I've never seen you before," he said. "I thought I knew all the lovely ladies of Rome."

"I am Giulia Farnese," I said. "And you are?"

He sketched a little bow. "Lorenzo Piccolomini, Cardinal Piccolomini's grandson. And as Dionysus, I will take pleasure in refilling your glass." He motioned to a servant who poured from a glass decanter.

"Thank you," I said, "but now I cannot dance with my hands full."

"Drink up and then dance," he said. I finished the glass quickly. The room seemed warm and sparkling, the dancers beautiful in their turns, like wandering stars come to earth. Lorenzo made some little joke, and I looked up over the rim of the glass.

Cardinal Borgia was on the other side of the dance floor, a beautiful blond woman at his side rather than the red-haired woman I had seen before. Her gown was aqua and teal, seashells ornamenting her hair and dress—Venus, Queen of the Seas. He smiled, looking down at her since she was quite petite. Men rarely looked down at me, or at least it took an exceptionally tall man. He was only of medium height. When I had spoken with him, there were only two finger-widths of difference between us. He looked up as though he had felt my gaze, his head tilting, a little smile at the corner of his mouth, and I looked away quickly.

"I said, would you like to dance again?" Lorenzo Piccolomini asked.

"Yes, that would be lovely," I said, putting my empty glass on the table edge. I let him lead me onto the floor, trying to match the steps of the lady ahead of me in the figures.

Cardinal Borgia had disappeared again. I tried not to be too obvious about looking for him. He did not tower over other dancers, but the ram's horn mask should be visible. I had not seen anyone else here wearing something like it.

I missed a step and nearly collided with the man who was stepping up to take his place as my next partner. "Excuse me," I said, and he bowed very correctly. He was also wearing a bedsheet toga. "And who are you this evening?"

"Achilles," he said, and I laughed. "Why is that funny?" He looked vaguely offended.

"There just seem to be many Achilleses here tonight." I couldn't stop giggling. "A host of Achilli. A gaggle of Achilli."

He disappeared as soon as the set ended. A waiter offered me another glass. "Thank you," I said, and turned.

Cardinal Borgia had been right behind me. I was almost nose to nose with him. I tried not to squeak in surprise. "La Bella Farnese. I am so pleased you attended," he said with a courteous nod.

"I am delighted to be invited. I've never been to a party like this," I said. "We do not have them in Montalto, and I have not been asked to any since I came to Rome."

"Something we must remedy," he said. His costume was beautifully made. He must have spent as much on it as on good clothes. The embroidery on the cloak was real, not painted on with paint that would not wash.

"And you are Alexander, of course."

"Of course." He really did look wonderful in the costume, and not a bit like a cardinal. He was dark instead of fair like Alexander, but he had presence.

"Have you all the rubies of the Ganges at your disposal?" I asked.

"Sadly, no. But greater than all rubies is a peerless woman," he said. He looked at my simple costume. "And you are?"

"Proserpina," I said, holding out the pomegranate on its ribbons in my left hand. "Awaiting abduction."

He closed his eyes for a second, his smile showing teeth for a moment. "Of course you are," he said.

"Adriana is Ceres," I said. The world seemed bright in his good grace.

"Naturally." He offered me his arm. "Will you permit me to show you the beauties of the palazzo?"

"I would be delighted," I said, and took his arm, transferring the wineglass to the other hand.

There were indeed many treasures. It was actually hard to look at the sculptures or tapestries with him because he was constantly assailed by people who wanted to talk to him. Because he was the host, or the vice-chancellor, or simply the kind of person that everyone felt they either wanted or were required to speak to, we couldn't move four feet without another conversation. I would have slipped away into the crowd if I had not been on his arm.

Cardinal Orsini, who I had not yet met but had seen at the wedding, greeted me like an old friend. "Orsino's little bride," he said proudly. "La Bella Farnese, or so I've heard. You must grace my palazzo some time."

"I should be delighted, Your Eminence," I said. "Nothing would give me greater pleasure than to know you better."

At that the old gentleman coughed. "Lovely girl," he said to Cardinal Borgia. "Wonder where he found her?"

"At Montalto on the Via Aurelia," I said, taking another sip of my chilled wine. The glass was nearly empty again, but it was quite hot in here with so many people. "A most placid and bucolic estate where the beauties of nature are surpassed only by our humble piety."

Orsini looked at Borgia. "And clever too." He tapped my wrist. "Not too pious, young woman. We need some handsome heirs!"

"One can pray, Your Eminence," I said truthfully.

He dropped his voice, leaning toward Cardinal Borgia. "We need to talk about this business with Ficino," he said.

Borgia shrugged. "What is there to say?"

"You know the man's as pious as a monk. If Ficino overreached, it was in error. My uncle, the Archbishop of Florence, supports him completely," Orsini said. "Whoever denounced him for heresy, it's politics."

"Of course it is," Borgia said.

"If the pope acquits him…." Orsini shrugged. "We may all express opinions to His Holiness, may we not?"

Another man who had had his back to us turned. "Are we talking about Ficino?"

Orsini cast his eyes heavenward. "Obviously."

He was a portly man of forty or so, smooth shaven, and dressed as Orpheus complete with lyre. "The archbishop stands behind him?"

"Yes," Orsini said. He looked annoyed. "If you'll excuse me?"

"Of course, Your Eminence," I said, and Orsini turned and disappeared into the crowd.

The gentleman winced. "I am afraid the good cardinal does not love me," he said.

"You know he never reads." Borgia looked amused. "May I present Giulia Farnese, a young lady newly come to Rome? Giulia, this is Ermolao Barbaro, Venice's newly appointed ambassador to the Vatican. He is a scholar of note, as I am sure you've heard."

I had, even in Montalto. My brother and I had studied his translation of Aristotle's *Ethics*, made accessible to us in Latin rather than Greek. I swallowed hard as he bent over my hand. "I am deeply honored, Signore. I am also indebted, for it is your good work with Aristotle which has made it possible for me to read and study his words."

Barbaro looked delighted. "You have read my Aristotle?"

"Your *Ethics*," I said. "I confess I have not yet gotten my hands on your *Politics*."

"Ermolao is currently working on an updated and annotated version of Pliny's *Natural History*," Borgia said. "A massive undertaking, but worthy and absolutely necessary."

"I have read two parts of it," I said. "The volume of zoology with beekeeping and oyster farming, and the botany section with viticulture and olive production."

"A country girl then," Barbaro said delightedly. "Pliny is as good on those things as he was when he wrote fourteen hundred years ago. Sadly, he is incorrect or out of date on many other things, and his work needs updating. Have you not read the other volumes?"

"My father did not have them," I said. We had only ten books in Montalto, and it was reckoned a library there. I suspected the Pliny had been bought by my father when he inherited Montalto and having been a mercenary soldier he had no idea how beekeeping or olive groves worked.

Barbaro looked at Borgia with mock indignation. "You must get this young lady some books!" he exclaimed. "A beautiful mind must be nurtured."

"I have just gotten her Plutarch," Borgia said. He put his hand over mine on his arm for a moment. "Would you have me drown her in books?"

"I should not mind that!" I said. To converse with such a scholar—Alessandro would be green with envy.

Barbaro laughed. "Cardinal Borgia always appreciates a good book. It has been twenty years since he supported the printing of my translation of Aristotle's *Politics*. My first book." He glanced at the cardinal. "But this business with Ficino—I'm not convinced it's just a swipe at the Medici. Florence is complicated, and even if the archbishop supports him, there are plenty who don't like the Academy he's built."

Borgia's voice was low, and the room was crowded. "And his latest book was heretical and you know it. Magic, demonology, sigils to invoke the power of old pagan gods through their astrological conjunctions...." My ears pricked forward metaphorically. Barbaro shrugged, smiling. "Of course we'll get him acquitted," Borgia said. "But I don't think you have to look far for who denounced him. Anyone who read it could see what it was."

"I've written a formal letter to His Holiness in support," Barbaro said.

"You and every noted humanist in Italy," Borgia said. "It will all be over before Lent." He patted Barbaro's shoulder. "Don't worry so much. It's taken care of."

"Then I will put my mind at ease on the matter," Barbaro said. He made a little bow to me. "Donna Giulia, it was a pleasure."

"It was my very great honor to meet you, Signore," I said, and let Cardinal Borgia steer me away into the crowd. I had so many questions and no idea how to ask them without saying far too much. "Ficino...."

"Marsilio Ficino is a great scholar," he said. "He was the protégé of Cosimo de Medici and was the tutor to his grandson, Lorenzo the Magnificent, who rules Florence now in all but name.

He's a Neoplatonist, a humanist, and unlike Barbaro who translates and comments on ancient writers, he is a towering writer himself." Cardinal Borgia dropped his voice. "His closeness to the Medici makes him a political target for those who do not love the Medici and his recent work on the nature of the soul offends others."

I glanced sideways at him. He was watching me attentively, the way he watched Lucrezia when he wanted to see if she would understand some concept. "And what does he say about the soul?"

"Among other things, that the soul is immortal. All souls that have ever existed, existed from the first day of creation, rather than coming into being before birth. Thus, the soul is truly eternal and only temporarily embodied in human form."

"And where was it then before our births? Do we all mill around in a great crowd in heaven waiting for a body like sheep going through a gate?"

The cardinal laughed. "It's possible. Ficino doesn't say, though one scholar he cites, Plethon, believed that souls transmigrate—that we live many times in different bodies as we seek to become closer to the divine."

I felt a frisson on my back. "Do you think that could be true?"

"It's heresy, isn't it?" Borgia shrugged. "But I see no harm in discussion of the nature of the soul. We cannot know or prove anything, and so there are bound to be different opinions. Debate is good for us. How do we learn except through reading and disputation?"

I nodded. "And so you wish for Lucrezia to learn disputation even though she's a girl?"

"Why not?" He glanced at me sideways. "If there are specific books you want to read, you are welcome to borrow them from me if I have them. You might have the Pliny if you want it."

"Thank you, Your Eminence," I said. There were volumes of the *Natural History* that I had not read. "I promise I will be very careful and not eat while I'm reading."

"A fault of Lucrezia's," the cardinal said.

We passed back through the saletta. The stacked plate was grand to the point of ostentatious, gold and silver mingled in reckless abandon. It was, in fact, a bit much even as the customary display of wealth. "You are very rich," I murmured tactlessly. "Where did it all come from?"

The corner of his mouth twitched. "I rescued a princess from durance vile and conveyed her safely to the man she wished to marry. When she became a great queen, she rewarded me handsomely." I glanced at him sideways, unsure how to take the jest. "You don't believe me?" the cardinal asked. "It's entirely true. But no matter." He shrugged. "New money is respected and reviled at once."

"Why would anyone revile you?" I could see why he might stand as a barrier to Bracciano, but surely that did not rise to the level of revulsion. I could certainly see nothing revolting about his person.

The cardinal laughed. "You have not been in Rome long."

"I truly do not know," I said. Lucrezia had mentioned the marrano rumor months ago, but that hardly seemed either plausible or relevant.

He put his head back, looking up at the elaborately painted coffered ceiling as we went into the gallery, windows down the side beneath the loggia. The Borgia bull ornamented every other square of the coffers. "I am Spanish, an interloper, and most of all not related to any of the great families. For seventy years since the Papacy got out from under the thumb of the French crown, it has been controlled by the great families—the Colonna, the Orsini, the Sforza…the high nobility. They have made up most of the College of Cardinals. And they have proceeded to act as though it were the year of Our Lord 1100."

We progressed along the gallery together, my hand on his arm. "The world has changed," he said. "Constantinople has fallen to the Turks. Al-Andalus is all but conquered by the monarchs of

Aragon and Castile, and only Granada remains. We print books instead of copying them. Great banking houses have more wealth than kings. If our Church is to survive in this new world, we must first acknowledge that the changes have come, then decide what we will do with them." He patted my hand as we walked toward a statue in the center of the room. "As vice-chancellor, I cannot be blind to the realities of banking and trade. I have opinions. I make them heard."

I nodded slowly. "So they hate you for it."

"They hate me because I am not one of them." He stopped as we reached the statue. "It's that simple. But the future does not belong to them."

"Fortune favors the bold," I said.

He looked delighted. "Indeed, Donna Giulia." He stepped away, looking up at the statue. "This is what I particularly wanted you to see."

It was a woman, life-size, seated with a baby in her lap and a crown of stars upon her head. The little boy suckled at her left breast, reaching for her with chubby fingers that looked entirely realistic, each fold of his baby flesh perfectly rendered. The pleats of her gown were lifelike. Her face was serene and beautiful, long-nosed and fine, and she looked at the viewer as though speaking while nursing. It was utterly exquisite. "That is the most beautiful Virgin and Child I have ever seen," I said quietly, walking around her. She exuded a deep sense of peace.

"That is not the Virgin," he said. I glanced back at him. His gaze rested on her face. "It was dug up two years ago not very far from here. Isis and Horus."

"An ancient goddess." I continued around her.

"We can learn from the past," he said quietly. "And surely such beauty can never be evil."

"Certainly not." I returned to his side. "One can feel it. Just as one can at any well-loved chapel."

He looked at me sideways, a half-smile on his face. "I wondered if you would think so." He offered his arm again. "I should not absent myself from my guests for long."

"No," I said. "You are the host." I felt oddly disappointed, but of course he could not let one guest monopolize his attention. He pointed out several paintings as we went, but I barely caught what they were. It occurred to me with a sudden and breathless clenching of my chest that his arm was warm beneath my hand, his classical garb exposing his forearm. His shoulder next to mine was broad beneath Alexander's purple cloak. If he was not young, he was exceedingly handsome. I liked the way his hair curled just a little only behind his ears, dark streaked with gray. He talked to me as if I were important and interesting. He wanted me to read and understand the world.

It was in this welter of emotion that we returned to the dancing room. With a bow, he left me and turned to another guest. *As he should*, I thought savagely. I could not spend all night on his arm, even if I wanted to.

Orsino appeared as if out of nowhere. "Where have you been?" he demanded.

"Why? Did you miss me?" I snapped.

"I wanted to dance."

"Aren't there plenty of women to dance with?" I asked.

"Who were you with?" Orsino said.

"If you must know, I was talking to Lucrezia's father," I said testily.

"Oh." His expression changed. "Well, you should be careful. People will talk."

"Talk about what?" I said. "I walked into the next room with Lucrezia's father."

"He has a reputation with women," Orsino said seriously. "Even though he's old."

I felt a blush rising in my face. "Better an old bull than a young ox." Orsino gaped. "I'd like some wine," I said. "I'm going to find another glass."

"You do not mean that," Orsino said in a furious whisper, following me.

"I certainly do mean that I'm going to find a glass," I said.

"I mean the ox part."

I stopped, turning to face him, the pomegranate in my hand. "Orsino, you have a choice. But I am not going to wait forever for you to find your courage." I stalked away.

Did he know about my summons from Bracciano? It was hard to believe he did not. Surely he had reached the obvious conclusion and knew nothing of the demons and mirrors. He was willing to let his wife be used by his cousin without a word of demurral and yet objected to her speaking with another man? I knew I would never forgive him, not if we were married forty years. He believed his cousin used me against my will and would not even speak up. One could not respect a man like that, much less love him.

Unlike Cardinal Borgia. I ducked behind a column and stood still. What absolute idiocy on my part! Infatuations with dead men were well and good, but infatuation with a living man who had never said one improper word to me? A cardinal? A priest? The father of a child I knew? A man old enough to be my father? I had utterly lost my mind.

And yet of all the men here, of all the possible partners one could seek, I found him most desirable. My fingers dug into the skin of the pomegranate. And what was I playing at, dressing as Proserpina waiting to be abducted? Did I mean to tempt? Had I dressed for him without admitting it to myself? Had he dressed as Alexander for me? Of course not. He had said that he admired Alexander. Why should he not dress as him for a costumed revel? What had that to do with me? Nothing. I was infatuated because I was unhappy in my marriage. A confessor would tell me to place my hopes upon my husband, where they belonged.

Of course, a confessor would also take a dim view of my husband renting me out to summon demons, the other part of me said.

I took a deep breath. I went through the saletta and out the doors into the courtyard. It was cooler outside. The crowd by the gates had dispersed and servants were sweeping up the debris from the fireworks and the crowd. I took a deep breath. The smell of gunpowder lingered in the air mingling with dung from the horses. A stableboy was going about with a pan and twig broom for that as well. Above the haze of the city, the stars were bright. Lights showed in neighboring buildings. This great city did not yet sleep.

What would it be like to be the consort of such a man? This party was the merest taste of it, learning and society and the currents of intrigues just beneath the surface. If I were the hostess, I would note the stableboy with approval, go inside and make certain that glasses left lying around in various rooms were whisked away, check on the preparations for a midnight supper if there was to be one, answer the steward's questions about which wines were to come out now, and then return to my lover's arm, greeting the powerful and the wise. I could do that, I thought. I was raised to rule over a household, not to be an ornament. I could talk about Pliny and see that the courtyard didn't smell like dung. I would be an exacting mistress of the house as my mother was, a conscientious master who got hands dirty as my father had been.

And yet Orsino wanted neither. If I had a husband who would give me scope for my talents, I could lift him up. I could be an asset for a man who wanted to distinguish himself, and instead I was yoked to a dud, a man with no ambition and no wit. If I were Cardinal Borgia's consort instead....

I took a deep breath. That was pointless speculation. I nurtured a foolish infatuation. It was best to put it aside.

Chapter Six

I went back inside, to the saletta where the potted palm trees drooped lushly over the lavish display of plate and carpets. The crowd was less there. I looked around for Dr. Treschi. Perhaps I could question him about the ritual we had done. Of all the men there, he had seemed the most sympathetic, and he had been friendly earlier in the dance. Was he still dancing? Surely his floppy wig should be visible. I made my way through the saletta to the dancing room.

Raised voices made me turn aside. In one of the salas Bracciano was holding court for several other gentlemen, including Cardinal Orsini. Tall and imposing, Bracciano wore a gilded breastplate and a helmet with a red plume, a sword at his belt. "...and when has Rome not thus prospered?" he asked. "Under the Caesars, Rome ruled the world. Now we are ruled by every petty merchant with money to lend." There was a laugh around the circle. "The Medici," he said. "Should we answer to them? We, the Orsini, are the true heirs of the Julio-Claudian Caesars. If the Caesars ruled Rome, bankers would answer to us rather than we to them."

Cardinal Orsini frowned. "Surely the pope rules in Rome."

Bracciano put his hand on his kinsman's shoulder. "Your Eminence, dear uncle, we know that the Pope is an old man. An old man needs a prop to his throne, just as he leans upon a cane when he walks. I mean no disrespect to Pope Innocent. But he is our Heavenly Father's representative. He is no king, no Caesar.

He is best suited to a life of prayer and contemplation, not to the muster of armies and the politics of the world. Those things are the province of a secular ruler. Did not our Lord say to render unto Caesar that which is Caesar's?"

"And you shall be Caesar because you dress as Augustus?" Cardinal Borgia's voice was mild but it cut through the conversation. He put his head to the side as though amused at a quirk of dress. "Poor man, too seasick to wave a sword at Actium, so Plutarch tells us. The lesser nephew of a greater man, laying claim to things he could not attain for himself. Is that your model?"

"The greatest Emperor of Rome," Bracciano said. "And the most enduring."

Borgia strolled over to stand by Cardinal Orsini, Alexander's embroidered tunic and purple cloak in contrast with Bracciano's scarlet. "He said he found Rome in wood and left her in marble, and yet you may walk through the ruins. We endure not as the seat of empire, but as the home of our Mother Church." He spread his hands. "We are the Holy City, gentlemen. We are unique. We are eternal. We are not for petty warlords and condottieri to claim. We are the Throne of St. Peter!"

"Indeed," Cardinal Orsini said, putting his hand on Bracciano's arm. "Dear boy, a staff is only to help a man to walk, not to tell him where to step."

Bracciano looked daggers at Borgia. "And if Jews and bankers contrive to gain the upper hand?"

"Do you see any present?" Cardinal Borgia asked lightly. "Oh, I do believe that there is a Medici in the saletta. Shall I get him?"

There was a murmur of laughter. "Please not," Cardinal Orsini said with a smile. "I owe him money and I'm avoiding him this evening!"

I heard a movement of cloth and looked around. Adriana had come to stand behind me. "I wish he wouldn't play that game," she said quietly.

"Is it a game?" I asked in the same low tone. For all the casualness of Cardinal Borgia's pose, I thought that he was not as easy as he wanted to seem.

"Rodrigo makes enemies," Adriana said.

"And friends," I said.

"That too." She lifted her chin. "But the enemies are more powerful. The Orsini have all but run the Colonna out of Rome. The only question now is who will rule—the Orsini or the Sforza."

I nodded. "I see," I said. "So he cultivates Cardinal Orsini and plays him against Bracciano."

"You do take to this," Adriana said, her painted mouth elongating. "Come. Give Orsino one dance at least."

"Of course," I said. Proserpina followed after Ceres meekly, and if she looked back, what of it?

However, to Adriana's annoyance, Orsino could not be found. "If he's in the gambling room, I'll stuff him," she muttered. Adriana had minimal patience with losing money and gaining nothing from it. She left me at the foot of the steps to the floor above to seek out her wayward son.

I finished the fourth glass and put it down carefully in the corner. I did not usually drink anything like four glasses of unwatered wine, and the world seemed a bit hot and crowded. Perhaps it was getting late. The music was louder, people's voices more raucous. When I looked at the dancing floor, the figures were no longer stately. Couples danced too closely, skirts lifted too high.

There might be a door to a garden where it would be cooler? The courtyard was outdoors but was hardly scenic. Besides, it seemed that some people had begun to leave and the courtyard would be full of people calling for litters and horses.

Perhaps this way? I turned a corner. It was not a door but an alcove occupied by a couple locked together, her skirts raised and one of her legs around his as one of her hands roved beneath his doublet in the front. I backed away quickly, muttering my apologies, though I had no indication they had even noticed me. From the balcony above I heard a feminine giggle, a man's voice replying lower in a husky laugh. It seemed another kind of dancing took place off the main floor.

I ducked around another corner. I was turned around. Where were the rooms in this house? Where was the garden and where was the necessary? Surely there was some place ladies were supposed to go? The candles were burning down, some of them drowning in pools of their own wax, making a dim and fitful light.

"Looking for someone?" I practically ran into a tall man in a bronze half-mask. He had brown hair a shade darker than the mask. Beneath it, the lines around his mouth placed his age at forty or so, and he had a swordsman's scar on his chin.

"I was looking for the garden," I said. I wasn't about to ask him for the necessary.

"I'm happy to show you," he said. There was a note I didn't like in his voice. "It's this way." He gestured to a door into a passage.

"Thank you, but I...." I was not about to go anywhere with him.

He took my arm, propelling me along. "It won't take but a minute," he said. "You're a pretty little bird."

"Signore, I don't...." I began as he all but shoved me through the door, real fear kindling suddenly.

"There you are!" came a voice behind him. "Giulia, my dear, I've looked all over for you." I stumbled with relief as Cardinal Borgia stepped around him and took my arm possessively. "Franceschetto, I must relieve you of your burden."

The man looked as if he might protest. Then he laughed. "I apologize for interfering with your latest fuck, Vice-Chancellor." He sketched me a little bow and ambled off.

The cardinal looked at me, a little frown on his face. "I hope my interference wasn't unwelcome."

"No, it was very welcome," I said. I took a deep breath. "Who is he?"

His mouth twitched. "Franceschetto Cybo, His Holiness' son."

That man was the Pope's son. "He does not do his father credit," I said, pleased my voice didn't shake at all.

"No. He believes he can get away with anything because he usually does." We were standing very close together. He smelled of incense, but then I suppose he bathed in vast clouds of it most days. His eyes looked black beneath the gilded half-mask in this dim light. "You should go home. The hour is late and the company not entirely safe."

"I am entirely safe with you," I said. Safe was not the word, but I was certain nothing would happen that I did not want. He could not make me safe from the things within myself.

"Are you?" His eyes were on my lips, flicking up to meet mine.

Somehow I had taken a step closer, my arm still on his. "There is nothing I am afraid of."

Like iron to a magnet, I leaned toward him and he toward me, lips meeting, his arm around my waist. He tasted of sweet red wine and the iron of flesh, and I yearned into it, a sensual and practiced kiss, my mouth opening under his like a flower opening to the sun for the first time. The solidity of his body against mine, my hand on the embroidery of the tunic, his heart beneath it. His arm around me tightened and he leaned into the kiss, devouring and needy.

And then he stepped back, his eyes on my face. Was I too innocent to be attractive? Was I doing it wrong? His expression was intent. "It is very easy to fall into the abyss."

"*Facilis descensus Averno*," I quoted. *It is easy to descend to the underworld*. Virgil, of course.

His mouth twitched sideways in an ironic smile. "But ascending is the difficult part." He offered me his arm. "I will return you to the party. And then perhaps you had best say good night."

"Of course, Cardinal," I said, and if I held to his arm tighter than necessary, it must be that the late hour made my steps unsteady.

The next morning I woke with a foul headache. Needless to say, I was on tenterhooks all the next day. And yet everything fell into its usual routine. I awoke alone. Orsino took himself off to his fencing lesson or wherever without so much as saying good morning. Donna Adriana was sleeping. I "helped" Lucrezia with her lessons as soon as Father Antonio arrived, and thus spent a quiet morning immersed in mathematics and Latin. Lucrezia was doing declensions, but Father Antonio had more interesting work for me. I had begun Greek, but was only learning vocabulary, though my Latin was becoming fluent. He had a series of famous passages from the Aeneid for me to translate.

"*Musa, mihi causas memora quo numine laeso,*" I read aloud. "*Muse, bring to my memory the reasons that a damaged spirit....* Is that right? Damaged? Hurt?"

"I should say offended," he said. "But damaged is permissible."

"How can a spirit be damaged?" Lucrezia asked.

"Declensions," he said, and she bent her golden head to her paper again.

"*Quidve dolens regina deum tot volvere casus insignem pietate virum tot adire labores impulerit.*" There was quite a lot in there. I bit my lip. "*Whose sorrow turned the queen of the gods against such a pious man that he endured such hardship.*"

"Very good, my lady," Father Antonio said. He gave me a shy smile.

I felt more confident of the last line. "*Tantaene animis caelestibus irae? Can a heavenly soul hold such rage?*" I could well imagine that Juno might. The queen of the gods put up with quite a lot.

"Are they all in Hell?" Lucrezia asked.

"Are who in Hell?" Father Antonio asked.

"All the Romans. The old Romans. The ones who lived and

died before Christ was born." She put her ink aside and sat up straight as though prepared for disputation.

He blinked. "I believe they are in Purgatory."

"Why?" Lucrezia put her head to the side. "It's not as though they rejected Christ. They couldn't possibly have been Christian if they lived and died before Jesus was born. So why should they get punished for something they couldn't help? That's not fair."

Father Antonio looked dumbstruck. "I can't say," he muttered.

"Well, why?" she asked. "It's not fair to punish someone for something they don't know. My father would never punish me for something I didn't know, and surely God the Father is as good as Cardinal Borgia!"

It was all I could do not to fall off my chair laughing. I think that I maintained a serene deportment. Father Antonio opened his mouth and shut it again. Then he opened it and shut it a second time. Lucrezia waited, her hands clasped and her expression attentive.

I had to save the poor man. "I believe it is almost time for Father Antonio to leave," I said, getting to my feet. "Father, thank you for your time this morning."

He almost leapt up. "You are very welcome, Donna Giulia. I will see you ladies tomorrow." He practically bolted.

I waited until he was out of earshot to laugh until my sides hurt. Lucrezia joined in. "He is so helpless, is he not? But I still do not know why they should be in Purgatory."

"Perhaps you should ask your father," I suggested. "He is much wiser than a young priest." I would enjoy watching her put her father on the spot that way, though I imagined his answer would have greater theological substance to it. Surely it was a matter he had considered.

That seemed to satisfy Lucrezia. She began putting her ink and paper away. "What did my father say last night?" she asked.

I nearly choked. "Your father?"

She looked up at me. "You saw him at the party, did you not? I wish I were allowed to go to parties."

"You are not yet ten years old," I said. "So you are still too young. In a few years I am sure you will go to plenty of parties." At the party. Of course.

"So what did he say?"

"Nothing in particular." I busied myself putting away her things. I had a hundred feelings, and none of them possible to express to Lucrezia. *I kissed your father? I kissed your father and wish I could kiss him again? Was he with any of the women I saw him with at the party? Does he have a mistress? Ten mistresses?* Sometimes it was possible to find out things from Lucrezia if one were careful, and I had so many questions. "Lucrezia, what is your mother like?" I didn't look at her.

"She's really nice," Lucrezia said. "And strict. She's a lot stricter than my father. He's easy to talk into things, but she has all kinds of rules." I glanced at Lucrezia, and she shrugged. "Even Cesare can't push her around. She makes you feel guilty if you do something wrong so you don't want to do it again. She loves me."

I smiled. "That's good." Lucrezia was a very loving child, so of course she had been loved. "What does she look like?"

"She's pretty," Lucrezia said promptly. "Everyone says so. They're all surprised she's nearly fifty. Carlo says she's his beautiful girl. She's blond but not as blond as me. And she's really smart. She has a head for business. She runs a vineyard and a boarding house and rents space to two osterias. She's got her feet on the ground, she says. She always tells us to keep our heads out of the clouds." I wondered how that had played with the occasionally fanciful cardinal. Still, they must have been together fifteen years or more.

"She got really mad at the way Juan was acting last summer," Lucrezia continued. "She said that if he couldn't respect the rules of her house and be polite to his step-father, he could go live with our father and get up for Lauds like Papa does instead of lying in bed all morning. She was so mad that my father had to come out from Rome and get him. So he lives at the vice-chancellor's palazzo now. There's only Gioffre with mother now." She dropped her voice, leaning close like a great lady with a confidence to share. "You know people say that he's not my whole brother. That he's Carlo's son, not my father's."

"Ah," I said. Heaven forbid a woman have a son by her husband rather than her lover! "And what does your father say about such things?" I asked coolly.

"He says Gioffre is my brother and not to listen to such nonsense." Lucrezia closed the cabinet. "But Gioffre lives with Carlo and Mother, and I'm here with Donna Adriana. It wouldn't be decent for me to live at the vice-chancellor's palazzo when it's all men there, but it's only four blocks away so Papa can come to see me all the time." She shrugged. "It doesn't matter much, does it?"

"No, sweet," I said. She had not yet discovered exactly how much it mattered. For all her beautiful clothes and expensive tutors, she was a bastard and worth nothing in the eyes of the world. My family might have little money, but I was respectable. I had value, if only of a certain type. Once one fell from the precipice, what was there between one and the abyss below?

"I expect my father will come tomorrow," Lucrezia said cheerfully. "He says he misses me when he doesn't see me, and I did not go to the party."

She seemed about to return to the unfairness of not being able to attend masquerades at the age of nine. It was much too adult a party for Lucrezia. I had found it fascinating, even the part that had been a little scary at the time, when Cybo tried to get me off alone with him. And yet somehow Cardinal Borgia had fortuitously appeared. How had that happened unless he had been watching me as closely as I had watched him?

Lucrezia was staring at me. "I'm sure he does miss you," I said quickly.

She turned and hugged me tight about the waist. "You're always so sweet, Giulia. Does nothing ever ruffle you?"

"It is not hard to be sweet to you," I said, and hugged her back.

"I told him you were always kind and clever," she said.

I blinked. "Told who?"

Lucrezia put her hands on her hips. "My father. Who else are we talking about?"

"Oh. Yes."

"He asks about you," Lucrezia said. She jumped up, ready to run outdoors. "Don't worry. I wouldn't say anything bad." She dashed off, leaving me to wonder what she said, and why he had asked.

Chapter Seven

Lucrezia's father came to see her the next afternoon. It was a pleasant day despite the season, and Adriana had well-watered wine and fruit sent to the garden so that her distinguished cousin could take his ease while Lucrezia sat on the grass beside him or lit on a chair for a moment like a blue butterfly before she took off again. I occupied a third chair, my head bent over my needlework. I only looked at him through my eyelashes. I did not speak of anything that had occurred at the party, and after one quizzical look, he also said nothing. It seemed we had decided to pretend that it never happened.

He had come from the Vatican, clearly. He wore his full red robes in all their billowing folds, though only the little skullcap instead of the blocked hat. His hair beneath it was dark streaked with gray, and the ruby on his finger was worth more than my entire dowry. He had made the mistake of asking about Lucrezia's studies, a week's explanation once she got going.

"...and Father Antonio says that you can prove things with mathematics but that it requires Euclid and he probably shouldn't teach me because the pope hasn't said whether it's real or not and some of the cardinals say it isn't. So I said that I would ask you to tell him to teach me," Lucrezia finished.

Cardinal Borgia looked bemused. "You want me to order Father Antonio to teach you geometry?"

I smiled and bent my head. I understood from Alessandro that many students would rather have their tutors ordered not to teach geometry! "I believe the controversy he referred to is the question of the size of the Earth," I said quietly.

"Ah." The cardinal leaned back in his chair. "Well, my heart, the pope hasn't taken a position on it because it's not a theological question. It's a mathematical question."

Lucrezia's brow furrowed. "I don't understand."

"It's a bit complex for a nine-year-old," he said. He picked up an orange from the fruit bowl on the table. "Suppose you were as tiny as an ant. You are crawling on the surface of this orange and you want to know how big it is." Lucrezia came and perched on the arm of the chair. "But you are very small, and you can't crawl over the entire thing. You can just crawl from this place to this one." He pointed to the orange. "But you can count how many paces it takes you. You can know how far it is between these two places. There was an ancient scholar in Alexandria who did this. He measured how far it was from Alexandria to a city called Syene and then used the difference in degrees in the angle of the sun at midsummer to see what portion of a sphere that distance was."

Lucrezia squinted at the orange. Her nose was freckling from the sun despite all attempts to keep it shaded. Her eyes were as blue as her dress. "How many degrees is it?"

"I don't recall without finding the book," he said, "but since we know there are 360 degrees in a sphere, if the distance from here to here is a particular portion of the whole, we know how big the sphere must be. So he knew how big the world must be." I had never heard this, and in my interest I forgot to ply the needle.

"How big is the world?" Lucrezia asked. She took the orange from him, turning it in his hands.

"Big," he said, smiling. "Everything we know of the world is only about half of it."

"What's in the other half?" Lucrezia said.

He shrugged, glanced at me, and I quickly looked down at my work. "We don't know," he said simply. "An endless ocean? Or lands we have not even imagined? But we know that something is there. It's a mathematical certainty."

Lucrezia frowned. "But it's not in the Bible."

He picked up the glass of wine. "The Kingdom of Scotland isn't in the Bible. Yet you believe it exists."

"Of course the Kingdom of Scotland exists!" Lucrezia said, tossing the orange from one hand to the other.

"How do you know?" I looked up through my lashes again. He was smiling. "Have you ever been there?"

"No!" Lucrezia said, "You know I have not, Papa!"

"Then how do you know Scotland exists?"

"Lots of people have been to Scotland," Lucrezia said.

"Who?" He took a sip of the wine. "Who do you know who has been to Scotland?"

"Nobody I know," Lucrezia said. "It's a long way. But everybody knows Scotland exists."

"So you believe Scotland exists because everybody believes it does? That's a dangerous line of thought, Lucrezia."

She looked exasperated. "Lots of learned men have written that Scotland exists."

"And lots of learned men have written about mathematical modeling of a sphere," Cardinal Borgia said. "Eratosthenes and Cleomedes and Ptolemy and many more have proved the size of the world. So you will believe others that say that Scotland exists but not that they have it aright?"

She put one hand on her hip, the other holding out the orange. "They weren't Christian and they lived a long time ago?"

"And?"

She tossed the orange to the other hand, suddenly laughing. "You win, Papa. I am not very good at disputation yet."

"You are," he said fondly.

Lucrezia glanced at me. "Giulia, what was it you said I should ask Papa because Father Antonio didn't know?"

I was caught paying attention. I nearly stabbed myself in the thumb with my needle. "Whether people who died before the birth of Christ were in Hell or Purgatory."

"Or whether it wasn't fair to blame them if they lived before Jesus," Lucrezia said. "I remember now. Papa, are they?"

"We are taught that they are in Limbo," he said. "And yet there are some Church Fathers who dispute that, Clement of Alexandria, for example." He smiled at Lucrezia. "He would agree with you that it's not fair to blame them for when they lived."

"Dante shows them in Limbo," I said. "In the outermost circle of Hell, where he is guided by Virgil. Which does not seem so different from how Virgil describes the underworld in the Aeneid. I suppose Dante was being self-referential to write of his imagined journey with Virgil to what is essentially Virgil's underworld." As I was reading the *Aeneid* with Father Antonio at present, it seemed an obvious statement.

The cardinal blinked. "Yes," he said. "That's certainly true." He looked at me, his head to the side. I was learning that was his quizzical expression, when something actually astonished him. Had he expected me not to make the most of the opportunity to study with a tutor? I loved my studies as much as my brother, Alessandro, did. Were I a boy, I would gladly have gone to the university at Pisa as he did.

"So does that mean Virgil was as wise as the Church Fathers?" Lucrezia asked.

Cardinal Borgia frowned. "That's a very complicated question." He took a sip of his wine. He only took it well-watered in the afternoon, and that abstemiously. I suppose it would look bad for a cardinal to be a drunkard, but then it also looked bad for him to have a bevy of acknowledged children in the face of supposed chastity. "It goes right to the center of one of the most difficult questions the Church faces now." He glanced at me. "La Bella Farnese's cousin, Cardinal Orsini, and some others are of the mind that the learning and literature of the ancient world are not truly compatible with Christian doctrine."

"He is my husband's cousin," I said shortly.

He nodded to acknowledge the point. "While others attempt some greater reconciliation. There are scholars who present the idea that these ancient beliefs also reflect the hand of God, and thus may be rendered compatible. That it is simply another language, as it were. That even the stars tell God's truths."

"As they did to the Magi," I surprised myself by saying, and he looked at me. "Guiding them to the Nativity."

"Just so," Cardinal Borgia said. His eyebrows had risen. "The Magi were astrologers. Therefore astrology must be a blessed science." He looked back at his daughter. "So, my Lucrezia, there is even a scholar who tries to explain the universe through what he calls the Cabbala, the teachings of Jewish scholars formerly in al-Andalus, but who now roam the world once more."

That had clearly gone over Lucrezia's nine-year old head but not mine. In fact, an idea had struck me. "Does this scholar have a name?"

"He is Pico della Mirandola," he said. "And he is in Florence. But one of his students has come to Rome to teach, Dionisio Treschi. Why do you ask, Donna Giulia?"

"I was simply curious," I said, bending my head over my needle virtuously. Treschi. Dr. Treschi again, the young man at the scrying, the one chalking the circles.

Lucrezia threw the orange up in the air and caught it. "I don't understand." She was growing bored with this subject.

"Simply, the question is whether we should study the ancients or abjure them," the cardinal said. "Whether they lead us to God or away from Him."

"What do you think?" Lucrezia threw the orange again. This time she missed the catch and she chased it across the grass.

"I think there is no sin in knowledge, just in the application of it." He looked at me over the rim of the glass. "Just as there is no sin in beauty." *Only in the application of it*, I thought. I blushed as I stabbed the cloth. Even the most off-handed compliment from him warmed me to the core.

Lucrezia had retrieved the orange. I got to my feet, managing to drop my needlework. "Your face will freckle if you stay out here much longer. We should go in." I picked up my sewing, my back to the cardinal.

"Of course, Donna Giulia," he murmured.

The next week was unusually cold and dismal. I awoke to ice crusting the garden grass in the morning, and trickles of water froze in the gutters. There were no more warm days in the courtyard. Lucrezia was cranky and Cardinal Borgia did not visit. I spent much of the day in my camera reading on my bed before the fire. Father Antonio did not come on his accustomed day and Lucrezia joined me instead, both of us lying under my green coverlet with our respective books in our hands. In the evening we played cards.

She was a good companion, but I did wish for adult company. At Montalto I had often spent the evenings by the fire with my mother, talking of all the practical problems of the estate, or listening to my parents when my father was alive. Alessandro had discussed his studies with me, divine and secular alike—all the ideas he culled from every book he read, every book he could lend to me. My grandmother had told stories. My father had too, when he'd had a cup of warmed wine with spice in the winter, long and rambling tales of his years as a condottiero which were sometimes funny and turned unexpectedly to blood. My family had talked constantly, my hands moving with the needle as my mother and grandmother and I sewed. My father had whittled or fletched his own arrows with quiet, expert hands. Even Alessandro had trimmed reeds for pens. There were always toddlers and dogs underfoot. And all the while we talked and talked and talked. There was never silence. There were forty people in the household, all of them busy.

This household was unnerving. It was a grand palazzo. Forty could have fit easily. And yet instead of a big family, relations and hangers-on, retainers and tutors and servants, there were but nine of us. Adriana, Orsino, Lucrezia and me constituted the entire family. Then there was the cook and her husband, Beneo, who served as majordomo. There was Adriana's maid Maria and two young maids who did the heavy work. I understood that in a great city it was not necessary to provide room and board to tutors, since they could go home easily. Nor was it necessary to provide constant work for the gardener who trimmed the bushes occasionally, or the seamstress who made Lucrezia's clothes. And yet it was disturbing. All of this space, all of these rooms unused—it was like something out of a tale, a castle caught sleeping. What would it take to awaken it?

In the stories, it was a kiss. And yet I had only had one in my life, at the masquerade, and it did not seem likely to be repeated. Why should it be? A momentary mistake, clearly. It could go nowhere. I could hardly imagine I would seem attractive to a man who knew as much of the world as Cardinal Borgia, who clearly had beautiful women vying for his attention! I should starve this infatuation and it would go away in time.

On the 19th of February a messenger came from Bracciano saying that I would be wanted that evening. It had been three months and I hoped that he had given up on me, but apparently not. This time, since I was less astonished by the entire situation, I was better able to concentrate on what was happening. Expecting rape at any moment does not leave one space for observation. Now that I knew what was wanted of me was entirely different, I watched closely, trying not to be conspicuous about it.

There were eight men, including Bracciano and Dr. Treschi. Two of them were young, their dress noble. The other four were older and had the air of military men. Some of Bracciano's officers? At least one of them wore papal devices rather than Orsini. That man seemed decidedly skeptical of the entire business. He was the one who had said before that I reported nothing that was not common gossip. Perhaps he was one of the gonfaloniere's men, part of the Papal Army, rather than an Orsini?

Bracciano was clearly in charge, but Dr. Treschi seemed the expert. It was he who directed people where to stand and chalked the lines on the floor. Once again, I was directed to sit on the three-legged stool holding the mirror while he did this. There was a square around the chair, then a circle around the square, each section between thick with chalked symbols. Then, last, there was an outer square around the circle. As he drew it and wrote symbols, he addressed the unseen. Who did he ask for protection? It was indeed Greek, which I did not have, but I thought he called names of angels. Gabriel was familiar, of course. Did the names of angels constrain the demon if all this was to keep it within?

In my hands, the handle of the mirror was cool. Surely it was not meant for this! It was far older than the rites they practiced, I thought, something familiar about it, as though I saw some common household object repurposed for dark magic. I closed my eyes, feeling the shape of the handle. *I once had something like this.* The thought rose like a whisper from deep within. I could see it on a table, a mirror with a lotus handle lying among faience boxes and glass jars of paint and creams. It was no part of Bracciano's evil. A lady's mirror, the face darkened by time....

Bracciano said the final words, "*Ecce*! *Venite*!"

The mist in the blackened mirror cleared. The twisted face looked up at me, a face of smoke that shifted as I watched. "You may begin your questions," Dr. Treschi said.

Bracciano nodded sharply. "Who now are the leading contenders to be pope?"

It smiled hungrily. "Carafa and della Rovere, as he well knows."

I looked up. "Cardinal Carafa and Cardinal della Rovere, My Lord."

"What will sway their allegiance?" Bracciano asked.

"Pardon me, My Lord," Dr. Treschi said. "That question is too complex. Assuredly many things may sway their allegiance in many directions. You must be specific when you direct spirits."

Bracciano tried again. "What will sway della Rovere to support my cousin, Cardinal Orsini?"

The demon smiled. "Nothing. Della Rovere means to be pope, and he will support no one except himself."

I repeated it. Bracciano frowned. "What then will sway Cardinal Carafa to support my cousin?"

"If he is convinced that he cannot win, and that Orsini is the only one who can defeat della Rovere or Sforza." The wispy face grew teeth. "Greedy men all, these prelates. How many ducats for a red hat?"

"If he does not think he can win," I said. "And that Cardinal Orsini is the only alternative to Cardinal della Rovere or Cardinal Sforza."

Bracciano nodded thoughtfully. "So it's possible, but my cousin must put up a good showing first."

"Indeed," the creature said. It grinned at me. "And what do you want, little Dove? You have more talent than any of this lot, except that fool, Treschi."

"I don't understand," I said.

"Understand what?" Bracciano asked.

"Something about ducats for a red hat," I said. I was cold. The mirror frame was like ice in my hands.

"One more question, My Lord," Treschi said. "She is weakening."

"Will the pope die of the cold in his chest he currently suffers from?"

The mirror cleared. I saw the old man sitting by the fire, his long beard over a rich, warm robe. He drank a tisane, his feet on a stool, slippers embroidered in white and gold. Color had returned to his face. "I do not think so, My Lord," I said. I shivered. "I see him out of bed and gaining strength."

"You may dismiss the creature," Bracciano said, apparently satisfied with my answers. He looked at the other men. "So not yet. It seems I have more time, gentlemen."

Time for what? I thought as Dr. Treschi began the tedious process of undoing all he had done. Time to prepare for the pope's death, surely. In arms? With money? Through persuasion? I cast my eyes down, a simple maiden who cared nothing for what they planned. I gathered from this that Cardinals Carafa and della Rovere were unalterably opposed, but since I knew nothing further of either of them, I could not prefer one. I had gathered as well that the Sforza and Orsini families were rivals. This was politics on the highest level—control of Rome and control of the papacy. I was not such a fool as Bracciano thought, but I did not know enough to draw the conclusions that Bracciano no doubt did.

And where was Cardinal Borgia in this? No one mentioned him at all, and yet previously he had been the obstacle to Bracciano's hopes. Perhaps that rested on his power as vice-chancellor, but one would expect his support to be worth something to someone. I put that thought away, resolving to inquire of those who would not tell Bracciano.

Two days later at dinner I interrupted Lucrezia's chattering. "Donna Adriana, who is Cardinal Carafa and why does he not like Cardinal della Rovere?"

Her eyebrows rose. "Why would you ask such a question?"

"I heard someone speak of it at My Lord Bracciano's palazzo," I said truthfully. "I wondered what it was about."

Adriana sighed. "Those are dangerous waters, and I tell you only so you will not inadvertently give offense. Cardinal Carafa believes that the printing of new and old works is a great good, as is the printing of popular works in Italian. Cardinal della Rovere believes that before any book is printed, the printer should have the permission of the local bishop, and that any work which does not receive this approval should be destroyed. They have argued at great length about it."

That did indeed seem to be a serious matter, and one I certainly had an opinion about. "And what does Cardinal Orsini say, as he is my new kinsman?"

"He is not much concerned with the matter," Adriana said. "He does not think there are so many books or so many readers that it is important."

"My father likes Cardinal Carafa," Lucrezia put in brightly. "He says that Cardinal Carafa is a great humanist and della Rovere a donkey because he wants universities not to teach about the nature of the rational soul. What's the nature of the rational soul, Giulia?"

"That people are able to think for themselves," I said. "And to make decisions based on logic and learning."

Orsino snorted. "More of that."

"You would do well to learn more of that, Orsino," Adriana said. "You must prepare for some sort of position."

He stood up. "I'm not a clerk, Mama. So who cares what books are printed?" He pushed his chair in and strolled out of the sala.

She looked after him worriedly. "My cousin and Cardinal

della Rovere are not friends," she said, "for all that they have been colleagues for many years."

"That's probably why," Lucrezia said brightly. "Papa says he's been yoked to that horse's ass forever and that della Rovere could have stayed in Paris as Papal Legate where he troubled him less and didn't encourage the pope to ridiculous courses."

"Lucrezia!" Adriana said. "You must not repeat things your father says in private. Discretion is a virtue."

"Thank you for your answer, Donna Adriana," I said. I certainly now had no doubts as to who Cardinal Borgia might support, but what that had to do with Bracciano was still a mystery. Perhaps Bracciano hated Borgia because he supported Carafa instead of Orsini? And yet it was possible that Carafa would support Orsini if there were no alternative. Or was it that Borgia would be a more acceptable alternative to Carafa than Orsini? I did not know enough to know which was true, but I began to see the shape of it.

It was a little more than a week later that I dared to try to find out. Lucrezia had gone out with her father to see a traveling performer who had exotic animals and was bringing them to the vice-chancellor's palazzo, and Adriana had likewise gone to visit a friend. I was alone in the house except for Orsino, who could be counted on to avoid me. I slipped into Lucrezia's room and borrowed her deck of cards.

I need not have been stealthy. If I had asked, Lucrezia would gladly have loaned them to me, but it was my guilt and discomfort that caused me to sneak. When we had played at telling fortunes with them, I had felt the familiar frisson of sight, of reaching beyond what was, only rendered less catastrophic, less enormous and more controllable. I wondered what would happen if I tried to use them thus but without the distraction of Lucrezia? In any event, I took the cards back to my camera and closed the door.

It was a beautiful day in early spring, chilly but sunny, and the light through the window made a warm stripe across the foot of my bed. I sat down and shuffled the cards carefully. They felt cool and pleasant, not frightening as the mirror always was, more like when I had asked Proserpina for her help in the Etruscan tomb. I had not been afraid of her. Could she hear me here, far from her tombs? *Lady of the Underworld*, I thought, *if it is by your help I have come to Rome, will you help me understand what is happening?* I shuffled and cut the cards again. I took a deep breath and addressed myself to them. *What is Lord Bracciano's purpose?* I turned over the top card and laid it gingerly on the bed covers.

A blindfolded woman stood at the center of a wheel. To her right, a man climbed it eagerly, the words coming from his mouth "I shall reign." At the top, a prince sat in state, his gown gilded, while the words read "I reign." To her left, a man tumbled down the wheel, head down, the words beneath him reading, "I have reigned."

"Fortuna's Wheel," I said aloud. The wheel of fortune, whereby some ascended and others descended. That was clear enough. What Bracciano desired was the ascension of the Orsini family fortunes. And how much higher could they go? They were already the most powerful family in Rome, boasting both the gonfaloniere and a cardinal. They had vast and lucrative estates. Where might they rise except to the papacy?

And I knew that, of course. It was hardly a surprise that Bracciano sought the papacy on behalf of his cousin. He had said as much. Yet this gave me little insight into what he hoped to accomplish or how, if the pope was not going to die in the near future. I phrased my thought carefully. *What does Lord Bracciano do at this time to further his plans?* I turned the second card over.

It was the chariot driven by the woman with red gloves, her face serene though the horses looked to bolt in opposite directions.

My eye was drawn to them as it had not been before, when I saw this card when Lucrezia and I told fortunes. Two horses, yoked together, yet hating each other, each rolling their eyes to the whites, stamping and jostling. Cardinal Borgia and Cardinal della Rovere? Lucrezia had said they were yoked together, but that della Rovere urged the pope to decisions that Cardinal Borgia did not like. At the very least, if one of them were cut loose, the other would be grateful. Perhaps that was what the demon had meant in showing me Cardinal Borgia as the obstruction to Bracciano's plans? If he were not vice-chancellor, perhaps Cardinal Orsini would be? It would be another step toward the papal throne.

I took a deep breath. *How does Lord Bracciano hope to accomplish this?* I turned the third card and shivered. The Devil grinned at me, wings spread behind him, while at his feet a man and woman stood enchained, heavy collars around their necks. *By means of black magic*, I thought. Well I knew that he conjured demons! I pressed the deck to my lips. *What may I do to thwart him?* I turned the next card.

A woman stood barefooted in a wild landscape, a silver bow in her left hand. In her right she held aloft the crescent moon. *Diana*, I thought, *or Luna herself, the goddess of the moon. The Moon, then. But what might this mean in this context?* I wished I had someone to ask. This friend of Lucrezia's mother would know, but I had only the most tenuous connection to her and could hardly ask a stranger about something which was at best foolish and at worst heretical. Once again, I did not know enough to understand.

I put the cards back in the deck and shuffled them. Again and again it was the same—my ignorance left me at loose ends. And yet before me was a world of learning and mystery! The whirling society I had seen at the Carnival party was right here, just a few blocks away behind the doors of other houses and here I sat, unable to reach it! I had talked with Ermolao Barbaro. I had managed conversations with Cardinal Orsini and other worthies. I was not incapable of being part of the world I craved. If I were more often in Cardinal Borgia's company....

I cut off that thought. No, what I must apply myself to was extricating myself from Bracciano's schemes. I could be certain that whatever his plan was, I wanted no part of it.

Chapter Eight

Lucrezia's tenth birthday fell on the Sunday after Easter. She celebrated it at her mother's house with her brothers and stayed overnight, returning on Monday morning with a basket of treats and a pile of presents. Our celebration was to be more modest—a dinner that evening with just Adriana, the cardinal and me. Orsino wouldn't be present. Bracciano had sent a tersely worded invitation for Orsino to have dinner with some of his officers that night. Adriana pointed out that this was no doubt so they could meet him and decide if he was suited to joining some regiment under their command. Orsino was sent off late in the afternoon, impeccably shaved and dressed, and thoroughly scolded about making a good impression for the sake of his future. Lucrezia would not miss him at her birthday dinner.

Cardinal Borgia arrived before sundown with his customary two guards, whom he promptly dismissed to the taverna down the street with enough coins to purchase dinner of their own and instructions to return for him after Compline. As usual, he spared Donna Adriana the expense of feeding them in the kitchen; a kindness, since two extra men was costly. After all, the staff was small and except for old Beneo who was the cook's husband and served as an arthritic majordomo, we were all women.

We were four at dinner in the sala, a silver bowl of narcissi and wood hyacinths in the center of the table on a white cloth, inexpensive but beautiful. Lucrezia wore her newest dress and I my blue velvet cotta over my best camisa. Cardinal Borgia was not wearing his red robes tonight. In a short coat of good brown cloth slashed with brown velvet and embroidered with gold, he looked like any prosperous gentleman until you saw his cardinal's ring.

Lucrezia received her presents first—a cherrywood lap desk from her father with little glass bottles holding different colors of ink. She pronounced it utterly beautiful, and I felt my present was exceedingly modest in comparison, but I knew it would be. I gave her a set of red ribbons. I had painstakingly embroidered a bouquet of yellow flowers on the ends of each one.

Lucrezia threw her arms around my neck and hugged me, proclaiming them the most beautiful things she had ever seen, and insisted on unlacing her sleeves and putting them on immediately. Her gown was yellow, so they matched well. I had kept the gown in mind when I worked them at night after she was asleep.

"A beautiful gift," the cardinal said. "And thoughtfully chosen." He smiled at me over the table. We had not talked alone since the masquerade. I had tried to starve this infatuation, but apparently I had not starved it enough. His smile made me giddy, though his words were nothing but common pleasantries.

Beneo and one of the maids brought in dinner then, Beneo yawning even as he served. Sunset had come, and the bells of St. Peters were ringing Vespers, the light from the open balcony doors in Donna Adriana's camera coming into the sala.

The lamb was beautifully prepared, and the nice sallat of fresh spring greens was delicious. Lucrezia told a funny story about her music master, and the cardinal told one in turn about how he had completely failed as a choirboy. "I can't carry a tune with a bucket," he said with a self-depreciating shrug. "Alas, since I was thwarted in making my fortune as a troubadour, I was for the Church instead."

Adriana and I laughed, as we should. Lucrezia frowned. "But

would you really want to be a troubadour, Papa?"

"It's all performance, isn't it?" he said. "Whether you are creating a song or a rite or a revel?"

"They are all mysteries," I said. He looked at me sharply. I went on, words tumbling out, for so often I thought things and had no one to discuss them with. "Designed to transport the emotions and to teach by creating an experience. Whether they are holy or profane, they take you out of your ordinary life and bring you into a different state of being." He looked as though he might say something, then stopped with an unreadable expression on his face.

"Surely they are not the same," Adriana said. "The most holy rites are touched by the divine, whereas a play is simply a mortal thing. An entertainment."

The cardinal glanced at Lucrezia. "And what do you think, my heart?"

"I think holy rites must be divine," she said, then hesitated. "Unless he is no true priest."

"But can a play not be divine as well?" I asked. "The Greeks believed that Apollo blessed the performance of plays pleasing to him, and we speak of the muses inspiring song and dance. Is that simply a conceit, or do we believe the muses exist?"

"A figure of speech," Adriana said. "For how can we allow that spirits exist which are neither angelic nor demonic?"

"Not necessarily true," Cardinal Borgia said. "There is a mode of thought called *prisca theologia* which says that God has always spoken with His creation in many times and places, and that a single, true thread of belief exists which passes through all religions, as through the centuries men have always sought union with God. Therefore, there may exist spirits which are neither angelic nor demonic, but which often prove beneficial to mankind. They hold a lower place in the hierarchy of heaven because they are of the fallen world, but they are not evil." He shrugged. "When we speak of the muses inspiring song, perhaps that is what we mean."

Adriana looked scandalized. “You’re a cardinal. How can you repeat such heresy?”

“It is my job to study theurgy as well as theology,” he said. “Surely you allow that, Adriana?”

“What is that, Papa?” Lucrezia asked.

“Take the words apart,” he instructed. “What is theology? What does it mean?”

“God-knowing,” Lucrezia said. “So it’s studying God.”

“So theurgy?”

“God-working,” I said. I felt a shiver up my spine. “I do not know what it might be, but I am curious.”

“Do you plan to leave us for the convent then?” Adriana said wryly.

“Certainly not,” I said. “I am ill-suited to such a life. And how should it differ from marriage to Orsino?” There was a bitter note in my voice, and the cardinal looked at me, a little frown between his brows.

Adriana changed the subject quickly. “Lucrezia, will you tell your father of your latest studies with Father Antonio?”

She pouted prettily. “I am much put out with him just now, Papa. He will not teach me Ovid!”

Her father laughed. “There I will not intervene. You are too young for the *Metamorphoses*.”

“Giulia is allowed to read it,” Lucrezia pointed out.

“She is a married woman, not a little girl of nine,” the cardinal replied.

“Ten,” Lucrezia said.

“Ten,” he allowed. “In a year or two. There are too many murders and abductions and things which you do not have the experience of life to understand.”

“The Rape of Proserpina,” Lucrezia said brightly. “And yet Giulia dressed as Proserpina for the masque.”

“Lucrezia!” Adriana exclaimed. “Little girls do not discuss

rape at the dinner table."

Cardinal Borgia leaned forward on his elbows. "To my mind, that story is about marriage. The Greeks called it a *hieros gamos*, a sacred marriage between gods, but it is the experience of many young women to be given in marriage to a man they do not know well and to find their wedding night shocking and their first months of marriage difficult." He glanced at me sideways. "They leave their mother's house and live in their husband's house, under different rules and without those who they love. Of course it's hard."

He meant his words for me as much as Lucrezia and misunderstood completely. If only that were the trouble! He thought that Orsino's attentions in the bedroom were distasteful to me rather than nonexistent.

"But it is part of growing up," he said to Lucrezia. "To become the lady of the house, queen of your own realm, you have to become a wife rather than a daughter. Pluto's chariot—do you know the marriage customs of the old Romans? Like us, they had a wedding procession from the bride's family house to the groom's. That's what the chariot is. It's Proserpina's wedding procession. We still keep this custom."

"Giulia didn't have a wedding procession," Lucrezia said. "And she was very sad." My mouth opened and shut. I had not said so to her, but it was true.

"Usually we keep it," his dark eyes rested on my face for a moment, and I thought he read my expression. "It's difficult," he said quietly, "to become part of a new family and to care for one's husband. But think, my Lucrezia, how Pluto must feel. Men do have feelings as well."

Lucrezia put her head to the side. "But he has all the power."

"He has a young woman who has been given to him, perhaps against her will, who is now in the most intimate parts of his life. His house is hers. She is mistress of all around her. If she hates him and raises their children to hate him, his life will be a misery.

Somehow he must win her. Perhaps his person is displeasing to her and she thinks him old or unattractive. Perhaps she finds him boring! She nods politely while he talks about things which do not interest her, railing against him in her mind the entire time. Perhaps she lies with him gritting her teeth while he tries to please her. Should he fail or mistake her, she will never forgive him. I put it to you that Pluto doesn't have it easy either."

And how should I find Orsino old? He is not but half a year my senior, I thought. No, he spoke of himself now. Lucrezia looked quizzical. "Why would she not just say what she thought?"

"Well, he is after all Lord of Riches, King of the World Beneath. There are many women who will grit their teeth and make themselves agreeable for gold." He did not look at me. Instead he toyed with the stem of the wine glass. "Men are not always very good at knowing when a woman dissembles."

"And is there no hope of happiness then?" I said. If even a man with money and power could not find satisfaction, how could anyone?

The cardinal's voice took on the tone I thought of as priestly, as though he counseled a stranger. "Perhaps if they are gentle with one another and try to understand each other's tempers, respect may grow."

"And love?" I challenged. "Where is one to find that?" He did look at me then, mouth opening as though to speak.

Lucrezia cut in. "Well, I will make my husband love me. And if he does not, I'll get an annulment and pack him off to the country!"

"You will do no such thing," Adriana said quickly. "No one is getting an annulment or going anywhere." The light was waning, the golden path across the floor quenched. It was growing dark in the sala. "And where is Beneo? He is supposed to light the candles."

"Probably in the kitchen," I said with some relief. One could count on Adriana to change the subject from anything difficult.

"Do you want me to get him?"

"There is no need," the cardinal said, reaching for the decanter of wine and topping up mine and Adriana's glasses. "We have family and good conversation."

Lucrezia yawned. "I'm sleepy," she said. "I was up late last night at mother's. Giulia, will you take me up?"

"Of course," I said. I got to my feet. "If you do not mind, Donna Adriana?"

"Good night, Lucrezia," her father said. "Give us a kiss." She went and kissed him and thanked him again for her birthday present, and we went out together.

The candles had not been lit on the stair either, but it was not full dark yet. Lucrezia's room was around the corner from mine, looking into the garden at a different angle. I helped her undress, shaking out her beautiful gamurra and laying it to air, telling her what a lovely birthday it had been. "And your lap desk is wonderful," I said, and turned. Lucrezia had already curled under her covers in her camisa, her head pillowed on her arm, her eyes closed and her breath even. "Asleep," I said. She looked so peaceful in sleep, not the whirlwind she was awake. I straightened her covers, brushing my fingers across her brow. "Good night, darling," I said. Was it sister or mother I felt? What need to define this tenderness? I blew out the candle on her table and went out quietly.

The hall was entirely dark. Surely Beneo should have lit the candles by now? Or if he were busy, someone would have? I listened. The house was completely quiet. I stood still, hushing even my breath. I heard nothing. I should hear something. There were too many people here not to, but I heard not even the murmur of conversation from Donna Adriana's sala on the floor below.

I went quickly down the stairs by feel. The door to the sala was open, and a lighter patch beyond showed where the door to the camera and the balcony were. I could see two figures slumped in their chairs. "Donna Adriana? Cardinal Borgia?" I hurried in.

Fear clutched at me. It was as though I had suddenly slid into some nightmare, the kind where ordinary things become awful.

"Donna Adriana?" She leaned back in her chair, her head against the rest, her white throat bared. I put my hand to it and felt her pulse beneath my fingertips, but she didn't stir. I shook her gently. "Donna Adriana?"

I went to Cardinal Borgia. He slumped forward, his arms resting on the table, his forehead on his arms. His wineglass had spilled, wine soaking the white linen. "Cardinal?" I put my hand on his shoulder. "Please. Please." He snorted, a snoring sort of noise. "Please wake up," I said. "Cardinal Borgia, please!" I put my hand against the side of his face, the evening's beard prickly under my fingers, but he only snorted again in his sleep.

Poison? A potion in the wine? I had heard of such. But I had drunk wine from the same decanter, poured by the cardinal's own hands, and I felt perfectly fine. Well, other than terrified. And Lucrezia had not drunk wine at all and she was sound asleep. There was no other dish we had not all shared.

"This is not right," I said to the sleepers. "Something is very wrong." I ran out of the sala and down the stairs on my way to the kitchen. The garden was dark, but a light came from the kitchen door. I hurried in, nearly tripping over Beneo on the way. He was asleep just inside the kitchen door, his snores loud in the empty kitchen. The fire was burning merrily. The remains of the servants' supper stood on the table. They had not been served wine from the same cask that we had, and yet there was Maria and one of the maids sound asleep at the table.

I pinched my own arm. It hurt. Well, so this was not a dream. And yet it seemed like one, though I was sure I was awake. My heart beat so rapidly I was sure I could not sleep. *Calm*, I said to myself. *Giulia, think!* If this were poison, how could it have been administered? Could it be some foul air or smoke? It was certainly possible for people to fall into sleep and death from a blocked flue or a fire in a confined space, but the kitchen fire was burning normally and there was no smoke in the room. Besides, the door was open to the passage. Upstairs, the balcony doors were wide open in the camera, doors and shutters both. No one could suffocate next to double doors wide open! And Lucrezia was in still another room on the floor above. Not foul air, then.

I paced out of the kitchen, going up the passage to the portico around the garden. It was very dark even outside, a night with no moon. An enchantment. Were there such outside of stories? Well, and were there mirrors with demons in them? Part of me was shocked to the core. Could an enchantment hold a holy cardinal? Apparently it could. How did one break enchantments in stories?

There was a movement in the garden, and I froze, slipping behind one of the pillars. Two men were climbing over the roof, their feet quiet but not silent on the tiles. They were dressed in dark clothes, but there was the glitter of a dagger at the waist of one. Not the cardinal's guards then. They would come to the gate when the time arrived for them to return for him. After Compline, he had said. Sometime after, as he was at a family party. I had heard Vespers rung but not Compline.

If they were not the cardinal's guards, they were up to no good. One climbed down the arbor, the other following. I caught a bit of their words, my back pressed against the pillar. "...nice and quiet. Think they're all sleeping?"

"That's what he said," the other man replied. "So let's find this priest and do the job."

"Not much sport to kill a sleeping man," the first said. He was coming closer. He would pass me if he went to the stairs.

"It's not sport. It's work," the other said. "Upstairs, do you think, or around the side?"

I tried not to breathe. The second man had a drawn sword in his hand. *This priest. Kill a sleeping man.* They were here to kill Cardinal Borgia.

"Round this way, maybe?" the first said. He came toward me, the second behind him. I turned around the pillar as they came around it, silently keeping it between us. They went toward the ground floor rooms. I heard a muffled curse as one of them tripped over something. They dared not kindle a light. And that was a gift, I thought. They did not know the house and I did. But what could I do? I had no weapon.

There were knives aplenty in the kitchen. I ran swiftly in the opposite direction from the way they'd gone, back down the kitchen passage and past Beneo sleeping. There was a filleting knife on the butchering table still bloody from the lamb. I grabbed it up. Anger made me clear, as though everything were bright and fine, time elongating. If I went up the servants' stairs, I could come around past Orsino's rooms and back to Adriana's sala from the other side. Once inside, I could bar the door with one of the candlestands and wait until the cardinal's guards arrived.

I went up the stairs quickly and quietly, listening. I heard no sound. Around the hall, past Orsino's door. There were the formal stairs, there the open door to the sala. I stopped.

I could indeed go in and bar the door. And what about Lucrezia, sleeping on the floor above? They would find her if they searched the third floor. What would they do then? I was going to have to think of something else. And there were their voices climbing the stairs. I had no choice. I ducked into the sala, pulling the doors shut and shoving a candlestick through the handles.

"Did you hear something?" one said.

"I don't think so." This unnatural quiet muffled my movements as much as theirs. It did not muffle the sound of someone pulling on the door. The candlestick clanked against the handles. "This door's locked."

"We'll come back to it if we don't find him elsewhere. It looks like a gentleman's room down here." I squeezed my eyes shut for a moment. Orsino's rooms. That would take them a few minutes to search. "You go on up. I'll check in here."

Up. Lucrezia. I unjammed the door. Fast as a waterbird when the dogs are loosed, I flew up the stairs to the third floor, leaving the sala door closed but not locked behind me. I was ahead of him. I heard him coming up the stairs. He was much larger and stronger than I. I stood behind the tapestry, my blue velvet invisible against the hanging. He stumbled over that step two from the top where the center of the tread was worn. He swore, turning toward her rooms.

No choice. No fear. He heard my first step, began to turn, but it was too late. I thrust the fillet knife full into his side, through doublet and shirt beneath. He bellowed. It was a scream of pure pain. I drew the knife out, the blood following after, and ran. I ran down the stairs, ducking into the stairwell going down to the ground floor as the other man ran up.

"What's going on?" It wouldn't take him long to see. There was a trail of black drops on the white marble. The knife in my hand dripped with blood from his companion's liver. I dropped it.

I heard their voices above. They were on the flight to the third floor. I must get them to come down, away from Lucrezia. I took a deep breath, then let out the most horrible scream I could imagine. Then quickly I ran down the stairs to the ground floor and to the other end through the garden and back up the servant's stairs that came out near the suite next to Donna Adriana's that had belonged to her husband.

One of the men must be helping the other down the stairs. "Go on down if you can," I heard him say. "There's something in here besides us."

"I'm going to die, aren't I?" the first said breathlessly.

Probably, I thought, *if I stabbed you in the liver. Though it could take you a while*. I didn't feel a bit sorry. Was this what my father had meant by fighting fury?

"You stay there. I'll check this floor for the priest."

You just try that, I thought. There was a floor stand with two fat unlit candles in the corner of the sala. I slipped in the door and took the candles off, setting them quietly on the floor. There were long spikes that held them, and the stand was wrought iron and half my height. I stood behind the door.

It was only a few moments before it opened. One man came in, walking quietly and cautiously, a big man, dagger drawn in his hand. One chance. If he closed with me, I would die. He straightened as he saw the figures slumped at the table. I swung the candlestand not at his head. There was too much chance of a glancing blow. I swung it at the back of his neck.

I heard the sharp crack and he dropped like a sack. I stood there holding the candlestand. He didn't move. I couldn't bring myself to bend over him. It would probably be stupid anyway if he weren't dead. Far away, in another world, I heard the bells of St. Peter's ringing Compline.

I ran to the table instead. I seized Cardinal Borgia by the shoulders. "Wake up! Please wake up!" I begged. "Cardinal, please!"

He was heavy. I couldn't hold him like that, and he slumped over again, dragging the tablecloth with him. The bowl of flowers tipped over and crashed to the floor, taking the tablecloth and the wineglasses with it.

And then I heard a welcome sound. There was a knocking at the street gates. The cardinal's guards. I heard the gates open, the urgent, frightened voice of the man I'd stabbed. "Thank God you're here!" he said. "Somebody's tried to kill the cardinal! Upstairs, quick!"

There were running feet on the stairs. "In here!" I shouted. "It's Donna Giulia. I hit the man with a candlestand!"

The guards rushed in, one of them tripping over the man in the dark. "Donna Giulia?"

There was a moan behind me. I spun around. She had moved in her chair. "Adriana? Adriana, can you hear me?"

"A light," said one of the guards.

"There is a fire in the kitchen," I said. My hands were suddenly shaking. "But please don't leave yet. That man broke in. I hit him. I don't know if I killed him." Adriana moaned again, and I took her hands in mine. "Adriana?"

Behind me was another sound. "What is going on here?" Cardinal Borgia said. I spun around. He was sitting up, one hand on his forehead.

"These men came to kill you," I said. "Two of them."

"He's dead all right," one of the guards said. "Broken neck."

Cardinal Borgia got to his feet. "You killed him?"

"No, Your Eminence. Donna Giulia did."

"I don't feel terribly good," I said, and bent over and lost my supper.

The next hour was a blur. The second assassin, the one I had stabbed, had gotten away out the street gate after he directed the guards upstairs. They'd assumed he was Donna Adriana's man and had paid him no further attention. I went out onto her balcony to breathe in the fresh air. It was cool and dark, and I leaned against the rail for a long time looking out at the lights of the city. Behind me, through the camera and in the sala, there was a great deal happening. I watched the moonless sky.

After a while I heard a step behind me. "Giulia?" the cardinal said. "Are you all right?"

"I killed a man," I said. I could hear the terrible crunch when I hit his neck. I didn't think I would ever forget it.

"So you did," he said gently. He came and leaned on the balcony rail beside me, a foot between us. "But if you had not, he would have probably killed us all. To kill in defense of others is a sin you may be absolved of."

"It was you they were after," I said. I had no proof, but I knew in my heart this had to do with Bracciano. And what could I say about that?

"Probably." He glanced at me sideways. "I had no thought that my presence brought danger to this house."

"I know," I said. "You'd never endanger Lucrezia."

"No." He was still looking at me. "I have offered Adriana the use of my guards on a permanent basis. Eight men will rotate, with no less than two here at any time. I will cover the expense, of course." He stopped, then went on as though he spoke to Lucrezia. "You were very brave."

"I had no fear," I said, "until it was over."

"And now?"

"Now I am empty, like an instrument that has been played." I put my hands flat on the balcony railing. I looked at him sideways. "I couldn't do anything else."

"Actually, you could have run," he said, rubbing his head. "Most people would have."

"I didn't think of it," I said.

Cardinal Borgia nodded slowly. "Your love for Lucrezia held you back."

"Yes," I said. "How could I leave her?" *Not just Lucrezia*, I thought, but I had more sense than to voice that.

"Will you come in now?" he asked. "They've taken the body out. Come in by the fire and have a little wine."

I nodded. He gave me his arm, and we went back into the sala. The room was brightly lit, every candle glowing. One of the maids was getting the broken glass off the floor with a broom. The tablecloth was half-off the table, red wine stains running down it like blood. The silver bowl had rolled onto the floor, the flowers scattered.

The cardinal frowned. "What's that?" he said, picking something up off the middle of the table. He turned it in his hand. "A human tooth?"

"It would have been under the tablecloth," I said. "Under the stem of the flower bowl." I had knocked the bowl over and dragged the tablecloth off when I tried to wake him the second time. On the floor, the maid gave a sob. I landed next to her, my knees just missing the broken glass. I put my hand over hers. "Cecilia, what do you know about this?"

She looked up at me, her eyes red. "I put the tooth there."

The cardinal's eyebrows rose. He made to kneel down, but I looked at him and shook my head. "Cecilia, why did you do that? You can tell me. I know you meant no harm."

"Indeed I did not, Donna Giulia!" she said.

My voice was very even. "Is it a charm? What was it meant to do?"

She began to cry. "It's a love charm, Madonna! A young gentleman came to me in the market and said he knew I worked in Donna Adriana's house. He said he knew you were unhappy in your marriage. He said that he loved you true, and if you noticed him, he'd make you happy. Well, I heard what you said the time you threw the water on Signore Orsino and about how he carries on, and I thought what was the harm in maybe a young scholar who admired you? It wouldn't make you do anything, just notice his suit."

The cardinal's eyebrows were somewhere around his hairline. I tried to ignore him. "What did this young scholar look like? Does he have a name?"

"He didn't give me his name, Donna Giulia. He was not much older than you. Dark. Handsome. Nicely trimmed beard. Not expensive clothes but neat."

Dr. Treschi, I thought. *That bastard*. I took a deep breath. "And what happened then? He gave you this charm? This tooth?" She nodded. "What were you supposed to do with it?"

"Put it beneath the tablecloth when you sat down to eat," she said. "That's all. Just put it under the tablecloth."

"So you put it there, and then put the bowl on top of it so we wouldn't see the bump in the tablecloth," I said.

Cecilia nodded miserably. "I thought it was a love charm!" she said.

"I know." I put my hand on her shoulder. "I understand. You had no idea this would happen. It's all right. Isn't it, Cardinal?" I looked up at him to put him on the spot.

"It is indeed," he said, making the sign of the cross over her head. "*Ego te absolvo*."

"You are too good to me!" she said, weeping.

"Don't meddle with any more love charms," he said. He drew me to my feet, taking me aside, turning the tooth over and over in his other hand. "A strange business," Cardinal Borgia said. "I think I don't know all there is to know about this."

"You do not," I said. I took a deep breath. And now was not the time and place, not with Orsino coming home and Adriana and the maids and the guards.... "Cardinal Borgia, may I confess to you?"

"If you would like," he said. His brows drew together somewhat. "You need to put this under the seal of the confessional?"

"I do," I said. My back was straight.

He nodded gravely. "Then come to me day after tomorrow at St. Peter's in the third hour. I will expect you."

"Yes, Cardinal," I said, and bobbed a curtsy.

Chapter Nine

At the appointed time one of Cardinal Borgia's guards escorted me to the Vatican. I had been in St. Peter's only twice since I had arrived in Rome. Donna Adriana did not attend Mass often, and when she did she preferred the small parish church. I had certainly never been into the Vatican proper. It was a beautiful sunny day in the season of Easter, and the basilica was filled with light. Every surface gleamed, the gilt and paintings shining in the spring light. The high altar was practically blinding. Pots of greenery added to the celebratory atmosphere.

So did the veritable army of priests, laymen, clerks, choirboys, nuns, penitents, and visitors clattering across marble floors or gathering in groups to talk. Some lit candles in the side shrines, while a black-robed choirmaster attempted to bring twenty boys to order in the choir stalls to practice. It was utterly breathtaking, the beating heart of Christendom. I stopped, simply taking it in.

Through this, like a barge on the Tiber parting lesser river traffic, swept Cardinal Borgia. Down the entire length of the nave he came, a ship under sail, red robes billowing. Three clerks scrambled after, one taking dictation and one waving some document. A pair of priests were following. A slight clerk wearing eyeglasses and carrying a heavy book pursued. A tall man in the purple robes of a bishop walked beside him attempting to keep up with the quickness of his step. He stopped to reply, unerringly finding a beam of light through one of the upper windows. It illuminated him as sharply as the hero onstage, flashing off his ring as he gestured broadly, his good regard a benediction. The light caught him in perfect profile, silhouetted against the splendor. He had a rather large nose, but he would play Agamemnon or Caesar to perfection.

And then he was off again, silk robes flowing, the entourage pursuing, visitors crossing themselves as he passed. The clerk with the book caught up, and he stopped again to hear what the man said, some matter of procedure perhaps as his voice carried. "Find a precedent, Burchard. Nearly fifteen hundred years of Church history. You can find a precedent." He swept on again, all eyes following. He walked straight to me. "Donna Giulia," he said.

I sunk into a deep curtsy as the moment demanded. "Your Eminence."

"Walk with me. I will hear your confession in my study." He waved a hand toward the confessional booths far down the nave. "It's loud in here today."

"Of course, Your Eminence." And so I joined the entourage, the man named Burchard giving way for me with a smile and a surprisingly courtly gesture.

Out through one of the side doors, across a garden square, in through a scriptorium and library, down a splendid passage—I was hard-pressed to keep up. "One must run like a terrier," Burchard said quietly. "Good for the humors, I suppose."

I nearly laughed, but he was not doing it in skirts. Though I suppose the cardinal was. His skirts were broader than mine. Burchard peeled off at another gallery, as did the bishop. The rest of us pursued. Around another corner, up a set of stairs, through a corridor with a black and white floor like a chessboard. And then into another scriptorium or the like, four desks holding ledgers, clerks popping up attentively.

"Don't let me disturb you," Cardinal Borgia said as he sailed through the room. "Brother Feliciano, I'd like that report on the building expenses at Santa Maria del Popolo this afternoon without fail. Who has been paid and who has not? I want to see the receipts and know for certain if we are being double-billed."

"Yes, Your Eminence," a young man said.

And we swept through another door into the study on the other side. He stopped. "Gentlemen, enough. Donna Giulia has the hour." He closed the door in their faces.

I took a deep breath, as much from our mad dash as from nerves. The room was not small but it was quite full. A large table took up much of the space beneath the window, the top of one side tilted like a copyist's desk, the other side filled with correspondence. There were three red leather chairs, one larger and two smaller, with a small table to the side, and a large book shelf with perhaps twenty volumes. The top of the shelf was taken up with many small items which I wished I could examine: a tiny marble head, a curving sphere with uncut amethysts in it, some square metal pieces I could not identify, a painted tile with a bird in flight on it, a dark steel arrowhead shaped like a leaf, a blue stone in the shape of a beetle, and a little clay bull. *Curiosities*, I thought. I wondered what each of them meant to him. The room smelled like parchment and wax, a hint of incense clinging to it. The light came in through the many paned window. It was quite a beautiful room in its way.

Cardinal Borgia sunk into the large chair. "Now," he said, gesturing to one of the other chairs, "sit down and tell me what you wished."

I sat down gingerly. "Your Eminence, is this under the seal of the confessional?"

"Yes, of course. I thought you would prefer somewhere private rather than in the nave. You may rest assured that I hear your confession as part of my priestly office, and that your words will go no further." He steepled his hands. "Why don't you begin at the beginning?"

"I was born in Montalto," I began.

He was trying not to smile. "Perhaps not that far back to the beginning."

I took a deep breath. "I know who sent the assassins and why. They came to kill you and they were sent by the gonfaloniere."

His brows twitched. He was all attention. "And how do you know this?"

I could have lied. I could have said that I heard it said among the Orsini, but surely lying to a priest in the confessional would only compound my sins.

"My Lord Bracciano required me to be part of a sorcerous ritual intended to see the future and determine the best way to do you harm." His eyebrows rose and I rushed on. "I have no proof, Your Eminence. I realize this is an outrageous charge. And I swear I did not know what he intended or expect the assassins. I had no part in that, and if I had known I would have told you. I would never endanger Lucrezia!"

"Yes, I believe that," he murmured. "And If you had wished the assassins to succeed, all you would have had to do was lock yourself in your room."

"Your Eminence, I would never have contrived at your death!" I said. "You must believe that. I am coming to you because I have no wish to be part of Bracciano's schemes and I have no means to deny him!" My voice rose.

"Calmly, calmly, Giulia," he said. "What part did you play in this operation?" His voice was soothing.

"Bracciano and his men made many squares and circles with chalk upon the floor to call a demon into a mirror. I sat upon a three-legged stool like the sibyls of old, to repeat what it said and to interpret the scenes it showed me. They called me a Dove." My hands twisted together in my lap. "Because I have seen things in mirrors before."

"Did you promise this creature anything?" he asked gravely.

"No, Your Eminence."

"Did you offer it anything or make any agreement with it?"

"No, Your Eminence," I said again. "I swear that I did not." I thought about it. "I think some of the men might have, or Bracciano himself. But I did not promise, offer, or agree to anything." I leaned forward. "You must know this is not by my free will."

"I understand that," he said. "But you have seen things in mirrors before?"

I could not dissemble. "Always," I said simply. "All my life. Not anything frightening or cruel. Just scenes, sometimes. Things from the past or the future. Fancies, I have thought. Sometimes small things that come to pass, but nothing important. Nothing frightening, not at all! Little things. And then after my father died...." I stopped.

"What happened after your father died?" he asked gently.

It all poured out. My father's death, my grandmother's, my little brother's. The summer sickness and how I had gone from my sickbed to my mother's childbed, and everything that came after. Every bit of fear and anger and pain came pouring out. How I had despaired of ever leaving Montalto. How I had gone to the tomb and what had happened there. How Bracciano had come to Montalto and seen me with the mirror. I had wished someone to confide in, and his quiet invited confidence. Perhaps it was something priests learned.

"And so Bracciano arranged this marriage, but he forbids Orsino to touch me." To my horror, my eyes filled with tears. "Eleven months I have been married, and he will not come to my bed but goes instead to brothels."

"Unfathomable," Cardinal Borgia muttered.

"He will not defy his kinsman; he believes that Bracciano ill-uses me, yet he will say nothing. What kind of man would let his virgin bride be despoiled by his kinsman and do nothing?" I demanded. "How can this be allowed?"

The cardinal put his hands together thoughtfully. "If Bracciano did indeed ill-use you—but he does not. If Orsino were cruel to you, I would speak with him. But I cannot order him to your bed."

"You could order me to his," I said bitterly. "Wifely duty and such."

"You could be granted an annulment on the basis of non-consummation if he is incapable or unwilling," he said thoughtfully. "You could be released from this marriage with no harm to you."

"Except what would I do then?" I asked. "Return to Montalto to grow old as a maiden aunt? I have no dowry anymore and no powerful kin to make a connection with me valuable. Go to a convent? I am sadly unsuited to a convent, Your Eminence."

"I see the problem," he said, and his eyes dropped. "Is there no one that you are close to, no friend you may rely on who might bring comfort to you?"

"There is my brother, Alessandro," I said. "But he is finishing at the university in Pisa and prepares to take holy orders. I have no idea where he will be sent."

He nodded gravely. "And you have not been able to make friends in Rome other than Lucrezia, and she is a child. However, the heart of the problem is Bracciano, it seems to me."

"He arranged for Orsino to be away dining with his officers. They would have done away with you; and Donna Adriana, Lucrezia and I would have been incidental damage. Your Eminence, he intends to kill you." My fear of that eclipsed all else.

"And I intend to kill him." His black eyes were sharp, though his voice was even. "He crossed a line when he sent his assassins near Lucrezia. But I am a patient man." He leaned forward in his chair. "It must not be quickly or intemperately done. He will show his hand in time."

"He will send for me again," I said. "And I cannot refuse him. I said I was sick last time, but he will not believe it again."

"Will they tell you what they intend?" the cardinal asked.

I shook my head. "No, but there may be a way." An idea had occurred to me. "Perhaps Dr. Treschi is bribable. You said he was a student of that scholar you knew of in Florence, della Mirandola. Students are often poor. If Bracciano pays him well, surely you can afford to pay him better."

Cardinal Borgia smiled. "As clever as you are lovely."

"You do not think that I am dissembling this entire time," I began hotly.

He waved a jeweled hand. "No, no. Giulia, I believe you. But if you can indeed convince Dr. Treschi to alter his allegiance, it would be extremely useful. Even if you can only find out what Bracciano intends, it is much easier to counter assassins when one expects them."

"Of course," I said. "And you cannot seek him without being noted. You are…rather noticeable." I gestured at his scarlet robes and general demeanor. No one could fail to see him, even if he were disguised.

"And yet you are supposedly the recipient of his love charm," he said. "Surely an infatuated young woman might seek out the man who interested her?"

"She might indeed," I said, a furious blush rising. There was only one real and living man I had an interest in seeking out, and I sat this moment in a small room with him.

"Giulia, I cannot ask you to do this."

"I would free myself," I said. "If the way to do that is to thwart Bracciano's plans, then I will do it."

He put his head to the side. "Even knowing there is danger?"

"There was danger the other night. And I killed." I glanced down.

"In defense of others, including a child," Cardinal Borgia said. "I will absolve you of that, and direct you to pray for the soul of the man you killed. I will also set a penance for you for your converse with the demon, though it is simply prayers and I think you will not find it onerous. It is clear you had no desire to do these things and that you only did so at the insistence of a man who you could not refuse."

"Thank you," I said, and bent my head.

"*Ego te absolvo*," he said, making the sign of the cross above me. It came with a kind of peace.

That afternoon I caught Donna Adriana's maid, Maria, in the kitchen. "I have a question for you," I said. I had a silver soldo in my hand. I dropped my voice as she stood waiting, phrasing carefully. "As you may have guessed, Orsino has not come to my marriage bed."

Her eyes were warm with sympathy and just a little amusement. "Madonna, I have guessed." How not? She had been one of the witnesses to the water-throwing incident.

"Then perhaps it is something in our stars which are incompatible," I said. "I have heard of such. I know he might not approve, but I would consult an astrologer who can cast our charts together and discover what the impediment to our happiness is. More than anything I desire him to be a real husband!"

Maria hesitated. She scratched her chin. "Donna Giulia," she said carefully, "I have known Orsino seven years now since I came to work in this house. I'm not sure that an astrologer can help."

"Why not?" I asked.

"Orsino is not what you might call forceful. A young woman wants a man who knows his own mind. And who has some guts in his belly."

I made my eyes very round. "Then what am I to do?"

"There's more than one fish in the ocean, is what I say," Maria said. "If you take my meaning. What Orsino doesn't want, somebody else would be happy to have. And better a lusty man than a coward."

I could not have agreed with Maria more, but it hardly served my purpose. "He is my husband," I said breathlessly. "I have heard of a learned doctor who consults to see if a man and a woman may be happy together. His name is Dr. Treschi. Maria, would you be so good as to find where he lodges? I hope he can help me."

She clearly thought a lover was a less doomed method of achieving satisfaction, but the coin glinted in my hand. And what harm could it do for me to talk to some charlatan who would give me useless advice? "Very well, Madonna," she said. "I will see if I can find him."

Maria was able to fulfill my commission amazingly well. It was only two days before she brought my clean and folded camisas to my room, shutting the door behind her. "I've found the man."

I had been sitting on the bed reading and I jumped to my feet. "Truly?"

She put the basket of clothes down, her hands twisting together. "He's an astrologer, Donna Giulia. I'm not sure I ought…."

"Maria, Cardinal Borgia himself called astrology the blessed science because it was practiced by the Magi. There is no harm in astrology." I put the book down. "The reason I want to consult with Dr. Treschi is because I have no idea how to win my husband's regard. Orsino is young and should be high-blooded. And I do not think I am displeasing. So why will he not do as he should?"

Maria sighed. "I do not know, my lady. You are very beautiful."

"Perhaps it is something in our stars," I said. "Perhaps this Dr. Treschi can tell me what to do."

She nodded. "I hope so, my lady," and gave me the directions to his lodging.

The next morning I slipped downstairs early, before Lucrezia was awake and certainly before Donna Adriana. I put a brown cloak that was hanging in the pantry on over my oldest dress and took up a market basket so that I would look like a maidservant doing the shopping. Quietly, I drew back the bar on the heavy kitchen door and slipped out, pulling it shut behind me and walking quickly away.

I had not generally been out the kitchen door before, and I stopped to get my bearings at the first corner, just down a short, steep street. Ahead of me was a little square with a church, San Salvatore in Lauro, where the servants generally attended. To either side, the street twisted between overhanging buildings. A dog nosed hopefully outside a closed osteria. The houses looked gold in the morning light, some shutters painted bright colors, all of them closed against the night's chill. No one was about, though I did hear a baby crying on some upper floor, a fretful, dirty clout kind of cry very familiar from my little sister. It stopped in a moment; someone must have gotten up to tend the baby.

The morning was chilly, the sky blue with a few clouds blowing away, the streets slick with last night's rain, a few puddles in the middle where they were rutted. No one knew me or where I was. I felt freer than I had in months, since I had come to Rome and been bound as a bride to propriety and unaccustomed confinement. Of course it was not that all Roman ladies were as cheerless as I was; most palazzos were brimming with life, friends and families and clients in and out all day. Certainly that must be true of the vice-chancellor's palazzo. If I lived there.... I cut that thought off immediately. I was not even going to speculate on what such a life would be.

With my head high, I started down the street following Maria's directions. It was quite a few blocks, though the streets turned round and round rather than running in straight lines, and I thought I must be getting near the river. It was a house with a wine-shop on the first floor, she had said, and Dr. Treschi consulted with clients in a room rented above.

I found the wine-shop without difficulty, a rickety staircase going up from the alley to a door. A sign hung beside it, a sun and moon drawn in blue. I rapped on the door sharply. All was silent. I rapped more loudly. "Who's there?" a man's voice called. I thought it was Dr. Treschi.

"I am a client who has come to consult Dr. Treschi," I replied loudly. "I have come to pay for his time."

Another man's voice said something too low to hear. "No," Dr. Treschi said. "I can't afford that." There was a low laugh, and I wondered what was going on. I had nearly decided to leave when the door opened. Dr. Treschi wore hose and a shirt, pulling a gown on over it quickly. Another young man was doing up his points and glanced up at me appraisingly.

"I am here to consult with Dr. Treschi," I said to him. "If the gentleman is not interested in the work...?" I let my voice trail off.

"No, of course not," Treschi said. He adjusted his gown, attempting to look professional, then turned and saw me. "Donna Giulia!"

The room was small and smelled of sex. Anyone with four brothers knew what a tiny room where men had been getting off smelled like. I went over and opened the window. "Dr. Treschi, I have an important commission for you. If you are not otherwise occupied?"

The other young man took the look Treschi gave him. "Later then," he said, and went out carrying his boots, no doubt to put them on sitting on the stairs.

Student vices, I thought. *Well, perhaps that makes me safer alone with him*. Treschi looked wary. "Donna Giulia, I don't know where to begin."

"You may begin by sitting down and answering my questions," I said, sitting down on one of the two stools at his table and laying a silver soldo on it. "I wish your professional consultation and I am prepared to pay for it."

"Of course." He took a deep breath. "Do you mind? I haven't..." He gestured to a pitcher of last night's wine and half a loaf of bread.

"Break your fast," I said. "But talk."

At that he smiled engagingly and sat down opposite me. "You're not at all what I expected."

"What did you expect?" I asked.

He shrugged, tearing off a piece of bread and putting it in his mouth. "A meek girl. Malleable. A Dove."

I pushed the coin toward him. "What is a Dove? Explain it to me."

"A Dove is a girl who, like the ancient oracles, has the ability to hear and speak with spirits," he said. "Because of her purity and malleability, she can serve as a conduit, a vessel, for them."

"I see," I said. I had guessed and wished to check whether it were true. "A Dove must be virgin?"

A blush began to rise on his half-shaven cheeks. "Yes. Absolutely. She must have never known a man carnally." He really was no older than Alessandro.

"And that is what gives her power?"

He tore off another piece of bread. "Well, maybe. Yes and no. Some of the oracles of old were ancient beldames. But it is generally accepted today that a Dove must be virgin. She must know as little of the world as possible because it is her purity that protects her from the evil of the spirits she encounters."

"So it is for her protection?" I asked.

Dr. Treschi nodded. "These spirits are both puissant and evil. They will attempt to trick men into losing their immortal souls."

"Surely it is far too dangerous to speak with them at all," I said.

"There are operations which render it safer," he said.

"The squares and circles you draw in chalk?"

He nodded again. "There was an ancient sage of Egypt, Hermes Trismegistus, who codified means of speaking with various spirits. Lately his work has been translated by a Florentine scholar, Maestro Ficino, and the wisdom of the Hermetic systems may again be employed."

"Ficino," I said. I had heard the name most recently at the masquerade. Cardinal Borgia had assured his friend, Barbaro, that Ficino would be acquitted of heresy though he was certainly guilty. "And do these Hermetic systems require the use of a Dove?"

"I think that is a modern adaptation," he said. "After all, in Hermes Trismegistus' era the great oracles of the ancient world were contemporary and there were many temple priestesses."

"Who presumably were not innocent maidens," I said. I found that quite irking.

Dr. Treschi squirmed a little. "Who presumably had their own titular patron gods, and thus could rely on the protection of friendly entities to preserve them from unfriendly ones."

I felt my eyebrows rise. "So you are allowing that ancient pagan gods could hold sway over demons?"

"A demon is an order of evil spirit," Treschi said. "Many ancient gods were credited with power over such. Isis was styled Mistress of Magic and said to hold back such night creatures. Presumably her protection was sufficient for her priestesses." He warmed to the topic. "The circles and squares I render call upon the protection of various entities as is appropriate. Generally, a working square invokes angels, but there are various operations that invoke the energies and planetary influences of others. A Square of Jupiter invokes Jupiter, obviously."

"Obviously," I said. "And Ficino teaches this?" If so, no wonder he had been denounced as a heretic. Cardinal Borgia certainly knew this. He did not seem a man to be hoodwinked into foolishly supporting someone whose work he did not understand.

"He does. Lorenzo de Medici has given him a small estate where he could set up an Academy for the young men of the Republic away from the distractions of city life, as Aristotle did at Mieza. He is the Academy's patron."

"Does he fancy his son another Alexander?" I asked.

Dr. Treschi snorted. "Piero is no Alexander. But there are many fine scholars there. I would have liked to study there myself but...." He broke off, shrugging.

"But you are not noble by birth," I said.

He met my eyes. "My father was a draper. He died when I was nine and my mother arranged for me to be educated so that I might be a clerk or go into holy orders. I made my own way to the university. But I've risen as far as I can without a patron, and since I have no kin to be my patrons, I must find one another way."

"Bracciano," I said.

Treschi nodded. "I owe him my livelihood."

I leaned forward. "I do understand what it is to have little and to try to make one's way in the world. Do you think Bracciano could use me thus if I were not a poor relation?"

"I..." he began and stopped.

"You are a philosopher even if you must curry favor with a great lord. After all, were not the sages of old beholden to kings and emperors? Every philosopher requires a patron. But I think you are not happy with yours." I smiled encouragingly. "Dr. Treschi, come clean with me. Tell me what I do and to what end. You are better than this. We are both better than this. We must stand before God and answer for what we do."

He dropped his eyes. "I don't know where to begin," he said. "And you are right, Donna Giulia. I never meant for it to go this far. I thought it would be simple. A respectable commission with a great patron. I didn't think it would be this." He took a long gulp of last night's wine.

"Dr. Treschi, tell me in simple words what purpose this serves."

He looked up at me. "My Lord Bracciano means to kill the vice-chancellor by means of black magic."

"So I understand," I said. He looked at me blankly. "Were you not the author of the enchantment by which everyone was to fall asleep at dinner and thus be helpless when two assassins arrived?" Treschi nodded. "It was only by good fortune that two of the cardinal's guards who had not dined with us returned and killed one of the assassins and ran off the other." I raised one eyebrow. "But it was you who gave the sleeping charm to a maid in the household, was it not?"

His eyes dropped. "It was."

"So you did not attempt to kill us with your own hands. Merely prepared the way for the men who would."

"Donna Giulia, no one was supposed to die but Cardinal Borgia!" he protested.

I kept my voice level though I should have liked to leap across the table and slap him. "And assassinating a cardinal while he sleeps—is that the act of a philosopher?"

"No," he said miserably. "But how can I refuse now? I'm in too deep, Madonna."

"Just call me Giulia," I said. "And you are?"

"Dionisio." He shook his head. "I don't know what to do. If I tell Bracciano that I won't do it again, I'll be dead. You don't just walk away from his service. He's the gonfaloniere. There's no need for assassins. Just an arrest and somehow I get killed. I don't have a rich family or influential friends to protect me, and you know as well as I do that the civil law of Rome is nothing when the great families are involved."

"I do," I said. "No more can I simply refuse him." I put my hand over his. "But we cannot just do this because we are too frightened not to."

"What else is there?" he said. "Besides flee to Florence."

"I cannot flee to Florence," I said sharply. "Dionisio, think! How much does Bracciano understand of the Hermetic rites you perform? Could he do them himself without you?"

He shook his head. "Not a chance. He and his kinsmen and officers who participate are barely competent as working magi. I am the one who sets up the wardings and the summonings."

"And could you do them wrong?"

"The demon would not be confined to the mirror and would run loose." He scratched his head. "Instead of Bracciano killing us, the demon would kill us."

"That doesn't seem like an answer, no," I said. "Very well. What would deny him his purpose without setting a demon loose?"

Treschi took a long drink of his wine. "If it simply didn't work."

"You mean as the assassins did not?" I asked.

He nodded. "My Lord Bracciano is going to want to know what went wrong."

"Nothing went wrong with your charm," I lied. "We were all asleep." I did not trust him enough to say that I had not been or ask why. I expected he could make some guesses but not give me certainties, and it was not worth the risk yet for only that. Besides, that would mean telling him that I thought that Proserpina had extended her protection to me, as he had said was true of priestesses in ancient times. It was a disturbing thought, but I had asked for her aid. I could hardly complain that she gave it. "The cardinal's guards interrupted them and killed one of the assassins. It was pure luck."

Treschi shrugged. "Or bad planning. One might have guessed Cardinal Borgia had guards close by. That's on Bracciano, not me." He looked at me. "That's a question he's sure to ask in the next session."

"Then I will tell him the absolute truth," I said. I wondered how to go about a bribe. I paused, looking up as though I had just had an idea. "I have a thought, Dionisio. You need money, no doubt, but more than that you need protection. What if Cardinal Borgia gave you money to leave and return to Florence? After all, his life is certainly worth a lot to him!"

"You want me to shake down Cardinal Borgia for protection money?" He boggled at me. "Have you lost your mind? I might as well let a demon loose on me! Do you have any idea how dangerous and ruthless he is?"

"Not really," I said. "I do not know him well." And yet I thought of his even tone when he'd said that he intended to kill Bracciano. I completely believed it. And I believed he would be patient. No, Cardinal Borgia would not show his hand too soon, but he would kill Bracciano in good time. If he weren't killed himself.

"I can't do that," Treschi said.

"Let me think on it then," I said offhandedly. "My friend, can you think of any other way to prevent your rite from working that does not seem to be your fault?" My life was so full of men with great moral courage. At least Cardinal Borgia wasn't simply blown around by every wind.

"If your husband would...you know." He stopped.

"If Orsino would consummate the marriage despite Bracciano's orders?" I asked. I refrained from saying that if Orsino was going to do that, he'd have done it eleven months ago.

Treschi nodded. "The Dove must be a virgin."

I couldn't resist. "So in theory, you and I could take care of that right now."

He nearly turned purple. "No. I mean, absolutely not. I mean, Lord Bracciano.... I mean...."

I let him off. "That was not a serious question."

"It would not be seemly," Dr. Treschi said primly.

"No, of course not." I couldn't give it away, could I? "Well, let us see what opportunities present themselves. But if we are united in not wishing to be used as tools for murder, at least we each have an ally."

"Indeed," he said, and gave me his hand.

Chapter Ten

It was nearly a month before Bracciano summoned me again. It was a perfect evening in mid-May, the sort of evening when even the air feels soft. A perfect evening for love, if I had ever known it. My first wedding anniversary had passed with the marriage still unconsummated. I was ready to strip Orsino, tie him to the furniture and ravish him, or would have been if I had liked him. Unfortunately there was no more to like than ever.

On the other hand, Cardinal Borgia.... The idea of kneeling penitent at his feet occupied a rather larger place in my mind than it should have. Surely I should be punished for such wicked thoughts! I imagine he could think of a way to do it extremely pleasantly, too. Which would beget more wicked thoughts in turn.... Oh, I was a mess. It was hard to manage a coherent conversation when he came to see Lucrezia.

But for the moment, my problem was Bracciano. His guards escorted me to his palazzo as the bells rang Vespers. There was the same room, the same gentlemen, the same stool waiting in the middle of the floor, the blackened mirror sitting upon it.

Dr. Treschi looked up when I entered and I nodded coolly to him, hoping that he wouldn't behave any differently. He nodded back. "Donna Giulia, if you will take up your place, I will begin chalking the square."

"Of course," I murmured.

Bracciano sized me up, his hands on his hips. "Before we begin, what happened the night that the cardinal's guard killed a man in your husband's house?"

I was well prepared for this question. "I do not know, My Lord," I said. "I was asleep like a baby. After dinner Donna Lucrezia was very tired and I took her up. Then I went in my own room and thought I would just sit down for a moment, but I fell into a sound sleep myself. When I woke there was a great bustle and it was all over." I looked up at him with big, innocent eyes.

After a moment he nodded. "We will find out tonight."

"As you wish, My Lord," I said demurely.

Dr. Treschi chalked square and circle. The man with the censer bathed everything in smoke. I held the mirror on my lap, curls of vapor around me.

"*Ecce*! *Venite*!" Bracciano said loudly.

Once again the misshapen face appeared in the mirror, leering at me. "He has come," I said. What might have been a mouth shaped into a toothy smile.

"Show her how the plan went awry," Bracciano demanded. "What was the cause of its failure?"

The demon grinned. "Not until he pays further," it said. "Five more years."

I repeated what it said, and Bracciano frowned. "I don't agree."

"Then I will give you nothing more," the demon said. Once again, I repeated.

Bracciano shook his head, then gestured to the man beside him. "Angelo?"

"My Lord, I...."

"Now!" Bracciano said.

The man straightened. "I will vow five more years of my immortal soul's service to Asmodeus."

The demon smiled. "Done," it said. "I will show her what you wish to see."

"It says it will do it," I said, and Bracciano nodded. The man stepped back, sweat pouring down his face.

In the mirror there was a smirk, a whirl of smoke, and I looked into the darkened sala of Donna Adriana's house. I saw her lean back in her chair, her head against the back as she fell asleep. I saw Cardinal Borgia slump forward, his head on his arms against the table, his glass tipping over. And then I saw myself, a slender shadow in blue velvet, enter and run to Donna Adriana. I saw myself, saw me shake her and check her pulse. I saw me go on my knees beside the cardinal, begging him to wake.

"What are you seeing?" Bracciano asked.

"The household going to sleep," I said. "Donna Adriana and the cardinal are asleep at the table." And there was the garden, the assassins coming over the wall. Then they were climbing the stairs with bared blades. They checked the sala door. It didn't move. Of course not. I had blocked it within.

"Two men are in the house," I said. "They go from room to room." That was true enough as it went. I saw one of the men climbing the stairs to the third floor. I saw him stumble, then turn hearing a sound behind him. A shadow moved, a blade stabbed out in the dark, a young woman fleeing down the stairs, blood dripping behind her. She seemed perfectly confident and lethal.

"What do you see?" Bracciano asked.

"They are looking on the third floor," I said, "But have not found what they seek." That was technically true. I heard the high, raucous sound of the demon's laughter. It knew. It knew how I lied. What would that cost me?

Now I saw the men confer on the stairs. I saw the wounded man's face twisted in pain, his hand coming away from his side black with blood. I saw him limping down, the other man turning toward the sala. He pushed the doors open. I heard again the sickening crunch of the candlestand striking the back of his neck. Perhaps I made some noise, for Bracciano demanded, "What are you seeing?"

"The cardinal's guards have come in," I said. I did not have to make my voice tremble. It did so on its own. "They are killing a man. He is slain."

"And the other?"

"Stabbed and running away." They knew that. Surely the man had reported to his master.

"So the charm worked," Dr. Treschi said. "Only the cardinal's guards returned too soon."

"It would seem so," Bracciano said.

In the mirror the demon grinned. "Liar, liar," it said. "Who do you serve?" I did not reply. If it did not know, I would certainly not tell it. Instead, I swayed on my stool as though I were faint.

"Look," Treschi said. "She is weakening. Have a care, My Lord! If she falls and breaks the warding…."

Bracciano nodded. "We've found out what we needed to know. Treschi, you can dismiss it."

Dr. Treschi began his chanting while I slumped forward as though exhausted. I was not. But it was disconcerting to see myself kill calmly. Was I so ruthless? I had not thought so. When the circle had been opened, he came and raised me from my stool. "Are you well, Donna Giulia?" he asked.

"Just a little dizzy," I said. "I am sorry I was not more help, My Lord Bracciano."

He glanced at me, deep in conversation with another man. "Another time," he said.

"Yes, My Lord," I said with a curtsy, and left as quickly as possible.

The next morning I waited about downstairs until Orsino came down. I stepped out from behind the saletta door and very deliberately stood in front of him. “Orsino, I want to talk to you.”

He hesitated. “I’m not sure....”

“If you’re allowed to talk to me?” I asked. “Truly?”

“We can talk,” he said. We went into the saletta. He stood so far away from me I couldn’t have touched him without lunging.

“Orsino,” I said, “why do I displease you so much? Aside from your kinsman’s restrictions, why don’t you want to make me your wife in truth?” He turned bright red. “Since you visit whores, I assume it’s not that you’re incapable. So why do you not do your duty by me? Bracciano would never know.”

He opened his mouth and shut it again. “I suppose I don’t like you much,” he said.

“Ah.” I lifted my chin. “And why is that?”

Orsino looked away, at the floor, at the walls. “I like girls who don’t make me feel stupid,” he said. “Not like you and Madonna Princess of Rome Lucrezia. I like girls who like playing cards instead of talking about religion and who don’t spend all their time with their nose in a book or chattering about dead men. Girls who like horseracing. Girls who aren’t boring. It’s like spending time with a tutor, not a woman.”

“I see,” I said. My face was flaming.

“And you’re not very bouncy, are you? I like breasts and a nice big bottom. You’re kind of...” he hunted for a word, “...average.” He shrugged. “Also hairy. I mean, you can see where you’d have hairy arms under your sleeves, like a man.”

I was mortified. “Hairy arms.” I supposed they were. I didn’t think about them much. But I supposed I might be hairy. Certainly I had hair in all the usual places in dark profusion. I didn’t bleach my arms or legs with lemon juice.

“And with that business with the assassins,” Orsino said. “Who wants a woman who hits men over the head with candlesticks? You killed that man.”

“In self-defense,” I said hotly.

"A woman is supposed to need to be saved," Orsino said, "not run around killing assassins! It's like being married to a tall, hairy condottiero."

"Well," I said. "Thank you for your frankness." I took a step back, colliding with the table. It reminded me that Cardinal Borgia hadn't seemed to mind my hairy arms when he'd seen them in the Proserpina costume. But maybe he just hadn't said anything about it.

Orsino shrugged. "You asked. But we're stuck with each other whether we like it or not."

"Yes," I said. "I suppose we are."

"Besides," Orsino said more cheerfully, "as long as we don't do it, it can be annulled when something better comes along."

"Is that what Bracciano says or your mother?" I asked. His jaw dropped but he didn't say anything. *Both of them*, I thought. *As soon as the little country bride's dowry is used up and she's no longer useful to Bracciano, easy enough to annul the marriage and send her packing.* "Do you even see me as a person?" I asked him.

Orsino looked confused. "I don't know what you mean by that."

"You probably don't," I said, and exited with at least some of my dignity intact.

The next day I professed a desire to confess. Adriana looked at me suspiciously but could think of no reason to forbid it. Would I say things that made the family look bad? She would not know if I said it under seal of the confessional, but Father Andrea, our parish priest, would know. He would know, and he would judge her.

And yet, when I sat in the tiny booth with Father Andrea on the other side of the screen, I hardly knew what to say. He had to prompt me. "What weighs upon your mind, my child?"

Then it was easier, there in the private semi-dark. "Father, I am unhappy in my marriage. I have been married for a year and my husband will not touch me or consummate the marriage. He goes to brothels, so I do not think he is incapable, but he will not touch me." There was a long silence. "Father?"

"That is...unusual," he said. "Why will he not do so?"

"His kin want the marriage unconsummated so that it can be annulled if a better match is possible," I said. "Father, I am very unhappy with this. I often wish myself free of Orsino! I do not want to be married to a man who will have no true marriage!"

He cleared his throat. "If it is true that he will not consummate the marriage because he does not intend for it to last, the sin is on his doorstep, not yours. He vowed to be your husband, did he not?"

"He did," I said.

"And if he took that vow falsely, in the eyes of God and man, you have no sin in wishing that either he would make it a true marriage or end it." His voice was kind.

"I wished at first he would make it a true marriage," I said. "But now if it is a sham, I simply wish it done. And I desire another." I felt my cheeks heat.

"Do you desire another who wishes to marry you?" Father Andrea asked quietly.

"No. It is not possible," I said. "And I yearn for him. I wish for him night and day, though I know it is wrong."

I heard him sigh. "It is natural for a young woman to wish for normal congress with her husband. Since your husband denies you, you think of another. I pray that your husband will do as he should—or, if not, release you so that you may marry fairly. You will say twenty pater nosters for your lustful thoughts of another. *Ego te absolvo.*"

And that was it. He did not ask who. He did not seem overly concerned in any way. One would think that young women came to him daily lusting after men who were not their husbands! If it gave him a bad opinion of Orsino, he deserved it. I was not about to aid their deception any longer. Let it be known that the Orsini married me under false pretense! I would not protect the reputation of those who thought they whored me out. A thought slipped in. *Perhaps someday they would find me a bad enemy to have.*

Lucrezia had heard from her father that he was to celebrate the Pentecost Mass that Sunday at the Church of St. Mary and the Martyrs and begged to go there instead of our parish church. Adriana raised an eyebrow when I volunteered to accompany Lucrezia. "Do you really wish everyone to see you in her company?" she asked.

"Do you really wish no one to see me? Sometimes I wonder. But then it would be easier to annul a marriage no one knows about, wouldn't it be?" Adriana drew a quick breath. "That is the plan, isn't it?" I said quietly. "When my dowry is gone and Bracciano is done with me, the marriage will be annulled and I'll be packed off home. If I have no friends and no one has seen me, it will be much less awkward to explain that Orsino was married to me for more than a year without consummating the marriage." I didn't give her time to reply, and my voice was perfectly even. "I have no intention in cooperating with that. I am certainly not going to protect Orsino's reputation while he destroys mine. I am not a prisoner and I intend to go about town as freely as a decent woman can. Even the strictest person could find no wrong in attending Mass with a child! I am going."

"Of course," Adriana said. She looked a little pale. "I am certain you and Lucrezia will find Mass at St. Mary and the Martyrs impressive."

I had not quite realized that the Church of St. Mary and the Martyrs was the ancient Pantheon. I had read about it, and Cardinal Borgia had mentioned it at the masquerade. We were in the street outside, joining the throng of brightly dressed, cheerful people when I saw the shape of the Roman columns, the inscription above the door, and its bronze dome rising behind unmistakably. It gave me a chill. Like the tombs near Montalto, like the statue Cardinal Borgia had showed me, age sat upon it gracefully, adding to its presence.

Of course in Rome many things are old, but often they are either ruins or so changed by their use that their original form and purpose is lost. This was not. It had been a place of worship for nearly fifteen hundred years, give or take a fire or two and rebuilding. As we walked under the high portico, I caught my breath. The sense of the numinous was so real.

There was the sound of music, the choir beginning, and everyone around us pushed forward to take their places. Lucrezia grabbed my hand, dragging me along. Inside, it was like no church I had ever seen. There were the red vestments, altar cloths and banners for Pentecost, bright candles everywhere, but the brightest light streamed downward from an oculus in the ceiling, a round circle in the bronze dome showing the sky. The light made a pool just in front of the altar. Gilded candlesticks shone unbearably bright. We took our places among the people, and even Lucrezia was still.

The procession began, the censer thuribles swinging, great clouds of incense billowing over us. There was the crucifer, and behind him Cardinal Borgia, his face solemn and his red robes flowing, the cassock topped with a white rochet with lace that fell to his knees, and over that a long cope, the full red cape that fastened across the breast, thick with gold embroidery. His face was not stern. Rather, his step was light though his clothes were heavy. He looked ahead with an expression of anticipation. *He enjoys this,* I thought. *This is not a duty. This is a pleasure to him.*

Before I could consider this entirely, Mass began. I tried to keep my thoughts pure, and after a bit it was easier to. His voice carried well. It was easy to hear him as priest and think of nothing else. Sometimes the Mass seems rote, as though there is no force behind it. I cannot say why, but one can feel it, and the congregation stirs and looks about and wonders at the time passing. When the force is there, people are rapt. I was rapt. It was as though I had never heard these words before, though of course I had many times. They seemed fresh and new, inspired just today by the Holy Spirit. When he elevated the Host, I felt my heart lift.

Then there was silence. He simply stood there, a column of smoke from the thurible ascending toward the oculus. With one clear treble, the musical sequence began, one pure voice rising into the air. "*Veni Sancte Spiritus.*" *Come, Holy Spirit*, I thought, listening to the words unfold. A second choir boy joined, two voices melding. *Come, father of the poor. Come, giver of gifts. Come, light of the heart….*

The cardinal bent, taking something from an acolyte who had come forward. I craned my neck to see. He held a white dove carefully in his hands, whispering to it to still it.

In labor, rest. In heat, temperance. In tears, solace. I had Latin enough to simply understand. Now more voices came in, the full choir, the music swelling. *Cleanse that which is dirty. Water that which is arid. Heal that which is ill.*

He lifted the white dove, holding it carefully aloft, and then released it. There was a vast sigh as its wings beat, dipping low over the crowd and then more strongly, circling upward toward the oculus, disappearing into the clear sky.

…and grant us eternal joy! The choir's last bright notes hung in the air. We were still looking upward. Rose petals fell from the oculus, great showers of them, red and pink and yellow and

white, turning as the dove had on the wind, raining down upon us. Cardinal Borgia was looking up, too, raising one hand to catch a petal, his mouth opened in a broad smile, a petal sticking on his hat.

So bright. So beautiful. Surely I could find no harm in this. Surely I could seek nothing dark or wrong! I felt pure, transported, clean of all confusion and anger.

"You see, Giulia?" Lucrezia said, tugging on my arm. "My father is a very good priest."

"He is indeed," I said. How could I feel this peace, want this love, and his at the same time?

Chapter Eleven

I did not expect to see Cardinal Borgia soon, but he turned up on Monday morning. I heard his voice in the garden and ran down quickly, only taking the time to smooth my hair by feel. It was still early and the garden cool. Lucrezia was alternating between sitting on the arm of his chair and running about waving fresh bread in her hand. Adriana stood by while Beneo put a tray of bread and butter on the little garden table. Adriana looked flustered. "Rodrigo, I had no expectation you would visit this morning."

"Simply stopping by. I hope it is not inconvenient." He gestured to his full red robes. "I am on my way to the Vatican and thought I would see Lucrezia." His eyes went past Adriana to me. I couldn't help what I feared was a silly smile.

"It is never inconvenient to see you, Papa," Lucrezia said, coming back for more butter like a a honeybee to a flower.

"I know you have a great deal to do, Adriana," he said. "I don't mean to interrupt. I will visit with Lucrezia and you do not need to entertain me. After all, we're family."

"Well, if you do not mind." Adriana looked relieved. She no doubt had plans. She glanced over and saw me approaching. "Perhaps Giulia will join you."

"Of course," I said demurely, simply a young relation appropriately deputized to entertain a distinguished guest who was in fact family. In truth, I had no idea what to say.

"If it does not inconvenience you, Donna Giulia."

I sat down in the other chair. "Not at all," I said.

Lucrezia picked up a pair of apricots from the bowl of fruit on the tray. "Papa, how do you learn to juggle?"

"Why do you need to learn to juggle?" he asked.

She shrugged. "You never know when it might come in handy."

"I suppose." He looked bemused. "I have come tell you that your mother would like you to come to the country with her earlier this year, before the Feast of St. John the Baptist on the 24th."

Lucrezia put her head to the side. "Why?"

"Because she is going earlier and loves your company," the cardinal said. He glanced at Adriana. "And it is safer from the river fevers." *Or a pack of assassins*, I thought. He wanted Lucrezia well away from whatever happened. "You might even stay with her for a few days before you go."

She shrugged. "When are we going?"

"I'm not certain of the day yet. Soon."

Adriana shifted from foot to foot. "Is this meant to be a permanent arrangement?" Obviously the loss of Lucrezia would be an enormous blow to her household economy.

"No, no," he said airily. "Just a summer jaunt. And I will be happy to continue my guards here and their upkeep." An outrageous expense, and I knew who it was for.

"Is Juan going?" Lucrezia asked.

"Yes, and he has sworn to behave," he said. "So you will all three be together, Juan, you and Gioffre."

"I'm going to go pack! I'll be back soon, Papa!" Lucrezia streaked away, followed by Adriana remonstrating that her maid should pack because of care with her clothes and she was a lady and....

Which left me sitting across the breakfast table from him in the middle of the garden, visible from every window and door. Cardinal Borgia reached for one of the roses in the small vase at the center of the table. "Rosa mundi," he said, turning the pink and white striped rose in his hands. "It's a shame to cut them. They last much longer on the bush."

The metaphor was obvious. "But then I would not see them and they would not delight me," I said. He glanced up, a little smile playing around the corner of his mouth. "They are not statues to be kept pristine forever but living things to endure wind and rain. If tonight's storms rip the petals from it, would you say it was better for it to stay on the vine than to come into my room where it will bloom for days? It might not say so, but then roses cannot speak."

"As you do so eloquently," the cardinal said.

I almost said more, but I did not. He was not a young woman and could idealize roses if he wished. He did not know that innocence is powerlessness. The only way one can remain pure is to remain inviolate, disengaged from trial and striving, doing nothing. "I am glad you think so, Your Eminence."

And Lucrezia was back. "Donna Adriana says there is no need to pack when we do not know the date and Maria will do it." She picked up an apricot in each hand for another juggling attempt. "Papa, why does St. Augustine hate everything?"

The abrupt change of subject had caught her father off guard. "What?"

"Father Antonio was telling me about St. Augustine and it just sounds like he hates anything nice or fun. Why does he?" She threw one apricot into the air and caught it with a hand full of another apricot. It was not like throwing oranges. Sooner or later they would squish.

He settled back in his chair. "Well, my heart, St. Augustine lived in a very unsettled time. The fourth and fifth centuries of Our Lord were full of enormous upheavals. Rome herself was taken in Augustine's time by the Visigoths. The city was pillaged and thousands of people killed or made slaves. Even St. Peter's was not spared but stripped of every valuable."

Lucrezia was listening with intense interest, as a child will to horrors they do not understand. "What happened?"

"When I was not too much older than you, I copied the words of a monk named Pelagius who described it." His voice shifted to the old-fashioned tone of recitation. "In every house there was a scene of misery and equally of grief and confusion. Slave and gentleman were in the same circumstances and felt the terror of death the same." He picked up an apricot from the table and the little knife to cut it with. "When an entire city, a whole people, pass through times like those it changes them. It makes them view the world as a dark room we are passing through with torment waiting on the other side for all save a few, for is it not their experience of the world?"

I put my hands together, fascinated. "So you are saying that faith is shaped by experience?"

He smiled. "Saints are but men and women and creatures of their time and place, as are we all. Many have been called to Christ in nearly a millennium and a half, but each has that experience tempered by the circumstances of their life. Imagine our Rome in such distress! Imagine the sack of a city of eight hundred thousand, a sack of such brutality that only half remained when the barbarian armies retreated with their spoils and slaves. It darkened our faith as surely as ash and smoke blackened our walls." He looked at Lucrezia. "If such a thing happened to you, what would you be afraid of?"

"That it would happen again," Lucrezia said promptly.

Her father nodded. "That you would endure such suffering again, now or in the life to come. And when people fear, what do they do?" He looked at me.

"We fight," I said.

The Cardinal agreed, "Yes. You find someone to blame for your misfortunes, and if you cannot take on an army of Visigoths, you find someone nearer by to blame. A neighbor who has transgressed, a stranger who is different…."

"Like the Jews," Lucrezia said. "Everybody always blames the Jews."

"Yes." He crossed his legs beneath his flowing robes. "And those who have not the mettle of courageous young ladies, what do they do?"

I knew that well enough. "They hate themselves. They destroy themselves in sorrow and despair. People usually react to bad things by hurting others or by hurting themselves."

His eyes were gentle. "Many people think it is better if they starve themselves or flagellate themselves or deprive themselves of sleep or food or sunshine or friendship—all the things that make people happy. After all, it does no other person harm. But it harms them, and they too are beloved children of Christ."

I had never heard such a thought in my life. "You are saying that fasting is wrong?"

"Not in moderation." He cut a sliver of apricot. "We eat no meat in Lent so that our bodies learn that they obey our spirits, and so that we may show our devotion. But to fast so extremely that one harms oneself is another kind of sin, the destruction of God's unique creation. We are meant to be happy."

"Of course we are," Lucrezia said, settling on the arm of his chair. "God is our father and he loves us, just as you love me and want me to be happy."

"Which does not mean he lets you do everything you want," I said slowly. "Because letting you stuff yourself on treats or climb on the roof would not be good for you."

"But within reason," Cardinal Borgia said.

This was a side of him I did not know. "How do you understand people's hearts so well?"

There was a sideways smile on his face. "I have been a priest for more than thirty years. I have heard a great many confessions and given counsel."

Lucrezia tossed the apricot again. It squashed in her hand. "Oops." Her hand was covered in ripe fruit.

"Do not wipe that on your dress," I said. "Go into the kitchen and wash your hands properly. It will not come out if you stain that cloth."

"Yes, Giulia." She ran off.

"You truly believe," I said. "It's not a pose or a pretense. When I saw you on Sunday, it was real."

"Is that so odd?" He gestured at his crimson skirts.

"Isn't it?" I asked. "It does not seem to me that there are so many sincere cardinals. And you…." How to say that he broke all the rules, or at least so many of them?

"I am a flawed man, venal, ambitious, and carnal. But I am better than I might be." He took a bite of the apricot. "I have tried celibacy, and like meat in Lent I can do without if I must, but not for a lifetime. Not without misery." He turned the apricot in his hand. "I am not Christlike. But I can choose to deal fairly with my lovers. I don't rape chambermaids or prey on choirboys. I can be better than the worst."

"And that is virtue in this Rome?"

"That is virtue in this world," he said gently. He looked toward the kitchen door where Lucrezia had disappeared. "I sire illegitimate children. And I see them raised with love and advantage. I am ambitious. But I do not consort with demons to kill my enemies. I intend to be elected Pope when the time comes with sharp deal-making and bribery, not murder."

"Sometimes it must come to murder," I said. "Bracciano…."

"Bracciano began it. And he is not about to beg forgiveness." He took another bite of the apricot. "But for now we must hobble him so that he cannot use this method any longer."

There was something that had been in my mind since the Mass and it worked its way to the surface now. "Dr. Treschi's methods call upon spirits," I said slowly. "They ask them to be present or even to enter into people. How is that different from what you did on Pentecost when you asked the Holy Spirit to come? *Veni Sancte Spiritus*. Is that not also an invocation?"

His eyebrows rose. "It is indeed an invocation."

"So what is the difference, other than intent, between calling upon saints or angels or the Holy Spirit, and demons?" I asked. "Your intent was to bring joy and comfort, and theirs is to bring pain. But is not the difference the intention, not the form?" I leaned forward. "And when a player begins a play with a speech to invoke the muses, is that not the same again? Is this not all part of the same cloth? That these are all our human reachings for that which is beyond sight?"

He looked utterly stunned, and then he smiled, a long, slow smile. "I believe so. *Prisca theologia*—the golden thread that runs through all humanity, seeking true understanding of the divine. When someone asks me for a blessing, that is what they ask—that I open a door between them and this light. But it is intent. That is the difference. If someone asks for a blessing on their baby or their horse or their boat, there is no harm to anyone in it. These demons they call, these intentions to kill—there is real and genuine harm. The form may be similar, but the intention is all."

"And if we speak of the player, whose intention is simply to entertain? Or of ancient spirits that existed before Christ?" I asked.

"Perhaps that is neutral," he began.

The rest of the thought was lost as Lucrezia came running back. "I have washed my hands," she said. "I am clean now. See?"

"I see that you are," I said, and we spoke of it no more before he had to go.

The next week was very quiet. I joined Lucrezia at her lessons, though my Latin was much more advanced than hers. I was doing

Aeneas in the underworld, something that seemed a little too appropriate. Cardinal Borgia came to see her once. Apparently he was very busy, and he did not stay for dinner. Consequently, I had no opportunity to speak with him except in front of Lucrezia. We talked about giraffes and hippopotamuses and other strange animals, as she had heard from a friend at her music lesson that some traveling company had a giraffe. This seemed to be the most interesting thing that had ever happened.

I sat in my chair with embroidery in my lap and wished I could talk to Cardinal Borgia alone. He wore a good coat in a summer weight dark red wool and did not look like a cardinal. It made him look younger, I thought. Also trimmer. He had a bit around the waist, and the coat complimented him rather than adding layers. Not that I minded. I would rather spend an hour in his presence, in witty discourse and discussion of interesting things, than watching Orsino clumsily swing a sword around. Besides, I had seen how fast he could move. One had to practically run to keep up.

Of course no one kept up with Lucrezia. Watching him dote upon her, I thought how unusual it was for a father to spend so much time with a daughter. He raised her as carefully as a son, giving her his attention and tutelage. My father had as well. Like Lucrezia, I had been the only girl in a pack of boys, my father's delight.

Heir of a good name but nothing else, he had been a condottiero, a mercenary soldier, in his youth. He'd not made his fortune at arms, though he'd been in one petty war after another for nearly twenty years. My father had never expected to inherit Montalto, but his half-brother had died unexpectedly without an heir. Montalto had allowed him to retire and marry. My mother was more than twenty years his junior, eighteen when he was thirty-nine, but I still remembered how his eyes had lit when he looked at her, how secret smiles had passed between them over our heads, flirtatious and warm though they had five children. He'd certainly loved us, his children. He had loved me no less than my brothers.

It left a lasting mark. I did not believe myself inferior to Alessandro in any way, except perhaps that he was taller than I. Nor did Alessandro think himself my superior. If I did not have Lucrezia's education so young, it said more about my family's wealth than my value. Certainly I intended to soak up every moment of opportunity to learn while I could.

I was in a cheerful frame of mind when the cardinal left and I went up to my room to wash my hands for dinner. I poured water over them and looked up.

The demon looked back from the mirror.

I nearly screamed. Instead I caught my breath sharply. "What do you want?" I asked.

Its face frayed sideways, laughing. "The question is, what do you want?"

"I want nothing that you can give me," I said.

"Untrue," it said. The surface of the mirror changed. I saw the sala downstairs, candlestands lit at the corners of a body laid out for the funeral. It was Orsino, his fair hair combed, wearing his best doublet. Adriana wept on the shoulder of a friend while others crowded about. "He slipped and hit his head on the steps," the demon said. "Or he might. It would be a terrible pity for you to be left a young widow, the owner of this house." It smiled. "You might do as you like then. You could take a lover. Why not? If your only guardian is your brother, away in Pisa, and all this was yours?" Orsino's face was still, a little slack-jawed. He looked like he did when he didn't understand something at all. Now Cardinal Borgia came to comfort me, his arm around my back over-familiarly. "A young widow," the demon said. "All alone in the world, but with wealth and beauty."

I looked away. "No. Not at the cost of Orsino's life."

"And what use is he to you?" the demon asked. "He won't bed you, much less make a good father for your children."

"I will not deal with demons," I said, though a chill ran down my back.

"You already do," it said. "You have already lost your immortal soul by such congress."

"I have been absolved of it," I said.

It laughed, a raucous and terrifying sound. "By whom? A priest who is no true believer? A cardinal who breaks his vows daily? I tell you that hellfire waits for Rodrigo Borgia. It waits for you as well, lusting after a priest."

The scene changed. I stood on Adriana's balcony looking out over the city at night, wearing only a fine camisa embroidered with gold. Cardinal Borgia came up behind me, his arm going around my waist and I leaned back into him as he buried his face in the long fall of my hair. I turned in his arms, meeting him in a kiss.

"You could have this," the demon said. "I only show you what may be."

My hand shook and I stilled it. "I have not summoned you or given you cause to speak to me. I will make no bargains with you."

"I don't need you to summon me, Dove," it said. "Any glass will do. Any still water. You know it's true. I can find you anywhere. You will never be free of me. Your dowry is spent and Adriana has nothing except what she gets from Borgia and Bracciano. Do you think Bracciano doesn't pay her well for your services?" The demon sneered. "Whatever she thinks they are. Your husband is content to sell you to his cousin. And I will speak to you whenever I want."

"Not if I don't see you," I said, and turned the mirror to the wall. Then I went out into my sala and shivered.

This was too much. If it could reach me, if it could kill Orsino or anyone else.... Surely a demon knew all about Hell? What if it was right? What if I was already so sunk in sin as to be beyond forgiveness? It was true I lusted after a priest. It was true I wished myself free of my marriage vows. It was certainly true that Cardinal

Borgia was not chaste and was more venal and epicurean than a priest should be. It was true that the image of what we might do caused me to feel thrill and shame at once. What if I was already lost?

I stood in the sala pressing my hands against the wall. *No*, I thought. *One can never believe a demon. They lie. Even when they tell the truth, they twist it to their own ends. It wants me to make a bargain or else destroy myself in despair. Which meant it fears me. My father had said thus of an enemy in arms. When they are assured of their superiority, they will not treat with you. If they treat, it is because they fear that you may win.*

But I could not have it leering at me from every mirror or pool. I could not live with its threats. I did not want it at all. I straightened up. Rightly or wrongly, I only knew of one way to be rid of it forever. It would not think that I dared or it would not have attempted to push me away from it. I must no longer be a Dove.

The next afternoon I slipped out to find Dr. Treschi. It was a little more than a week to the next dark moon, when I expected Bracciano would send for me. Dr. Treschi was with a client when I arrived, a woman older than myself who wanted to know if she would ever have a daughter as she had three sons. I sat down on the steps outside and waited while he did her consultation.

It was a warm day, and through the alley I could see the street and the plaza beyond. Truly the life of the city was beautiful beyond belief. And how wonderful to slip away like this, as I had in Montalto, and simply go about as I wished! Of course a wealthy woman didn't do that in Rome, not without attendants, but I looked like a servant in a good house, perhaps the personal maid of a great lady. As such, I was unremarkable.

Rome, I thought, the city of the Caesars. How many others had sat where I did—or not precisely where I did, since these wooden steps were only decades old? How many others moved like ghosts around us, the past separated only by a thin veil? That beautiful statue of Cardinal Borgia's had come from somewhere near here. What had the city looked like then?

With my eyes half-closed, dozing in the sun, I could see it shift, the street for a moment fading into another version of itself, the plaza now with a fountain in the midst, a woman in a litter borne by slaves passing, while beyond a columned portico had shops beneath.

I started up. Of course it was just fancy. I was in my Rome, not the Rome of long ago. And yet for a moment the other had seemed real. Was this, I thought, part of being a Dove? To see things with the eyes of the heart? Was it as simple as reaching for it, no chalked symbols or incantations necessary?

"Donna Giulia, I am ready for you," Dr. Treschi said.

The woman was coming out with him, a broad smile on her face. "Thank you, Maestro," she said, and we passed one another on the steps.

I went in and sat down at his table. "I need to understand what we are doing," I said. "And I will pay for you to explain to me how this works. Is the mirror special or would any mirror do? What rules does this demon follow?" I laid three silver coins on the table.

He looked at them. "It's complicated."

"Then begin," I said.

"A woman may not study magics."

"She perfectly well may," I said. "If she is paying for it. So get on with it, Dionisio. I'm not asking you to do it. I'm asking you to explain it. You said that this followed the teachings of an ancient sage, Hermes Trismegistus."

"As translated by Maestro Ficino, yes," he said. "My own master, Pico della Mirandola, was Ficino's prize student. He has put into service those concepts Ficino theorized."

I had guessed as much. "What practical applications are you attempting?"

He took a deep breath. "Very well. You understand that there are five planets in addition to our own and the moon, yes?"

"Yes," I said. "Mercury, Venus, Mars, Jupiter and Saturn."

"Each of those planets rules different spheres of life and aspects of public and private events," he said. "For example, Mars rules war but also conflicts between persons." I nodded and he continued. "Jupiter rules commerce, but also how men rise to positions of distinction. Venus rules love and fortune. When we speak of a Square of Venus or Jupiter, it is a sigil that invokes the planetary energies to do something in particular. In this case, the squares are to protect us from the demon that we summon."

"So that the demon may not harm you because it cannot leave these circles and squares," I said. "In short, you lock it in a box with me. I can't say that I like that much."

"The Dove's innocence protects her," he protested.

"And the mirror?" I asked.

"Is simply to facilitate communication," he said. "Any mirror would do. We use an ancient mirror because it is more… atmospheric."

A beautiful thing, but not truly necessary. I had guessed as much from my conversation with the demon in my mirror. "And if the Dove is not innocent?"

"If she is not virgin, it cannot speak with her," Dr. Treschi said. "But the more worldly she is, the less she is protected."

Wonderful, I thought. So the more I knew, the more jeopardy I was in. Yet knowing less made me helpless. However, I had been correct that if I were deflowered, I would be safe from it. "What other rules does this demon follow?"

"It cannot leave the square and circle if they are properly done," he said. "It cannot take things that are not bargained or offered. It cannot harm someone without payment."

"Without payment," I said. "As though a demon were a street assassin?"

Dr. Treschi shrugged. "It cannot act in the material world except under certain conditions, and that includes payment that provides the energy to do it."

I nodded slowly. I had brought bread and a pomegranate for Proserpina and Pluto in the Etruscan tomb as my grandmother had instructed. "Like an ancient offering."

He looked startled. Men kept looking startled around me. "Yes. Incense is the minimum, which is why we cense the space so that it may manifest. Wine is usual. But most potent..."

"...is blood," I said. I could guess the logical end. After all, the old Romans had practiced animal sacrifice. And there were darker tales, stories whispered that children should not hear, of evil done with human blood.

He nodded miserably. "Yes."

"And you think that is where this will end?" I asked.

"My Lord Bracciano wants it to kill. Life for life is the usual bargain. He ordered one of his men to cut his hand and use his blood to enchant the tooth that we used in the sleep charm. And the tooth came from a hanged man, so I suppose that's death too. But if he wants something that will actually kill Cardinal Borgia, it's going to require more than blood from a man living or a tooth from a man already dead."

"And you are going to help him do this?" I demanded. "Dionisio, you cannot do this."

He met my eyes. "If I don't, he'll kill me. I am trapped with no way out. If I refuse him, his bravos will do me in before I can leave Rome. My hope is to somehow turn the rituals so they don't work but seem that they might."

"So that eventually he will decide you are a charlatan."

"Better a charlatan than a corpse."

That was inarguable. "What does Bracciano want? Ultimately.

What is the goal?"

"He doesn't confide in me." Dionisio looked away.

"You have an opinion," I said. "You have worked with him these many months. What is the point of this?"

He sighed. "He wants to make Cardinal Orsini the next Pope. Right now Pope Innocent is pulled this way and that by Cardinal della Rovere and Cardinal Borgia. If Cardinal Borgia were to die, Orsini might be vice-chancellor because he is essentially a neutral party. Then the Orsini would control both the pope's army and his foreign policy through the Chancellery. From there, it's a logical step for Orsini to be the next pope. Bracciano's kinsman will keep him as gonfaloniere. You know that office is appointed at the pope's pleasure, and while it would be politically difficult to discharge him without cause, he could be dismissed. Cardinal Orsini would keep him and he thinks he is the stronger man, so he would control the pope."

"I see," I said. "And barring that?"

"If Cardinal Orsini can't be elected, he would intrigue to elevate someone old and infirm who will readily be his puppet, through either senility or inaction." Dionisio shrugged. "It's all one to me."

"It is not," I said hotly. "The question of whether your master, della Mirandola, is arrested for heresy is not unimportant to you! The question of whether you are is not! Who the next pope is and what he believes is vitally important to every scholar."

"Well, yes." He looked sheepish. "Pico is nearly broken by the heresy charge. I honestly don't know if he'll live. He's stopped teaching. Everything's changed." He shook his head. "It's one reason I left Florence. I can't stand it now."

"Then change it," I said. I leaned forward. "The pope's word can dismiss the heresy charge. Of course it matters who's elected! That's what an election is. It's choosing the future."

"I thought God chose the pope."

"Sometimes God needs help," I said.

Chapter Twelve

Three nights later, the cardinal stayed for dinner. There were five of us to begin, but Orsino left as soon as was polite, and Lucrezia retired soon after. Only Adriana and Cardinal Borgia remained. I said good night prettily, but instead of going to my room I slipped down the stairs to wait at the bottom before the street door. Cardinal Borgia came down the stairs soon after. He had been on his way home from the Vatican, and his red skirts flared at the quickness of his step. His guards were waiting just outside the door in the portico.

I stepped out of the shadow. "Your Eminence? Might I have a word?"

"Of course." I drew him a few paces along, into the darkened saletta. "Is this more of the business with Bracciano?" he asked quietly.

"In a manner of speaking," I said. My heart was suddenly beating very fast.

"What is it?" he asked. He was not a foot from me, worry on his face.

"The demon," I said quietly. "It appeared to me in the mirror in my room. It says that it can speak to me from any mirror and reflective surface." I looked down at his hands, the ring on them black in the dim light. "It made an offer. It showed me Orsino laid out for a funeral in this house. It asked me how I would like to be a young widow, with money and the house and a lover of my choosing." I did not dare look at his face.

"Giulia."

"I said no! I would not have it at the cost of Orsino's life, no matter how much I might want it." I felt tears choking my throat. "I can't do this! I can't have it pursuing me, looking out at me all the time, following me everywhere!"

"You did not promise this creature anything?" His voice was calm, patient.

"No." I dared a look at him then. We stood so close together, his expression concerned. "I promised nothing. It tried to bribe me. It showed me...." I halted, then went on, my eyes on his face. "It showed me with my lover. Here. In this house. Happy. But I told it that I would not make a bargain and I took down the mirror and turned it to the wall in another room."

"That was well done."

I had to charge forward. If I did not, I would lose courage and not say it at all. "I know of one way to place myself out of its reach. If I were no longer a virgin. If you..." I stopped. He looked as though he tried not to smile. It hurt. I remembered everything Orsino had said. "Am I not pretty enough?" I said sadly. "Not pretty enough to want, not even once?"

His face changed, the smile rueful. "Giulia, I am laughing at myself, not at you. You are incomparably beautiful and I was trying to be good, but now you offer me your virginity and the justification that I take what I want to save you, not out of selfishness! How can I not laugh at myself?"

"You want me?" That he said so was like balm. Had I heard correctly?

He took my hand, turning it over, palm up resting in his. "Very badly. You would tempt a saint, and I am no saint."

"My husband does not desire me at all," I said.

"Orsino is a fool. But think." He still held my hand in his. "If

I simply deflower you now, Bracciano will know when the next session doesn't work. He will be angry."

"Yes, but…."

"A moment. Let me finish." I nodded, and he went on. "At best, and he certainly may do worse, he will have Orsino repudiate you in the most insulting terms. You will be sent back to the country in disgrace, a whore whose marriage was annulled by an outraged husband. You will never marry. You will spend your days as a maiden aunt, the embarrassment of your kin."

"Better that than a demon's pawn," I said. I looked down at his hand and mine, his great ruby ring glinting in the dim light. He waited, and I went on. "When I came to Rome," I said, "I hoped for learning and beauty and art and love. I wanted plays and politics and interesting people and to know the world and everything in it. I can't have that. I can either be Bracciano's Dove until he is done and then be packed off, or I can choose to thwart his plans and be packed off. I would rather have the latter. At least it is on my terms, even if no one in Rome will remember I was ever here."

"I would remember," Cardinal Borgia said. His expression was inscrutable. "But I think there are alternatives to a life as a maiden aunt tending sheep." His eyes were very dark. "And Rome needs you. You are too fair and bright to deprive her of you. Dazzling brightness." He drew breath, taking a step back. "Let me think on this a few days. There are ways to solve your dilemma without destroying your prospects. Can you be patient for a few days and trust me?"

I nodded. "Will you have me?" I could not quite manage "deflower me." I would not beg.

"Think, Giulia. Not now. Not here. Even if we were to do this, Adriana or Lucrezia might come downstairs at any moment. Or Orsino. To have you over the table now is not the answer."

"I see that," I said, though my pulse leaped at the idea. Over the table in the saletta with my husband and mother-in-law upstairs….

He took a step back, then raised my hand to his lips. "I should go." His mouth brushed my fingers and I shivered.

"I will do as you say," I said. "I will wait."

There was a step on the stair. "Rodrigo? Are you still here?" It was Adriana's voice.

"Just leaving," he replied loudly, hastening to the door of the saletta. "Nature called."

"Ah." I could just see the hem of Adriana's skirts through the balustrade. "Good night then."

"Good night, Adriana," he said, and went to the outer door. He looked back at me in the darkened saletta. "Good night."

I waited until all footsteps had gone before I sought my room, my body still ringing with his touch.

The next day I was on tenterhooks, but nothing whatsoever happened. I did lessons with Lucrezia, who was bored and restless and tormented her tutor with unanswerable questions while I tried to read Pliny. I had borrowed a volume of the cardinal's copy of the *Natural History* and was endeavoring to learn about mineralogy. I found it very interesting indeed, as I had never learned of the properties of metals and their uses, but it required rather closer attention than I could give it with Lucrezia constantly jumping around.

Saturday, the twelfth of June, was the first really hot day of the summer. The garden was too hot to sit in by midafternoon. At least indoors there was shade even if there was no breeze and not a leaf stirred. Donna Adriana had taken Lucrezia to visit her mother and would not be back until after the night meal, as I expected they would be asked to stay for dinner. I was reading in my room, wishing that the clouds on the horizon might bring a thunderstorm to cool us off, when Maria knocked on the door. "I beg your pardon, Donna Giulia. The cardinal is here and Donna Adriana and little Lucrezia are not. He expected to see them. I told him perhaps there was some mistake, but he insists he has the day correct. Will you come down and speak with him?"

"Of course," I said, getting to my feet. I think my face was serene. My heart was anything but. He knew perfectly well Lucrezia and Adriana would be gone, and probably Orsino as well, if he thought of him at all. I followed Maria downstairs like a woman who wishes to spare a devoted servant the task of saying no to a distinguished visitor who is confused.

He was waiting in the garden wearing his full red robes, even the short cape that came down to his waist front and back and red gloves that covered his wrists up to his tightly buttoned sleeves. I smoothed my hair back into its snood before I went out. I was not dressed for guests, and certainly not for any I wished to impress, but his eyes lit when he saw me. "Cardinal Borgia," I said loudly for the benefit of Maria, "I am so sorry you have arrived at a time when the household is out. I beg your pardon if there was some confusion on our parts. I understood that Donna Adriana was taking Lucrezia to her mother's home for a visit today."

"Was it so?" He took off his cap, rubbing the sweat from his brow. "I am the one who is confused. Such a hot day, and I have hurried to see my little girl." Maria was hovering near.

"You must be perishing," I said. "Will you not come inside where it is cool and take some wine? We cannot leave our guest sweltering!" I looked around. "Maria, please bring wine and water to my sala. I will entertain the cardinal." After all, what else could one do in courtesy and propriety? I had never entertained anyone in my sala before, but then it would seem officious to take over Adriana's without her leave. I was simply a young woman attempting to step up to her responsibilities. "If Orsino is about, will you ask him to join us?"

Maria twisted her apron. "He has gone out," she said. "And I don't expect him back until late." To a brothel or something else she disapproved of, I almost heard her say.

I sighed. "Then we shall be two. The wine, if you please." I shook my head a little at her as if to say, *That is my irresponsible husband! Leaving me to entertain his mother's distinguished guest alone!*

"Of course, Donna Giulia," she said, and left us.

I led him upstairs to my sala, little used as it was. There was a table and two chairs, the door to my camera open behind it, light-filled from the window on the garden. My heart raced as he followed me saying some pleasantry or other about how he did not mean to trouble us.

"It is no trouble at all, Your Eminence," I said, and marveled at how cool my voice was. The sala was quite dark. "It is so warm. If you'd wish to take off your morzetta?" That was the short, buttoned cape he wore, and far too many layers in the heat.

"If you do not mind such informality," he said. He was smiling. We gave each other lines like players, a comedy enacted for the servants.

"Not at all," I said. "And your hat?" I took his hat and put it on the side table. "It is very hot."

"Terribly hot," he said.

"And your gloves, Your Eminence?"

He laid his buttoned gloves with hat and cape. He dropped his voice. "Are you planning to undress me completely?"

I choked trying not to laugh and succeeded only in a coughing fit. He pounded me on the back. "I beg pardon, Your Eminence," I said between gasps as Maria brought a tray in with wine and water both in carafes for mixing and a pair of glasses.

"Allow me to pour for you," he said, lifting the pitcher and pouring chilled wine and water into a glass. "You are in distress."

"Do not disturb yourself, I pray," I said between gasps. I sat down in one of the chairs. "I am well, Maria." No doubt she assumed me nervous at entertaining an important guest by myself, as I never had before.

"Yes, Donna Giulia." She departed. After a moment, the cardinal crossed the room and closed the door.

"Let us go into my camera," I said in a whisper. "Maria may wait on the stair in case I want something." Picking up my glass, I led him into my room. He followed after, an expression of amusement on his face. There was, after all, nowhere to sit except on the bed.

I sat down on the near side. He went around and sat on the other side at the foot near the window. I took a deep breath. "Have you thought about...." I wasn't sure how to even phrase the rest of the question.

"I have." His voice was businesslike. "There are two options which I wish to put to you. First, since your marriage to Orsino has not been consummated and you are a virgin, it would be easy to procure an annulment on grounds of non-consummation. Orsino is a man, not a child, and he has had more than a year to do it. If he will not or cannot, you may be released with all honor." I started to speak and he held up his hand. "A moment, Giulia. You need not fear you will be packed off to the country with no prospects. I will arrange for your dowry to be returned, and I will find you a better husband here in Rome, a man more to your taste who will appreciate you."

"I see," I said. It was a handsome offer, and yet I felt oddly disappointed. With his wide circle of friends among the wealthy of Rome, surely he could find a good husband for me if he tried. "And what sort of husband do you imagine for me?"

One shoulder twitched, half a shrug as though he hadn't considered the matter closely. "Older than Orsino. Well-educated. A man with experience of the world that will stimulate your mind. A man who wants an intellectual companion, not simply a beauty." He warmed to the topic. "Generous, intelligent, capable of patience with a young woman. Possibly a man with children who is seeking a kind stepmother. A man with enough money to guarantee your comfort."

"In short, a man like yourself," I said.

He stopped, glancing aside. "Well," he said, "the second option is that you could be my concubine." I thought for a moment my heart stopped entirely. I fear my expression was a sly smile. "Hear me out," he said, and I nodded. "You are as clever as a Vatican clerk, brave, eager, and utterly beautiful, which Vatican clerks are not. You are wasted on a boy who cannot appreciate what he has. I can offer you comfort, learning, and sensual fulfillment if you find my person pleasing." His eyes searched my face.

"I have found your person pleasing these many months," I said. "Since the masquerade." How could I say that he left me breathless? I did not want to sound either desperate or lukewarm. "You are very attractive."

"Ah." He smiled, and it seemed like the world lit on fire. "That does help, doesn't it? It's a fair offer. My complete support, clothes, books, tutors, whatever you need, to be my acknowledged mistress."

"And what about your vows? Are you not supposed to be chaste?" I asked.

"In theory." He shrugged cheerfully. "All the cardinals have mistresses, except those who have boys. Last year the Pope even issued a statement that canon law didn't prevent cardinals from having acknowledged concubines. But it is not respectable for you. If you cross the line, even with the fiction that you are still married to Orsino, you will cease to be a good woman in the eyes of the world." He sat back. "Which is why I want you to think about it. Don't make your decision today."

"But I want..."

"Not in passion," he said. "Coldly. Decide what is best for you. Annulment and a new marriage, or me. If you choose the annulment, I will arrange it and see that your dowry is returned to you and do all I have promised."

I nodded. He was right, of course. I would gladly let him have me now, right here in this bed with the afternoon sun streaming in the window, but it was better to think. I had not considered, had not hoped, for such an offer. The best I had imagined was that he might help me rid myself of demon and virginity alike. And yet there was one thing I must know. I raised my chin. "Do you think," I asked quietly, "that you might come to love me?"

The corner of his mouth twitched as though he laughed at himself. "Giulia, do you truly not know how rare and wonderful you are? Clever and kind both, using your wit to amuse rather than wound, desiring learning rather than gossip, daring and hungry, with an infatuation with Alexander the Great and the face of a Madonna? Do you think such women are common?"

"I wouldn't know," I said simply. "I have seen little of women in Rome."

He took my hand in his, glancing down at it with a rueful smile. "Even in Rome, where there are many women who love learning and the treasury that is the past, I have never met one like you. No, not in all the cities of Italy and Spain. Other women who are wonderful in different ways, yes, but I have never seen a creature like you." He looked up, dark eyes resting on my face. "One might well believe that lilies bloom where you tread."

A year ago I had hoped that my husband might come to love me in time. That Cardinal Borgia might, a man who I admired and desired, was more than I had allowed myself to imagine. He had always seen me. From the first time when I had met him at my own wedding, he had listened to me and conversed as though I were of worth, but I had not thought that this infatuation might be mutual. I had thought myself a foolish young woman madly in love with a man decades her senior who had his choice of beauties. Now it all twisted about.

I might refuse him. There were women who would, or who would take the jewels and clothes and whatever else was offered and then spurn him and laugh. I could hear them clearly—how the Spanish cardinal had begged, an old libertine making a fool of himself over a young beauty, as though her fresh charms were for him! I could well imagine the laughter and gossip. *His cousin's daughter-in-law! My dear, he has children older than she is! What could that silly man have been thinking? She took him for all he's worth, but can you blame her? He's rich as Croesus!* I saw all of that in his face.

And yet he asked. He gave me a choice. I had no doubt that if I said I wanted an annulment and a new marriage, he would do as he offered. Otherwise, how would he truly know if I chose him or simply wanted to be free of the demon and Orsino alike?

"We might suit very well," he said. "With me you will find wealth, pleasure, learning, and possibly power." He lifted my hand, his eyes meeting mine. "But assuredly you will never find safety or peace. Those were not the first assassins and they won't be the last. That is what it is to be a Borgia." He did not kiss my fingers, only held them. He looked at me directly. "I have told you I am ambitious. I will be pope."

"Yes, I expect you will be," I said. I believed it when he said it. And I also had an idea of how dangerous that might be, with so many other powerful contenders at least one of whom had supporters ready to kill. "Do you think that I want a quiet life? That I have not yearned for this—to try myself on the greatest field and see what I can do? Should I simply retire without having drawn sword, saying the game is too dangerous?"

"If you are my concubine, you will be a player in this game, not a witness to it. You do not yet know how bloody the game can be or how high the stakes."

"That is what I want," I said. "I care whether printers require the approval of the Church to print books or may do as they like! Or that universities can teach the ancient philosophers as well as Augustine and Aquinas. And yet do you think it matters to anyone what I, a young woman, want or think? If I am your concubine, what I think will matter. If I can help you be pope, I will. For the love of you, and for my own interest, but more so because I believe that you are right."

"I am astounded you put such faith in me."

"Should I not?" I asked.

His eyes were grave. "This is not a decision to make lightly. It is your life. If you are my concubine, that is what you will be forevermore. Everyone will know you, whether to cultivate you or revile you. Even if we do not suit, even if you decide differently in a year…"

"…or you do," I said.

"That's not terribly likely," he said. "I was with Vannozza for sixteen years and before that with Catalina for nearly nine. I am unchaste, but I am constant in my affections."

I took a deep breath. "And in the last few years?"

He settled with his back against the bedpost, letting go of my hand. "When Vannozza and I ended, I had every expensive courtesan and bored wife in Rome throwing herself at me. I've caught a notable number."

Admittedly, I found the idea intriguing. After all, if so many women found it desirable, surely it must be. Even in Montalto, women speculated on how various men might be in bed! A reputation did mean something. I put my head to the side. "So why not continue to do so?"

"Bored wives are all very well, but if there is not an understanding between her and her husband, it will bring her to ruin. I have no interest in being the downfall of someone's happiness for a few hours of pleasure. And the courtesans…." He shrugged, playing with the tassel on one of the pillows. "It's a purely financial arrangement. I am very rich. But it does not particularly suit me."

"Having been loved, you want a woman who adores you," I said.

He shrugged. "I want to be loved. As I deserve." His mouth

twisted into a smile on the last words. "I'm very lovable, actually."

"You are indeed," I said, with that now-familiar clenching of the chest. "I could love you." *Do love you*, I nearly said, but he had said to think about it coldly.

"I hope you might in time," he said. "But remember, it is easy to descend to the underworld...."

"...Pluto's doors stand open night and day," I quoted back, "but to return, to retrace your steps to the air above, that's the trick."

"And you wonder why I want you!" He looked delighted.

I scooted closer. "Then may I at least sample what you are offering? Even if I am to haggle as though it were a market, in the market at least I taste the figs before I buy them." I thought I could not bear it if only our hands touched.

"You want to taste my figs?"

"You could taste mine."

He shook his head. "Do you have any idea how tempting you are?"

"I'm trying to be." How did one move a man to passion? I wanted to see him look as he had at the masquerade when he had kissed me.

"You are certainly succeeding. How has Orsino managed to leave you virgin for more than a year?"

I glanced away. The humiliation still rankled. "I understand he prefers women who are more sporting and talk less. And who don't make him feel dumb."

"Ridiculous boy." He sat forward, face to face, our knees not quite touching. "If he can't keep up, he needs to run faster."

"Perhaps he doesn't want to," I said. "Not everyone wants to know things."

"Of course not. But that is as unfathomable to you as it is to me, isn't it?" He took my hand in his, caressing the back of it with his thumb. "You are hungry for the world and everything in it." He lifted my hand. "Let us see how you like this." He kissed my hand. He didn't touch his lips to the back of it gallantly. He turned my hand in his, kissing the palm sensuously, then each fingertip, then back to the palm, then lingered at the juncture of my fingers.

I caught my breath, leaning forward, my other hand against his crooked leg where he sat on the bed. "Oh yes."

He looked up at me over my hand, wicked black eyes smiling. "Kiss me."

I slid forward to be close enough, knee to knee. I had never deliberately kissed someone before. He simply waited for it. I lifted my hand to his face, laying it along his cheek, feeling the shape of it, the creases at the corner of his eyes, the faint prickle of beard, the softness of his hair under my fingertips, the fullness of his lips with my thumb. I saw him react, a sensual smile. There was power in this, the power to make him want me, make him desire me, control the moment, control the game. Control him. It was intoxicating, this powerful, self-possessed man waiting for my touch. I leaned in and kissed him. He tasted of the wine I had served and of himself. A long kiss, and then I let go.

He took a deep breath. "You are a very dangerous woman," he said. I am afraid that I giggled. "And an irrepressible flirt." He reached for me. "My turn."

I believe we could have exchanged kisses all afternoon. Sprawling on my bed with our heads to the foot, the sunlight striping across our bodies like a band of warmth, I tilted my head back as he kissed the hollow of my throat. I shifted, trying to free my skirts enough to raise them. His hand was beneath the cloth, stroking my bare thigh, but I lay on too many folds to lift them, to get his fingers where I wanted them. The sunlight came through the window, golden and bright. We could simply do this, warm and quiet in the afternoon, naturally and generously, without fanfare. I wanted his weight on me, his body against mine without silks between.

"A moment," he said. He sounded breathless, his face still against me. And then he sat up, eclipsing the stream of light. "We are not going to do this today."

If this was what being his concubine entailed, all offers of support were superfluous. Which of course was why he wanted me to consider his offer when he wasn't here. Perhaps my head would be clear enough. I took a deep breath. "I am going to think about it," I said. "When you are not here."

"Yes," he said. I had undone the five buttons on one of his sleeves and it hung loose. I am sure my hair was a disaster, my camisa and cotta pulled to the side where he had kissed my breast.

"And consider it rationally."

"Yes." He got up, pacing to the window, his back to me. "Rationally." His voice sounded strained.

"Are you in distress?" I asked, propping up on one elbow.

He huffed. "You have no idea."

"I am sorry to cause you distress, Your Eminence," I said.

He turned around. "Don't you think under the circumstances we might progress from Your Eminence to something more personal?"

I stood up, rearranging my clothes and taking a deep breath. I came to stand by him at the window. The garden was quiet, only the buzz of bees on the blue rosemary flowers. "Rodrigo," I said, lifting my hand to the side of his face again.

"My sweet Giulia," he said, and turned his head and kissed my palm. "I had best go before all our good resolutions come to nothing."

"Yes, of course," I said. We straightened our clothes and I saw him out very properly. Then I went to my room and handled my frustrations in the manner of women everywhere. It did not stretch the imagination to think he must have done so as well.

Chapter Thirteen

The next morning, when all was cool and quiet, I sat down with paper and pen. I put two columns on the page as though to keep accounts—For and Against. I would consider this offer completely rationally.

In the For column I put the obvious things. Money. Tutors and learning. Books were a separate line item. Clothing and jewelry. Should those be two separate items or one? I paused, not certain how to phrase the next thing. Perhaps society? Married to Orsino, I lived a very retired life and I was bored to death. And yet Rome was full of excitement, interesting people, and all that came with living in a city of sixty thousand! There were plays, but I did not see them. There were scholars, but I did not entertain them. There were surely other women my age with an interest in letters and arts, but I did not know them. The fascinating world I had seen at the vice-chancellor's palazzo was right there if someone would open the door for me. Rodrigo would open it.

But there was more than that. The heart of the question was what the world would be. Would the beautiful things made long ago, the stories of the ancients, their plays and poems and epics and scientific theories, be remembered and embraced, or would they be rejected as unchristian? And would new ideas, like della Mirandola's, be rejected and suppressed? I knew what I wanted. I knew what direction I wanted the Church to take. I wanted all the beauties restored. I wanted all the knowledge. But what could I, a young woman, possibly do to influence events? I had no power.

I could have it. The concubine of a powerful cardinal—or even the pope—was a voice. Rodrigo embraced the past with both arms, collected and preserved and tried to understand the wonders the ancients had wrought. If he were pope, would he censure della Mirandola or prohibit Euclid? Would he require universities to stop teaching about the rational nature of the soul? Hardly.

All power lies in patronage in this world, I thought. To be his concubine was to be his client as well as his confidant. And Rodrigo had said I would be cultivated. I would have clients of my own, people who sought my patronage. I could support artists, scholars, and playwrights. I could dispense commissions. Carefully, I wrote "Power" in the For column.

Of course he had also said I would be reviled. I wrote "Reviled" in the Against column. There were those who would hate me out of jealousy and those who would despise me because I was a whore, a kept woman rather than a good wife. They would hold me up as an example of dissipation and sin. I wrote "Sin" in the Against column. I was unsure which column "Dissipation" belonged in.

And was it sin? Obviously not if the pope allowed it. Or did that only allow Rodrigo, not me? I pondered. Surely breaking my marriage vows was my sin. On the other hand, a marriage unconsummated or entered into under false pretense (intending it to be unconsummated) was no true marriage by canon law. I couldn't be breaking my marriage vows if I wasn't really married. So that made it merely fornication rather than adultery.

I wished I could talk to Alessandro about this. But writing to him would take two weeks to get an answer, and how much of this would I want to put on paper anyway?

Well then, what would my mother say? I propped my chin on my hand. She would consider the good I could do for the family. A powerful man, a powerful patron, could guarantee my brothers good careers and my little sister a better marriage than mine when the time came. Money in my hands could filter north to Montalto. I could help them all, and my mother would count that important. No, her worry would not be for my soul. It would be that he might desert me, pregnant and disgraced, proving a scoundrel rather than a solid support. Love does not pay creditors or take care of children. I wrote "Love" in the For column and "Scoundrel?" in the Against column.

There was a cogent argument in the For column, however. Certainly he took care of Lucrezia beautifully, and while I had not met her brothers they seemed well provided for. I wanted children, and children were simply a fact of life unless one were very unfortunate and they died. "Good father" went in the For column.

But one could not provide support if one were dead. In the natural course of things I would outlive him by decades. I considered that for a moment, chewing on the end of the reed pen. I was acquainted with death. It took young as well as old. I might die in childbed next year. If so, I would be a fool not to live now! Why borrow tomorrow's heartache?

No, the real question was whether Rodrigo would keep his promises. I put the pen down. The only person who might be able to illuminate that was Lucrezia.

I found her in the kitchen hunting for treats despite having had bread for breakfast and dragged her out to the garden seats where no one could overhear us. "Lucrezia, I have a very important question," I said, taking both her hands in mine. "Does your father keep his promises?"

She looked thoughtful. "Usually," she said scrupulously. "Except when he can't. Sometimes he promises he'll visit on a certain day and then something happens with the Chancellery or the pope wants to meet with him or something and he sends word that he won't be here."

That was fair enough. He was in charge of the diplomatic relations of a city-state. That could hardly wait on a child. "Does he keep his promises to your mother?"

Lucrezia looked at me, tilting her head to the side. "Why?"

"I'm curious," I said.

She smiled like a self-satisfied kitten. "Yes, he does. I think so, anyway. But sometimes they quarrel." Her eyes widened. "Very loudly."

"About what?"

"About whether it's his job to keep Juan from misbehaving because he's Juan's father and should discipline him, and he says how is he supposed to do that when Juan lives with Mother? And they argue sometimes about which of us is supposed to be with which of them when. Sometimes they yell," Lucrezia said.

"Does he strike her?" I asked.

Lucrezia made a face. "My mother would never put up with a man striking her! If he did, she'd throw water at him like you did at Orsino that time!" We both started laughing, simultaneously imagining the gorgeously dressed cardinal dripping with soapy water. "My mother throws water at cats that fight, not at husbands! That's what she said when I told her!" Lucrezia giggled.

"You told her about that?" I was embarrassed. It was not my finest moment.

She nodded, still giggling. "I told her all about you! I always do."

"Oh." I felt a bit nonplussed. "What does she say about me?"

"She says there's no fool like an old fool." Lucrezia tossed her long hair. "And what does that mean, Giulia?"

It means she knows Rodrigo better than he knows himself, I thought. *And far better than I do. She fears I will hurt him*. Which was indeed useful information.

Cardinal Borgia came to see Lucrezia the next day and stayed to dinner. He wore the summer-weight red wool again, which I had admired before. He sat in Orsino's accustomed place on the short side, while Orsino sat between Lucrezia and his mother on the long side opposite me. Only Adriana and Lucrezia talked much. I was afraid to utter a word. Sitting down with my husband, his mother, the churchman I wished would deflower me, and his daughter was—well, quite a lot.

Cardinal Borgia had very little to say either. He twirled his wine around in his glass, watching it as though it were fascinating, while Lucrezia told him a long and possibly accurate story about snails. It was exceedingly awkward.

I shifted in my seat uncomfortably. He looked up at me as though the smallest sound I had made was a clap of thunder. There was an expression of such raw desire in his eyes that it took my breath away. I dropped my fork. "Excuse me," I said and dived under the table after it.

"Allow me," Rodrigo said, and also bent to pick it up. We nearly cracked heads under the table. I tried to convey something with a look, but I have no idea what it said.

Instead I emerged with the fork. "There is no need to trouble yourself," I said coolly.

Lucrezia frowned. "Papa, I do not know what you and Giulia have quarreled about, but must you? Cannot we all be friends?"

"Lucrezia!" Adriana said. "That is rude."

"It is ruder still to sit glaring at one another without apology," Lucrezia said. "That is what my mother says. She always makes us apologize to one another and make amends."

"Your mother is very wise," Rodrigo said. He nodded to me. "Donna Giulia, I am sorry if I have offended you in any way.

Please accept my heartfelt apologies."

I opened my mouth and then shut it again. His eyes were smiling at me as though this was all a glorious jest and we two the only ones who could laugh. I smiled as well. "Your Eminence, you have not offended, and I pray you pardon me if my rough country manners have in any way offended you."

"Donna Giulia, your manners are exquisite, as is your courteous speech. It is beyond you to give the slightest offense," he said.

"Your Eminence surpasses all in your graciousness," I replied. "Who could wish to trouble you in any way?"

"Dear lady, if you trouble the tranquil waters of the mind, it is simply because your delightful presence renders courtesy impossible." The corner of his mouth twitched.

"It desolates me that I might trouble Your Eminence's tranquility in any way," I said. "I must apologize again."

"Donna Giulia, please do not disturb yourself with my tranquility," he said. "There is no need for apology, or if so, the error is mine. I am but a flawed son of Adam, and your lunar serenity is beyond me."

"And yet you outshine the sun in the glory of your gracious presence, Your Eminence," I said.

Adriana was staring at us like we had lost our wits.

"You can stop apologizing now," Lucrezia said. "That's enough."

"It is more than enough," I said, laughing.

"Courtesy taken to extremes is unfortunately funny," her father explained to Lucrezia. "We are making a joke."

"Oh!" Lucrezia smiled. "Then you are not angry with each other?"

"Not in the least," he assured her.

"Of course not, my dear," I said. Once again, my husband uttered not a word.

The morning of June 18th dawned hot and muggy, unseasonably so, with the almost white sky that presaged thunderstorms later. In mid-afternoon I received a note requiring me at Bracciano's palazzo that evening. I was not surprised. His guards escorted me there just before sundown, Vespers ringing as I arrived. The clouds had piled up, but as yet no hint of breeze stirred. I wore my blue velvet, sweltering in the heat and looking decidedly unseasonable compared to lighter silks. Surely in Rodrigo's promises of fine clothes there would be new summer gowns!

That thought was occupying my mind in what had now become almost routine, being escorted to the sala upstairs where Bracciano's gentlemen were getting ready. Today I was earlier than usual. There were only two men already present, both in good clothes, one with a face I thought I recognized from the masquerade. They were talking and barely spared a glance for me as I entered and sat down in one of the chairs that had been pushed to the walls. After all, they had seen me for months. I was of no more account than the implements waiting, the thurible on its chain, the mirror shrouded in black cloth, the aspergillum, the book on the table.

I stopped. I had seen the book before, but only cradled carefully by Bracciano or Dr. Treschi. I had never seen it left alone before. It was hand-copied rather than printed, and it lay open to a page marked with a ribbon. I couldn't quite read it at the angle I was sitting. I waited.

After a few minutes, the two men walked out into the hall, still discussing something. As soon as they did, I got to my feet quietly and went around the table. I did not touch it, but the words were plain enough in Latin.

"To Cause A Fall Which Shall Prove Fatal. Take a black dog and cut its throat by a dark moon. Take its blood in a chalice and mix with rue and the ashes of a burnt page of Psalms. Form the Square of Jupiter with the name of the one whose fatality you desire. Say...." And there were lines in Greek or another language I did not read. I shook my head, then picked up at the end of the quotation. "Take the chalice and pour it out by night over the place you have selected."

A steel hand closed around my wrist. "What are you doing?" Bracciano asked.

I looked up at him as innocently as possible. "I was looking at the book, My Lord."

He bent closer, overbearing me entirely. "Why?"

"I was curious," I said. "But I have no Latin, or nothing beyond *Pater Noster.*" His hand was bruising, and I tried to look as young and small as I could.

"I see." He released me, stepping back. "Curiosity is a flaw in a young woman."

"Well I know it, My Lord," I said.

Bracciano looked at me levelly. He didn't believe me. It was plain. And yet he nodded, stepping away. "Sit down and wait for your part," he said, and I did so.

When the circles and squares were chalked and I sat in the center with the mirror, it fogged immediately as I looked into it, the demon looking back. It leered at me. "So, wanton girl, have you decided to stretch out beneath a priest? You and I might come to a profitable arrangement."

"What is your lordship's question?" I asked Bracciano, ignoring the demon's words, though I felt my cheeks color for all I knew that no one else could hear it.

Bracciano seemed to be phrasing his question carefully. "If the operation is performed as written, will the trap be sprung within a single moon?"

The demon's mouth blurred into a smile. "Assuredly. Assuredly he will die within a moon."

"Assuredly he will die within a moon," I repeated, though a chill seized me. Did he mean Rodrigo?

The demon took it as though I had put a question to it, Rodrigo's face swimming before me in the mirror. "What a short time you will have with your lover," the demon said. "It is to be pitied." I glared at the glass but could not speak, for of course the whole room could hear me.

"Who shall be vice-chancellor next?" Bracciano asked.

Another face appeared, one I recognized, and I said his name clearly aloud. "Cardinal Ascanio Sforza." Bracciano winced. The Sforza were the enemies of the Orsini. If he would be rid of Rodrigo, he would not be replaced with someone Bracciano liked better, and certainly not with his cousin, Cardinal Orsini. I felt a kind of grim triumph in that, despite my fear.

"Will the Pope authorize additional funds?"

I saw Bracciano smiling over a paper. "It seems so, My Lord. I see that you are happy." I made my voice waver. I tried to keep it to no more than four questions, though truly I could have done more. The mirror was ice in my hands, but I could hold it still. I was growing used to this.

"Practice makes perfect," the demon said sarcastically. "You make quite a nice little minion. I might have an offer for you that you would like. After all, if you are damned already, why not enjoy life?"

"And will the man who is the impediment know anything of this?" Bracciano asked. Once again, Rodrigo's face appeared, grave and concerned, as though I spoke to him.

"No, My Lord. He will not," I said.

"Liar," the demon said. "What an accomplished little liar you are! If he does not, it is because you lie to him as you lie to everyone. You lie to your husband, to your mother-in-law, to your family, and even to your lover. You are a natural-born daughter of Eve." I ignored it, though my hands shook.

"My Lord Bracciano," Dr. Treschi said, giving me a meaningful glance. "The Dove tires."

"The Dove tires, the Dove tires," the demon said. "Or are they tired of the Dove?"

Bracciano nodded sharply. "Dismiss the entity then. We will allow our Dove to leave before we continue further."

I put the mirror face down on the floor and waited while Dr. Treschi did his part, reciting and then erasing part of the circle. I stepped out over the square. Everyone stood at ease for a bit, several of the men helping themselves to wine on one of the side tables, talking together. Dr. Treschi approached me. "Are you well?" he asked loudly.

"Yes, thank you," I said. He was making strange expressions that were no doubt supposed to be meaningful, but I could think of no way to talk to him privately.

Bracciano appeared at my elbow. "You are done," he said. "I will have my guards escort you home."

"Thank you, My Lord," I said, and let him lead me away from Treschi.

We went out into the hall and he turned to two of his guards. "You will see Donna Giulia home." His voice was very bland and he did not look at me. Another guard was leading a half-grown hound on a leash up the stairs, a black pup that was looking around eagerly. He nosed at my hand and I closed my eyes.

"This way, my lady," one of the guards said, and preceded me down. I lifted my skirts on the stairs. Unlike the dog, I had an inkling of my fate.

We went out the main doors to the street, one guard ahead and one behind. Both wore sword and dagger, and each had a good leather jerkin over sleeves in Orsini red and white. One was no taller than I, but both were clearly stronger. One carried a lantern to light our way.

I was glad I had brought a cloak because the storm looked to break soon, a freshening wind scouring the dark streets. It was still early as these things went, probably lacking an hour until midnight. Normally there would still be people about but the impending rain seemed to have sent them scurrying home. I pulled up my hood, letting both guards get ahead of me by a step or two, wondering how I would lose them. I would have to. It was possible Bracciano hadn't given them orders to kill me, but I certainly wasn't going to bet my life on it. I knew too much. He suspected my loyalties. And after all, girls are cheap.

I walked as slowly as possible. I had no ideas. How would I escape two armed men? I could not outrun them, not in skirts and both of them young and fit. I could certainly not fight them. Even if I could get a knife, they wore leather and I did not. Could I appeal to someone for help? Who? The streets were all but deserted, market stalls closed, even tavernas and osterias closing against the rain and the hour. A church? We were not near any, nor would we pass one on the way. And they would not wait until we were nearly there. They would not risk the cardinal's guards at Adriana's house hearing. Also, that neighborhood was safer and there would be more guards at the gates of palazzi in general. If it looked like a young lady was being set upon, there were those who might interfere. No, it would be soon.

A flash of lightning split the sky, the thunder following after. As though it had opened the gates of heaven, the rain began, fat drops spattering off the street.

One of the guards swore. They'd be soaked. And so would I. There was a plaza ahead, in ordinary day holding a market around a fountain. The stalls were closed, but three streets led off from it. One led to Dr. Treschi's lodging. I had been that way. Of course he was not there. He was still at Bracciano's, but I knew the place. I marked the way, a sharp right down the alley coming into the plaza. On the next flash.

The lightning cracked. The thunderclap came so close it was almost deafening, the rain whirling around us. I ran. I could not see;

the lightning had been so bright that its afterimage remained. But I had marked where I was going. I ran. It would give me a few moments.

I heard one of them shout behind me. I gained the mouth of the alley, running for all I was worth on the slippery stones, trying to keep close to one of the buildings where I would be less visible. Dark blue velvet with a dark cloak was at least not conspicuous. I kept running. At the next corner I turned sharply right again, then left as soon as I could, down an alleyway that cut between two streets. I heard them calling to one another. "This way! She went down here!"

I had a little lead but not much. I must get off the street. But where? There were the closed gates of a palazzo, closed ground floor doors to a building with rooms above and shops below, all closed against night and rain. There was a portico ahead, columns where a passage ran through along a greater building. In bright daylight I had seen peddlers here.

Tonight there were women. There were three of them standing beneath it, waiting for the rain to stop, their camisas pulled down so far most of their breasts showed. One had her hand on her hip, looking at me. Her eyes met mine.

A risk, but worth it. I dashed out of the rain, my hair fallen and my cloak soaked. "Please!" I said in a low voice, "Please, there is a man chasing me who is trying to force me! I got away but I can't lose him!"

She looked at one of the others. "Here," one of them said. "Crouch down behind us. We'll stand together." Their skirts when they stood side by side were wide enough. I scooted down between them and the wall—and just in time, for one of the Orsini guards came pelting around the corner.

He saw the first prostitute, his eyes checking but clearly she was not me. "You there," he demanded, "have you seen a girl in blue?"

"I'm a girl in blue," she said, putting out her hand. "What other girl do you need?"

He was having none of it. “Tall, young, in a blue cloak,” he said.

“No, captain,” one of the women in front of me said, the one who had invited me behind her skirts. “This is our corner.” He shook his head and turned, going back the way he had come. I nearly collapsed against the wall.

The woman who had answered bent down and helped me up. “He’s gone,” she said. “Come out now, chickie.”

“Thank you,” I said getting up. Her hands were warm and kind. “Thank you so much.”

“Orsini guard,” the first said. “You work in an Orsini house?”

My clothes must look somewhat battered. Also they were quite provincial in cut, as I had previously noted. They thought I was a maid in her mistress’ castoffs. “Yes,” I said. “He offered to walk me home.”

“That’s always a good line,” the other woman said. “You won’t fall for that again.”

“I won’t,” I said. “I don’t know where I should go.” Which was true. They’d be searching for me between here and Donna Adriana’s house. Even as I said it, I knew there was only one option. “Actually, do you know the vice-chancellor’s palazzo? I have a friend who works there.” Which was absolutely true. He certainly worked there.

The first woman nodded. “I can tell you how to get there. But you might be best to stay here.”

“He’ll keep looking for me,” I said. “When he doesn’t find me, he’ll be back.” The vice-chancellor’s palazzo was only a few blocks from Adriana’s, but I was turned around. My voice shook and it was not an act. “I don’t know this part of the city well. Can you tell me how to get there?”

She did. And she let me wipe my soaked face on her shawl. “Be careful,” the other woman said. “The streets are dangerous.”

“I will,” I said. “And thank you again.” The rain was still pouring down in sheets, but that wouldn’t discourage my pursuers.

I had no doubt they'd persist. Going back and telling Bracciano that they'd lost me would not be easy. They'd hunt for several hours at least. Dr. Treschi's lodgings might be nearer, but first I could not be certain any friend of his would let me in. Second, I was not at all certain that Dr. Treschi's loyalties could be counted upon. Bracciano was his patron, and it seemed he was prepared to enact a spell for murder, killing that poor pup in the process. No, I would not trust Dr. Treschi. Better to trust my own feet and mind and try to get to Rodrigo. At least I knew I would be safe there.

Also, while I knew who they meant to kill and by means of a lethal fall, I did not know where or how. Not in his house tonight, presumably, if they had to get their bloody mixture onto the stairs in question. Nobody would let someone in to asperge his stairway with blood in the middle of the night! But where and what might be done about it—I had to warn him before he went wherever it was or did whatever might spring the trap. I plunged back out into the rain.

Chapter Fourteen

The lightning and thunder had lessened but the rain fell in sheets, washing the streets and making swirls of offal, debris and night soil in each depression. The oldest streets were humped so that water ran toward the gutters, keeping the center cobbles clean. Which meant I was walking ankle-deep in the worst of it, trying to keep to the side inconspicuously. The water ran through my shoes, occasionally something nasty hauling up against my ankles until I shook it off. My skirts were sodden to the knees and quite a lot above.

Here and there a light still showed in an upper window, or a lantern glowed in the vestibule of some great house. For the most part the city was dark. I am certain I would never have reached the vice-chancellor's palazzo without greater harm except for the rain. Even the most hardened footpads expected no one to rob in the downpour. Still, I started at every sound. Was it one of the two guards or simply another sort of predator? I was shivering with cold and apprehension by the time the palazzo came in sight. I ran across the street in front.

There were two guards behind the ornamental iron gates at the portico, and I practically threw myself against the gates. One of the guards looked familiar. He must have rotated through duty at Donna Adriana's. "Please let me in!" I begged. "It's Donna Giulia. I have to see Cardinal Borgia immediately!"

"You're who?" the other guard asked skeptically.

"La Bella Farnese," the one I recognized said. "You know."

"Oh." The guard opened the metal gate. "What's going on?"

"There's a plot to kill the vice-chancellor," I said. "Please, I must tell him. I was nearly killed." My hair had fallen from its pins in a sodden mess to my waist and I was soaked to the skin. I looked half-drowned.

The first guard, the one who had called me La Bella Farnese, took charge. "Come this way, Donna Giulia," he said. "I will take you up." He looked at the other guard. "Close and bar the gate. Don't let anyone else in."

I heard the bar fall into place as I followed him. I slipped and nearly fell on the stairs, my ruined shoes giving me no traction on the marble, and the guard caught me under the elbow. "Here, Madonna," he said. He steadied me. I was shaking with cold and with the shock of it all now that I was safe. "Not far."

We went on to the second floor where I had never been the night of the party, down a grand loggia that looked on the courtyard, another guard coming to attention at the top of the stairs and running ahead of us to open the door to a fine sala. I went in, dripping on the elaborate carpet. "Wait a moment, Madonna," the guard said, and went to the far end to knock on another door.

I waited. It was only a few moments before the door opened wide, Rodrigo hurrying out pulling a velvet gown over his long shirt. "Giulia! What in the world has happened?"

My knees nearly gave way with relief. He caught my elbows. "The man I told you of. He is trying to kill you," I said.

"Come in by the fire. I will tend to the guard." He led me into his camera, where indeed there was a fire burning merrily against the chill of the rain. As soon as he saw me there, he turned about, going back into the sala, giving orders to the guard and a servant who had been wakened. It must be very late. He had clearly retired, as had the senior servants.

I stretched my hands to the fire, then took off my shoes. My clothes were not only soaked but also stinking and filthy at the hem from the refuse of the gutters. I undid the blue velvet and dropped it on the floor. I had little hope it could be repaired. The light blue cotta followed it. Regretfully, I remembered how carefully my mother had sewn it for my wedding.

Rodrigo came back in, shutting the doors behind him. "I've doubled the guard," he said. "And had them lock the kitchen entrance entirely. Now what is going on?"

"Bracciano had me to scry for him tonight. They were going to kill a dog and use its blood to do something to cause you to have a fatal fall," I said. I was shivering, standing before the fire in my soaked camisa, yet all I could feel was the puppy nudging my hand hopefully. He was dead now. "They were going to do a spell. Bracciano had his guards take me home, only they weren't supposed to actually take me there. They were going to kill me."

"My dearest." He looked shocked. Perhaps there were things that did indeed shock him.

"But I got away from them in the streets. I hid and made my way here."

"They?"

"Two Orsini guardsmen."

"Giulia." He seemed at a loss for other words.

"So I came to warn you," I said. "I don't know how or exactly when. It's supposed to be sprung when you go somewhere or do something, but I don't know what. It's blood. On stairs." I wasn't making a lot of sense.

"You're freezing," he said. "I have a dry shirt. A moment." He went to go rummage in a press.

I stripped off my soaking camisa and simply climbed into his large, curtained bed. It was warm from his sleeping body, and I pulled the covers up around me as I sat among the pillows. He turned around with a long shirt in hand and stopped dead.

"This is warmer," I said. The covers just concealed my breasts.

Rodrigo shook his head ruefully. "Plot," he said. "To kill me." He sat down beside me, the shirt on top of the covers. "Then pull the covers up so that you're warm. And try to tell me what is going on from the beginning."

"Yes," I said, pulling them over my shoulders.

He spoke very slowly. "My chastity, thought, and common sense are all sorely tried by having you naked in my bed. It is my failing, unfortunately, to be rendered nearly witless and speechless. However, recognizing my weakness, if it is important that I know what you came to tell me, please refrain from naked embraces until you have imparted whatever it is."

I started laughing and wasn't sure I could stop. "I will do that, Rodrigo. Recognizing your frailty."

"Thank you," he said gravely, sitting with his back against the pillows and headboard so that he could see my face. I pulled a pillow against my chest to lean on, the covers up to my chin. "Now," he said. "Calmly. I am sure tonight has been trying. Tell me what happened from the beginning."

"Bracciano sent for me tonight," I began, and I told him all that had occurred, truthfully and in order. It was easier to talk thus. He did not interrupt, only asked a question here and there when I stopped. The fire was warm, the firelight flickering, the rain still pattering occasionally against the window. The bed was very comfortable. When at last I finished, he was silent, leaning against the headboard. "Is something wrong?" I asked.

He shook his head. "You are very brave," he said. "Quick thinking." He looked down at me nestled among the pillows. "This leaves me with a conundrum. Obviously this trap is set. Presumably it will spring when I go to some particular place. Not in this house, I think, but I cannot stay in my house forever!"

"It could be anywhere," I said.

"Nearly anywhere," Rodrigo said, raising a finger. "Not in the

Vatican. Demons cannot abide holy ground."

"Anywhere besides here and the Vatican," I said. Which left a great deal of Rome. There was one thing that bothered me. "Does not your holy office protect you from such evil?"

"Would that it did," he said. "If all evil were averted from churchmen, life would be much easier." He reached down, stroking my drying hair. "But I am no more immune to the malice of men than anyone else. Bracciano has made a bargain with this demon, and the consequences are real." At least he did not doubt me. I leaned against his hand like any other creature gentled and reassured by comforting presence. He smelled of civet and tuberose, warm and rich. "Ah, Giulia," he said. "It is very late. You have warned me as you meant to, and you are safe here. Rest, and we will consider in the morning. You will be as secure here as in your own bed."

By which he meant he would not touch me, save this hand on my hair? I sat up, letting my hair fall to cover me where the sheet did not. "I have made my choice," I said. "I choose you."

His eyes did not leave mine. "To be done with the demon tonight?"

"No," I said. "And probably best if we do not consummate this right now. It is still possible that there will have to be an annulment if Orsino is difficult about this."

"And for that it is best if you are *virgo intacta*," Rodrigo said.

"I am not saying I wish to leave your bed," I said. The cold and fear had left me. Danger had left a hunger behind. "Even if we do not...." I tried again. "The kissing was very good. It is just that the annulment...." I felt myself turning red.

"If your husband did not completely lack imagination, he would be able to think of things that would please you while leaving you technically virgin," he said.

"Are there such things?"

"A great many," Rodrigo said. "And well worth exploring, even after you are no longer a maiden."

"Things that please you too?" I asked.

"Oh yes." He gathered some of my heavy, damp hair in his hand. "If one wanted to avoid pregnancy, or if it were the wrong time of the month—there are plenty of reasons, including pleasure." His voice was falsely light, casual so as not to press me if I wished to put him off.

"You might show me some of them," I said, and took his hand and brought it to my lips as though I kissed his ring, reverently and with tenderness. Of course he did not wear his ring to bed, and I saw his face change. "I will follow where you lead," I said, and then with a smile, "for you know I am innocent in these matters and require your good instruction."

He shifted, turning on his side toward me so that I faced him and he leaned on one elbow. "Do you indeed?" That was flirtation, but there was a dark glint in his eye. What would it take to truly see him transported with lust? What would he be like if he finally lost his careful control, became unthinking and unreasoning? That was a thought heady as wine. "Are you so innocent as all that?"

"Well," I said, ducking my head with false modesty, "I do know how a few things work. I have…explored…as the result of lustful thoughts."

"Perhaps you should tell me more about these lustful thoughts." He gathered my hair again, baring my shoulders, running the weight of it through his fingers.

"Should I confess lustful thoughts for a cardinal?" I said. *How does one seduce? Or does it come naturally to say aloud things I have said in my own mind?* "Sometimes when I think of a certain cardinal, I am overcome with carnal desires."

"Are you?" He traced the line of my neck with one finger. I could see his pulse jumping in his own throat above the open drawstrings of his shirt. "And what do you do about it?"

"I touch myself." I leaned into his hand.

His mouth twisted in a smile. "A grave sin."

"Then perhaps you will assign me suitable penance," I said.

"I presume you don't want me to tell you to say ten *Pater Nosters*," he said, amusement in his voice. That was probably what he actually told women. When I had really confessed to him, telling him of my dealings with the demon, he had been entirely priestly.

"Cannot you think of something better?" I asked, somewhat breathlessly.

"I expect I might. Kneel for me." There was a smile in his eyes and he did not move. I could do it or not.

Pushing the covers back, I knelt up as though I were at the altar rail. My hair fell down my back and over my right shoulder, my left breast uncovered, my belly and all beneath it. There was nothing hidden. He could see all that I was.

He let out a breath that might have been admiration or disbelief. "Lovely," Rodrigo said. "Utterly lovely." He sat up beside me, his head at the level of my breast, simply looking at me. Learning me.

There in the firelit quiet, time seemed to stand still. His hands arranged my hair, pushing it back over my shoulder, and all the while my private parts throbbed with desire. To be naked before him, to be seen, to be known—the expression on his face was not hunger, not purely that, but the same longing desire with which he looked at his statue, as though I were an ancient goddess come to life, a dream made flesh.

"So beautiful," he said. He ran his hand down my side to the curve of my hip, and I arched against his hand. "La Bella Farnese indeed."

"You began calling me that," I said. It was he who had named me The Beautiful, and I had wondered at it at the time, if it was meant in jest. Now I knew it was desire.

"Still," he said, one hand on my hip. "Still," and parted my knees, arranging them almost fussily so that I sat on my heels. "Penitent, remember?"

"I do," I said somewhat breathlessly.

"And for what should I punish you?"

"Touching myself," I said. I could feel the beat of my own pulse there.

"Then do it," he said. "Show me." He lowered his voice on the last.

I took a shuddering breath. To do that, before him.... I had done it thus many times, but with someone watching it was dizzying. With him watching. And yet there was something curiously freeing about it, though there was no spur but his voice. He could see all. I put my hand to my breast, lifting it and stroking, the nipple hardening under my fingers, round and ripe in my hand. My eyes did not leave his. I offered it to him as gracefully as I had offered the pomegranate at the masquerade, and he leaned forward and took it in his mouth.

I swayed, nearly falling. His hand on my hip steadied me. Sensation. Heat. Pride in my daring. The movement of his mouth on my breast.

And then he withdrew. I looked down at him. He was smiling, his eyes dark with pleasure. "And what else do you do?" he asked.

"This." I put my right hand where I wanted it, where the pulse jumped between my legs. Rodrigo could see the working of my fingers, the expression on my face as naked as anything else. And then sensation. My fingers on my own folds, spreading warmth, pressure on that center of pleasure.

"Gorgeous," he said. His voice sounded a bit strained. "My lovely penitent. Don't stop."

I closed my eyes. Firelight. Warmth. His voice. My hands. Something was changing inside, something deep taking root.

I felt the movement of the bed, and then he was kneeling up behind me, velvet robe and linen shirt against my skin where my hair did not cover it, and I leaned back against him as his hand came around my waist. He bent his lips to my neck. I turned my head and met his mouth with mine. Starving, hungry, devouring me—I had wanted to be kissed like this, and yet it was better than any imagining, the taste of his mouth, the prickle of his cheek, the hardness against my buttocks where he embraced me. We swayed, locked together as though in dance, leaning back against him. Our mouths parted. We had to breathe. Then again. Timeless. Deep.

And his hand on my belly and then between my legs, fingers touching mine on me. "Like that," he said. "Is that how you like it?" I made some incoherent noise. I opened my eyes. "Like that?" His fingers stroking me, taking up my own rhythm.

I bore down against his hand. "I do sincerely repent," I said. I didn't. Of course I didn't.

"Ah, but you'll do it again." His hand left mine to do its work, holding me instead. "Won't you?"

"I will, Your Eminence," I said. It was building, so sharp, so bright, the transfiguration of every fantasy.

"And how shall I punish you for recidivism?"

"Severely," I whispered. The world went bright and dark, muscles clenching, and I ground down against my hand. I might have screamed. I would have fallen if he hadn't been behind me, held against him as though he were an angel to bear me up to heaven.

And then I was through. He let me down to the pillows where I sprawled bonelessly, my body throbbing. "There, my Giulia." Rodrigo gathered me against him, velvet robe against my cheek, one hand open on his chest, feeling his heartbeat beneath his thin shirt. "There, my beauty."

I opened my eyes, opened my mouth. "So intense."

"Yes." His voice was rough. He must be holding back.

And yet he waited, that expression on his face as though he looked into my soul. "I am too passionate," I said. To want such things, to crave them…

The corner of his mouth quirked. "My love, you are exactly as God made you."

Freed, unchained, perfect in his sight—what else could I be when he looked at me like that? I leaned into him seeking another kiss. Could that be repeated, so raw, so consuming? I could feel him hard against me. Surely he wanted to take me. Surely he needed release. "Show me," I said breathlessly. "Show me what to do."

"Gladly." Robe and shirt up, a line of hair down his stomach leading to his groin.

"Oh my," I said. "How is that all supposed to fit?"

He laughed, his head thrown back on the pillows. "That is the kind of compliment a man likes. You're a country girl. Haven't you watched?"

"The Borgia bull?" I said, smiling into his eyes. "Of course I have." I brushed my hand over his member. "Show me as I did you."

"Like this." He took my hand in his, curling my fingers around him. "Gentle. You're not milking a cow."

At that I couldn't help but laugh, half-collapsing on his shoulder, my hand on him. "I'll be gentler than with the cow, I promise." Skin so soft, so warm, so sensitive to sensation. I had never touched a man before. Tentative exploration turned bold, light touches firm.

"Faster," he said, and I moved to get a better angle, leaning over him. It would be easy to straddle him, wouldn't it? I could see how it should go. A lover beneath me like earth while I arched above him like the night sky.

His eyes were closed, an expression of intense concentration on his face. He looked as he had at the Pentecost Mass, transported, refined. *Inspirati*, I thought, filled with spirit. Could God be lover as well as father and son?

"Look at me," I said my hand moving on him steadily. "Look at me." He opened his eyes, raw and intent.

And that was the moment, sense abandoned. His face tensed almost as though in pain, and he spilled his seed against me, against my belly where I leaned against him, thrusting into my hand. A groan, and he lay like a stringless puppet among the pillows. I lay down against his side, my hand now open on his chest, listening to him breathe. "My dearest," I said. "My love." It was new to say these words.

"My Giulia," Rodrigo said, and folded me in his arm. He kissed my brow, my hair, my nose. "All right?"

"Yes," I said. "More than all right."

He smiled and closed his eyes again, holding me tight. I pulled the covers up over us both, warm and safe in the bubble of firelight. Outside, the rain was heavy again, a steady drumbeat against the glass. Distant thunder rolled from a flash of lightning unseen. In here it was safe and warm. He held me against his heart, and I smiled against his flesh. *If this was the antechamber to passion, what lies within?* I closed my eyes too. *I will never regret this*, I thought.

Chapter Fifteen

I woke for a moment uncertain of where I was. There was a horrible noise I could not identify. Then it came back to me, the velvet bed curtains, the fire dying away to coals—and Rodrigo snoring loudly. I turned over. He lay on his back, mouth open, dreadful snorts emanating. I sighed. There was no perfection in the fallen world.

I turned over, hugging a pillow and closing my eyes. *Snort. Snort. Snuffle.* Silence. The silence continued. Was he dead? Had he suddenly expired in his sleep? I turned over. *Snort! Snuffle. Snort snort snort.* I put my hand to my brow. Clearly there were still more things I had to learn about the ways of men.

And now sleep had fled. I was instead thinking of all the frightening moments earlier, the guards and the street and the rain. I was very lucky not to be dead.

Beyond that, what did Bracciano intend? I did not doubt he would kill Rodrigo if he could. Could he? The demon seemed to think so. Or at least it pretended so. Was that a lie or truth? How could I know? How could I sleep wondering? Perhaps if I found nature's necessity, I would sleep after. I got up, pattering barefooted around the great bed. Rodrigo didn't stir other than to snort again. His mind was untroubled. Mine was not. His dark red robe lay discarded on the floor and I picked it up and put it on.

There were several doors off the room and I chose the first one, hoping it didn't lead to a hallway full of guards. No, it was a study. I slipped in. There was a great desk visible in the faint light through the rain-swept window, a window seat with a red cover, the desk covered in papers. The shelves held at least a hundred books.

"Oh," I said quietly. I examined them, trying to tell what they were in the dim light. I took down one at random and carried it to the window, flipping it open to the title page. "*Amadís de Gaula*," I said. It was in Spanish, a language I did not read, but of course I knew of the famous adventures of the perfect, gentle knight who wept when his lady chastised him, then sired a son on her without marriage, and was exiled ten years in Constantinople. The book looked well-worn, some of the pages a little loose. How long had he had it? I put it back where it belonged, picking up the next one and taking it to the window as well.

This one was hand-copied rather than printed, page after page in neat, elegant Latin, a trained scribe's hand with all the lines perfectly squared. I gently turned to the first page. "Wherever Ptolemy and Aristobulus in their histories of Alexander son of Philip have given the same account, I have followed it on the assumption of its accuracy. Where their accounts have differed, I have chosen the more interesting."

I looked at the page before. "The Alexander of Arrianus," it read. Where a copyist might put their initials, there was a neat *RLB*. Another story of Alexander, one he had copied out himself? I closed the book, running my hands over the cover. When he was my age, there had been no printed books, he had said. Copying even this much must have taken him many months. I found it hard to imagine him sitting still that long.

I put the book back where it belonged. I had to find a way to confound Bracciano's plan. It was simply not acceptable to do nothing while he was in jeopardy. I slipped back out of the study and tried the next door.

It was a dressing room with all neatly arranged for the bath, a big empty copper tub to one side, a toilet chair, basin, and all the necessities. I availed myself, looking around the tidy little room. Bathing sheets were neatly stacked on a shelf. There was a basin and over it a mirror for shaving. A mirror.

I got up, going to it carefully. It had said it could manifest in any surface, and it certainly had in my mirror at home. I glanced back to make certain the door was shut. Then I stepped in front of it. "Asmodeus?" I said quietly.

The surface clouded, and then the face appeared as if out of smoke, obscuring my own. It leered. "Still alive, little Dove? Bracciano underestimated you."

"Apparently," I said.

"And now you stand in front of me with a cardinal's seed on your naked belly and you want to make a bargain. Let me guess. You want your lover's life. I can do that. It's simple for me to make certain that Bracciano's plan doesn't work. But it will cost you." It smiled.

"No," I said levelly. "I don't want to make a bargain. I mean to compel you." I had passed through fear and out the other side. This me, this new me born in killing with knife or candlestand, eluding men meant to kill me, choosing my lover as I wished and wearing his seed like a badge—I was not afraid.

Its smoke eyes widened. "Compel me? You cannot compel me, mortal girl!"

"Actually, I can," I said. "You are a demon, and you must make bargains and keep them fairly. That is what you do with Bracciano. He and his men promise you years of their soul's service for your counsel of dubious worth. But I am a Dove and I am virgin yet. I promised you nothing and yet you used me. You borrowed my tongue without my consent, and for that I am owed."

It hissed. There was no other word for it. It hissed like a cat that has been stepped on. "I will not hear this," it said.

"You will," I said. "You have claimed that because I am a

Dove, you may appear in any reflective surface at any time and hound me all my days. I say that a binding works two ways. I will hold you to this mirror. I have learned the signs from Dr. Treschi, and I will keep you in this glass unable to depart until you do what I wish." I had learned no such signs, nor knew of any, but such must exist. If it was possible to bind the demon to the area inside the chalked wards, it was possible to bind it into the glass.

"I will show you nothing," it said.

"Then I will hold you here by what you owe me, bind you here, and throw this glass in the river," I said. "And you may hope that someday someone will find it who has the wit to release you."

"You think too much of yourself, girl!" it snarled. But it was frightened. It was frightened more than I.

"Or, you may show me what I wish, and then I will call your debt to me paid. You may depart, all business between us concluded." I put my head to the side. "I daresay exorcism would be unpleasant. And I happen to know a cardinal."

It laughed, its mouth elongating. "Well played," it said. "I will show you one thing at your request, fairly and honestly, and then I will depart, all business concluded."

"I will have no further call upon you, and you will have none on me," I said. "We shall not see one another again."

"Agreed," it said. "There will be no talk of bindings."

"Agreed, and you will never again trouble me or mine, my servants, my friends, my lovers, my children, or anything that is mine," I said, "or my promise that there shall be no bindings is null and void."

"Agreed," it said. The mist in the mirror coalesced again. "What would you see?"

"I would see the death Bracciano plans for Cardinal Borgia, the manner, time and place of its occurrence."

The mist swirled, and once again a scene appeared. It was night. Two bearers walked with torches streaming, a party following after: four of the cardinal's guard, and between them Rodrigo and Lucrezia. They passed through a narrow street, then a broader plaza with a garden wall along one side, a square tower rising at the end of it. There was a set of stairs leading down as though it went through the building. They started down.

I saw him sway. I saw him fall, reaching out but grabbing nothing, simply slipping and falling on his back. I heard the crack as the back of his head hit the stone step. I heard Lucrezia's scream. "Papa! Papa!" I saw his eyes still open.

The demon's face appeared, the scene twisting into his smile. "Are you satisfied?"

"Yes," I said. If there was horror in me, my voice did not betray it, a gambler's face still and quiet. "I hold our bargain concluded."

"Then I will be gone," it said, and with a shift the mirror cleared. I stood shivering in Rodrigo's bathing chamber, sick with what I had done.

I took a deep breath and went back into the bedchamber. Rodrigo was still snoring. I sat down beside his feet. I shook them gently. "Rodrigo? Wake up. I need to tell you something."

He came awake swiftly. He must be used to being roused in the middle of the night. "What is it, Giulia?" he asked, sitting up. His shirt was still up around his chest, and he pulled it down.

"I know where Bracciano intends to murder you," I said. "Or rather, I know what the place looks like though I have never seen it."

He frowned. "What do you mean, you know what it looks like?"

"I called the demon into the mirror and made it show me."

"What mirror?"

"The one in your bathing room," I said.

"Giulia!" He got to his feet, his face a study in disbelief. "You summoned a demon in my bath? What in the name of Heaven?"

"I wanted to find out...."

"You said that you had only had converse with them against your will," he said, angrily striding around the room. "You said that Bracciano made you. And now you tell me you called it?"

"I did, but—"

"Giulia!" he shouted. "You may think me a very wicked man, but I am no fool and I do have limits. I do not deal with demons. At all. Ever. You summoned a demon into my rooms? I am a cardinal of the Holy Church. I do not have demons in my house!"

"I needed to find out what Bracciano intended," I said. He had never shouted at me before, or at anyone in my presence. Tears prickled in my eyes. I thought he would tell me I had been brave.

"You know what he intends. He intends to kill me. And so you summoned a demon?" He went around the bed, throwing his hands up to the heavens. "No demons. Not ever. Not for any reason." He loomed over me. "Do you not understand that they will lie and it will always seem like a good reason? It will always seem like a good bargain and that the harm is acceptable? That is how they strike. It is one little step at a time. One small evil. Just a drop of blood. Just an animal's blood. Just a man's life."

"I know, but...." I burst into tears. "It is your life!" I covered my face with my hands. "I could get this one thing from it and maybe save you. I compelled it to answer and then agree that we would never converse again. I don't want to be evil. But I did it. I did it, and now you will hate me." I sobbed hopelessly into my hands, sitting on the end of his bed.

"Giulia." Now his voice was gentle, and he came and sat beside me, putting an arm around my heaving shoulders. "Giulia, sweet. I shouldn't have yelled at you. Dearest, come here. I'm sorry." I turned, burying my face in his shoulder. "There now, sweet. You made a mistake, and I shouldn't have shouted. It's just that a demon can be a very serious mistake."

"I didn't promise it anything except that I would leave it alone if it left me alone," I sobbed. "I needed to know how they were going to kill you. Because I can't stand that. I can't stand it. Everybody dies and leaves me alone." I hadn't meant to say the last, hadn't known I meant it until that moment. My father on his deathbed, the skin stretched taut over his face, gray beard and slack jaw....

"Dearest." Rodrigo's arms were tight around me. "Dearest, I'm not going to die anytime soon. I'm not going to leave you alone."

"You will," I said. The tears would not stop.

I felt him take a breath, as though he considered what he would say. "Eventually," Rodrigo said. "Everyone dies eventually. But I am hearty and hale and I hope I have a good many years left to me. And when I go to pay the piper in Purgatory, I expect I will spend long enough there that you will join me in due time." He ducked his face, kissing the top of my head. "Surely we can find enough to amuse us in the company of sinners and ancients. I'm rather looking forward to the discourse."

I hiccoughed. So like him to imagine Purgatory as an endless symposium! But I was more concerned with the pain of losing him in this world. "I cannot lose you," I said, holding onto his shirt.

"You are not going to lose me anytime soon," he promised. "We will foil this plot. Bracciano isn't going to be the end of me. God himself may bring me down, but it won't be the Orsini!"

"I know how the curse is supposed to work," I said. I put my head on his shoulder.

"Good." He pushed my long hair back from my face. "We will talk about that in the morning. You were nearly murdered, then spent your first night in a man's bed, then summoned a demon, then had your first lovers' quarrel. It's a lot for one night."

"I suppose it is." I tightened my hand on his shirt. "No more demons. I promise."

"You give your solemn word?" He lifted my chin so he could see my expression. "No calling or summoning demons, ever, anywhere?"

"Yes," I said. "I promise, Rodrigo."

"Then let's see if we can have a few hours of sleep before we begin it all," he said. He reached around me on the covers and found the clean long shirt of his that he had offered me hours ago. "Put this on and get into bed. There's no need for tears. I am not going to die and I will not shout at you."

"I know you have a temper," I said as I pulled it over my head. It was soft and smelled like him. "I do too."

"So I gathered from you throwing washing water on Orsino."

"You heard about that?" I said. Had everybody heard about that?

"Lucrezia."

"Of course." She heard everything and told everyone indiscriminately.

"Tuck your feet in and come lie next to me," he said. I curled up against him, face to face, warm and comfortable, his chin against my forehead. I felt entirely drained. And this was so warm. "I suppose I'll have to exorcise the room," he said contemplatively.

"Well, at least you won't have to send out for an exorcist," I said. "I understand they're expensive."

He laughed, his arms tight around me. "As a matter of economy, yes. Besides, it is a little difficult to explain why an exorcist is needed in a cardinal's dressing room!" He kissed the top of my head. "Ah, Giulia. Never a dull moment."

"I expect not," I said, and fell asleep listening to his heartbeat.

When I woke again it was to light streaming through the windows. There were sounds outside, as though servants were going about their business or people were in the sala. I lay on soft linen sheets in Rodrigo's bed, the bedcurtains not drawn but hanging loosely from the ceiling rods that suspended them around the bed. The fire had died out. From the quality of the light it was certainly mid-morning.

And there was Rodrigo's voice outside the door speaking to someone. Quite possibly he didn't want them to know I was there, so I shrunk down among the pillows so that I couldn't be seen from the door. It opened. Voices came in, then were muffled again as it closed. "Giulia?" Rodrigo couldn't see me either.

I sat up. "I'm here," I said. "What time is it?"

"Nearly noon," he said. He looked amused as he approached the bed, a bundle in his hands. "I trust you've slept well. I, on the other hand, have been up since dawn."

I winced. "Why?"

He sat down on the side of the bed. "Sweetness, I have work to do. There are things I do besides visit Lucrezia and debauch young ladies."

"I am so terribly sorry." He couldn't have slept more than two hours after the demon. "Perhaps you need a nap?"

Rodrigo started laughing. "There you are in my bed wearing nothing but my shirt, suggesting I need a nap? Should I say, *Cancel my appointments today, I have a new mistress and I need a nap and an exorcist*?"

He was laughing about it, so he wasn't angry anymore. I smiled back. "That would certainly set people talking."

"Well, let's not have them talking yet," he said. "There is Bracciano and your marriage to resolve first."

A thought hit me. "Oh no! Adriana! Lucrezia! They'll be frantic that I didn't come back last night. Adriana will imagine that something terrible has happened to me. And how am I going to get home? My clothes are probably ruined."

"Matters I have already taken care of," Rodrigo said. "When the guards went to relieve the night guards at Adriana's, I sent a note to her that you had been set upon but were safe with me. I also asked for her to find some dry clothes of yours and send them back with the guards." He held out the bundle, unfolding it to show my green cotta. "Dry, clean clothes."

"You are a marvel," I said.

"That's what Pope Innocent says," Rodrigo said. He looked quite self-satisfied. "So if you're awake, would you join me for the noon meal before you return to Adriana? We need to talk about Bracciano."

"Of course," I said. "Give me a moment to dress." I looked at him a little boldly. "Unless you'd like to watch?"

"In the interest of getting out of bed sometime today, sadly not," he said, getting up. He leaned over and kissed me on the top of my head to soften the refusal. "Come out when you're dressed." He ambled out into the sala, walking like the cock of the run.

Well, I thought, gathering up my clothes and going into the dressing room to wash, *so this is what it's like having a lover. I could get used to this.*

By the time I joined him in the sala a table had been laid for two and the servants were just leaving a tray of bread, fruit, cheese, and thin-sliced smoked ham. Rodrigo was not in full robes, just a black embroidered doublet over a fine linen shirt. It complimented his coloring to wear black like the Spaniard he was, and he handed me into my seat with a courtly gesture. The servants closed the door behind them.

I poured from the decanter on the table for both of us. "This is lovely," I said. Certainly the servants would talk, but perhaps he didn't mind that kind of gossip.

He raised a hand as if it were nothing, but he clearly looked pleased. If he sought to charm me, perhaps I should try to charm him too. If we were both charming to one another, things could be quite pleasant. And so I made myself as amiable as possible while we began the noon meal, fully aware that he was indeed taking time away from other things and it would be remarked upon.

At last, with a sigh, he put his glass down. "Bracciano," he said. I nodded. "Tell me what you saw."

I composed myself, hands in my lap. "I saw you and Lucrezia. It was night and you were walking with four guards and two torchbearers. It was a city street. There was what looked like a garden wall and a square tower at the end of it, and then a very strange staircase that went down like it was a tunnel going under a building. You and Lucrezia started down the steps and then...." I stopped, feeling the horror of the moment as I had not when the demon had shown me.

"And then?" he prompted.

"You fell," I said. "I heard the back of your head strike the stone step. You died." I did not add that I had heard Lucrezia's screams. I did not need to say it. It made it more real, and this was something that absolutely wasn't going to happen. "I don't know where it was, but there can't be very many places in Rome that fit the description."

"Fortunately, I know exactly where it is," Rodrigo said. "That's Vannozza's house, approaching it from one side and going down the old stairs that pass through. Of course I would go there and of course Lucrezia would be with me. I would be taking her to her mother's." He rested his chin on his hand. "The steps are very old—before the Caesars, actually. There was a famous murder there a thousand years ago and more. They're dark but in a public place. Someone could certainly asperge them or spill blood on them without being noticed."

"And they would be certain that sooner or later you would go there," I said.

"Sooner or later I must," he said. "I can't simply avoid the home where my children live."

Anyone who knew anything about him would know that. "We can't leave a curse against you active and working," I said.

"We?" Rodrigo's eyebrow rose.

"I am partially to blame for this," I said. "So I must make amends."

"Very well." He didn't attempt to dissuade me at all. "But you must also be careful. After last night, Bracciano knows that you are no longer his."

"He tried to kill me," I said.

"So he did. A loose end. But not, if you will pardon me, a terribly important one. If you accuse him, no one will believe you. And you are not a magus." Rodrigo toyed with a piece of bread. "Nor am I knowledgeable about such matters. I am a priest, not a Cabbalist."

"A what?"

"A Jewish scholar who has studied the map of the universe and might be of assistance. Nor do I know a Cabbalist currently in Rome. Rome is not welcoming to Jews at present. Were we in Valencia," he spread his hands, "I would know where to inquire."

"You know Jewish scholars?" The idea that a cardinal would know such seemed extraordinary.

"My dear, when I was a boy less than half of the people in Valencia were Christian. I knew many boys who were Jews, and Muslims too. Rome can be remarkably uncosmopolitan for a great city." He took a bite of the bread. "So a Cabbalist is unlikely. I imagine Pico della Mirandola could certainly undo what his student has done, but he is in Florence."

I put two pieces together. "What about Maestro Ficino?" I asked. "Surely he owes you a good turn for getting him acquitted of heresy?"

Rodrigo stopped, the bread in hand, smiling. "Aren't you fast? Ficino does owe me a good turn—as well as to the other cardinals who spoke to the pope on his behalf, but he too is in Florence. Also," he paused, picking up a bit of cheese, "Lorenzo the Magnificent's daughter is married to Bracciano's heir. Ficino is Lorenzo's man. He'd think twice about crossing Bracciano."

"I did not know that connection," I said, flushing. Had I sounded entirely ignorant?

"Of course not." He chewed with gusto. "How would you? You will learn the connections—who serves whom, who owes what, and who needs or desperately wants what another thinks little of. Politics is a web."

"And you are the spider at the center."

"I hope so. Consider rather that there are many spiders, and that small spiders are devoured by larger ones as surely as any unwitting insect that blunders into the web." He smiled. "You shall be my little spider."

That sounded intriguing. "And shall I poison your enemies?" I asked teasingly.

"I hope that will not be necessary." Rodrigo wasn't laughing. "I prefer other means of negotiating." He reached for another piece of bread. "So, my little spider, what do you imagine we should do next?"

"It seems to me," I said slowly, "that the best course of action would be to turn Dr. Treschi against Bracciano. He can surely tell us exactly what was done and how to undo it. He is certainly unhappy working for Bracciano, and I think he will be horrified that his master tried to kill me."

"You think? Enough to trust your life to it?"

"I think it is possible," I said slowly. "He said before that he might be willing to return to Florence if he had the money to do so. I suggested that he should consider you, but he was as frightened of you as of Bracciano. Now…." I shrugged.

"He may be more frightened of Bracciano than he was," Rodrigo said.

"Why was he so frightened of you?" I asked.

Rodrigo shook his head, though he smiled. "Giulia, don't make the mistake of thinking that because I am nice to you, I am a nice person."

"I have never seen you be anything other than generous and kind," I said stoutly.

"No," he said. "You have not. But just because a dog does not bite you does not mean it doesn't bite. Perhaps it just likes you."

"I would be very glad if you bit Bracciano," I said.

"I shall," Rodrigo said. "But not today. He is the gonfaloniere and the head of the Orsini family. I do not yet have the power to take him on. Today, I will cost him his Dove and his magus, a significant setback. But biting him will have to wait."

"Then I will talk to Dr. Treschi if he will talk," I said. "I will appeal to him and offer him money if he will desert Bracciano, enough money to return to Florence?"

He nodded. "That will do. The money's no object. Any amount he would consider reasonable is well enough. The important thing is that we undo this and he leaves. That is a condition of the money. He will return to Florence." He stopped. "Giulia, be careful. If you go to see him, take one of my guards with you. I will tell them to obey your requests."

"I will be careful," I promised. It was something to be deputized as his agent. "And I will not fail you."

"I know you won't," he said, and lifted his glass to me.

Chapter Sixteen

I arrived home at mid-afternoon. Lucrezia ran to me the moment I came through the vestibule. "Giulia! Donna Adriana said you were set upon by footpads. Are you well?"

"Very well," I said, hugging her tightly. "I escaped them in the streets because it was raining. When I had finally evaded them, I realized that I was near the vice-chancellor's palazzo. It seemed safer to ask your father for refuge than to try to get back here."

"And my father would protect you," Lucrezia said. "I am sure you were quite safe there. I was worried when you weren't here this morning but then my father's note came."

"Was Orsino worried?" I asked. Perversely, I wanted to know.

"I don't think so," she said. "He didn't say anything."

It was certainly good to know I could have been murdered and my husband wouldn't notice! For that matter, he didn't seem to care that I'd spent the night with Cardinal Borgia. He wasn't here at the gate remonstrating with me, was he?

"Well, I am perfectly fine," I said. I gave Lucrezia another squeeze. I would not let her scream as she had in my vision. I would make certain she didn't lose her father as I had lost mine.

"Giulia, I would like to speak with you." Adriana stood on the stairs, one hand to her breast, her voice cool.

"Certainly, Donna Adriana," I said.

"In my sala."

"Of course." I followed her up demurely.

She shut the doors of the sala and let me out onto the balcony where we could not be overheard, the city unfolded beneath us. "Giulia, has my cousin had you?"

I could answer honestly and truthfully, if not fully. "No, Donna Adriana." Some of the tension left her body. "He allowed me to stay in the vice-chancellor's palazzo, but he did not seek to fornicate with me. He was gallant and kind."

Adriana took a deep breath. "Giulia, there are things you must understand, things which are no doubt alien to life in Montalto. I know that you do not like My Lord Bracciano and that his summons are a burden to you. You do not wish to be his mistress. I understand that. But it will not last long. He will tire of you very soon. A few months, and then he will be done. You will have the rest of your life ahead of you."

"So I must tamely submit to him?" I asked. If he were using me thus, I would not simply put up with it until he grew bored! I would contrive at his downfall at every opportunity.

"It is the best course," Adriana said. "Should you conceive, the child would be an Orsini. Orsino would accept the fiction that his firstborn is his."

"And then he will have me, his cousin's leavings, when Bracciano is through?" The rage in my voice could not be contained. "He thinks then he will plow my field and we will go on as though nothing happened? I tell you, I will never bed Orsino. Not in twenty years! If he would not bed me for more than a year and would not demand that his cousin give up his wife, I will never make him happy. Never."

Adriana's brows rose, an expression rather like her cousin's. "Giulia, he cannot."

"He will not. How would Bracciano know if he slept with me? He is a coward. I will never give him anything. And he does not have the balls to take it." I was filled with fury now. "You will have no grandchildren. He will have no heir that is his. I will never yield to him, and if he should manage the courage to demand it, he will die. I will kill him before I yield to him, just as I killed that assassin." I put my hands flat on the sun-warmed railing of the balcony, trying to control my voice. "You have given him bad counsel, Donna Adriana. I married him hoping that he would be a good husband and that we would be happy together. But since he has proved himself a sniveling boy, he shall never have me."

"I see." She had gone pale at the mention of the assassin. "And so instead you hope for my cousin, Cardinal Borgia. Giulia, do you not understand you are a pawn in the game? The vice-chancellor and the gonfaloniere play with Rome as their chessboard. Rodrigo wants you because you are Bracciano's. He will tweak his enemy by stealing his mistress, but that is all it is. He will use you. Perhaps he will give you lavish presents for a few weeks, but he will not give you more. He will not stay with you or make you happy. It is not his way."

I said nothing. Had not Rodrigo said he was not as kind as I thought? How could I know if he told the truth? I had nothing but Lucrezia's word.

Adriana shook her head ruefully. "We are women. We are tossed here and there by powerful men. We do not choose. We are chosen. But if you play with my cousin, you will regret it. I have known him far longer than you have. He will use you against Bracciano and he will enjoy your youth and beauty. Then he will be gone. And what will you do then?" Her voice was sympathetic. "You are a pawn, Giulia. You cannot play games with the great."

I raised my chin. "Sometimes pawns become queens."

"You know as well as I how hard it is for a pawn to reach the crown row."

"I will reach it," I said. My hands were shaking. "Now if you will excuse me, Donna Adriana, I am quite fatigued."

"Of course," she said, and I fled to my room.

I threw myself on my bed. Perhaps I should have cried. The girl I had been a year ago would have. But if I was not yet Pluto's bride, I was at least no longer the girl who had descended to this underworld. I had eaten two of the three pomegranate seeds, I thought. I could still leave, but I was no longer innocent.

And did I want to leave? If a handsome young man showed up today, promising me a life I ought to find ideal, the lady of a rich country property with my children and my good husband and my people to rule over, would I want that? Or did I want this game, this dark and brutal game of assassins and black magic, of blood and sex? Did I truly think I could reach the crown row and transform into a queen? Rodrigo wanted to be pope. Popes have no queens. There was no Lady of the Vatican. Cardinals' concubines were seen and not heard, dirty little secrets that weren't so very secret. And that was if he succeeded. He might fail. Then I would have less than nothing. I would be disgraced and without a protector. I might be killed. My children might be killed, if I had any. Did I really think I could play this game and win?

I stared at the ceiling, dry-eyed. If I did not try, I knew what my life would be. Perhaps, if I were lucky, Bracciano would consider me beneath his notice and I would continue here, harnessed to Orsino unless I asked Rodrigo for an annulment. But even that was being of his faction, whether I technically lay with him or not. If last night had taught me anything, it was that Bracciano did not leave loose ends if he could help it. I needed Rodrigo's protection. I'd be a fool to turn that down, whether I loved and trusted him or not.

No, it came out the same either way. A pawn is defenseless until it reaches the crown row, constrained in its movement, capable of taking a major piece only if it is ignored to the player's regret. If I did not move forward, I would be taken sooner or later. Therefore, it only made good sense to defend the king until I could say, *Make me a queen.*

There was a knock on the door, followed by Maria's voice. "Donna Giulia? There is a man here who says he needs to see you." I got up, patting my hair back into place. Who could it be? Surely not Dr. Treschi seeking me out. Probably a messenger from Rodrigo about some part of this. I came downstairs hurriedly.

A young man was standing with his back to me, a sword at his side, a sharply cut doublet of good blue cloth with yellow laces on the sleeves, dark hair trimmed shorter than the fashion. For a moment I had no idea who he was, and then he turned. "Alessandro!" I shouted, flinging myself into his arms.

He caught me and swung me around. "Giulia! You're looking well."

"Alessandro, you have no idea how glad I am to see you," I said, kissing his cheek and holding him tight. "I have missed you so much."

"I'm glad to see you, Sorellina," he said. His smile said as much. There was a step behind me, and he looked over my shoulder. "And there is my good brother, Orsino! How are you?"

I turned. Orsino was looking daggers at me. "Have you come to take her home?"

Alessandro frowned, looking from Orsino to me and back again. "Should I?" he asked.

"Did she ask you to?" Orsino asked.

"Not yet," Alessandro said. His smile had evaporated. "Should she?"

"That depends on whether she's told you she's a whore yet."

Alessandro loosened his sword in the scabbard, all good humor fled. "If you call my sister a whore, you will answer for it."

"Alessandro, no," I said.

Orsino looked at Alessandro, tense and ready, his hand on his hilt. "I misspoke," he said, and turned and walked away.

Alessandro looked down at me. "Sorellina, what in the name of Heaven is going on?"

"Take me somewhere other than here," I said. "I know a taverna. We need to talk."

"As you like," he said, and gave me his arm.

We went out the back door and down the street to the taverna that the cardinal's guards frequented. It was clean and well-kept, with a good board. We asked for bread and cheese to go with our wine since it was only the middle of the afternoon and found a quiet table with no one near. Anyone who saw us would think us a young bravo and his girl, sitting knee to knee with the plate between us.

When the serving girl had gone, Alessandro leaned forward, his voice low. "Giulia, what happened? Your letters didn't mention Orsino often but I didn't think it was this bad."

"I am still a virgin," I said flatly. "Orsino won't consummate the marriage. Not that I want him to at this point. I am done with him. I told him months ago that I would not wait on his courage much longer, and I am finished."

Alessandro looked at me keenly, his eyes so much like my own in the mirror. "Is there someone else?"

I glanced away. "Yes. It's complicated."

"Then begin at the beginning," he said.

"First, I want to know why you're here," I said. "I have wanted to see you so much! I wanted to talk to you and I didn't dare trust any of this to a letter. You being here—it's just what I needed." I squeezed his hand across the table. "I thought you were in Pisa waiting to be assigned to a parish somewhere."

"I was assigned to a clerkship at the Vatican," Alessandro said. "It's crazy. They're very competitive. You need serious influence to get one. I have no idea how I got it. I was called in and told I'd been given the clerkship and to get on the road to Rome! I stopped at home on the way for a few days to see Mother and the little ones, but I thought I'd surprise you. And maybe stay with you, since I don't have lodgings in Rome, but it seems like that's awkward." He stopped, reading something in my face. "Giulia, did you have something to do with this?"

"I had no idea he was going to do this," I said. I'd said weeks ago that I missed Alessandro above all else, and that it would make me happy to see him, the time I'd gone to Rodrigo in the Vatican to confess that I was Bracciano's Dove. He must have put through a clerkship for Alessandro immediately and not even told me.

"He who?" Alessandro asked.

I took a deep breath. "Cardinal Borgia."

"The vice-chancellor," Alessandro said flatly.

"Yes." That's certainly who he was.

Alessandro dropped his voice. "Giulia, are you sleeping with a cardinal?"

"Not precisely," I said.

"Not precisely?"

"I told you I am still a virgin. We have not technically lain together." I pursed my lips, waiting for whatever he said.

"And a handshake isn't sodomy," Alessandro said. "A fine parsing of canon law, Sorellina."

"What do you mean, a handshake isn't sodomy?" I demanded. "Alessandro, I thought you'd given that up!"

"Technically," Alessandro grinned, "oh, technically virgin sister!"

I shook my head. "You are so much trouble."

"Says the woman who's shaking hands with a cardinal!"

I felt myself blushing. I suppose what I had done for him last night was what Alessandro meant that he liked a friend to do with him. "It is fun, isn't it?" I said, tossing my head.

My brother doubled over laughing, nearly spitting his wine everywhere. "We're too much alike," he said. "I've missed you, Giulia!"

"And I you," I said. "Alessandro, you have no idea how much I need you now."

"I'm here," he said simply.

I nearly started crying. "And you have a clerkship at the Vatican, so you're staying."

"Unless your cardinal throws me out."

Which of course gave me another good reason to be of Rodrigo's faction. Now my brother owed Rodrigo his job. On the other hand, Alessandro would love being a clerk at the Vatican, and I had my doubts about how he'd like some rural parish somewhere, not my brilliant Alessandro who wanted ideas and excitement as much as I did. "Let me tell you from the beginning," I said. "It's a long story."

We sat there for hours. Sunset came and the Vespers bells of St. Peter's. Adriana would be worried. *Let her worry*, I thought. *Let her worry that my brother is taking me home and my lover is procuring an annulment that would embarrass Orsino and incense Bracciano. "We are leaves in the stream" is a lovely excuse for doing nothing!*

"And so I have chosen," I said to Alessandro. "I will be Cardinal Borgia's concubine. Perhaps he will play me false. I don't know. But I know that this is my chance to play, and if I leave the table, it will never come again."

"And you love him," Alessandro said, leaning back in his chair. "Can't fool me, Sorellina. I know that look."

"Well, yes," I said. "But it's also advantageous."

"Very sophisticated," he said. "But you're blushing. Is he that good?"

I looked up from under my eyelashes. "You have no idea. And you're not about to find out!"

Alessandro laughed. "More's the pity, apparently." He sobered. "As long as you're happy and he treats you well, you know I'm with you."

"He does," I said simply. It was so good to have someone to confide in. Perhaps Alessandro could even understand. "Even if

Orsino wasn't useless as a husband, we wouldn't have suited. He has no interest in learning or the arts or anything, and I do mean anything. He doesn't want to learn and he doesn't want to work and as far as I know he doesn't do anything except sometimes go to horse races! I would never be happy with him. If he'd consummated the marriage last year, I'd be looking for a lover by now. Rodrigo...." I stopped. I didn't even know how to describe him. "He's what I want," I said. It was inadequate but true. "I'm not going to stand around helplessly. I'm going to get what I want."

"Spoken like a condottiero," Alessandro said. "You sound like Father."

"Do I?"

"I mean that in the best possible way," he said. "And yes, I still miss him too." He looked away, and it occurred to me that it must have been hard for him at seventeen to be the man of the family. He'd had to leave the university and come home to take care of us all, with Mother sick and me the only help for him, and I wasn't but turning fourteen then. We'd managed, Alessandro and I. And when we could do without him, he'd gone back to school. If I could help his career in any way, I would. I wasn't the least bit sorry Rodrigo had gotten him a competitive clerkship. To rise in the Church, Alessandro needed a patron, and Cardinal Borgia was a good one. Alessandro sighed. "You've got a mess and no mistake. Well, what do you need me to do?"

I took his hands across the table. How wonderful it was to have someone who was absolutely on my side! "We need to find Dr. Treschi," I said. "If you can help me with that, I would appreciate it. It will be safer to go to him with you. Also you have more education." It galled me to say it, but of course it was true. "I have no Greek, and I know that's needed for some of his Hermetic operations."

He nodded seriously. "I've never done this kind of thing, but I have good Greek. And I have read the *900 Theses* by Pico della Mirandola."

"Really? After they were condemned as heresy?"

"Only parts of them." Alessandro smiled. "Besides, isn't forbidden knowledge more tempting? I'll wager your cardinal has read them."

"Possibly," I said. *Probably*, I thought. Rodrigo seemed to know quite a lot about things that were on the edge of heresy, ideas that wasn't exactly embraced by the traditionalists in the Church. It was one of the things that intrigued me about him.

Alessandro was watching me, an inscrutable expression on his face. "You've grown up, Sorellina."

"I hope so," I said. "I've wanted to."

He nodded. "Then let us find this Dr. Treschi."

Compline had not yet rung when we arrived at Dr. Treschi's rooms. Not a light showed, though the stars had appeared in the sky. The moon was a rising sliver just a day past the dark.

"Maybe he's not here," Alessandro said.

Maybe he's dead, I thought, but didn't voice that aloud. Who was to say if he'd been allowed to return peacefully home last night? I certainly hadn't been. I knocked again. "Dionisio?" I said quietly. "It's Giulia." There was no sound. I looked at Alessandro and he looked at me. "Dionisio?" I said again.

There was the sound of the bolt drawing back and Dr. Treschi looked out through the crack. He nearly shut the door again when he saw Alessandro. "This is my brother," I said. "We're here to help."

"Then come in." He pulled the door open, motioning us in quickly, then closing it and bolting it behind. He stared at me. "I'm surprised you're alive."

"No thanks to you," I said. "You could have warned me."

"I was trying to," he said.

"You could have been more plain," I said. "I was nearly killed." I shook my head. "But I wasn't. So did he try to kill you too?"

"Not yet." Dr. Treschi looked drawn and grim.

"But you expect it," Alessandro said. "Alessandro Farnese, late of the university at Pisa."

"Dionisio Treschi," he replied. "Of Florence. You are Giulia's brother?"

"Yes, and recently ordained a priest," Alessandro said. "So maybe I can help with your problem."

"My problem is temporal rather than spiritual," Treschi said with a hollow laugh.

I felt we were rather missing the point. "What happened after I left? What did they do?"

He drew himself up. "They…we…did a rite to kill Cardinal Borgia."

Alessandro crossed himself. "That is evil, but you may yet be forgiven if you help undo what you have done."

"I would with a very great will," Dr. Treschi said. "But…."

"But you are in fear for your life," I finished.

He shook his head. "I am already a dead man. I would do it, but I cannot."

"What do you lack?" I said. "If this rite can be undone, what do we need to do?"

"It's too late," he said. "The trap has been laid."

"Dionisio, pull yourself together! Just because Bracciano means to kill you does not mean he will succeed! I am not dead. Cardinal Borgia himself will give you money to leave Rome and return to Florence in safety if you undo this."

He looked at me with surprise. "You speak for him?"

"He has made me his agent in this matter," I said. "And I have played Bracciano false from the beginning. My allegiance was never his."

"You've been working for the cardinal all along." He sounded almost admiring.

"Yes," I said. "It was I that killed the assassin sent to kill him while he slept. I deceived Bracciano about how the spell worked. Now how shall we save my patron from this plot?"

Alessandro had already heard that part and didn't even flinch this time. He'd already said that our father would be proud. "If it requires more than one man, I have good Latin and Greek and some familiarity with della Mirandola's teachings."

Treschi took a deep breath. "Then we might have a chance."

"So what did you do and what does it take to undo it?" I asked. "That poor pup..." I couldn't quite complete the sentence.

"...was bled into a chalice," he said. "We created an inauspicious Square of Solomon for the downfall of the great and a sigil with the name Rodrigo Borgia. They were burned, some of the ash going into the chalice and some into wax to make a wax sigil. We called upon the demon to empower them. Then we closed the operation." He shivered. "Then I went with several of My Lord Bracciano's men to put it where it belonged—to asperge the steps and put the wax sigil there in some inconspicuous place."

Alessandro looked alarmed. "You made a blood sacrifice? Of a dog?"

Alessandro had a soft heart and loved dogs, and I did not want him so incensed with Dr. Treschi that they could not work together. "How do we undo it?" I asked quickly. "That's the thing we must concentrate on."

"I'm not precisely..."

"What about holy water?" Alessandro said. "If you've asperged something with blood to taint it, asperge it with holy water to cleanse it. That's basic."

"I don't have any holy water," Dr. Treschi said.

Alessandro looked at him incredulously. "I'm a priest. Give me some water!"

"I do have blessed salt," Treschi said.

"Good. Then we're halfway there," Alessandro said. "Water. Salt. What else do we need, Giulia?"

Obviously, Dr. Treschi was too frightened to think clearly. "If you made this wax sigil, can't it be broken or melted?"

"There needs to be a counter-sigil," he said. "With the Square of Jupiter in an auspicious formula and the name of Rodrigo Borgia."

"So we make this, putting some of the ash into the holy water, take it to the place, and Alessandro asperges it?" I said. "What about the demon?" I had promised Rodrigo I'd have nothing more to do with demons.

"We call the angel in relentless opposition to the demon," Dr. Treschi said. "That is the Archangel Raphael. I can write out the invocation." He looked at me apologetically. "The Dove will have to deliver the invocation. Unless Father Alessandro is a virgin?"

Alessandro smiled. "I'm afraid not. And it's too much to hope that you are?"

"Fine," I said. I hardly felt pure enough for calling angels, but I had promised Rodrigo no demons, not no spirits of any kind. It seemed doubtful that an angel would listen to a prayer for the safety of my clerical lover, but perhaps my virtue would matter little in removing such evil. "Then write it out and let's do this without delay." I handed him paper from his table. "Dr. Treschi, do you have water?"

"In the pitcher there," he said, motioning to the wash basin.

"That will do," Alessandro said. "It's not what kind of water. It's the words. Give me the salt."

"Do you need a light?" I asked. There was only very dim light coming through the window.

My brother gave me a narrow smile. "Blessing water for the font is something we're literally supposed to be able to do in the dark. Just put the pitcher there and be still."

Alessandro was newly ordained. I'd never seen him in his priestly office. Now he closed his eyes, bringing his hands together in prayer. "*Exorciso te, creatura aquae, in nomine Dei Patris omnipotentis, et in nomine Jesu Christi filii ejus Domini nostri....*" I closed mine as well. His voice was direct, clear, and I felt a frisson down my back. Whatever it was that made one a true priest, Alessandro was one. What would it be like, I wondered, to experience that? I would have to ask him, or Rodrigo. He went on, and I could mentally translate at least some of it. "...may everything this water sprinkles be delivered from all that is unclean and hurtful..." What would it be like to know the union a true priest was supposed to feel? A woman could never experience it. After all, we were not made in the likeness of God. And yet once we had been thought so, had we not? In the ancient tomb near Montalto, Proserpina and Pluto sat side by side, receiving reverence together, ruling the Underworld together.

Dr. Treschi shifted from foot to foot and I opened my eyes, glancing around. Alessandro was no doubt audible if one listened at the door, but surely no further.

Now he raised the dish of salt, pouring it into the washing pitcher, his hand making the sign of the cross. "*Deus invictus, trementes supplicesque deprecamur, ac petimus....*" His back was straight, and there was nothing hesitant in his motions. He finished the prayer, putting the pitcher before him on the table, then smiled at me. "That's done," he said.

"You are lovely," I said.

Alessandro had an expression of sheer delight. "I wish I could show you what it's like, Sorellina."

"So do I," I said.

Dr. Treschi seemed to have calmed down. Perhaps Alessandro's prayers had soothed him. "I will write out the invocation and then we make the sigil," he said. He got a reed pen and ink, paper and the end of a candle.

He tried to hand a pen to Alessandro. "Her penmanship is better," Alessandro said, and I sat down on the stool, dipping the tip.

"Make a square of the letters," Dr. Treschi said. "Three down and four across, that reads Rodrigo Borgia."

"There are thirteen letters in Rodrigo Borgia," I said.

"Are you sure?" he asked.

"Count them," I said.

"How do we do this?" Dr. Treschi passed a hand over his eyes.

"I'll put the d and r in the same square," I said. "It's one sound. Also four by three is not a square. It's a rectangle. You need sixteen letters to make a square."

"Well he can't have more letters in his name," Alessandro said. "Giulia, you can't just give him three more!"

I looked at it. "Three by three," I said. "There are letters repeated."

"What?" Treschi said.

"Give me a moment." I could see how to do it neatly. ROD across, then down to the R beneath, then over to the I, up to the G, down to the O, and so on.... "Thus," I said, showing them the square. "Do you see?"

R O D

B G R

O I A

Dr. Treschi looked dumbstruck. "That's brilliant. It's on a Square of Saturn rather than Jupiter, but perhaps better for protective functions this way."

"Another thing women cannot study?" I asked tartly. "Why don't you write the invocation while I ink this neatly?"

He wrote out the invocation and handed it to me. I glanced at it; it was not long, but difficult to read in the dim light. I folded it and put it in my bosom. Then Dr. Treschi molded the wax with his hands into a small ball, kneading and rolling it, while I inked the square neatly. "There may be some life in the coals," he said. I went to the fire and rummaged about with a splinter until I could light it, the sudden flare illuminating the dark room. It must have gotten late. I hadn't heard Compline, but surely we were well past its hour.

"Now burn the paper," he instructed. "Let some of the ash fall in the water and give me some to incorporate into the wax."

I did so, holding the paper carefully by the corner as it burned. Alessandro held the pitcher beneath it, catching a falling bit of paper that was extinguished by the water. Suddenly, his head jerked around. I was about to ask him what, but he put his finger to his lips.

Dr. Treschi froze as well, and I listened. There was a faint creak, as though someone were trying to climb the steps quietly. I leaned against Dr. Treschi, so close to his ear that Alessandro couldn't have overheard. "Is there another way out?"

He nodded. I reached out and touched Alessandro's hand. He nodded, glancing at the pitcher. He would need his hands free for his sword. Dr. Treschi had a dagger. I had a pitcher of water that I shouldn't spill.

"Show her," Alessandro mouthed at Treschi.

He went across the room and opened a door that led down a steep stair, triangular treads going down in a dark space that smelled of urine. The way to the privy, no doubt, and probably one shared by all who lived in the building. Treschi went first, I followed, and Alessandro brought up the rear. When he closed the door it was utterly black on the stair. Still, the door to the exterior stairs was barred. They'd either have to break it or force the shutters on the window. Or try to raise the bar through the crack quietly if they hoped to catch Dr. Treschi sleeping. We had a few minutes.

I stumbled and nearly fell forward onto Dr. Treschi. The water sloshed. I stopped my fall against his shoulder and he grunted. Alessandro nearly ran into me from behind.

"This is the downstairs..." he whispered. I presumed there was a door in the side wall, but I couldn't see it. We went on a few more steps, my hand on Dr. Treschi's shoulder. He stopped again. I heard a faint sound, and then an outside door opened a crack. Dark as it was, it seemed like blinding light after the stair. There was the privy to the side, unmistakable from the smell. And there was the little yard behind the building, the smell of a chicken coop competing with the privy. Dr. Treschi looked out cautiously. We should be ninety degrees around the building from the stair. But if they'd left someone to watch the corner....

Dr. Treschi slipped out, and I followed, Alessandro behind me. We cut across the yard along the edge of the house, trying to put it between us and them. Unfortunately, there was a shed. You couldn't get into the street from this side. We huddled together in the shadow of the shed. "What now?" Alessandro whispered.

"Back," Treschi said. "Toward the alley behind." The way I had come...was it only last night? I nodded.

We had almost reached the shelter of the next building when I heard a shout behind. "There!" a man yelled.

Alessandro glanced back, sizing up the wall of the next building. "Get behind me!" he said, "Stay between me and the wall, Giulia!" I did so, pitcher in both hands, as Alessandro drew his sword, Dr. Treschi next to me.

There were two men, Orsini guards most likely, though they'd taken off their livery and wore plain clothing. Well, assassins wouldn't need steel or leather to kill an unarmed man sleeping, and it was best if they looked like unremarkable thieves, wasn't it? They each held a dagger.

Alessandro stayed close in front of us, not going to meet them, in a high guard exactly as our father had taught him. I remembered how much my father had enjoyed sparring with him, circling each other in our courtyard at Montalto, my father old and Alessandro young, a thin stripling with long arms. This was the son destined for the cloth. He would have no need for the sword, surely. Had he kept up practice at the university? It seemed I was about to find out.

The first man checked. They had expected one person, a scholar. Now there were three and one a young man who held a sword like he knew his business.

"Get off with you!" Alessandro shouted. "I'll have no footpads here!" *Clever*, I thought. These men had been sent to kill Treschi. If they thought they had attacked some other people accidentally nearby, they ought to withdraw.

Unfortunately, one of them recognized him. "There's the man!" he said, circling around Alessandro's left.

The one in front made a move, and Alessandro parried knife with sword, the momentum of the heavy blade knocking the man back. Alessandro followed through, turning the parry into a slash to the left, the tip grazing the upper arm of the circling man. He yelled, backing away.

"Come on," the first one answered. "We need more." They backed off a few steps, one of them holding his bleeding shoulder, and then pelted off up the street. Alessandro waited in guard until they were out of sight.

"That was fantastic," Dr. Treschi said. "I mean really good. A fencing priest!"

"I'm glad you haven't forgotten everything Papa taught you," I said, more calmly than I felt.

"'Thank you, dear brother' is customary," Alessandro said, sheathing his blade. He looked at Treschi. "So how far is this and how are we getting there?"

"It's south and east," Dr. Treschi said. "Near the Quirinal Hill. It's half an hour's walk or so."

I looked at Alessandro and he looked at me. "Halfway across the city," I said flatly. Which meant there was plenty of time for them to get reinforcements and go there. Bracciano would guess where we were going if he knew Treschi had turned.

Alessandro shook his head. "Let's start walking," he said.

Chapter Seventeen

We weren't too far from the Basilica di Santa Maria in Ara Coeli on its hill, the steps leading up from the street to the church and the streets above. Dr. Treschi seemed to know where we were going. I had not been in this part of the city often, and never by night. If there was ever a time to regret how little I had gone about, this was it! If he led us wrong, I would not know. Nor would Alessandro, who had been in Rome precisely once.

Clearly Alessandro wondered the same thing as we hustled along the streets. "How far do they have to go for reinforcements?"

I could at least answer that. "The Duke of Bracciano lives at the Palazzo Orsini de Campo. It's not ten minutes from where we were."

Alessandro shook his head. "So they're close behind us."

"Probably," I said grimly. He didn't ask how many men Bracciano had. The answer was obviously as many as he needed. He was the gonfaloniere. I looked up the steps at the silent basilica. "Dionisio, what if we go up? Is there a way down on the other side? Can we cut time off by going over rather than around?"

"Yes, there are steps down the other side," he replied. "But they go down into the ruins of the old forum. It's a den of thieves at night. That's not a safe way to go."

"It is also not safe to be caught by a dozen of Bracciano's guards," I said. "Alessandro?"

He glanced back the way we'd come. "Better the theoretical foe than the manifest one," he said. "I was lucky there were two and they only had knives. I can't take on an army."

"Then we go up," I said, and started up the steep steps, the other two following swiftly.

We skirted around the closed church. Behind us, the lights of the city were bright— houses and workshops and tavernas and buildings. It was not terribly late. On the other side a dark gap loomed like a pit. Here and there a wall gleamed, white marble in the starlight. Broken columns jutted from the ground. Another flight of steps went down.

"The Gemonian Stairs," Dr. Treschi said in a curiously hushed voice. "The old Romans used to execute people here and leave their bodies to rot on the steps."

There was certainly a terrible feeling about it. Going down in darkness toward the forum, I could feel it like a miasma. There are no ghosts. Souls do not linger in the world, but go to Heaven or Hell or Purgatory as is suitable. And yet the steps were haunted. They were so sunk in misery that going down them felt impure. I slowed my tread. My feet wanted to trip. The stairs wanted to send me tumbling hurt and bruised amid the broken shards of the pitcher of holy water.

"What is this place?" Alessandro said quietly.

"Don't linger," I said, putting my hand on his arm. I could feel them pressing near, the spirits of this place. *It should be better in the Forum*, I thought. *Surely*. "Come, Alessandro."

We went down the steps together. The shadows played tricks. My brother stumbled once and I steadied him. "Sorry," he said. "I thought I saw something rolling. Did you?"

"Yes," I said. "Now come." It had been a girl's body, eleven or twelve, her throat cut, her eyes wide. Only of course there was nothing there. She had lived and died nearly fifteen hundred years ago, the daughter of Sejanus, killed for her father's ambition. *If you want me to remember your name*, I said in my heart, *I will find it. I am certain it is in Tacitus. I will find it. I will remember you. I will bring flowers for you here when we are done.*

At that the pressure eased somewhat, as if her shade kept the others at bay. Or perhaps all they wanted was recognition. We reached the bottom. Ahead the forum was a forest of columns, pale stumps in the starlight, larger walls and buildings further along. We started across as though we were in a dream. If a strange mist had risen from the ground, it would have been no more confusing.

"How far is it?" Alessandro asked, his voice oddly hushed.

"Not far," Dr. Treschi said.

And yet it seemed that we walked and walked. Were we going the wrong way, following the forum the long way instead of cutting across? Surely we should be on the other side by now. It wasn't far! And yet there were more mazes of broken stones. This couldn't be right.

"I think it's this way," Alessandro said as yet another wall blocked our path. "Around the end."

"No, it's this way," Dr. Treschi said.

"That's west," Alessandro said. "Back the way we came."

I stopped. The Forum wasn't that big! I should be able to see the Curia. It was famously intact. This wasn't right. Which way had we come? It was a dark night, but I should be able to see the Curia from anywhere in the Forum.

"It isn't," Treschi said.

Look with the eyes of your heart, something whispered inside me. *You do not need mirrors. Your soul is the mirror.*

I closed my eyes, trying to ignore Alessandro and Treschi arguing in furious whispers. They were trying to fight the strangeness, to block it. And yet the more they did, the more confusing it became. I took a breath. *Show me*, I thought. *Show me, oh heart.*

I opened my eyes. Ahead of me a row of columns reared along a flight of steps, and as though time flowed backwards, the tumbled columns healed, walls returning to the vertical, façade and carvings shining. A bronze statue appeared on a plinth that grew like a tree, Nike spreading her wings, her face raised to the skies triumphantly. "That is the Temple of Peace," I said. "We must go across its front and then past the ruined tower." Neither of them asked me how I knew. Perhaps they assumed I had been this way before. "Come, gentlemen," I said.

I walked half in the past. While it did not remain as clear as it had in that first moment, I could see the shapes of the buildings as they had been. I could see where tumbled stones obscured a clear path. This was a major street. It led north. It was as clear to me as anything seen by daylight. We walked from the Temple of Peace toward the Forum of Nerva, broken stones revealing themselves to be instead graceful colonnades. Steps no longer led nowhere, but to temples of gleaming marble, their façades decorated with bright colors, statues lifelike and beautiful.

Beyond, there was the ruined tower, not ancient but abandoned a century ago, stones tumbled and thrown down by an earthquake, jutting out of the darkness like a watcher on the edge of the strangeness.

"It can't be far." Dr. Treschi was breathing hard.

"It isn't," I replied.

"Just follow Giulia," my brother said. I don't know what he thought I was doing, but he trusted it. He trusted me.

The pitcher held to my chest, we crossed in front of the ruined tower, empty windows looking down on us. Beyond was the city. I nearly fell with relief. Lights showed at windows. The street ambled between older houses, ground floor shops closed. The strangeness was gone. There was only now.

Alessandro took a deep breath. He caught my eye. I shook my head. We would talk about it later. What I had seen, what he had seen—those were mysteries.

"Where are we?" I asked Dr. Treschi. "How close are we to

the stairs?"

He looked more composed. "Not far," he said. "Maybe three blocks on this street and then right."

We hurried along. The night was cool but not chill. Occasionally voices floated down, people talking in rooms above, their windows open to the pleasant summer evening. A thought occurred to me. "Tomorrow is midsummer eve, isn't it?"

"Yes," Alessandro said. "Why?"

"No reason," I said. I thought my grandmother had said once that spirits walked on midsummer eve, but that was not until tomorrow.

"This corner," Dr. Treschi said.

We cut down a street between two handsome buildings—palazzos, most likely, though this part of the city was not as fashionable as the quarter nearer the Vatican—with doors shut and barred against the night. A lamp burned beside one door. There was a little square a block on, windows overlooking it, including one with a pretty balcony. Two stories below the balcony the street turned, steps leading up and going through the building to emerge in a different street beyond, as though it were a tunnel. It was paved with square ancient pavers, and near the top of the steps a single lamp hung from an iron hook. The steps were dark. Their mottled surface revealed nothing.

"They could have been asperged with blood and how would we know?" I murmured.

"They were," Dr. Treschi said. "And last night, like tonight, nobody was around." It was getting quite late.

Alessandro shook his head. "Let's do this. We may not have much time."

Dr. Treschi pulled the wax sigil out of his shirt. "So first I'll put the sigil with the other one, the one it's supposed to counteract." He went to the side of the step, sliding it into a crack between the pavers and the wall.

We went up onto the steps. Once we were in this tunnel itself, we could not be seen from the windows or balcony above. "There's a side door here at the top of the steps," I said.

"It's probably a kitchen entrance to the building above," Dr. Treschi said. "Last night nobody paid any attention and there were more of us then."

"Get on with it!" Alessandro said testily. "We don't have all night! Bracciano's men will be back."

Dr. Treschi spread his arms and began his invocation in Greek, his tone low but echoing sibilantly off the stone walls. I shivered, holding the pitcher tight against my breasts. It seemed like the invocation went on and on. I supposed he was doing with words what he usually did with chalk, but chalk would not stay on these stairs where people walked and would hardly be inconspicuous. I wished I understood the words. Perhaps now I could learn. Surely Rodrigo would pay for a tutor to teach me Greek. Dr. Treschi slowly ascended the stairs past me, going up to the top. There wasn't a circle to walk as he had at Bracciano's palazzo, but presumably he could walk back and forth. I felt what he was doing like pressure in my ears, like the feel of an impending storm.

There was the sound of footsteps in the street below, the way we had come. Alessandro brushed past me, coming to stand five steps from the bottom, drawing his sword. "Stay behind me, Giulia."

"Yes," I said. I backed up two more steps. Where he stood, they'd have to come up the stairs at him while he held the commanding ground. I just needed to be sure I was beyond his reach because slashes were impossible to stop or change direction, heavy as his sword was. Dr. Treschi stood above me, still chanting.

They came around the corner, checking as they saw him. Four men this time, guardsmen in plain clothes, but with swords rather than knives.

"Get him then," one said, and two of the men began to advance on Alessandro. No more than two could approach at once, thankfully. He remained on guard. Our father always said to stay cool. Hot-headed men lose. Alessandro looked calm. He simply waited.

The first one attacked, trying to come in with a slashing blow left to right. Alessandro stepped back up the stairs. It did not connect, the man now off-balance, the momentum of his blow leading him down. Alessandro slashed downward, hitting the man hard in the back of the left shoulder, driving him to his knees, blood spreading over his sleeve. He kicked his sword free, boot connecting where he had just cut, the man tumbling down five steps with a scream. Alessandro returned to guard.

Dr. Treschi had stopped, watching rather than chanting. "Go on!" I shouted. "He's buying you time!" He took up his invocation again.

This time two men rushed Alessandro at once. He gave ground again, backing up the steps to only one before me, the steps narrowing as they went up. The tight quarters gave them less room to move. He caught a blow on his sword and they locked, face to face a foot apart, straining to push the other aside. The third man tried to come in from the side. Alessandro couldn't respond. I could see the strike he meant to make, a long slashing blow against my brother's unprotected side.

I hit him on the head with the pitcher. It was good solid clay and he hadn't been expecting it. He stumbled sideways, falling to one knee clasping his head, his sword on the ground. The pitcher slipped out of my hands, shattering against the stones in a rain of shards, holy water spattering over the stones. The man measured his length on the stairs, rolling backwards to lie face up, shaking his head to try to clear it. I grabbed his sword and threw it behind me, up the stairs and out of reach.

"That's one way to asperge," Alessandro said, his mouth twisting into a grim smile. We were side by side. "Now get back, Giulia. I need room."

I scrambled up a few steps. He returned to guard, waiting. Had I messed it up by breaking the pitcher? I wasn't far from the top of the stairs. The cranny where the sigil was hidden was below me on the wet steps.

The remaining two men with swords began to advance again. The one I had kicked got to his feet. "Giulia! The invocation! Now!" Dr. Treschi shouted.

I pulled out the paper I had stuck in my bodice. I could just see well enough in the flickering light of the dim lamp to read it. "Raphael, Most Holy Archangel," I began. "Angel of Light, Bright Star of Morning, thou art the implacable foe of Asmodeus." I had no idea if it would work or not, but there was no time to think, no time to consider.

They advanced. They were trying to force Alessandro back, or to make a move against one of them. If he did, the other could then close. Alessandro gave ground another step, declining to move against either. He couldn't keep that up. One would move and he'd have to respond. Then the other would come in.

"Most Holy Archangel, cleanse this place of befoulment…"

There was the sound of feet behind them. For a moment I prayed that some friendly passers-by had arrived, but then I saw the person I wanted least to see. It was Rodrigo and several of his guards, still in his full red vestments as he had been in the vision, in the one single place in Rome he should not be, a torchbearer leading.

One of the assailants turned, seeing him. The man had sword in hand. Rodrigo was one step from the bottom stair, armed with nothing but his furious expression. I saw the man turn from Alessandro. The guards were behind Rodrigo.

"…remove all ill-intention from it and purify it with your light! Come, Most Holy Raphael!" I shouted.

Three things happened at once. Alessandro slashed with his sword at the man who had half-turned, forcing the other assailant to parry low. The man who had turned to Rodrigo lifted his sword. And Rodrigo stepped onto the lowest stair, the torchbearer a step behind. The pavement sizzled where he stepped, blood and holy water and a shadow rising beneath his foot.

"*Veni*!" I shouted, raising my hands to the flickering torch, every bit of desperate will behind it. For a moment it seemed all stood still—the swordsman, Rodrigo, and a dark shape like a great black dog rising from the pavement.

And then there was something between. Flame. Wind. A sudden, breathless silence as though at the center of a mighty gust, red and gold and pure white light. It pierced, the dark shadow failing, so bright that I squeezed my eyes shut for a moment.

There was a shout. I opened them. The swordsman staggered back, his blow uncompleted, straight into the cardinal's guards. Alessandro pushed forward, using his shoulder to shove the man who had overbalanced. The torchbearer stepped in front of Rodrigo, sweeping out with the brand, clearing a path. I felt dizzy suddenly and put a hand to steady myself against the wall. It was as though lightning had passed through. I blinked like an owl by day.

A sharp melee was taking place at the foot of the stairs, the Orsini guards suddenly up against Rodrigo's. Alessandro stood in front of me, his chest heaving. Rodrigo took the steps up to him, quick as a cat on the slippery stones. "Who are you?" he demanded.

"Alessandro Farnese, at Your Eminence's service," Alessandro said with a sharp bow. "You may not recall, but we met at my sister's wedding."

"Giulia..." He looked around at me and I came to his side.

"I am well," I said. I realized I looked a bit disheveled. "No harm has come to me."

"Our new clerk," Rodrigo said. He glanced at me. "I see it runs in the family." I took his arm, feeling my heart still pounding, though the speckles of light before my eyes had stopped.

At the bottom of the stairs, the Orsini were in retreat, two run off into the night, including the one I had disarmed. One lay bleeding on the stones, while the fourth man lay still in the shadows.

"Don't pursue them," Rodrigo called. "Let them go."

Dr. Treschi came down the steps. "Dr. Dionisio Treschi, Your Eminence. May I say that I...."

"Yes, yes," Rodrigo said.

"What are you doing here?" I demanded. "This is the one, single place in the entire city where you shouldn't be! You know this is where the trap was. Why are you here?"

"Lucrezia came to my house having sneaked out of Adriana's. She said that you had left with your brother after he challenged Orsino to a duel and that Adriana was terrified and she and Orsino were shouting at each other and it had been hours and you hadn't come back. I thought I knew where you might be," he said. "If you had decided to do something about—"

"You are an absolute fool!" I shouted. "You are the last person who should be here! You could have sent your guards and not come yourself!" Alessandro looked nonplussed. Perhaps he wasn't in the habit of yelling at cardinals.

The door at the top of the stair had opened. A man leaned out, a handsome youth with the beginning of a mustache, a naked sword in his hand. A woman pushed out from behind him, her gown half-laced. "I should have known," she said. "Rodrigo, what is going on here?"

"I have no idea," he said.

"You have no idea?" She put her hands on her hips.

A small form came dashing up the stairs. "Mama!" Lucrezia said, "Did you see the angel?"

"Lucrezia!" Rodrigo yelled. "What are you doing here?"

"I followed you," she said cheerfully. "Who's the dead man?"

"One of the gonfaloniere's men, I believe," Alessandro said, sheathing his sword. "In ordinary clothes so as not to be recognized." He mounted the stairs and bent over her hand. "Alessandro Farnese at your service, Madonna."

She gave him a somewhat ironic smile. "Vannozza dei Cattanei," she said, as he bowed deeply.

The young man with the sword elbowed out past his mother. "Papa, did they ambush you? If so, I'll..."

"You will do absolutely nothing, Juan," the woman said. "Your father has clearly survived through some sort of fool's luck."

I attempted to make myself as inconspicuous as possible. I had known that someday I would meet Lucrezia's mother. I had hoped it would be in a less strange fashion. I let go of Rodrigo's arm and took a casual step away.

"The angel was extremely impressive," Lucrezia said. "Did you see it, Juan?"

"What angel?" her brother said.

The most senior of the guard drew himself up in front of Rodrigo. "One man of theirs is dead, Your Eminence. There is another who is wounded. What do you want me to do with them?"

Rodrigo's lips pursed. "Return them to the gonfaloniere's palazzo and put them at the gates. With my compliments."

"Your Eminence." He bowed sharply.

"Come in the house," Vannozza said. "Unless you'd like to stand in the street for whatever dramatic production this is. Honestly, Rodrigo. Do you know what time it is?" She took Lucrezia under her arm. "I can't believe your father put you in this danger."

"He didn't," Lucrezia said, her arm around her mother's waist. "I followed him. It wasn't hard. They had torches and a lot of people. He told me to stay at his house but I didn't. So it's my fault, not his. I wanted to see what happened. Mama, did you see Giulia call the angel?"

I winced inwardly but hopefully not outwardly. Vannozza looked at me, no doubt taking in my disheveled hair and the water splashed all down the front of my gown. "No," she said. "I did not." She had certainly seen me yelling at Rodrigo, however.

Dr. Treschi attempted to make his bow. "Madonna, I am Dr. Dionisio Treschi, late of Florence."

"Let's go in the house," Rodrigo said. "Vannozza, I am sorry to have disturbed your tranquility."

We went in through a strong door into a storeroom, then through another strong door into a kitchen. I hung back as much as possible. Alessandro seemed to have appointed himself ambassador and was attempting to engage Lucrezia's mother in conversation as we went upstairs. This was not at all the introduction I would have wished.

Dr. Treschi was the only one behind me except for Juan, who lagged back to bar the doors in turn. "It worked," he whispered. "I can't believe it worked! One can never be certain."

"Now you say that," I said.

"Donna Giulia, you are very forceful."

"So I have been told to my detriment."

"...and there was a plot to kill Papa and Signore Farnese is going to fight a duel..." Lucrezia informed her mother.

"I should rather not fight a duel unless necessary," Alessandro said.

"Then you have more sense than my sons," Vannozza replied.

Eventually we all emerged into a comfortable sala, the table cleared and the chairs arranged neatly. It was very tasteful and calm, good furniture arranged without ostentation. There was a tapestry runner in green, a single silver tray and pitcher on the credenza, rather than Rodrigo's taste for the maximum in everything. The room smelled like furniture soap and the lemons in a bowl on the table. Rodrigo was oddly quiet for him. I suppose he had lived here for many years when he was with Vannozza. If so, there was nothing of him in the room now. He liked bright colors, wall paintings and a profusion of objects that teased the senses.

"…and then I slipped out and went to the vice-chancellor's palazzo…" Lucrezia continued.

"Where you are going right now is to bed," Vannozza said. "It's midnight. No, you are not running around the city anymore tonight. You are staying here and going to bed in your room." She looked at Rodrigo. "Your father may run all over Rome in the middle of the night having adventures, but you are ten years old. Bed."

With a roll of her eyes, Lucrezia kissed her father's cheek. "Good night then," she said. "I'll miss all the rest, I suppose."

"Good night, Lucrezia," Rodrigo said. He took a deep breath as she departed. "Vannozza, I think it would be best if she stayed with you until you leave for the vineyard. She can get her things tomorrow."

"Now you think of her safety!"

"I had no idea she had followed me!" he protested.

A sleepy manservant brought wine and bread. Juan threw himself in a chair, looking up at Alessandro. "So who are you fighting a duel with? And did you kill that man?"

Alessandro sat down in the next chair. "Orsino Orsini, and I hope not to fight him," he began.

Dr. Treschi tried again. "Your Eminence, I am Dr. Dionisio Treschi. Allow me to say that I did not harbor any ill intent toward your august person…."

I sat down in the least comfortable looking chair, suddenly exhausted. The servant offered me a glass of wine, and I took it with thanks, taking one little sip.

"So you're Giulia Farnese." Vannozza was standing in front of me.

I sat up straight, meeting her eyes firmly. "I am," I said.

"Well, if you can yell at him, you'll be all right." Rodrigo seemed to suddenly find Dr. Treschi's conversation fascinating. Alessandro was talking with Juan.

"I have the greatest respect for Cardinal Borgia," I said. How could I possibly salvage this situation? I did not want to be her enemy. Rodrigo might deserve his own domestic dramas but putting Lucrezia in the middle would be cruel.

Her eyebrows rose. "Enough to die for him? Those men might have killed you."

"I did not think of it that way," I said honestly.

"The young never do," Vannozza said. "They think they're immortal until they aren't. Rodrigo's ambitions are the death of people. I try to make sure it's none of mine. The man who died tonight has a family."

"He was ordered to kill," I said. "It could have been my brother dead as easily. Given the choice, I'm glad it was him."

"I'm glad you recognize it could have been your brother." She glanced over at Alessandro and Juan in conversation. "My sons never do." She lifted her head. "This isn't the last time he'll put you in mortal danger. Just as long as you know what you're getting into. It's Rodrigo's world and we just live in it."

I wasn't sure at all how to reply to that. Vannozza turned. "Rodrigo, it's after midnight. Unless you and your entire entourage are planning on staying here, don't you think it's time to end this social call? Presumably you have places you're supposed to be in the morning. And surely Signore Farnese is expected to work even if you may spend the day in idleness?"

"I am certainly not going to spend the day in idleness," Rodrigo said. He put down his glass. "I will be awake for Lauds."

"Given that's five hours from now, get going!" she said, making a shooing motion.

He stood up, the corner of his mouth twitching. Vannozza was also tall, almost eye-to-eye with him as I was. "I beg your pardon, my dear, for this untimely intrusion."

"Try to keep from getting yourself killed on the way home."

"I always do," he said, and bowed over her hand politely.

I felt a stab of jealousy. Unworthy. Vannozza had made it clear that she pitied me more than hated me, a girl in over her head with a man Vannozza knew all too well. She thought I would regret this. Maybe I would, but not tonight.

"Alessandro, it's time to go," I said.

It seemed that Rodrigo had ordered more guards to follow the initial group, because when we went down there were six in the kitchen. Four went with us and the torchbearer, a party of nine with Rodrigo, me, Alessandro and Dr. Treschi. Even the most hardened footpads would avoid us. Surely Bracciano would. I thought sending him the bodies of his dead and wounded made a certain statement.

We kept to major streets, avoiding the Forum by passing well north of it. Vigil was ringing two hours past midnight as we reached the vice-chancellor's palazzo. It was still a blaze of light, guards at the gate and servants waiting for the cardinal's return.

"Father Alessandro, Dr. Treschi, I hope you will be my guests tonight," Rodrigo said. They both made pro forma demurrals cut quite short by the lateness of the hour. The majordomo led them away to guest rooms. No one made any suggestion about where I was to sleep. I stood in the grand saletta, suddenly bone-tired. "Giulia, if you will come up?" He offered me his arm.

I took it, leaning a little on his shoulder. We went up to his room. Was it only last night I had first slept here? Only last night I had run in the rain from Bracciano's guards to him? Only last night we had pleased each other, last night I had called a demon? It seemed weeks or months gone.

I took off my gown and slid in beside him wearing my camisa. "Come here, my Giulia," he said, and I curled onto his shoulder, my face against his long shirt.

"You're not dead," I said. That seemed like the important point.

"Not at present," he said. We were asleep before I could even answer.

Chapter Eighteen

Unsurprisingly, Rodrigo and I both slept through Lauds. I judged it to be an hour or more after Prime when I rose and dressed and slipped out. There was a guard on the loggia outside his private apartments who looked around. "Good morning," I said cheerfully. I wasn't going to slink about like I was ashamed of myself, so it was best to begin as I meant to go on, as though I were for all practical purposes the lady of the house.

"Good morning, Madonna," he replied.

"Have you seen Father Alessandro this morning?" I asked. It seemed strange to title him thus, but he had earned it.

"Yes, Madonna. He went downstairs just after Prime."

"I will find him," I said. I went down the grand marble stairs, the house cool in the morning, sunlight coming in through every window. Where it touched each tapestry, bright threads gleamed like jewels. The stairs were marble, the railing ornamented with gilded rondels that showed the Borgia bull picked out in gold. Even the ceiling was lavishly painted. In my light green cotta over a white camisa, my hair simply dressed in a snood, I imagined I looked very informal, but then even duchesses or grand courtesans surely didn't walk around dripping jewels early on a Sunday morning.

I found Alessandro in the gallery off the saletta, walking around the statue of the mother and child thoughtfully. "She's beautiful, isn't she?" I said, coming to stand beside him.

"Very much so," he said. "Mary, Queen of Heaven."

"Actually, Isis and Horus," I said. The room was full of light this time of day, as though we were in the basilica. "A different Queen of Heaven. Though I suppose not so different after all if one accepts *prisca theologia*."

Alessandro looked at me sideways. "Which of us has been studying theology?"

"Both of us, apparently." I took his arm.

He put his hand over mine comfortingly. "I suppose it's like the draper's wife knowing cloth."

"Someone has to keep the shop," I said.

"You'll do it exceedingly well," Alessandro said. We strolled around her toward another statue beneath the portico, a small and exquisite faun on a plinth. "I suppose Dr. Treschi will be off to Florence today. I hope he gets there safely."

"I hope he has learned not to conjure demons," I said. "Just because you can doesn't mean you should."

"You sound like Mother," Alessandro said. "And you get to explain all this to her in a letter. You're not pushing it off on me."

"I will," I said. "As soon as I know what to explain." It was still somewhat unclear how things with Orsino were going to be managed, though I was determined we would never again live under the same roof.

He nodded. "Well, in a moment I'm off to morning Mass at St. Peter's! My first morning living in Rome." He had a delighted smile.

"Was all that one day?"

"And what a first day in Rome! I nearly had a duel, rescued my sister, invoked an angel, had a fight with dastardly assassins, saved a cardinal's life, and got put up in a grand palazzo! Now I shall wash it down with Mass at St. Peter's. I challenge anyone to have had a better first day in Rome!"

"You are incorrigible," I said, and sent him off to Mass in high spirits.

I wandered into the hallway, where the majordomo found me. He held a brown purse. "Donna Giulia, His Eminence said to give this to you so that you may present it to Dr. Treschi." His voice was conscientiously devoid of either approval or disapproval.

"Thank you," I said, taking it. I understood completely. Rodrigo meant for Dr. Treschi to be my client rather than his. My first client. I did not have rooms to see him in. "If you will send word for Dr. Treschi to attend me in the gallery?"

"Yes, Donna Giulia," he said with a bow and withdrew. I returned to the gallery, standing by the statue. I took a deep breath. I was a patron.

When Dr. Treschi came in, he hurried across the marble floor and bent over my hand. "Donna Giulia, words cannot express my thanks. I owe you my deepest gratitude."

I handed the purse to him. "Dr. Treschi, your help was invaluable. As I promised, here are funds to help you on your way to Florence and allow you to reestablish yourself in that city."

His dark eyes met mine. "You are a fine Dove. It's a pity…." His voice trailed off as there was no good way to end that sentence.

"Perhaps we will see one another at some later date," I said formally.

"I hope so. Should you ever need a magus…"

"…I know precisely who to send for," I said with more warmth. "Take care, Dionisio. And Godspeed upon the road."

"I will speak widely of your kindness and your generosity," he said, "and that there is no greater lady in Rome than La Bella Farnese!"

A reputation already. Well, I had asked for it. "I will keep you in my prayers," I said, and meant it.

I went back upstairs to find Rodrigo in his study off the bedchamber, dressed in his red doublet rather than scarlet robes, eating bread with well-watered wine while he examined a paper before him. "Good morning," I said, bending over him and kissing his freshly shaved cheek. His expression of pleasure was worth savoring.

"My dear," he said. "I'd like you to look at this." He put his arm around my waist and I perched half on the arm of the chair, half in his lap to read it. "All Orsino must do is sign."

I read it twice. Then I looked at him incredulously. "A castle?"

"The castle of Vasanello," he said smugly. "An old and distinguished property."

"You are trading a castle for me? A castle?"

"With all its lands and incomes," Rodrigo said.

I nearly fell off the chair and would have if not for his arm around me. "That's a dowry for a princess! You think I'm worth a castle and everything in it? It's bigger than Montalto. It's worth three times as much!"

"My sweet, you are worth much more than a castle," he said, and had trouble finishing because I was kissing him. Everything is measured in gold in the world. My dowry set my price at three thousand florins. Vasanello was twenty times that much, at least.

I was laughing and crying at once. "I can't believe you're going to trade Orsino a castle for me."

"Well," he said, the corner of his mouth twitching. "It's not my castle."

I stopped. "Wait. You're trading a castle that doesn't belong to you?"

Rodrigo looked smug. "Vasanello is a former Orsini fortress, one of their traditional strongholds. Some time ago it was bequeathed to the Church. The Orsini have wanted it back ever since. In my role as vice-chancellor, I have the power to transfer deeds. I am simply restoring an Orsini property to a worthy scion of their line."

"You're trading a castle that doesn't belong to you to your mistress's husband to buy him off?"

"Essentially." Rodrigo gave me a squeeze. "Orsino gets an estate and the income from it. Adriana gets him employed for life as master of a great estate which is not dependent on the whims of his kin. Cardinal Orsini gets Vasanello back in the family, which he has greatly desired. Bracciano can't complain because his family has nagged for a decade to get Vasanello back and what can he say—that now he doesn't want it? You get rid of Orsino. And I get you." He waved a hand like a conjuror at a fair. "Everybody's happy."

I looked at him incredulously. He had the twistiest mind I'd ever imagined. "So Orsino goes to the country…"

"…and stays there…"

"…and I remain with Adriana and Lucrezia…"

"…a respectable married woman living with her mother-in-law…"

"…who happens to be a cardinal's concubine."

"Exactly," Rodrigo said. "And since you are technically married to Orsino, unless he wishes the public shame of admitting he's cuckolded, Vasanello will pass to our son as the legitimate heir."

"Our son?" My mouth dropped open.

"I expect there will be one, don't you? Or a daughter." Rodrigo smirked. "I do make good daughters." He had no opportunity to speak further, as I stopped his mouth for quite some time.

Donna Adriana looked up as we were shown into her room, the doors open to the balcony beyond, warm in the afternoon sun. She frowned, obviously surprised to see us together. "Rodrigo, I did not expect you today. Lucrezia has arrived and said that she was packing to go to the country with her mother." She looked at me, clearly torn between whether to remonstrate with me in front of Rodrigo or not. Where had I been? Did my brother intend to take me home? Where was my brother? Was there going to be a challenge to a duel?

"I'm not here about Lucrezia," he said. He put the paper down on her table. "That is the deed to the castle and holdings of Vasanello," he said, "which can easily be signed over to your son."

She looked at him incredulously and then at me. "Giulia," she said. "You haven't."

"I have," I said simply.

"Vasanello? A great holding?"

"Consider it my second dowry," I said.

"My Lord Bracciano," she began.

Rodrigo cut her off. "Adriana, you can't have two patrons. You know this. Either you are with the Orsini or the Borgia. I put it to you that I offer you the better arrangement. You've been seeking some sort of reasonable position for your son. Ownership and management of Vasanello is better than he could have hoped for."

She raised her chin. "And you will want me to vacate this house and go with him to the country permanently, I suppose."

"Not at all," he said pleasantly. "What could be more natural than that your son manage his estate in person while you remain in Rome with his wife? And of course Lucrezia. A very respectable arrangement. And Giulia will certainly have adequate funds to open the house and entertain in appropriate style. You may, of course, visit your son in the country whenever you wish." He smiled. "Come, Adriana. Will Bracciano offer you anything as good?"

She looked at me, and I thought I saw actual concern in her eyes. "And you?"

"One does not just trip and fall over a cardinal," I said. I looped my arm around Rodrigo's possessively.

She almost laughed. "A troublesome and clever girl," she said, but she said it kindly. "I wish you well with my cousin, then. He is not an easy man."

"I never said I was," Rodrigo said. "Will you call your son? I will sign this deed to him today."

She hesitated only a moment, then stood. "I will get him," she said, and swept from the camera.

I looked out the doors, then walked onto the balcony. Rome spread at my feet, roofs and houses and streets, the tower of St. Peter's against the sky. I heard his step behind me. He did not quite touch me, yet he stood too close for propriety. "A beautiful view," he said.

"It is, isn't it?" I said. The pots of jasmine were in bloom. I would never look at it the same way again. It was ours now.

There were arguing voices, and Orsino burst onto the balcony followed by Adriana. "You want to trade an estate for my wife?" he demanded.

Rodrigo shrugged. "You don't seem to have any use for her."

Orsino looked at me red-faced. "And you? You're my mother's cousin's whore?"

"That is not the word I would use," Rodrigo said in a tone that I had not heard before.

"Orsino, ours is no real marriage and you know it," I said. "We have been joined on paper but there is nothing between us and never has been." I had things to say, and it was time to say them. "I did not choose you and I did not choose this house or this sham marriage or any of the rest of it. I am done with others choosing for me. I have made my own arrangements for my own satisfaction. Now you have two choices. You can refuse this agreement and I will get an annulment based on non-consummation. You will be laughed at by all of Rome and required to return my dowry, which you have spent, and I will go on with my life. Or you can take this agreement and remain married in name only, with an estate that will provide you with a source of income for the rest of your life instead of hoping your cousin will use you as a pawn on his battlefields. If I were you, I'd take Vasanello. But it's your choice. I have made mine."

He simply stared at me for a long moment. "Orsino will sign the agreement," Adriana said. For an instant I thought he would actually defy his mother, but then his head dropped and he nodded.

"Good," said Rodrigo. "Adriana, let us go into the study. I'm sure you have ink there."

"I will bring it here," she said.

I stood in the light through the balcony doors while Orsino signed the contract spread on Adriana's table. More than a year ago we had signed the marriage contract in this room. Now I regained my freedom. I watched Rodrigo bend to sign. No, he was not young, nor the husband I had imagined, a man who belonged to God before me, and yet my heart sang when I watched his clever fingers on the pen, when his mouth moved in a smile as he looked up, eyes lighting as they fell on me.

There was a running step behind, Lucrezia coming in like a thundering herd. "Papa! I didn't expect you here today. I'm getting my things to go to the country with Mother."

"Just some bit of business," Rodrigo said, hugging her as she flew at him. "A contract about property."

"Oh," Lucrezia said. "I thought it might be important since Giulia looks so happy."

Rodrigo left soon thereafter, claiming pressing business, after being dragged off to confer with Lucrezia, who then peppered me with questions about the night before and insisted that I should help her pack for the country. Her father had left four guards to escort her back to her mother's, which I thought would be safe enough.

"Why are you packing too?" Lucrezia demanded. "You aren't coming to the country with us, are you?"

"I am going to stay with your father for a few days," I said, folding my clean camisas neatly, not looking at her. I hoped I wasn't blushing. "My brother will be there too." Which was utterly true. It was far too awkward for Alessandro to stay under the same roof as Orsino after nearly fighting a duel with him.

"Because it's safer or because of what Orsino said?" Lucrezia asked.

"It seems more convenient for everyone," I temporized.

Lucrezia bounced on my bed experimentally. "You mean you're going to lie with him."

"Lucrezia!" I felt myself turning furiously red.

She didn't even blush. "I think you will be very good for him," she said. "Papa sometimes does not have much sense." Her tone sounded just like her mother's.

"I am sure your Papa is quite sensible," I said. "I will only be there a few days, so I am finished packing."

"Also you don't have many clothes," Lucrezia said. "I'm sure Papa will take care of that. I told him you didn't."

"Lucrezia." I shook my head. "Is there anything else you told your Papa about me?"

She laughed, bouncing again. "I won't tell," she said. She pulled out the costume I had worn for the masquerade. "I think you should wear this."

"That is a carnival costume," I said. She shrugged, still smiling. "It is not carnival and I am not going to a masquerade."

"Please?" Lucrezia begged, a glint in her eye just like her father's. "You could put your gamurra over it." She pulled out the largest halberd in her armory. "Papa said he liked you in it very much." She held it up, simple white linen in a classical style, falling from the shoulders in graceful folds, though it did bare my lower arms.

"Well," I said, "with my green gown over it, if your father liked it." It felt ridiculous, but I supposed it didn't look like a carnival costume with the gown over it, just a very plain camisa.

"Now come help me pack," she said, popping to her feet. "I have a lot to do."

Indeed she did. Lucrezia's wardrobe and fripperies put mine to shame. She dawdled and dithered in a way that made me wonder how enthusiastic she was about going. Packing her for the country took three trunks, and that was with leaving most of her best clothes behind. "I won't need them at the vineyard," she said practically. "There are no elegant parties there." The number of elegant parties she was allowed to attend in town was zero, but she held out hopes. Vespers was ringing by the time we finished.

"Oh goodness!" Lucrezia said. "Mother will expect me soon. We should go. Do you have your things?"

"Are the guards escorting us both together?" I asked. It made sense. We could both go to whichever destination was easier and then the guards could go with the other one from there.

"We should go down," she said. She was smirking. It made me distinctly uneasy. I hoped there would be no awkward scene with Orsino.

We had just reached the stairs, Beneo carrying one of Lucrezia's trunks, when there was a loud knocking on the street door. Beneo put the trunk down with a sigh and went to it, calling out, "Who's there?"

"Alessandro Farnese," my brother answered. What in the world? Did he feel like he needed to fetch me? Or had I been so long that everyone was worrying?

Adriana came bustling down as Lucrezia and I went down to the vestibule. "I hope you will be happy," she said to me. "And that you will return."

"Donna Adriana," I said, and wasn't certain how to finish. She meant well but listening to her would destroy me. I hoped she would consider this change of fortune one more eddy in the stream and accept it as she had the others.

Beneo opened the gate. I am not sure who gasped first, me or Adriana. Alessandro wore his best doublet in Farnese blue, holding the reins of a gorgeous black Friesian parade mount, its mane braided with red ribbons and its scarlet saddle blanket embroidered with gold. Four torchbearers stood by in the falling dusk in Borgia livery, red with the bull in gold. There were ten guards as well, all in steel, the Borgia bull on their breastplates. A wagon decked in red waited for my modest bundles. "Sorellina," Alessandro said, offering me a crown of flowers—white roses and lilies entwined like a classical garland. Or a bridal wreath. I simply stared at him.

Lucrezia jumped up and down. "Put it on!" she said. "I'll do it." She grabbed it out of Alessandro's hands and I bent for her to put it on my head.

Adriana shook her head. "Really, Rodrigo?"

It looked like a bridal procession. Already a crowd had gathered in the street, curious and hopeful of alms. I had not had a procession when I married. I was married from the groom's house because my family had no town house, and in any event my wedding had been as small as was decent.

Alessandro grinned. "A horse suitable for Pluto, or so I've heard."

"His name is Memnon," Lucrezia put in. "He's a sweetie." She darted out to let the horse nibble at her hand.

"I presume this is your father's horse?" I asked. A ridiculous question. Who else's would it be?

Alessandro cupped his hands for me to mount. "Up you go."

I stepped in as I had when we were children and swung up, settling the rein though he held the bridle like a proper attendant. "I can't believe this."

"I'll see you when I get back from the country!" Lucrezia shouted, waving wildly.

Beside her, Adriana was actually smiling. "He's mad," she said.

My heart was singing. "A very stylish abduction," I said, and leaned over to kiss her. After all, she had been my Ceres. And then I lifted my face to the crowd, smiling.

They cheered. "La Bella Farnese!" someone yelled. And why not? I was young and beautiful and splendid and happy. There was indeed an alms basket as there should be for a bride, and I rode between the torchbearers, guards before and behind, with Alessandro walking before me holding the bridle. I threw the alms, tossing them far into the crowd. There were cheers. "La Bella Farnese!" I raised my hand to them, raised my face to the stars somewhere above the lights of the city. The torches streamed in the night air, just as they had in the reflecting pool before the painting of Proserpina. A very stylish abduction indeed.

The vice-chancellor's palazzo was lit with lamps on the loggias that made four sides of a square around the courtyard, and it seemed the whole household had turned out to see the commotion, including a dozen young clerks and every servant who wasn't required elsewhere. Rodrigo was waiting in black velvet with gold embroidery, a smile on his face as Alessandro led the horse in through the gates. Two of the clerks were dispensing alms at the gates behind me, to the cheers of the crowd. The fountain's droplets glittered in the torchlight and Alessandro led the horse forward as Rodrigo came down the steps and met us before the fountain. I suspect I was beaming.

"Welcome to my home, Giulia Farnese," he said, and stretched out a hand to help me down.

I slid off, and he caught me neatly around the waist, though this did have something of the air of falling into an embrace. I was nearly of a height with him, but he didn't seem to mind that I was tall. Rodrigo stepped back and bent over my hand with a courtly bow.

"What a very polite Pluto you are!" I said, nearly laughing with delight.

"How could one be else to such a lovely Proserpina?" His eyes were dancing with pleasure as he straightened up.

"All this for me?"

"All this and more," he said.

The household applauded and shouted. What in the world did they think they were witnessing? A celibate churchman's parody of a wedding? A pagan ceremony? Or simply one of the spectacles he was famous for? With Rodrigo Borgia, who knew?

"You had Lucrezia in on it," I said.

He spread his hands. "She was a great help. And she enjoyed it no end. She is quite devoted to you, you know."

"Lucrezia is a dear," I said, and my eyes misted a little.

I took his arm and he led me into the saletta, two of the younger maids throwing rose petals ahead of us. The credenzas were spread with costly carpets, stacked with gold and silver plate, bowls and platters and ewers as though all the wealth of the underworld were displayed, the bronze Nike nestled among them. It was even more magnificent than it had been at the masquerade. The servants were lined up as though to greet the mistress of the house. I tried to have a word for everyone, though I suspect I seemed dizzy with delight.

The balustrade of the stairs was wreathed in green swags studded with white lilies. The little maid scampered ahead, diligently pitching rose petals to crush fragrantly beneath my somewhat worn slippers. I was not precisely dressed as a great lady.

The doors to his sala were thrown open, more wealth displayed, tapestries and carpets and silver vessels brimming with fruit and flowers. Every lamp and candle was lit. Either they had gathered every treasure from all over the house, or Rodrigo was rich beyond imagining. He turned, making a little speech. "I am sorry to have kept you from your dinner, which I hope you will enjoy. My lady and I will dine alone." There was a somewhat raucous cheer from the clerks.

Alessandro kissed me on the forehead. "Good night, Giulia," he said, and went out. How had Rodrigo completely won him over in twelve hours? He was acting like the proud brother of a bride, not a scandalized brother of a ruined woman.

Rodrigo closed the doors, and I heard the thump as the guard came to rest outside, halberd handle against the floor. "Will you come into the camera?" he asked, holding out his hand.

"With great good will," I said, and rested my fingers on his.

The windows had been covered with tapestries and no light showed from outside. The Tree of Life rose from the Garden of Eden and turtledoves sang in its branches. A fountain was surrounded by poppies, three graces dancing nude about it. A field was studded with flowers, a unicorn at rest among the lilies. Twenty tiny lamps of colored glass hung from wrought iron stands, blue and rose and yellow and green, bright colored stars. The carpets beneath our feet were soft and thick, intricate patterns in scarlet and every other color. There was a table laid with golden dishes, and beyond it his huge bed hung in red velvet. "Welcome to the underworld," he said.

"It is lovely beyond imagining," I said.

"And so are you." He had every word perfect, a master player with an audience of one. To be the center of his good grace was intoxicating.

"I suppose I should dress the part," I said. "Lucrezia managed me well and I am wearing Proserpina's costume." I unfastened the green gown and laid it carefully aside, wearing only the white linen I'd worn to the masquerade.

"When you said you were awaiting abduction," Rodrigo said.

"Did I say that?" It was hard to believe I'd been so daring.

"You certainly did. It got my attention." He unfastened my snood carefully, releasing my hair in a loose wave below my waist. He stroked it once, and a shiver ran down my back. "One abduction, as requested. Though I could not manage a chariot on such short notice, so Memnon had to do."

I turned and he was smiling. "I believe you would have acquired a chariot."

"With two more days, yes," Rodrigo said. He lifted my hand and kissed the fingertips. "Chariots are not easy to find these days."

I laughed. "You delight me," I said.

"I am trying to. Let us hope we delight one another." He gestured to the table. There was a golden bowl and a little knife, and one round, red pomegranate.

"Well," I said. Neatly, I sliced it open, glittering seeds in their scarlet folds. It felt as though a profound silence had fallen. We were in a great house. There must be a hundred people about, and yet it was as silent as though we were indeed in some secret chamber far underground. He watched me, black eyes never leaving my face. I detached a pip, red staining my fingers, and put it in my mouth, tart and sweet at once. Then a second. Then a third. I closed my eyes and swallowed it.

He kissed me. My eyes were already closed, so I did not know until I felt his lips on mine, tasting the pomegranate on my tongue. I heard the knife clatter to the floor as I put my arms around him. What could one want besides this? It felt as though the world rotated around us, a dizzying swirl but we were the nexus, the point where all stood still, timeless and entranced.

I do not know how long we stood thus. It might have been a hundred years. It might have been a few minutes. How long to know one another? How long to touch his hair and smell the fresh-washed scent of him, to feel his hands beneath the thin white linen against my flesh?

We moved to the bed, sinking down together, dreamlike, as though we created an enchantment for one another. My hands on black velvet, seeing my pale fingers twisting in the laces of his sleeve as his mouth closed on my nipple, back arching as I leaned into him. His hands on my thigh, stroking upward as I reached for the points of his hose, alive with sensation. Leaning back on a feather bolster, my hair sticking on the raised embroidery, as his fingers sought that pleasant core, the rhythm I had shown him before. When I arched up against him, all sense leaving me, it seemed I might fly, only half-tethered to my body.

"So ready," he whispered, bending over me, and I tightened my hand against the small of his back. Stretching, wet, needy.... He pushed into me. Not sharp pain, just ache, overfilled. One slow thrust. I gasped. He held still. "Giulia?"

"Go on," I said. The last thing I wanted was for it to stop, for him to stop now. Not now, not at the end. I watched his eyes close, trying to relax into him. "My love," I whispered. "My darling." Tight, a little uncomfortable, but not pain. If I moved with him....

And there was the release, the moment when he stilled, unable to wait any longer, his face changing. I put my hand to his cheek, turned to the side against him as he rolled off, his organ against me and my body tight against his, not letting go. The world still spun.

"Don't let go of me," I said. "Don't let go."

"I won't," he said. "There, my sweet." This same strange quiet still enveloped us. I took a long breath. Warmth, and the glow of the lamps on my eyelids, the musky smell of us. A little aftercramp, just a twinge. The feel of his skin on mine. I almost dozed. It might have been moments or long minutes before he moved. "Giulia?"

I opened my eyes. "Well," I said with satisfaction, "that wasn't so bad."

"I'm glad to know I'm not so bad," Rodrigo said gravely.

That hadn't come out as I had intended. "That's not what I meant," I said, kissing his cheek and his chin and jawline as the opportunity presented. "I meant that after all that's made of it, I expected much worse. It was a little uncomfortable. That is all."

"I'm glad of that," he said, stroking my hair back from my face. And of course the reason it wasn't so bad was his care. His hand was soothing, but there was a teasing sound in his voice. "So do you feel debauched and depraved?"

"No," I said quite honestly. "I feel married." This was what I had hoped for on my wedding night more than a year ago: satiated, satisfied, happy. Close as breath to someone who loved me.

He was silent for a moment. Then Rodrigo's arms tightened around me. "Something new for us both."

That was puzzling. "New for you?"

"My dear, I've never been married. I've never had a virgin bride. I have always had experienced women."

Could he have actually worried that it wouldn't go well? That I would hate him after for causing me inevitable pain? As though a little pain wasn't entirely worth it? I ducked my head, nuzzling his throat. "I would never have guessed," I said. Everything about him stirred the senses, and his care was no exception. I raised my face to his, lips to lips. "I hope that you will be diligent in my education, for I am very eager to learn."

There was the kiss, sweet and deep, everything I could want. He shifted, half-sitting up. "I shall be the most diligent of tutors," Rodrigo said.

"I will need lessons every day," I said with my widest and most innocent eyes.

He laughed, getting up. "Perhaps not another until after dinner. I have a suitable repast waiting."

"You have thought of everything." I sat up gingerly. There was a thin, scarlet streak on the white linen gown where I had lain on it. Done, I thought, and no need to parade bloody sheets. But no doubt. Truly, I felt relieved.

"I have tried to." He returned with a fresh camisa, perfectly simple but so fine that it was almost transparent. "And this," he said, holding out a robe of figured gold velvet lined in satin of the same color, easy to make but of stunning material. "*Domina lucida fulgida mea. My lady of dazzling brightness.*"

I couldn't help but laugh with sheer pleasure in the beauty of it as I got to my feet and he dressed me, the camisa and the robe, my hair left long down my back against the plush material. "Proserpina could have no finer," I said, and he handed me to the table.

There were dishes left under covers, morsels that would keep until we wanted them, cheeses and rice balls seasoned with long pepper, slivers of ham thin as glass, olives and candied almonds and dates stuffed with sharp cheese, and marzipan hearts tinted pink with rosewater. And sweet red wine, cool in a golden goblet.

"For my lady's pleasure," he said, and seated me gallantly.

"So," I said, popping a rice ball into my mouth, "how many things are there? So I can size up the lessons."

Rodrigo almost choked on his wine. "Do you mean positions or everything that one can do?"

"Beginning with positions," I said decisively. "Everything that one can do seems a large field of study. Best to break it down."

"One must be organized about these things," he said. "Well, there is the most basic, with the woman beneath the man, as we did."

"Yes," I said. There might be a better alternative. He was heavy and I was quite squashed.

"There is front to back, like a stallion mounting a mare." He waved his hand in the air as though to sketch out something.

"I'm a country girl," I said. "I know how a stallion covers a mare. Or for the fuzzier version, a ram and an ewe." That did have quite a lot of potential.

"Or a bull, if one wishes to extend the metaphor."

"Really?" I said teasingly, eating a stuffed date very slowly. "Thinking well of yourself?"

"It's my family's device," he said. "The Borgia Bull. So…."

"Then by all means, a bull rather than a ram."

"There is reclining, with the man beneath and the woman atop," he continued. "And there is standing, either against a wall or with a table or such to sit or lean upon."

I tried to visualize it, wine glass in hand. "A table seems safer," I said. I didn't entirely trust him to hold me up against a wall. Perhaps it would work for a small woman and a burly man. For us it seemed likely to end in a fall. Nor would the extra jeopardy add spice.

Rodrigo selected a triangle of cheese, his voice was thoughtful. "Tomorrow I must see to your support."

"I don't think the table in here is sturdy enough," I said.

Rodrigo looked at me perplexedly, then started laughing again. "I meant financially."

"I'm still fixed on the table," I said. Of course it was funny and charming too, as I meant it to be. He laughed, pleased that I was more interested in the sex than the money, which frankly I was just then. I had no doubt he would spend money generously. "I make you laugh," I said.

"You delight me," Rodrigo said. He put his hand over mine on the table. "How you are supported speaks to your value," he said seriously. "Just as a dowry does. If support is scant and grudging, you will be treated as of little worth. I intend to keep you as if you were a princess."

"That is ridiculous," I said, though of course there was an appeal to books and fine clothing and the kind of luxuries I had never had.

"Perhaps a duchess then." He looked amused.

"I understand Lucrezia said I have no clothes," I said. It was not true that I had none, only considerably fewer and less expensive than hers. "I hope I can do you credit." I did worry a bit. "Orsino said that I was too tall, quite hairy, and very average in shape."

Rodrigo shook his head. "He has no taste at all. My dear, you are perfectly classically proportioned, the ideal ratio in every way. As for tall, if one wants tall sons, one does not get them from short mothers! You are a great beauty, and as soon as you are set off by lovely clothes as a gem is set in gold, you will have Rome at your feet."

I blushed. He meant every word of it. Whether it was infatuation or truth, the opinions of others would have to reveal. "Then I will need a maid of my own," I said thoughtfully. "Maria only manages to do for me as well as Adriana because my needs have been simple."

"They will not be anymore," Rodrigo said, "if you are to be hostess in this house as well. I mean to flaunt you." He lifted his own golden goblet.

"And I to be flaunted," I said. "How else will people know there is patronage to be had?"

"Aren't you a quick study!"

"I mean to be a good instrument for you," I said seriously. "So I must learn how, and I must have the tools to do it."

"I would have you adequately armed for war," Rodrigo said. In black velvet, golden goblet in hand, he looked like a king indeed. "It is war, my sweet." He paused, enumerating again. "You will need a riding horse to go about town. I will put two of my guards at your disposal to escort you where you wish."

I blinked. For more than a year I had been discouraged from going anywhere, even to Mass. "To go where I wish?"

Rodrigo took another drink. "Printers, cloth merchants, dining with your brother or with friends—whatever you want to do. But you know that some parts of the city are not safe, and I have enemies."

I could hardly credit I had understood correctly. "I may go wherever I want without asking you?"

He looked at me over the rim of the cup. "I'm not your husband. A concubine is her own woman." He shrugged. "I do ask you to take the guards, not to constrain you, but for your safety."

In Montalto I had gone about as I wished, but I'd never thought I could do so in Rome. The only times I had been able to do what I wanted was when I slipped out looking like a servant. To go where I wanted, a great lady with private guards and no restrictions....

"Of course I will take them," I said. "I am not Lucrezia, and I am sensible of the dangers of the city." I paused, phrasing my question. "You told her that we were going to...."

"Lucrezia questioned me closely on the subject and informed me that I should make you my concubine without delay, as you are, in her words, nice, pretty, and not going to do what I say."

"Lucrezia said that?"

"She is very direct." The corner of his mouth twitched.

"I will certainly do what you say," I replied indignantly. "Unless it beggars good sense."

Rodrigo started laughing. "Which means that you will not, while professing sweet obedience."

"I have pretended to be nothing other that I am," I said, somewhat stung.

"Giulia, Giulia." He took both my hands in his on the elaborate table. "You are my treasure. I would never want you meek and spiritless."

"I never shall be," I said. I took a sip, glancing at him across from me, rumpled and louche in black velvet and his white shirt. There was still something I didn't understand. "Why are you so good to me?" I asked quietly. "You need not have gone to so much trouble to have me. I would have taken your offer without all this."

Rodrigo's expression was inscrutable. "Perhaps I enjoy doing it."

"I see that you do." An answer that was true, but not the whole truth. I took another sip, considering how to best put it. "You offered when you could have demanded. Even given that this was for your pleasure as well as mine, you could have carried me off in truth and none could have protested."

"That would not have achieved my goal." He busied himself with the silver serving tongs, putting delicacies on each of our plates.

"Which is?"

"Your devotion." He glanced up, a little smile on his face. "I want you to adore me and dedicate yourself to my happiness and interests." I must have stared at him mutely, for he went on. "Women, or men for that matter, may be terrified into doing all manner of things, but they will stop doing them the moment they may. Fear, intimidation, demands—these things may bring immediate results but not lasting ones. I want your loyalty, not merely the use of your body, as lovely as it is." He shrugged. "I want you to be mine completely."

I did not say what came into my head, that such things bind both ways. Surely he knew that when he created this rite or play or whatever it was. "Proserpina?" I said, with a raised eyebrow.

"Consider it a matter of self interest," he said, leaning back in his chair, taking an olive with his fingers and then removing the pit from his mouth. "A woman in my house, in the most intimate parts of my life, could do me great harm if she hated me."

And again that was true, but not the whole truth. Lucrezia's mother had known the right of it, I thought: *There's no fool like an old fool.* He was utterly, foolishly, besotted with me, knowing every danger that came with it. I might play him and use him or even betray him to his enemies. Yet sitting across the table, the candlelight shining on the golden folds of my robe, I knew he had seen me rightly. I was exactly who he imagined me to be, his Lady of Dazzling Brightness, not an innocent girl, but his consort and queen.

I reached for his hand. "You are my Pluto." I lifted his hand to my lips, kissing his finger where the ring would be. "And I will love you forever."

"I hope so," he said, and if it sounded more a prayer than a statement, it did not worry me in the slightest.

It was three months before I saw Bracciano again, and then it was across the crowd in the sala of the vice-chancellor's palazzo. September had come, every vessel filled with grapes to celebrate the harvest, the wine flowing freely. In the square before the palazzo there had been a fireworks display paid for by Rodrigo for the pleasure of all comers—certainly everyone who lived nearby attended. His servants had gone round with wine, dressed in classical garb with wreaths of vine.

Musicians played in the reception room and the courtyard as well, the latter enjoyed by the crowd outside the gates. Inside, the party was a vision of bright celebration. Lamps glittered in every corner. In the sala, dancers filled out a set, ten couples beautifully dressed, bowing and circling like wandering stars. I did not dance. I stood beside Rodrigo at the far end near the gallery entrance, chatting with a Medici who was here to discuss money with the vice-chancellor. We were being mutually charming to one another in the way of people who have nothing to say but must appear engaging.

Bracciano looked about the room, dignified and stern in Orsini red. And he saw me. He began to make his way around the edges of the room, through the throngs watching the dancers and the servants refilling glasses. At my side I felt Rodrigo stiffen. "Shall I prevent him if he tries to speak with you?"

"No," I said quietly. It was, after all, a great crowd. The music was loud, the dancers glittering with jewels and bright colors as they turned.

Rodrigo's mouth twitched in approval. "Scream if you need me," he said quietly, and turned to speak to Cardinal Sforza, both of them gorgeous in flaring red silks.

I smiled at the Medici and accepted his polite excuses that he must speak with someone he had just seen. It took Bracciano some time to make his way across the room. I waited, serene in a midnight blue cotta of heavy satin, a gown embroidered with silver lilies over it, my hair caught up in a caul with pearls. They matched the pearl-encrusted cross I wore around my neck.

At last he stood in front of me, looking me up and down as though ascertaining my price. "La Bella Farnese," he said with only a perfunctory nod.

"My Lord Bracciano," I said, with the same.

"You've done well for yourself," he said. "My kinsman off to the country and you installed most lavishly."

My eyes were very wide and I said disingenuously, "My Lord, I am afraid I do not know what you mean! I am a simple young woman, flotsam on the stream carried wherever the water takes her. How could I stand up to the force of a Borgia?"

He snorted, but what was there to say? He strode away into the crowd without another word.

Rodrigo turned and I took his arm, watching Bracciano disappear into the crowd. Obviously he'd heard every word. "Aren't you a hungry little spider," he said in a low voice.

I smiled. "This is going to be interesting."

Coming soon:
the second book of the Memoirs of the Borgia Sibyl

THE BORGIA DOVE

Jo Graham

Renaissance Woman

1492: Giulia Farnese is the mistress of the powerful Cardinal Rodrigo Borgia. Educated, brave and ambitious, Giulia revels in the art and ideas of the Renaissance and in her newfound influence as the consort of one of the leaders of the humanist movement within the Vatican. The gifts of prophecy and magic that made her a weapon against Rodrigo but allowed her to save his life are gone with her virginity—or so she thinks.

Now the pope is dying, plunging Rome into lawless chaos until a new pope can be elected. The most likely candidates want to purge Rome of heresy, endangering both Giulia's friends and the fragile Renaissance itself. A dark horse candidate who most people underestimate to their peril, Rodrigo is ruthless and clever; but to seize the ultimate prize of the papacy, he'll need all the help he can get. He relies on Giulia to be his eyes and ears in the world of powerful women and to negotiate on his behalf when the voting cardinals are locked in seclusion.

Drawn into a high-stakes game of bribery and bargains, Giulia discovers all too soon that losing means paying a deadly price. Her only hope of protecting those she cares about from Rodrigo's enemies lies in mastering the magical gifts she once thought lost. For Giulia to claim the divine power of a pagan priestess may be the ultimate heresy—or a way to win her lover the papal crown.

Acknowledgments

In leaping into the Borgias and a new Numinous World book, I have so many to thank, including my long-time readers who have encouraged me at every step. I would particularly like to thank my pre-readers Joss Davis, Victoria Francis, Jennifer Roberson, and Lena Strid for their feedback as I worked.

I am also indebted to Samantha Morris, who has kindly shared her original research on the Borgias with me and steered me to various sources. I also appreciate her responses to occasional emergencies like, "what does the floor look like in there?" I am also appreciative of Dr. Katharine Fellows, who shared with me her doctoral thesis on Rodrigo Borgia in his years as vice-chancellor. All mistakes are of course my own.

As always, this book would not exist without my wonderful partner, Amy Griswold, who has put up with several years of Borgia-mania! I also appreciate the constant support of Melissa Scott, who read and made so many suggestions on this manuscript. I would also like to thank my editor, Athena Andreadis, who has made this book infinitely stronger by her canny insights.

Most especially, I would like to thank Janet Frederick Rhodes, who died years before I wrote this, but who always knew I could when she generously and kindly edited hundreds of pages of a 15th century epic written by a sixteen-year-old who loved Virgil, Machiavelli, Richard III, and Neoplatonists. Rhodesie, I wish you could see what came of it!

About the Author

Jo Graham is the author of twenty-seven books and three online games. Best known for her historical fantasy novels *Black Ships* and *Stealing Fire*, and her tie-in novels for MGM's popular *Stargate: Atlantis* and *Stargate: SG-1* series, she has been a Locus Award finalist, an Amazon Top Choice, a Spectrum Award finalist, a Manly Wade Wellman Award finalist, a Romantic Times Top Pick in historical fiction and a Lambda Literary Award and Rainbow Award nominee for bisexual fiction. With Melissa Scott, she is the author of five books in the *Order of the Air* series, a historical fantasy series set in the 1920s and 30s. She is also the author of three pagan spirituality books. She lives in North Carolina with her partner and is the mother of two daughters.

Ingram Content Group UK Ltd.
Milton Keynes UK
UKHW011057310323
419467UK00001B/39